HOMEWARD
BORNE

a novel by
RUTH CHATTERTON

Simon and Schuster, 1950

For excerpt on page 195, Stephens: INSURREC-
TIONS Copyright 1909 by The Macmillan Company
and used with their permission. "What Tomas an
Buile Said in a Pub"

MANUFACTURED IN THE UNITED STATES OF AMERICA
BY THE HADDON CRAFTSMEN, INC., SCRANTON, PA.

To MY HUSBAND, without whose belief and guidance this tale could not have been told.

Long had he fancied each successive slope
Concealed some cottage, whither he might turn
And rest; but now along heaven's darkening cope
The crows rushed by in eddies, homeward borne.
Thus warned he sought . . .

Guilt and Sorrow
William Wordsworth

BOOK ONE

1

THE TRAIN with its three coaches and its single baggage car jolted and creaked its way along the Vermont countryside, the rippling gray banners of smoke curling back, then rising and mingling with the soft clouds that hung motionless over the gently rolling hills.

The old man in his worn, greasy uniform chewed impatiently on the toothpick between his yellow teeth and scowled down at the slim, dark young woman. She moved her head wearily against the dusty red plush of the coach seat and fumbled in her purse for her railroad ticket. She did not open her eyes. They were stinging with fatigue, and the sensation of sand persisted under her heavy lids.

"Come on, come on! I ain't got all day!"

She sat up quickly. As she opened her eyes a cinder flew into one of them and a hot twinge of pain darted through her head.

Damn that conductor! She didn't like being up at this hour any better than he did. Where had she put that ticket? Where the devil had it got to? Why did conductors always have to be so bad-tempered?

She groped blindly in her bag, found the ticket, and handed it to him.

"You're in the wrong coach, lady."

"What?"

"If yer goin' as far as New York, yuh gotta go in the car ahead. This car's bein' took off at White River Junction. And yuh can't leave your bag in the aisle, neither. Somebody'll fall over it and break their neck."

He punched her ticket and moved on to the next seat, blinking angrily through his spectacles.

Pax Lyttleton gathered up her belongings and reached for her valise. She staggered forward with her arms full, thrown by the movement of the train from one side to the other, and as she struggled with the handle of the door, her voice floated back to the conductor:

"I can't very well leave it in the aisle if I have to go into the car ahead, you silly old fool."

She settled herself in the next car, with her valise in the aisle as it

3

had been in the car behind—just for the hell of it!—and then wondered why she was so cross.

Of course, she'd hardly closed her eyes the night before. She had been too tired to sleep, too nagged by the anxiety which never left her.

There had been the usual chores of her average day and the plans for her return. The guest room had to be put in order. No one had occupied it since Robert's parents had visited them from the South, just before he had gone overseas. She had made up one of the beds with new sheets and clean white blankets which smelled of moth balls, and one of her own small pillows which she always tucked under her ear.

She had to find the right book for the night table, put plenty of hangers in the closet, and at the last moment she had hung an informal picture of Robert with his football team, class of '36, on the wall between the window and the dressing table. Jake was standing beside him in the picture—not in football clothes, of course—and Robert's arm was thrown affectionately around Jake's shoulder. How incongruous Jake looked among all those athletic giants. Strange, she hadn't remembered that he was in the photograph until after she'd hung it—or had she?

Tubby had been unusually difficult all yesterday afternoon. He had refused to play with his gang and was under her feet every minute. And those awful "why"s and "what for"s. Why couldn't she stop everything and take Luke to the vet's? He was sure that the dog had a canker in his ear. How'd she like to have a canker in *her* ear? How would she like to have her ear hang way down and walk with her head on one side? Why was she going to New York, anyway? She had something to do there. What? Never mind. Why couldn't he go too? Not this time, Tubs. Well, if he couldn't go to New York, could he sit up until nine just once? Why couldn't he save his bath for the morning and have fifteen minutes more with her?

She hadn't wanted one more minute with him. She wanted to talk to Philip.

Then when Philip had arrived and they were comfortably settled in the library, the phone began to ring. Was she really going to New York? Was she going for any special reason? They couldn't see why she wanted to go to New York alone. That wouldn't be any fun, would it? Why didn't she wait until Robert got back? When was he coming home, anyway? Why wouldn't she tell them why she was going?

She had finally banged down the receiver in sheer exasperation.

"Damn their inquisitive souls!"

Philip had looked at her soberly. "Why don't you tell 'em, Pax?"

"You know, Phil. You *know!*"

"Sure. But do you know?"

"Phil! Stop looking superior! I've told you over and over. It's a hard thing to explain. It'll be all right once it's all over—I mean, it'll be so much easier. You know that."

"Hope you're not fooling yourself, Pax. Nothing gets any easier."

But Pax had rushed on. "You know I don't want anyone to tell me not to. You know how easy it is for anybody to influence me. Why, you, yourself—Phil, you know what a coward I am!"

"A coward, Pax? It's pretty damned brave to be scared of something and still go through with it. You'll do all right."

Later, in bed, it was a little frightening to think that after the next day things might never be the same. She shivered and pulled the covers around her shoulders. Hour after hour, she lay there in the dark, trying not to think and dozing for brief intervals. She heard the clock in the church tower strike every hour and practically every quarter.

At three o'clock, just before it was light, she finally got up, put on her robe and slippers, and tiptoed down into the kitchen. She put on some coffee, let Luke out, found a day-old Burlington newspaper, and propped it up against the sugar bowl on the kitchen table.

She was sipping her coffee and trying to read when she heard footsteps on the gravel path which led to the back door.

"Hi," said Philip. "I saw the light go on so I dressed and came over. Anything I can do?"

"I don't think so. Everything's done except my bath. I couldn't sleep."

Then Philip had made her go upstairs and dress while he cooked some eggs and made some toast and took them up to her on a tray.

Amy Sanders was already at the station when they got there. As they waited for the train, none of them had very much to say. Philip made sure she had written down the name of the little hotel in the Seventies. He couldn't remember the exact street, but the hotel was called the Preston, and it was on the East Side. Pax had put the name of the hotel just above the address of the agency, which she must telephone the minute she arrived in New York.

Then the train had pulled in. Philip squeezed her hand so hard it hurt, Amy gave her a hug, and she was being pushed up the steps of the coach. Philip carried her bag in for her and found her an empty seat.

"You all right?"

Pax smiled wanly and nodded.

"Good luck, kid," he said briefly, and jumped off.

And now she was feeling terribly alone. The train was hot and smelly and drafty, and she couldn't find that bloody cinder. She clutched at her lashes, pulled the upper lid down over the lower one, blew her nose hard until she was tired. Nothing happened. The stub-

5

born speck eluded her and every time she blinked it scratched her eyeball until she wanted to scream. It hurt to read and it hurt to look out of the window, and she didn't want to sit there with her eyes closed, because she'd go on thinking and being afraid of what was waiting for her at the end of the journey.

The hours crawled on and small fears tapped at her brain and were quickly pushed away again. The plush of the coach seat was hot, and when she turned her head and put her cheek against it, in an effort to sleep, it prickled annoyingly, and the accumulated dust of many years dried her nostrils and made it painful to breathe.

The sun was high and beginning to move a little toward the west when the conductor threw open the door of the coach.

"Hundred and Twenty-fifth Street. Uptown New York."

Pax looked out of the window. How well she remembered that district, with all the dilapidated tenements leaning toward the tracks. The houses always seethed with people of all races and colors—mostly black —who hung out of the windows in passive curiosity, or lolled lazily on rickety fire escapes hung with soiled underwear, discolored diapers, and torn, faded bedding.

The few times she had passed this segregated section of New York, she had felt sick to her stomach with pity for those hundreds of thousands of unfortunates. Now, the only sensation she felt was the agony caused by the cinder in her eye.

The train came to a stop with a jolt.

"Grand Central Terminal! Last stop!"

There was no porter in the day coach, so once again she gathered up her various belongings and started for the door ahead.

"Passengers kindly use the rear door!"

Pax thought furiously that all railroad conductors must have chronic indigestion and that it was really very silly to have to go all the way back and then walk the whole length of the coach again. Might as well put her on a treadmill and have done with it.

Outside the train, there were hundreds of people searching for their luggage and calling for porters. Pax trudged the five long blocks of the platform, carrying her bag, then climbed to an upper level. For a moment, quite bewildered, she stood in that humming metropolis which is Grand Central Terminal, looking for an exit. There was a sign in neon lights over one door which said "Taxis"; she followed it and found herself in the lobby of the Biltmore Hotel. She walked out and hailed a taxi.

When she arrived at the hotel, she gave her bag and her topcoat to a bellboy, who led her to the desk.

6

"I should like a room with two beds," she explained to the clerk as she registered. "Did you receive a wire from Professor Philip Winslow, making the reservation? It was sent from Mapleton, Vermont. He's often been a guest here, I believe."

"Yes, of course, madam. We've put aside a small suite for you. I'm sure you'll find it very comfortable."

"But I don't want a suite," she said. "We'll only be here for one night."

"Very well, madam, I think that can be arranged. The boy will show you to your room."

"I don't think I'll go up. I'm in rather a hurry. If you'll just send up my valise and these magazines—"

She looked at the clock which hung over the desk. It was nearly two-thirty. There was plenty of time for the little she had to do, and she had all afternoon.

She pushed her way through the revolving doors and went out onto the sidewalk. It was a quiet street. On the block below there were a few small trees, and the cool April sunlight played through the young leaves. She decided she'd walk for a bit. She knew practically nothing about this part of New York. The next time she came it would probably be to meet Robert, and that would mean a noisy midtown hotel, a few nights of theaters and smoky night clubs.

She strolled leisurely down Madison Avenue, stopping now and then to look into the shop windows, until she came to a restaurant. Suddenly she realized that she had eaten nothing since early morning except the dry sandwich and watery milk she'd had on the train. She went in.

She caught sight of her reflection in the wall mirror beside her table and wrinkled her nose in disgust. Her face was drawn and white, and she looked every bit of her twenty-eight years. Why hadn't she had sense enough to go up to her room in the hotel and freshen up a bit? Well, she had been in a hurry—or had she? She took out her compact, powdered her nose, and rouged her pale lips; then she took another look for the cinder. It was still hopelessly embedded and invisible.

When she had finished her lunch and paid her bill, she went out through the side door. Across the street was a small movie theater.

It was only three-thirty. That agency office wouldn't close before five-thirty or six, surely. She'd just go in for half an hour or so.

As she walked up the ramp which led to the auditorium, she could hear the angry voice of Donald Duck quacking his heart out. She found her way in the dark to a seat on the aisle, keeping one eye on the funny creature on the screen. She gazed rapturously at him as he sailed through the air with the greatest of ease, landing on his chin with a

7

frightening thud, his beak flattening out, while his roars of rage filled the theater. Pax giggled.

What a godsend she had come out of the side entrance of the restaurant. If she hadn't she would be— She wouldn't think of that for the moment. She'd give herself an hour. Think how much more relaxed she'd be.

Resolutely she concentrated on Donald, who had picked himself up and walked away. As he brushed the dirt off his sailor suit, muttering furiously to himself, around the corner came his mortal enemy, Pluto.

Suddenly they clashed. There was a bellow from Pluto, a raucous, nerve-splitting howl from Donald, and a gigantic pin wheel of light flashes, gaping jaws, red tongues, sailor suits, and duck feathers, which gradually dwindled and dwindled to a pin point of light—and it was over.

Pax shook with laughter and settled back in her seat contentedly as an enormous camera wheeled around on the screen. The lens of the camera became two eyes, upon which were written "The Eyes of the World," and they focused on hers.

"MAYOR O'DWYER AND GROVER WHALEN
GREETING THE NEW CHINESE MEMBER OF THE SECURITY COUNCIL."

There was the inevitable flower in Mr. Whalen's buttonhole, as the smiling officials posed for the cameramen.

"THE UN-AMERICAN COMMITTEE IN SESSION.
THE HOLLYWOOD PROBE IS ON!"

What sour faces those Congressmen had. Wonder whether they're Republicans or Democrats. What's the difference, anyway?

The scene changed again.

There was a flat, treeless background and a crowd of people in the distance. Then the camera flashed to a boat. Down the gangplank people were trudging, bags and bundles in their hands and strapped to their backs. Soldiers in shorts alternately helped and pushed them along. Then back to the first scene and the camera traveled closer. Men, women, and children stood silently behind barbed wire. Most of them were youths and young women between the ages of seventeen and twenty-five. There were many children standing in front of them, clinging with their little hands to the wire fence, gazing out like monkeys from behind a cage.

For the most part, their faces were hard and expressionless, but a few of them were angry and wore a sardonic grin, and all their eyes appeared to be dead and hopeless.

8

The scene faded out to nothing and on the screen appeared one word: "CYPRUS."

Pax quickly got up from her seat. She felt a little sick. She stumbled up the aisle and out into the lobby. A hot wave of shame flooded through her, and she half walked, half ran up the street looking for a drugstore where there might be a telephone booth. She found one on the corner.

She pulled the door to, took out her address book, and dialed the number. There was an angry stumbling sound on the wire. She hung up the receiver and waited. Then she dialed again.

"Hello?"

"Is this Plaza 9-8721?"

"Yes. What can I do for you?"

"May I speak with Mrs. Harris, please?"

"Which Mrs. Harris do you want?"

"I don't know."

"Well, I'm afraid I can't help you, madam, unless you can tell me."

"Oh, dear! Is there more than one?"

The operator's voice sounded bored. "Two."

Pax's face felt hot and she began to suffer the first symptoms of claustrophobia. "I only know one. I mean, I didn't know there were two."

The operator seemed to thaw a little. "What's the name of your Mrs. Harris, miss?"

"I don't remember. What's yours?" This was too ridiculous. "I mean, perhaps if I hear both their names, I'll know. It's silly of me, but you see, I didn't notice particularly, and I didn't bring any of her letters with me."

"Well, there's a Mrs. Myron Harris and a Marguerite Harris."

"Oh. Well, would you be good enough to tell me Mrs. Myron Harris's first name?"

Pax heard a giggle from the other end of the wire.

"Her name is Margaret. I'm sorry, miss."

They both began to laugh. The strain was broken and the first contact was made.

"How would you like to speak to both of them? I think that's the best way to find out which one you want."

"Thank you."

She waited. I am the damnedest fool, she thought. But it was as if the iron bands that seemed to press around the power of her will and the sinking feeling in the pit of her stomach had disappeared as she heard the calm, detached voice.

9

"Hello. Mrs. Myron Harris speaking. Who is this, please?"

"I'm Pax Lyttleton from Mapleton, Vermont."

"Oh, hello, Mrs. Lyttleton. I've been expecting to hear from you."

What a warm, friendly voice! She was feeling better already.

"Are we going to have the pleasure of seeing you this afternoon?"

"Oh, yes. I'm on my way. Will it be all right if I come now?"

Then, just for the fraction of a second, it was as if a light, warning finger had tapped at her brain. "That is, I mean, in a little while. You see, Mrs. Harris, the silliest thing happened to me this morning. I got a cinder in my eye on the train, and I haven't been able to get it out. I thought I might just stop by a doctor's—" She felt her face getting hot again. Not for a moment had the idea of stopping at a doctor's occurred to her until now.

"Oh, don't bother to do that, Mrs. Lyttleton. We always have a nurse on duty here. She'll take it out for you in a second."

"Oh, will she? Then I'll come right along."

"Have you got the address?"

"Yes, I have it, thanks."

"Good. Come to the sixteenth floor. Sixteen-o-two. We'll be waiting for you."

Pax hung up the receiver, opened the door of the telephone booth, and started for the street. On her way she passed the candy counter. Almost without thinking, she stopped, bought a box of chocolate mints, and put them in her handbag. She hailed a taxi, gave the address to the driver, and pulled the door shut.

She was no longer afraid. What was there to fear, even in a world which was slowly destroying itself by fear? Philip, that stalwart enemy of fear, had said that. And he was right. Gone was the faltering uncertainty of the last forty-eight hours; gone that inexplicable panic which she had never been able to defeat, that panic which suddenly stabbed into her brain when she was off guard, attacking her like a virus from nowhere, eddying and whirling through her thoughts, clutching at her heart, until she wanted to sit down on a curb, in a closet, anywhere, and do nothing, hide, stop breathing.

Why couldn't she learn? Why couldn't she? It wasn't as if she didn't know. It wasn't as if Philip hadn't gently, patiently, sometimes brutally drubbed it into her stupid mind that there wasn't any reason to be afraid of things you didn't know.

She thought of her terror when her father died.

With that ever-recurring sense of guilt, she remembered the last time she had seen him, looking a little more frail than usual, sitting in his own particular chair beside the fire, reading. Absent-mindedly, but not without affection, he had turned his cheek for her good-night kiss, and while she and Robert and her young son slept, he had quietly slipped away from them. She had stubbornly locked herself in her room, and her father's last journey had been taken without any farewell from his only daughter.

And then, in the summer of 1940—Robert had been reading the newspaper very thoroughly, day after day. Robert wasn't particularly interested in newspapers. Robert wasn't particularly interested in anything except his family, friends, and football. Often she would come into a room unexpectedly and find him talking to Jake. He could always talk to Jake. Jake was his friend.

"God-damned bloody bastards!" she overheard him say one night. "Just wait till I get a crack at 'em!"

But he'd stop suddenly when she came in.

"Hello, darlin'. Anyone seen the evenin' paper round here?"

"No. Why, Robert?"

"Thought I'd have a look at the football news. You know, Jake, Harvard doesn't look so good this year."

"Doesn't it, Bertie? What's the matter with it?"

"Their God-damned quarterback—sorry, honey chile—doesn't know a football from an Easter egg. I was just tellin' ol' Jake here—"

But all the time she knew, and that clammy invisible hand began clutching at her throat.

"What'll I do, Phil?" she would say. "He'll join up! I know he will."

"Don't be an ass, Pax. We're not at war."

"Doesn't make any difference. He'll find a way. Talk to him, Phil, will you? I won't be able to bear it if he goes! I tell you, I simply won't be able to bear it!"

And then the blow had fallen. And it wasn't as bad as she thought it would be. It never was when she struck straight at the heart of her fears or they struck at her.

She hadn't as yet been driven to the center of her present dread, but still the attack had passed. She'd find out in a few minutes how groundless this one was. She must be nearly there.

She took out her compact again, with a little more interest than she'd had the previous time. A tired but rather lovely face looked back at her from the little mirror.

The large agate-colored eyes were set very far apart beneath level black eyebrows. At the moment there were blue shadows under them, the lids were heavy, and the left one was red and slightly swollen. Her chin was pointed, a bit too long and very determined, her mouth large and full, and her nose a little ridiculous. It started out being an ordinary, well-shaped feature, changed its mind, and continued on and up, ending in a round blob which sometimes quivered when she talked. Her hair was black and too curly. At the moment she was wearing it drawn up and off her ears, and caught slightly to one side of her head in a loose cluster of ringlets. Her ears were small and a little pointed at the top, her throat long and slender. The most arresting thing about her was her smooth, chalk-white skin.

She reddened her lips, felt about in her bag until she found a small bottle of perfume, put some on her temples and behind her ears, and felt better.

The cab was stopping. She had arrived.

2

PAX GOT OUT at the sixteenth floor, opened the door of the office, and went in. Somehow it was not at all as she had pictured it. There were bookcases, comfortable chintz-covered chairs, and small tables upon which were magazines, cigarette boxes, and ashtrays. It was lighted with softly shaded lamps, and in the corner was a low English desk, behind which sat a young woman receptionist.

"Good afternoon," said Pax. "Will you be good enough to tell Mrs.—er—Myron Harris I'm here?" This time she wasn't going to make any mistake. She had written down the name on the back of an old envelope. "My name is Lyttleton."

"Oh, yes, of course, Mrs. Lyttleton, will you step this way?"

The girl led the way into a private office. A short, stout woman, about fiftyish, with strong, plain features, stepped forward to greet her. Mrs. Harris had swarthy skin, large brown eyes, a suspicion of a dark shadow on her upper lip, and blue-black hair shot with gray. She was smartly dressed in a simple black dress and hat, with a heavy gold necklace around her throat, and in her ears she wore flat gold earrings.

She held out her hand to Pax and smiled; her smile was warm and sympathetic.

"I'm very happy indeed to see you, Mrs. Lyttleton. Come and sit down over here."

"Thank you."

"Did you just get into town today?"

"Yes. I took a very early train this morning. It was a slow one, but it was the only one that would get me in early." She hesitated a moment. "You see, there were a few things I had to do first."

"Of course. Before we go any further, Mrs. Lyttleton, I want you to know how very grateful we are to you. It's a fine thing you're doing. I wish we could find a few more like you."

"To tell you the truth, Mrs. Harris, I think I'm a little frightened."

Mrs. Harris looked at her seriously; then she reached across the desk and patted the girl's arm.

"That's not very difficult to believe. I should be frightened too. It's a grave step you're taking."

"I know."

"It will take patience and courage."

"I know that, too." Pax smiled wanly. "And I haven't got either of 'em. All I can say is, I'm going to try awfully hard."

"I don't think you'll find it too difficult," Mrs. Harris said with a smile. "Of course, there will probably be constant little irritations, you know, adjustment in your own life and your family's—"

"I know all that."

"And there will be times when people will try to hurt you. People can be awfully merciless, you know."

"I don't know very much about people, Mrs. Harris," said Pax simply. "I never have. But I've learned a lot in the last six years from one of the people who sponsored me in this—you know, Professor Winslow."

"Yes. I have his letter here. He seems charming—and intelligent."

"He's the best friend I have in the world," Pax said.

Mrs. Harris put on a pair of horn-rimmed spectacles and glanced through some papers which lay on the desk in front of her.

"All your sponsors seem to think you're doing the right thing."

"Oh, yes, they do. But it's lucky you only asked for three recommendations," Pax said impulsively. "You see, Mrs. Harris, there was no one else, really, whom I wanted to tell yet. Mrs. Sanders, Philip Winslow, of course, and Tubby's minister—Tubby is my son."

"Really?" said Mrs. Harris. "How old is Tubby?"

"He'll be nine in July."

"And what does Tubby's father think about all this?"

For an imperceptible moment, Pax hesitated; then she smiled a little nervously. "Well, he doesn't know about it yet."

Mrs. Harris sat up a little straighter and a look of surprise lighted her eyes. "Do you mean you haven't consulted him about such an important undertaking?"

Pax lowered her eyes and began to play with her wedding ring.

"Well—you see, Mrs. Harris, my husband is still in Germany with the Army of Occupation. You know how it is; three thousand miles is a long way and it isn't always easy to discuss things in letters. Well—to be very truthful, Mrs. Harris, I was a little afraid he might think I was taking on too much—"

"Are you quite sure you're not?"

"Oh, yes. I want so terribly to do it."

"But you were afraid your husband might dissuade you?"

"Oh, no, Mrs. Harris. If you knew my husband, you'd realize that he'd be the first one to approve of what I'm doing. I expect he'll be coming home very soon, now, and—" The slight uncertainty in her voice disappeared, and it seemed to take on a new firmness. "Anyway, it's really my responsibility financially and—well, morally. It won't make any difference, will it?"

"No, Mrs. Lyttleton, your three sponsors will be quite enough—" She broke off abruptly, reached for a box on her desk, and offered a cigarette to Pax.

As the woman lighted it for her, Pax noticed that the flame brought out the lines of weariness around the dark eyes and the strength and generosity of her mouth.

"I think we're pretty well set on all the technicalities, but would you mind if I asked you one or two questions which are not on the questionnaire?"

"Of course not, Mrs. Harris. Ask me anything you like."

Unconsciously Pax pressed her hand over her left eye.

Mrs. Harris got up quickly.

"My dear girl, how thoughtless of me! Your poor eye! I'm so sorry. Will you come this way?" She pulled Pax out of her chair and guided her to the door. "The surgery is just down this corridor. I think Miss Seldon has all her implements of torture in here." She opened the last door at the right of the corridor. "This is Mrs. Lyttleton; Miss Seldon, our nurse. Will you see if you can get that cinder out for her?"

"Let's have a look."

The nurse took Pax by the hand, put her in a chair, and pulled her head back gently until it rested on the back.

"I'll go back to my office," said Mrs. Harris. "Just send her along to me when you've finished, will you, Nurse? Don't hurt her."

Pax closed her eyes and relaxed. She felt strangely at peace, although she realized she was no nearer her ordeal than she'd been an hour ago.

"Try and relax your lid, Mrs. Lyttleton. I'm going to roll it back over this orange stick. I'm not going to hurt you. Dear me, it is inflamed, isn't it?"

14

With thumb and forefinger she began to open Pax's eye. It hurt. Pax jerked away, and as she looked at the ceiling, her eyes rolled back in instinctive defense against the light, and everything became misty.

She heard the voice of the nurse saying: "Now, now, it's not going to hurt!"

She smiled grimly to herself. What faraway memory did that recall? What was that odd sound? Like a harmonica. Now she remembered.

She had been playing in the back yard with Herman Schulte, the son of the laundress who used to come to the house every Tuesday. Herman was sitting on the back-porch railing, swinging his legs and making horrible sounds on a mouth organ.

"Go away now, Pax! I'll hurt yuh!"

"You will not. Give it to me, Herman! I want it!"

"You can't have it! It's mine. Get away from here!"

Pax ran up the steps and reached for it.

"Please! Let me play it just once! I'll give it back!"

Herman flung his arm high in the air, holding the harmonica out of her reach. She leaned over him and tried to grab it. The boy lost his balance and toppled over onto the ground. It wasn't very high and the fall couldn't have hurt him at all, but he lay there shrieking. Pax flew down to him.

"Are you hurt, Herman? Are you hurt?"

He stopped screaming suddenly. With a quick move he picked up a handful of dirt and threw it in her eyes. She let out a yell of rage and ran to Martha.

That was it! That was what had taken her back along the years. She had jerked away from Martha, too, and Martha had also said, "Now, now, it's not going to hurt."

That was a long time ago. Funny, she could *hear* that harmonica.

"There you are, Mrs. Lyttleton. No wonder it hurt. Hold still a minute. I want to put some drops in your eyes." It felt cool and soothing. "Don't wipe it out. Let it stay as long as you can."

Pax nodded. She sat up and tried to open her eyes. Everything swam in a watery haze; even sound was blurry. But she *did* hear a harmonica! Gradually her vision cleared. She started slightly, and stared.

Down at the end of the fairly large room, a little boy sat on the window ledge. He was softly playing a mouth organ. Strange she hadn't noticed him when she came in. He sat there quietly, the afternoon sunlight on his brown hair, watching without much curiosity, occasionally putting the mouth organ to his lips, playing those curious dissonances.

She smiled at him, but he didn't smile back. He looked at her gravely and went on playing.

Pax thanked the nurse; then she felt about in her handbag, pulled out her old leather cigarette case—Jake had given her that—and nervously lighted a cigarette.

"Isn't it funny," she said to the nurse, "how we always reach for a cigarette after an uncomfortable moment? Good-by, Miss Seldon, and thanks again."

She put her hand on the doorknob and looked back at the boy.

"Good-by," she said uncertainly.

The boy merely looked at her.

She hurried down the corridor and knocked at Mrs. Harris's door.

"Come in, Mrs. Lyttleton. How does it feel now?"

"Much better, thank you very much."

"Well, come along and sit down and we'll finish up these last few things."

"What do you want me to tell you that you don't know already?"

"Well," said Mrs. Harris, "if you don't mind my asking you, there is a paragraph here—" She took up one of the papers. "You say you don't belong to any church."

"That's quite true, Mrs. Harris. Does it make any difference?" Pax said anxiously. "You see, my father was an agnostic. There was no religion he hadn't delved into deeply. Of course, he respected them all—"

"Naturally," said Mrs. Harris quietly.

"He'd studied them in their own languages," Pax continued. "You see, he was completely familiar with all the Far Eastern languages and their various dialects. I'm afraid Father didn't live his life in this century. He lived it in those thousands of years before our Christian God was ever thought of."

Mrs. Harris looked at her steadily. "I see," she said.

"Please don't misunderstand me." Pax smiled a little. "I'm not like my father. I'm a very simple woman. It's just that my mother died when I was born, and it never occurred to my father to make me go to any church or Sunday school. I guess it was wrong." She paused. "But you mustn't worry about that. My son goes to a Presbyterian Sunday school, mainly, I think, because it is near, and because all the little boys he plays with go there. When my son is old enough, he will choose his own religion—and he will be given the spiritual guidance which will make him able to choose. Is that what you wanted to know?"

Mrs. Harris nodded. "Yes. And thanks for being honest. You see, we had to be sure."

16

"Next," said Pax, with a little smile.

"As we told you in our letter, your financial status naturally had to be investigated. It is quite satisfactory, but—please don't let this embarrass you—I'm sure you know that it will be a long, expensive undertaking, and, for your own sake, I want to be sure that you are not only able to but that you want to undertake this burden."

Pax looked at her thoughtfully.

"I want to be very honest with you, Mrs. Harris. I don't know anything except that I am here, that tomorrow will be another day, and that there is very little pity left."

"That is a very tragic fact, my dear."

"I don't need very much money for myself. My father left me the house we live in; my mother left me a small amount of money which I shall use for this—job of mine. My husband is fairly well off. We'll get along all right." Pax leaned over and touched the woman's hand. "But thank you for worrying about me and warning me."

"Well," said Mrs. Harris, "I guess that's it. I believe in you, and I think you'll make a go of it."

"Thank you. I'll try," Pax said. "Now, please, may I ask you something?"

"Of course."

"How did you get into this work?"

"Well, my dear, we all did war work. But when it was over, we realized it wasn't over for everyone. It isn't over for the people the world has forgotten. We found that there are a few merciful people in America who want to do something about it and find it very difficult to go through all the red tape. A few of us got together and formed this organization. Some of us have a little influence in Washington, and with our investigations thoroughly organized, and contacts in Europe, we are often able to succeed where the government agencies are not. It is that traditional drop in the bucket as far as this problem is concerned, but we do our best." She looked at the girl soberly. "Are you ready to take over?"

"I'm ready."

Mrs. Harris picked up the telephone and gave some instructions.

"Another cigarette, Mrs. Lyttleton?"

"Thank you, I don't think so. Not now."

Pax rose, and went over and looked out of the window. Now, with everything apparently settled, the waiting seemed interminable.

"Oh, Mrs. Lyttleton, would you think me rude if I asked you where you got that extraordinary name? Pax. It's very unusual."

"Well, I told you that my father was an unusual man. You see, I was born shortly after the first World War. Our old servant Martha told me that when I was a few weeks old Father leaned over the crib one afternoon and stared at me. Then he said to her, 'Well, Martha, peace on earth seems further away than ever. We may as well try to create a little around here. We'll call the child Pax and may God help her!' "

"I like it," said Mrs. Harris. "The Greeks have a word for it, too, but it's not so unusual."

But Pax was no longer listening. She turned quickly as she heard the door open.

3   STANDING IN THE DOORWAY, the mouth organ still in his hand, was the brown-haired boy she had seen in the surgery.

For a moment Pax didn't move. Then she said quietly, "Hello."

The child didn't answer. He stood there looking at her soberly. Mrs. Harris leaned forward and spoke to him in a strange language.

Swiftly Pax turned to her. "Doesn't he speak any English?"

Mrs. Harris laughed gently. "Did you really think he would?"

"But I can't talk to him! What does he speak?"

"A few words of many languages—mostly the Slavic ones, I should judge. Yiddish, of course." She paused as she saw the consternation on Pax's face. "These children learn very quickly, Mrs. Lyttleton," she said. "I shouldn't worry too much if I were you. He's already picked up a few words of French—in the Distribution Center, I suppose—and he knows quite a few phrases of German. The poor little devil has probably heard plenty of it, God help him!" Then she smiled. "He speaks quite a lot of Polish."

"Oh, dear!" said Pax.

Through all this, the boy leaned indifferently against the door. He didn't seem interested in anything except the instrument which he tried to play from time to time.

Pax tried again. "Er—*was ist*—*dein*—er"—she looked to Mrs. Harris for help—"er—name?" she finished lamely. Suddenly she remembered

18

a few phrases of the Arabic her father had tried to teach her. She said, "*Shu Usmack?*"

"He doesn't speak Hebrew," Mrs. Harris said quietly. "This boy is the product of a concentration camp, Mrs. Lyttleton. As far as we can find out, he has never known anything else since the first four or five years of his life. I don't think he can even remember his mother or father. At any rate, he's never spoken of them."

Pax watched him for a moment, her eyes filled with compassion. Then she opened her bag, took the box of mints out of it, and handed it to him. He studied it for a moment, then opened it gingerly.

"*Chocolat,*" said Pax, with her best French accent, and she took one out of the box and put it in his mouth. He swallowed it and then looked at her with interest for the first time, his eyes glittering. As rapidly as he could, he stuffed one after the other into his mouth until he nearly choked. Then he went slowly over to her and reached for her bag.

She started to draw it away, but Mrs. Harris said quickly, "Watch him. See what he'll do. That's the only way you'll learn."

Silently he took everything out of her bag, until he came to the cigarette case that Jake had given her. He put it up to his nose and smelled it, then almost smiled, but not quite.

"*Bitte?*" he asked.

She nodded. He opened the case, put a cigarette in his mouth, found the matches on the table, and lighted the cigarette. Then he took out three or four more and put them in his pocket.

Pax looked at him in horror. "Oh, he can't!" she cried. "He's so little!"

Mrs. Harris said, "I told you this job wouldn't be easy." She sighed. "Would you like to change your mind? It's not too late."

"Oh, no! No! But . . . Oh, the poor little thing!"

He stood against the desk, smoking as if he had smoked all his life—which he probably had. He inhaled the smoke deeply into his lungs, letting some of it escape slowly through his nose, then began to make smoke rings. He watched them intently as they floated out into the room, occasionally glancing furtively at the two women.

Pax said, "Is he showing off?"

"No, I don't think so," Mrs. Harris said. "He seems quite used to it."

"How awful!" exclaimed Pax. "How old is he?"

"We don't know, exactly. We think about eleven."

"Eleven! But he's so small. He doesn't look any more than eight."

"I know. He's undernourished."

"Of course. I'd forgotten."

"Don't be discouraged. I've seen several of these children. You'll be amazed to see how quickly he will respond to proper food and rest. The hardest job will be"—Mrs. Harris hesitated a moment—"his mind."

The old panic began to steal over Pax again.

"I have taken on a job, haven't I? Do you think I can do it?"

"I know you can—if you *want* to do it."

The boy finished his cigarette, carelessly threw the butt on the floor, and stepped on it. Mrs. Harris said something to him in Yiddish, and her voice was stern. He gave her a terrified look, picked it up hurriedly, opened the window, and threw it out. She smiled and said something that sounded like *"Danke schön*, Jan," pronouncing the last word as though it were "Yon."

"Jan. Is that his name?"

"Yes. Jan ben Rozov."

"Oh. Am I to call him that?"

There were so many things she hadn't thought about.

"You may name him what you like, but if I were you I think I'd call him Jan for a while. He knows that, and everything is bound to be strange to him for some time, at least."

Pax sat down in a chair near him.

"Jan," she said gently, *"veux tu venir ici et causer avec moi?"*

He paid no attention. Pax looked discouraged.

"My French is so bad, but my German's worse! It's going to be awful, isn't it?"

"He heard you. I think he understands more than you think. Jan," Mrs. Harris said, and again she spoke in Yiddish.

He listened. Then he raised his head, looked at Pax, and slowly went to her. She took his hand.

It was long and slender, but it might have been a little dead hand. His fingers didn't close around hers. He let his hand rest in hers and stared at the floor. She looked at him curiously.

His head was rather large for his body, but then he was so very small. His skin was pale gold and clear. His brows were straight and dark, his lashes thick and long and curling. His nose was strong and slightly arched, his mouth well cut but with the lower lip protruding a little. She couldn't see his eyes, which were still lowered.

Her eyes traveled down, taking in the small body and the pitifully thin legs. They looked even thinner than they were, because the short pants he was wearing were so short and so tight. His socks were loose and hung down over his shoes, which would have fitted a healthy sixteen-year-old boy.

She raised her eyes and looked at his head again, wishing he'd look at her, but he didn't. She saw that his hair was thick and a little wavy, and, on one side of his head toward the crown, one lock stood up re-belliously from an unmanageable cowlick.

A lump crept into her throat and she longed to smooth the lock in place as she often smoothed Tubby's, but she was afraid to.

"*Veux tu venir demeurer avec moi et mon fils,* Jan?" she asked haltingly.

Again Mrs. Harris spoke rapidly to him. He hesitated a moment, then looked up at her, and she saw that his eyes were large, soft brown in color, and that the lower lids slanted slightly in the far corners.

"*Merci, madame,*" he said in a low but childish voice.

Mrs. Harris laughed. "What did I tell you? I don't think you'll have much trouble."

Pax smiled automatically, but her eyes were troubled. She looked at her watch.

"I think, Mrs. Harris, if you are willing to trust him to me, we'd better be getting along."

Mrs. Harris was putting a set of papers into a large envelope. She came from behind the desk and handed the envelope to Pax.

"Read these when you get time," she said. "This is all the data about the child that it was possible to collect. It will help you." She patted the girl on the shoulder. "It will help you to understand, I mean."

"Thank you," said Pax, and put them in her bag.

"I wish I could do more for you, but I know very little about this particular boy. Not any more, I'm afraid, than you will know after you've read them. I'm sorry he hasn't any clothes except what he's got on. You see, he only arrived in this country this morning."

"I'll get him some. It'll be fun." She stopped abruptly. "Don't worry. We'll get along. Every time things get tough I'll try to remember how much harder it's going to be for him than it will be for me."

She turned to look at him.

He had put another cigarette in his mouth and had gone up to the desk to light it. The two women watched him quietly.

He put the box of matches in his pocket with the other cigarettes that were left. Then his eyes fell on the silver desk lighter. With a swift movement he had it in his hand and had slipped it into his other pocket.

Mrs. Harris spoke to him sharply. He took it out of his pocket with no embarrassment whatever and put it back on the desk.

"I forgot to tell you. They all steal."

"What?"

"It was their only means of survival. He's not a bad boy. He'll learn."

"What did you say to him?"

"I told him he didn't have to steal it. I said that if he wanted a light you'd give it to him."

"But that's not true! He mustn't smoke. It's bad for him."

"Take it easy, my dear. Rome wasn't built in a day. Jan is a very grownup little boy. 'Don't' means only one thing to him, a combination of guards and Gestapo and blows. Just try to make him understand. He will, if you give him time."

Suddenly Pax felt as if she were going to cry.

"I'll get his coat," Mrs. Harris said, and she went out and closed the door.

Pax was alone with this strange child; he would go back with her now to the hotel. He would go to Mapleton with her tomorrow. He would be with her from now on, all the days of her life.

"You and I are going to be friends, aren't we?" she said to him earnestly. He stared at her.

"*Amis, toi et moi.*"

"*Bitte?*" he said.

Then he took up his mouth organ and began to blow on it.

The door opened, and Mrs. Harris came in with a dark blue coat over her arm. She bundled the boy into it, buttoning it up around his neck.

"They say it's getting a little chilly."

She looked at Jan and began to laugh. Pax laughed, too. It was bitterly sad, but it was funny.

The coat hung nearly to his ankles. The sleeves came down four inches over his wrists. He stretched out his arms and looked at them, but he said nothing. He just dropped them to his sides again and stood there waiting.

Mrs. Harris pulled him back until he was leaning against her, smoothing his hair as Pax had wanted to do a few minutes before.

"I apologize for this coat, Mrs. Lyttleton, but I realized that he wasn't very warm, so I sent home for one of my sons' coats. I have two sons, but unfortunately for Jan, they're both quite a lot older, as you can see. But it will keep him warm for tonight. Are you going right back to Mapleton?"

"No. Not until tomorrow. Jan and I have some shopping to do first, haven't we, Jan?"

Jan reached in his pocket and pulled out his third cigarette. Impulsively, Pax started toward him.

"Jan, please! You've had—" She stopped. Then she reached for the lighter. "Here, let me light it for you."

Mrs. Harris smiled and nodded. She bent down and spoke to the

22

boy again in the language he could understand. Then she ruffled his hair, gave him a friendly little jab in the chest, took him by the hand, and led him to Pax. She opened the door and let them pass in front of her. Then the three of them walked to the elevator. Mrs. Harris pushed the button and held out her hand to Pax.

"If you have any difficulty, just phone me. You understand, of course, that we will make inquiries from time to time, and we'd be very grateful if you will let us know about his progress."

"Of course, Mrs. Harris. I'll write you."

"Remember, you have two years to make up your mind about adopting him legally, so if things should go wrong, don't feel that this step is irrevocable, will you?"

Pax looked down at the boy.

"Oh, no. I understand everything, I think. I'll send the coat back to you tomorrow. Thank you so much for everything, Mrs. Harris."

"That's my phone. Will you forgive me if I don't wait for the elevator?"

"No, please! Of course I don't mind. Good-by, Mrs. Harris. Thank you."

Mrs. Harris reached the door of her office and turned, with her hand on the doorknob, for a last look at the incongruous pair. She saw a tall slim girl in a conservative black jacket and skirt, with a white scarf at her throat and a small black hat on her head, holding by the hand the tiny boy in his ludicrous coat, calmly smoking a cigarette.

"Don't forget," she called to Pax, "he's very old."

The red light flashed, and behind the opaque glass doors the shadow of the elevator appeared, slowly descending, then coming to a stop.

Pax and Jan stepped in and stood facing the folding metal gates. The board to the left of the operator showed small red lights next to most of the floor numbers.

Several people got on at the fifteenth floor, including two young women, evidently private secretaries or stenographers, with their inevitable sheer stockings, high-heeled shoes, and well-cut tailored suits.

Pax pulled the boy in front of her to make more room. One of the young women glanced down at Jan. Her casual look slowly changed to an inquisitive one. She glanced at Pax, then nudged her companion. Their eyes took in the child from the top of his brown head to his ungainly shoes. One of them whispered behind her hand, and they both giggled.

When they reached the main floor, everybody pushed and shoved, trying to be the first to get into the street. No one else noticed Pax and the child.

Jan's big shoes shuffled along, tapping sharply on the stone floor. When they reached the street, a brisk wind had sprung up, and Pax's skirt swirled around her knees. She held on to her hat with one hand and to Jan with the other. As she pushed through the people on the sidewalk toward the curb to hail a taxi, she felt the boy draw back. She saw that he was looking over his shoulder, and suddenly he snatched his hand away and ran back in the direction from which he'd come.

When she caught up with him, he was standing in front of a legless pencil peddler, who was holding out his wares with one hand and a hat with the other.

Jan pulled up his ridiculous coat until he could get one hand into his trouser pocket. Out came his last cigarette, which he gravely handed to the vendor.

As she caught him by the hand, and once more made her way to the curb, the child's voice floated up to her.

"*Er ist durstig,*" he said.

She stopped a taxi, helped the child in, and gave the driver the address. She nudged Jan and pointed out of the car window to the tall buildings which stretched up toward the sky. He nodded, then settled back indifferently, apparently looking at nothing. She took off her hat, leaned her head against the side of the taxi, closed her eyes, and tried to think.

How had she got here? From where had she come? Irrelevant thoughts jostled and collided against each other as they leaped through her head.

Pity for a mass of suffering humanity. Philip had probed at the pity in her, the pity supposedly born in the heart of every human being; first probed, then forced it up and out into her consciousness.

That was it. That was where she had started from. That was what had brought her to this, riding up the Avenue of the Americas in a taxi, confused and alone except for this unknown child whose future she had so confidently taken into her ignorant and not particularly able hands.

No, it went back much further than that. Back to something she didn't want to remember.

Again she looked down at the small boy, who sat so silently beside her, and her thoughts traveled even further back, to the strange solitude of her own childhood.

Prelude

A SLEEPY HORSE, warmly wrapped in blankets, was hitched to an old sleigh which stood just outside the Gifford house. Great flakes of snow fell thickly and steadily, while clouds of it whirled and spiraled across the Green, rising and falling with the wind which swept down from Mansfield Mountain. For two days, practically no vehicle had ventured on the streets of Mapleton, and the blizzard had raged so savagely that it seemed as though some invisible Titan were standing astride the mountaintop, viciously hurling colossal shovelfuls of snow on the little town.

Inside the Gifford house there was a tense stillness. Suddenly, a wail like the mewling of a little cat floated down from the second floor. Then again there was an ominous hush.

And so, in the year of our Lord, nineteen hundred and twenty, Pax Gifford opened her eyes to a life which was destined to walk down lonely vistas.

Viewed from the cradle and the floor, that early life was a normal and uneventful one. Her mother having died when she was born, Pax never experienced that maternal warmth and instinctive sense of safety to which, like all small animals, babies react. And her father, deeply grieved by the death of his young wife, paid practically no attention to her.

Edmund Gifford was a scholar and an archaeologist. He spent most of his waking hours with his poets, his prophets, and his philosophers— philosophers of the early Syrians and Egyptians, the Chinese and the Semites, although he occasionally brought himself up to date with the Greeks and the Romans. The heavy, musty library of the Gifford home was his sanctum. The only concession he made to fatherhood was to allow his daughter to play on the floor, on the nurse's day out, while he pored over his books.

Once when Pax was about fourteen months old, she crawled over to the fireplace, attracted by the dancing sheen of the firelight on the hearthstone. With a baby's curiosity, she stretched forth her small hand

and picked up a glowing ember. The shock of that first agonizing pain was, in a way, a symbol that for many years both her bitter and her joyous experiences would be her own discoveries.

When she was two or three years old, her bored nurse would dump her in a sand pile which belonged to the children next door while she gossiped with the servants. Pax was a silent, obedient child, so she would stay where she was put, sedately filling her pail with sand and pouring it out again, completely indifferent to the noisy antics of Bill and Emily Bascomb.

When Professor Gifford's housekeeper, Martha Endicott, considered that the little girl was old enough to take care of herself, she dismissed the nurse and took over. Martha was a rawboned, forbidding, typical New England spinster. She was devoted to her charge, but, like so many of the old Puritan stock, she didn't believe in any outward display of affection. She had Edmund Gifford and the house to look after as well as the girl, so, during play hours, Pax was left pretty much to her own devices.

In spite of her shyness, Pax would be drawn reluctantly into the games of the two little extroverts next door, but she could usually be found standing by herself at the edge of their circle, watching them soberly, quite removed from their hearty normalcy.

Her kindergarten years were a fleeting memory to her. Her first signs of quickening interest appeared when she began going to a country grammar school about a mile away from her home. Martha sent her off every morning about eight o'clock, watching her as she ran down the garden path, swinging her lunch box, her black braids bouncing on her shoulders.

But it was not any desire for the knowledge in books that urged her along that country road, for that was not in her. There were paths which wound their way from that road into the woods, and in the woods there were the most amazing secrets.

She was nearly always late for class and sometimes she didn't go at all. The young country teacher hesitated to complain to the President of the College that his only daughter was a constant truant and not too intelligent in her classes when she did attend. So, until she was twelve, when Edmund sent her away to boarding school for two years, she continued to play hookey and to revel in it. She would get just out of sight of the town; then she'd worm her small body through a barbed-wire fence, scamper across a meadow, scramble through the underbrush and bracken, and make her way through the woods to her retreat.

It was a cave in the side of the mountain, about fifty feet up the slope. She loved it at all seasons and at all times of the day; the cobwebs in the dew of the morning, and at noon the good smell of the warm, sun-baked earth which lay just outside.

She waited eagerly in the autumn for the changing colors of the leaves, the October wood-smoke that floated to her from some distant bonfire, and the smell of the sap in the pines and maples. In the late summer she watched the golden dandelions turn into puffs, soar away, and melt into the air.

She took her dolls there, and she cut out pictures and hung them on the walls of the cave with adhesive tape. She wriggled her small body down into the soft earth until she made herself a kind of cradle. There she would lie and think of nothing in particular. She'd watch the sunlight outside, dancing on the grass, or, if there was rain, listen to the sound of the drops on the stones above her head.

The only place she was happy was in her cave, because she felt safe there; because no one else knew where it was or even of its existence.

She called it Finnegan's Cave.

She hated boarding school. Pax was never gregarious, and the child-herd spirit frightened her. She was desperately unhappy and continually wrote to her father, imploring him to take her away.

After two years, he finally allowed her to come home, to that ugly comfortable house with its mansard roof, its cupolas and verandas; home to Martha, home to loneliness and her father's indifference.

He was vaguely irritated and disappointed that Pax had not inherited any of his love of scholarship. He couldn't understand her hatred of school and study, and he insisted that she have some mental discipline.

Amy Sanders, who was a Middle Westerner and a widow, lived just across the Green from the Gifford house. She and Edmund were old friends and she was devoted to the girl. Amy had very little money, but she had a beautiful old house, most of which she rented out to students. She collected antiques from all parts of the countryside and sold them when she could. She just managed to make ends meet, so when Edmund offered her a weekly salary to work with Pax for three or four hours a day, she agreed. She was not an intellectual woman, nor was she in any way a teacher, but she had an alert mind and Pax liked her. She did very little, except to choose the right books and try to keep the girl's mind active.

One afternoon in the early spring, Amy and Pax were alone in Amy's charming drawing room. Amy never allowed the students in that particular room, but Pax had her lessons there.

Pax was chewing on her pencil, daydreaming, as usual, and wishing

27

she were at Finnegan's. Amy watched her as she drew indeterminate circles and little houses and animals on the pad she held on her knee.

"Pax, what was the date of the Battle of Bunker Hill?"

"Er—eighteen hundred and sixty-three," replied Pax vaguely.

"Really, my dear, that's very interesting." Amy closed her book with a snap. "Well, that's enough for today." She got up and started out of the room.

"Where are you going, Mrs. Sanders? Isn't that right?"

"You're just about one hundred years out of the way. Not quite," she added. "I'm going over to see your father."

Pax showed an unexpected flash of humor.

"It's no use," she said. "He wouldn't know."

Amy strode across the Green, pushed open the door of the Gifford house, and walked determinedly into the library.

Gifford sat in his favorite wing chair, beside the dying fire. There were bits of tobacco on his coat and on the carpet around the chair, and he was so intent on his book that he didn't hear her come in.

"Hello, Edmund."

A quick frown wrinkled his forehead, as though he were annoyed at being interrupted. He put his book on his lap, face down.

"Pull up a chair, Amy."

She settled herself comfortably and took out her cigarette case. She was one of the few women in Mapleton at that time who smoked.

Edmund smiled at her. "Bad influence for my daughter."

"Poppycock!" she said. "I might as well add to the general rankness in this room. How can you breathe in here, Edmund?"

"I do very well, thanks," he said dryly. "What's the matter?"

"What are you reading?"

"Antisthenes." He smiled contentedly. "He knew some of the answers."

"That's more than you do," she snorted. "Antisthenes, indeed! Edmund, you ought to be ashamed of yourself."

"What have I done now?"

"Nothing. Not now, not ever." She paused for a moment. "Has it ever occurred to you that Pax is well on her way to becoming an illiterate?"

Edmund leaned over, knocked the ashes out of his pipe on the hearth, and calmly refilled it.

"What's she done now?"

"Not a thing, the poor child. After two schools and me, she just doesn't know the difference between the American Revolution and the

28

Civil War, that's all! God knows when she thinks the World War was fought!"

Edmund grinned. "That piece of information isn't going to do her— or the rest of the world—a damn bit of good. Let her look to the future. Dates are no good to her." He pointed to his book. "The old boys proved that."

"Edmund, it's a shame and a disgrace to neglect that child the way you're doing."

"Really, Amy, I don't know what you're talking about."

"Why don't you know her, Edmund? She's worth knowing, believe me." She smiled wryly. "Even if she doesn't know whether Omaha's a state or a city. I've gone as far with her as I can."

Edmund puffed on his pipe and stared into the fire. Amy had struck at him more forcefully than she realized. He knew that he had resented the child when she had cost his wife her life, but that resentment had long passed. It had burned itself out into an acceptance and an indifference. His present neglect had sprung from sheer selfishness and a desire to live his life as he wished.

"Perhaps you'd be good enough to tell me one thing. How does one get to know a young girl? They're a little outside my ken."

"Love her, Edmund. She needs it desperately."

"Don't be absurd, Amy. I do love her. She's my own daughter."

"Oh, no, Edmund. If you did, you would know her, and you admit that you don't. You see, Edmund, with all your great wisdom, you don't realize that you don't have to know a person to love her. You love her in order to know her."

Amy left him beside his fire, staring into and beyond the dying embers.

When she returned to her own house, she found Pax still doodling on her exercise pad. Amy watched the girl for a moment. Pax's elbow was on the table beside her and her cheek rested on her closed fist. Amy noticed the stillness of the black head, the weary droop of the slim shoulders.

There was a disturbing quality about the child. She wondered if she herself were as much of a stranger to Pax as everyone else appeared to be, or was it the other way round? Was it the girl herself who was the stranger?

"What are you doing, Pax?"

"Nothing. What did Father say?"

"About what?"

"About what you said," replied Pax.

"What did I say?"

29

"That's what I'm trying to find out."

Pax stared at Amy with an anxious expression in her eyes. Through the organdy curtains, the sun shone across the girl's face and made the white skin seem much whiter. Amy saw that there were two or three tiny pimples on the pointed chin.

"How old are you, Pax?"

"Fourteen. Why?"

"Yes, of course you are!"

The idea went through Amy's mind that the girl must have passed that extremely difficult time of puberty. She wondered if anyone had explained it to her, or if it had come as a painful shock. She made a mental note to ask Martha tomorrow.

"Pax, what do you want from life?"

"I don't know. Nothing, I guess. What is there to want?"

"You know we all want to help you—your father, too—but we don't know how to, Pax, unless you help us to know."

"I don't want anything, Mrs. Sanders, honestly I don't."

"Dear child," Amy said, "you need companions of your own age, not an old woman like me. You need new interests, don't you see?"

Pax burst into tears. "That's what you told Father," she wailed. "You don't want me any more! You don't like me. I thought you liked me. Nobody likes me!"

Amy quietly gave the girl her handkerchief and let her cry it out. Pax blew her nose and handed the handkerchief back to her.

"Better keep it," said Amy. "You'll probably need it again in a minute."

Pax hunched further down in her chair and looked straight ahead.

"Do you know, I'm a little surprised at you, Pax. You're behaving like a small child instead of an intelligent young woman."

"I'm not intelligent. I'm a dope."

"You've got something there, but do you have to be? I simply told your father what I've told you: that there must be something you want and some way of getting it for you."

An hour later, Pax started for home. She walked slowly across the Green, then back again; down the hill, and up the other side; around the college, then back across the Green again. It took her the better part of an hour to get there.

She was confused and unhappy. That strange passivity behind which she had dwelt so long had been disturbed. She didn't want to see anyone, least of all her father. Now that he'd had a serious talk with

Mrs. Sanders, she knew he'd question her and ask her what she wanted to do.

Well, she didn't want to do anything. She just wanted to be left alone. The tears started to well up again. She knew—she'd steal around to the back and wait outside in the dark until she saw Martha go into the front of the house; then she'd sneak in the back door, up the back stairs. She'd say she had a headache and ask to have dinner in bed.

As she started across the lawn, the front door opened and Philip Winslow came out. Winslow was a tall, thin young man of about twenty-four. He was a graduate of Mapleton and had become a great favorite of Professor Gifford's. After his graduation, he had returned to the college as an instructor.

Pax was never shy with Winslow, but she didn't want to see him tonight, either. She stood very still, hoping no one would notice her, and watched Philip swing down the path. Then she started for the back of the house. Her father's voice stopped her.

"Come in this way, Pax. The grass is damp."

She was for it. He'd see she'd been crying, too. She ran up the steps, pushed by him, and made for the hall stairs.

"Wait a minute." He was holding open the door of the library. "Come in here for a moment, will you? There's a fine fire, and I'd like a little company while I have a drink."

Pax threw her coat on the hall seat, went over to the fireplace, and stood looking down into the flames. The Professor went across to the table and poured himself a whiskey.

"The years I spent in England got me into this very pleasant habit that I've never quite wanted to rid myself of. Sit down, dear child, but not in my chair."

As if she ever would!

"May I give you a small glass of sherry?"

"Oh, no, Father. I don't think so."

"Try it. It'll do you good. A little *apéritif* before dinner never hurts anyone." He handed it to her. "Very convivial too. We must do this every evening, Pax. I think I should like it very much."

Here it comes, she thought to herself, and she gritted her teeth and waited.

"Getting a little brisk out, don't you think? How you young women go about in this weather without hats is beyond me."

Pax didn't answer. Why couldn't she think of something to say? Why did she always feel such a dope when she was with her father? She sipped the golden liquid and was surprised to find how warm and pleasant it felt as it slipped down her throat. The fire was comforting. She liked the room, too.

"Sorry I didn't ask Winslow to dine with us. You'd have liked that, wouldn't you?"

"Yes."

She emptied her glass and twirled it around in her fingers. "Father, this is very good. May I have a little more?"

"Of course."

She didn't really want it, but it might put off that inevitable lecture a little longer. She took another sip. Strange, but she didn't seem to feel quite so nervous.

"If I were you, Pax, I wouldn't drink it so fast. You'll enjoy it more if you sip it."

"Yes."

"You like Winslow, don't you?" Edmund asked abruptly.

"Yes, I like him. Don't you?"

"Good man, Winslow, always has been. Takes a lot of work off my shoulders. I don't understand his subject, though."

"What is his subject, Father?"

"Psychology. He majored in it. He'll make a good professor for us someday."

"What's psychology, Father?" It had just slipped out. She hadn't meant to ask it. Why couldn't she keep her mouth shut?

"Psychology? Well, my dear, the psyche is the soul or the mind. Some people confuse them, but my belief is they're one and the same. Psychology is the science that treats of the mind. It investigates the phenomena of consciousness and behavior."

"Yes?"

The corner of his mouth twitched a little. "Someday, when you're older, Philip will explain it to you better than I can."

A gong sounded in the hall.

"That's dinner, Pax. Shall we go in or do you want to go upstairs first?"

Pax got to her feet and staggered a little. She'd forgotten all about that headache she'd been determined to have.

Gradually he broke down a great deal of her diffidence. He talked at random on easy subjects which he thought might interest her. In spite of the fact that he was a recluse and a scholar, part of his job was understanding how to handle young people. He knew better than to force her out into the open. He realized that one too abrupt move from him would send her back into that inner secretiveness for which, in a way, he was convinced he was responsible.

32

The evening rituals continued. Sometimes he asked Amy or Philip Winslow to dine with them. She liked the nights with Philip best.

There were many conferences between Amy, Edmund, and Philip which Pax knew nothing about. When they finally determined that the time was ripe, Edmund made up his mind to broach the subject of study.

"Pax, my dear," he said to her one night, as she sat on the arm of his chair, "how would you like to engage the President of Mapleton College as a private tutor?"

"I guess I'd like it."

She knew that was what he wanted her to say.

"I can only give you an hour or so a day, but perhaps we can organize that mind of yours a bit and I can refresh my tired old one on subjects which I haven't thought about for years."

And so her education began.

Edmund embarked upon his new undertaking with a certain amount of enthusiasm. It gave him a new interest and it gratified his ego to think he might shape this young mind the way he wanted to.

During those first few weeks, Pax was happier than she'd been at any time in her life. It was the first time in her fourteen years that anyone had taken a real interest in her. But Edmund Gifford had no warmth left. His self-imposed, sedentary life had taken toll of his tolerance and his temper, and, except in dealing with his own subject, he was an erratic and stern schoolmaster. He gradually tired of his new toy, and his interest in his daughter began to wane, so again Pax turned into herself. It was the birth of self-pity in her, and for the first time, in the secret depths of her young heart, she realized that she was lonely.

Pax was approaching her fifteenth year. In spite of herself, the compulsory exercise of her mind had done away with some of her shyness. And she had found one great friend, Philip Winslow.

One afternoon about five o'clock, she flung herself into his room at Amy's.

"What do you think he wants me to do now?"

"Your father?"

She threw herself on the floor and crossed her legs under her.

"Yeah," she said in disgust. "He wants me to learn Grecian."

"Greek, kid," said Philip.

"Why?" she demanded.

"Why what?" Philip grinned. "Why Greek or why does he want you to learn it?"

"Both," she said flatly. "Why is it Greek instead of Grecian? It's 'Ode to a Grecian Urn,' isn't it?"

" 'Ode *on* a Grecian Urn,' dope."

"It's Italian and Rumanian, isn't it?"

"Yeah. But it isn't Francian. It's French."

"Why?" asked Pax.

"Grecian is Hellenic. Hellenic is a classical Greek—oh, what the hell —and I didn't mean to make a pun. Ask your father, and let's get on with your gripe."

"He says I've got to learn Greci—Greek, or I won't be able to read real poetry. Well, I've had enough poetry! I've had enough of everything! And most of all, I've had enough of Father!"

"And honest to God, kid, I think he's had enough of you."

Suddenly her face cleared, and she crawled over to him, rested her forearms on his knee, and knelt there, looking up at him hopefully.

"Yes, I really think he has," he said thoughtfully, half to her, half to himself.

He picked her up off the floor, put his hands on her shoulders, and smiled calmly into her eyes.

"Oh, Phil, I can't stand this going on day after day being made to feel more and more of a fool."

"Look, Pax, will you tell me one thing honestly?"

"Of course."

"Don't you want to study? You're not fifteen yet, you know."

She began to walk up and down the room.

"Sure I want to study, but I don't know *what* I want to study." She stopped suddenly and her face began to pucker. "I can't learn what he tells me!" she wailed. "It just won't go into my head!"

Philip caught her by the hand and started for the door, pulling her after him.

"Let's go raid Amy's icebox. I'm hungry. And then I'm going to take you home."

Fifteen minutes later Pax was in the kitchen, perched up on the back of a chair, her feet on the seat, munching on a chicken sandwich. Between bites, Pax was still muttering her resentment at being treated like a bluestocking.

"First thing you know, he'll be wanting me to learn those Sem— Sem—Sem-something languages he's so crazy about."

"Semitic?"

"Yeah," she said, "what's that?"

"Well, the Semitic languages possess records of great antiquity. In other words, it's about as far back as you can go. The Semitic languages include Arabic, Phoenician, Hebrew, Aramaic—"

"Hebrew," she interrupted. "That's Jewish, isn't it?"

"Not necessarily, but it usually is."

She thought for a moment. "Do I know any Jews?"

"In Mapleton? I don't think so."

"Papa Leclerc's a Jew."

Philip looked at her sharply. "Who told you that? Papa Leclerc's a Roman Catholic."

She jumped down from the chair, put her fingers under the tap, then dried them on the hand towel behind the door.

"Em Bascomb said he was. It was last summer when we were having a chocolate sundae. Em said he was a dirty old Jew because he didn't put enough ice cream in 'em."

Philip looked at her gravely. "If I were you, Pax, I'd remember never to let anyone say a thing like that to me again."

He stared at her, trying to decide whether she was very ignorant or very innocent. She couldn't be trying to be funny.

"Philip," she demanded, "would I know a Jew if I saw one?"

"I hope not," he said, and pushed her gently through the kitchen door.

4

Pax was jarred sharply back to the present. As the taxi neared Fifty-seventh Street, the red light flashed. There was a shrieking of brakes and the driver pulled up so sharply that Pax was nearly thrown from the seat. Her first thought was for the boy.

He had fallen on his knees and had scraped along the floor of the cab, but he quickly picked himself up and sat back again. She saw that his knees were black with dirt and there was a little blood on one of them.

She looked anxiously into his face. Not even an involuntary twinge of pain had flashed across it. For a moment she thought of Tubby, of how he would have yelled with pain and rage, and how she wouldn't have blamed him, but this young stoic didn't even examine the bruises.

Pity for the boy suddenly became mixed with shame and contempt for herself for being surprised at his courage, and she heard again her young voice asking Philip if she would know a Jew if she saw one, and Philip's enigmatic reply: "I hope not."

Now she understood what he meant, and instinctively she put her arm around the boy and gave him a quick hug. He didn't respond, but somehow she felt that he liked it. She took a clean handkerchief out of her handbag, tried to brush off the dirt, and gently wiped away the few drops of blood. Then she folded it on the clean side and tied it around his knee.

When they reached the hotel she helped the boy out, and as she paid for the taxi she noticed—and was grateful for it—that the driver showed no curiosity about the pathetic figure who stood waiting quietly for her on the sidewalk.

Without thinking, she pushed Jan ahead of her through the revolving door and followed him. Instead of stepping out into the hotel, the boy continued around again. With an absurd sense of panic, she waited until the door made the complete circle, grabbed him, and pulled him out of it.

He looked at her, then back at the door, and just for a moment she

36

thought she saw a twinkle of interest in his brown eyes. To him, a revolving door must seem a new but not frightening monster.

As they started past the elevators, which were a few feet to the left of the hotel entrance, she caught Jan by the arm and gently pushed him up against the wall.

"*Bleiben sie hier*, Jan," she said. She wasn't sure that was correct or that he understood her, but she smiled, shook her finger at him, and tried to make him know that he was not to follow her.

She walked across the lobby to the desk and asked for her key, and then she felt something touch her elbow. She looked down and saw that Jan was standing beside her, his brown head just reaching above the level of the desk. With a quick frown of annoyance, she explained to the clerk that her luggage had been taken up earlier and asked the number of her room.

The clerk studied the register, but kept glancing at the boy in his silly coat, out of the corner of his eye.

"Just a moment, Mrs. Lyttleton," he said, and disappeared behind the panel of letter and key compartments. There was a low murmur of voices. She waited impatiently.

Another clerk appeared, and he too went over to the register, and he too kept looking at the boy.

Pax became more and more nervous as the minutes passed. After what seemed to her an interminable time, the first clerk returned, took a key from one of the compartments, and called a bellboy.

"Take Mrs. Lyttleton up to twelve-sixteen. Her luggage has already gone up." He turned to Pax. "You'll excuse my asking, Mrs. Lyttleton, but you did say that you only wanted the room for one night, didn't you?"

"We are leaving in the morning," Pax replied shortly.

"You see, madam, all the hotels are very crowded and we are booked way in advance. You understand our position, of course?"

She turned and walked quickly to the elevator, followed by the boy.

The bellboy opened the door of her room, switched on the light, and crossed to the window to open it.

"That's all right," she said, and opened her bag to get some change. Before she closed it she took out the long envelope given her by Mrs. Harris, and stood there with it in her hand, waiting for the bellboy to go.

"Will there be anything else, miss?"

"Nothing, thank you."

As he passed Jan, he leaned over and gave him a slap on his back.

"Hiya, feller! Goin' to like it here, huh?" He looked from her to the child, grinned, and left.

Pax tossed her hat onto a chair and pushed her hair back from her hot forehead. Her whole body ached with exhaustion and a pall seemed to be settling down over her. She looked down at the papers in her hand and decided to put off reading them until later. The child's past could wait; his present was more important. She walked over to the table between the beds and put the envelope in the drawer.

"Come here, Jan. Let me take off your coat."

He looked puzzled, shook his head, and gave a little shrug of his shoulders. She went over to him, knelt down, and unbuttoned his coat.

"Coat," she said distinctly.

"Ca-a-wt?" he repeated.

"That's it, Jan," she said, almost gaily. She felt better. Apparently he was going to try.

"Now, you sit there like a good boy, while I unpack," she said, putting him in a big chair by the window.

She lifted her suitcase onto the bed, pulled out her nightgown and dressing gown, and threw them over the foot. She took her bottles and toilet articles and carried them into the bathroom.

When she returned, Jan was no longer sitting by the window. He was standing at the foot of the bed, stroking the soft, shining satin of her nightgown. His big eyes looked up at her.

"*Nett!*" he said.

He hasn't anything to sleep in, she thought. He hasn't anything to unpack. He hasn't anything but me! Suddenly he began to tug at her arm and shifted from one foot to the other.

Dear God! she thought. What am I thinking of! The poor little thing. And I've lived with a small boy for eight years!

She took him by the hand and led him in the direction of the bathroom.

"*Wollen sie im Badezimmer gehen?*"

"*Danke,*" he said.

"Thank you, see? *Danke* is thank you." He looked at her inquiringly. "Never mind," she said, and pushed him into the bathroom and shut the door.

She remembered his knees. She rummaged in her valise and found the iodine. She had always made a point of carrying something of the kind ever since Tubby was old enough to collect scrapes and bruises. She stood with her back against the wall in the narrow passage outside the bathroom and waited.

After she had bathed his knees and painted the scraped one, he wandered over to the window, leaned his elbow on the sill, and, chin in hand, gazed out over the city. The tall, indeterminate gray buildings looked as if they had been cut out of cardboard and propped against an opalescent green sky. The windows were like washed-out spangles of light which slowly deepened into brilliant yellow as the darkness fell.

"Jan," she asked, *"vous avez faim?"* He puckered his forehead. *"Hunrig?"* Was that the word?

His face brightened. He nodded his head vigorously. *"Ja!"* he said.

She took him into the bathroom again, washed his face and neck and ears, scrubbed his hands, and brushed his thick brown hair. He stood passively and let her do it. She put on his thin little jacket, and they started down the hall toward the elevators.

Just as she rang the bell, she remembered the expressions on the faces of the hotel clerks as they looked at the grotesque little figure in the enormous coat standing with his chin above the desk. She took the boy's hand and walked swiftly back to their room.

When the floor waiter brought her the menus, she handed one to Jan without thinking. She drew it back quickly. What a fool! He's never seen a menu. He's probably never seen any food except scraps, just enough to keep that unwanted spark of life from flickering out altogether.

She hurriedly ordered a big meal for him and a chop and a salad for herself. She made gestures of eating.

"Soon," she said. *"Bientôt*—soon."

"So-oon?" Jan repeated with an upward inflection.

What was the damn word in German?

"Bald?" she said, questioningly.

"Ja, bald! So-oon, *ja."*

She gave him a copy of *Life* which she had brought with her on the train. She opened it, put it on his lap, and pointed to the pictures. She sat on the arm of his chair, turning the pages slowly.

They'd got halfway through the magazine when to her horror she turned to a picture of dead bodies, piled one on top of the other. The caption under it was: "1945." The opposite page showed groups of skeletonlike, despairing people behind a barbed-wire fence, the children half-naked, their little bellies distended from hunger. That caption read: "1947."

She didn't know whether to take the book away from him or to ignore it and turn the page as quickly as possible. She looked down at him and there was panic in her face. The child was looking at the frightening scenes with complete indifference, and she was stunned by the thought of what was locked away in this boy's memory.

When the dinner was served, he ate like a ravenous little animal. He took the soup plate in his two hands and drank the soup in four or five noisy gulps. He ate the steak and vegetables with his fingers. He couldn't manage the mashed potatoes that way, so he lapped them up like a dog.

Pax was appalled. But when he had finished, she couldn't resist ordering him some ice cream with chocolate sauce. When he tasted it, the expression on the small face delighted her, and she laughed happily when she wiped the chocolate off his face with a warm washcloth.

After the waiter had cleared away the table, Jan went back and climbed up in his chair by the window, took out his mouth organ, and put it to his lips.

What was she to do with him the rest of the evening? She looked at her wrist watch. It wasn't quite eight o'clock. She couldn't take him to see a moving picture. She wouldn't risk the snickers of people when they saw that long coat flapping around his legs. She'd have to stick out the evening somehow. She felt that remote, intangible loneliness begin to creep over her again.

She opened her case, took out a cigarette, and lighted it. Jan dropped his harmonica, ran across the room, and grabbed it out of her hand. Angrily, she slapped his hand and took the cigarette away from him. She saw a surly look come over his face and she remembered Mrs. Harris's words: "Blows—Gestapo."

She drew him to her, patted his cheek, and offered him a cigarette from her case. She lighted it for him. He took it silently, turned, and went back to his chair.

When he'd smoked it way down to the end, he opened the window and threw it out, just as he had done that afternoon when Mrs. Harris had scolded him. Then he sat and stared straight in front of him.

Pax went on reading. Soon she noticed that his eyes were closed and his head was drooping lower and lower. Naturally, he must be exhausted. She'd put him to bed immediately. That would solve everything.

"Jan. Jan, dear."

She shook him gently. Startled, he jerked his head up. His little fist tightened and he drew it back as if to strike. Pax took his small wrist in her hand and patted him on the shoulder.

"*Bett*, Jan."

He got out of the chair and swayed a little. His small face suddenly looked hurt and his skin was green. He began to gag.

Hurriedly she started to drag him to the bathroom, but before she had taken more than a step, he threw up all over her.

Oh, damn! Damn! Damn! Oh, the stupid little fool! Oh, God! What am I going to do with him?

She pushed him into the bathroom and held his head over the toilet bowl. Another retch and the wonderful dinner she had ordered for him was no more.

She slipped out of her skirt and threw it over the tub. Then she cleaned up the boy, took off his clothes except for his torn little undershirt, tucked him into bed, and turned off all the lights.

Pax lay in the bath. She put her hands on the floor of the tub, raising and lowering her slim body and floating it back and forth in the water. The tired mucles finally relaxed, the tenseness seemed to flow out of her finger tips, and her thoughts began to sort themselves out of the chaos of the last few hours.

What was this irritability which she couldn't control? Was it because there was no common language between them? Perhaps that was it. She wanted so much to get inside that little imprisoned mind, but she couldn't.

Was she unconsciously on the defensive for her own son? Would she so completely have lost control of her nerves if it had been Tubby who had been sick all over her? Would she have behaved differently if this child were not a stranger to her womb? Was it because he was foreign, alien? Was it because he was Jewish? *Was* he Jewish? Why had that thought come into her mind?

What would Philip have done these last few hours? How would Robert have handled it? Robert, sweet, strong, without nerves, and with that charming, nonchalant good humor.

Why didn't Robert come home? She wanted him so. The war was over, had been for nearly two years. The Army of Occupation didn't need him the way she did. Robert must have seen remnants of this horror of which Jan was an infinitesimal part. Robert would have leaned down and taken the little skinny body in his arms and all would have been well.

She got out of her bath, dried herself, and put on her nightgown.

She'd get to know him. She'd be damned if she wouldn't.

She tiptoed into the room and got quietly into bed. Jan didn't stir. He was sound asleep. She put on the bed light, opened the table drawer beside her as softly as she could, and took out Mrs. Harris's envelope. She drew out the papers and began to read.

JAN BEN ROZOV.

POLISH OR POSSIBLY CZECH. PROBABLY JEWISH.

PARENTS ALMOST CERTAINLY PERISHED IN THE CREMATORIUM IN
   BIRKENAU.

BOY SAVED FROM THE FURNACES BY A POLISH WOMAN, OLGA
   WIENOWSKI.

PICKED UP WITH HER BY THE RUSSIANS WHEN THEY ENTERED THE
   TOWN, BOTH ESCAPING FROM THE CAMP.

BOY THOROUGHLY EXAMINED PHYSICALLY.

GOOD HEALTH EXCEPT FOR UNDERNOURISHMENT.

NOTHING KNOWN OF FAMILY OR BACKGROUND.

That was all, but there was a short letter from a woman who was
undoubtedly an executive in a Distribution Center in France. It was
in French, but there was a translation attached to it.

To whom it may concern:

   *This child has been with us for six weeks, after having gone from
one Distribution Center to another in many parts of Poland and
Germany.*

   *He is unusually smart for his age and, we think, sensitive and
responsive. He is very different from many of the other children we
have had, who seem to be interested only in the physical comforts
they are just discovering. Naturally, the language problem may prove
difficult.*

   *He entered this Center with Olga Wienowski who, having been in
the trusted position of a* blocova *in the camp, was able to induce the
guards at Oświęciem at certain dangerous times to turn their heads
the other way, when she hid him under her bed and so saved his life
for several years.*

   *I will not go into the few details that I know of his experiences in
Oświęciem which were told to me by Olga. He will, I'm sure,
eventually tell you himself all he remembers.*

   *He is and, I presume, will continue to be very unhappy for a
time because of his separation from this woman. We located some
of her family, who were very averse to her taking the boy, insisting
that there were enough mouths to feed without his. So regretfully
we were forced to take him away from her.*

   *If there is any further information we can give you, I hope you
will let us know.*

I hope he will find a good home, for we think he is a fine little boy and in this short time we have become exceedingly fond of him.

He is entirely alone in the world, as far as we know, and he is very sad.

Sincerely,
Celeste   Blum

Slowly, Pax folded the papers and put them back in the envelope. Then, for the first time, she really let go and the tears streamed down her face. She stifled the sobs so as not to wake him.

Oh, Jake, Jake, it could have been you!

She took her handkerchief from under the pillow, dried her eyes, and was about to turn off the light when she heard a soft whimpering from the other bed. Jan's little body was twitching under the bedclothes and his head was whipping back and forth on the pillow.

Swiftly she got out of bed and knelt beside him. She put her hand gently on his forehead; it was hot, and damp with perspiration.

"Jan," she whispered, "oh, don't! Please don't!"

His body gradually relaxed and the small tortured face became serene again. He didn't wake and she knelt there, stroking his head.

What torment had he relived in that moment?

She leaned closer and looked at him searchingly.

The long dark lashes cast a blue shadow under his eyes. The bones of his cheeks were more prominent in this light. His lips were slightly parted. She wondered what his teeth were like. She hadn't as yet seen him smile.

Was that short arched nose anything like Jake's? No, it wasn't really —or was it?

She cupped her pointed chin in her hand and with the other she went on stroking his hair.

She'd take him home tomorrow and they would begin from there.

Interlude

PAX FIRST MET JAKE in her father's office. One autumn day she made her way across the Green and the campus, leaning into the brisk wind which had blown up suddenly and swept the rain away. The young trees that bordered the lawn around the college bent low over the stone wall, and the copper and carmine leaves rustled as they whirled and spiraled in the wind.

She went up the steps of the administration building and down the hall to her father's office. She was about to open the door when it was swung out of her hand by someone on the other side. It caught her off balance, and she fell into the arms of a young man who was just coming out.

He stooped to pick up the books she'd dropped, handed them to her with an "I'm sorry," and started out the door.

"Just a minute, Felder, I don't think you've met my daughter."

"No, I haven't. How do you do?"

"How do you do?"

He looked nice. He was neither tall nor short; thin—thinner even than Philip. He had a lean, humorous face, straight black hair, and eager, narrow green eyes, the under lids full, slanting definitely upward in the outer corners.

She looked away.

"You and Felder ought to know each other, Pax," said her father. "He's quite a poet in his way. Wish he took as much interest in some of his other subjects."

"I thought I'd had my lecture for the day, sir," the young man said, but he smiled at Edmund, and Pax saw that these two not only understood each other but liked each other as well.

"Here are your books, Father. Are they the ones you wanted?"

Edmund riffled the pages of one of them. "Thanks, my dear."

Pax smiled shyly at the young man as he held the door open for her. "Thank you, Mr.—er—Felder?" she said, with an upward inflection.

"That's it. Felder. Jacob Felder."

Pax left her father's office, walked slowly down the hall, and out of the building. When she reached the bottom step, the wind caught her and swept her onward across the Green in the direction of her house. It blew her crisp black hair into her eyes and buckled her skirt around her knees. Then it propelled her right by the house and up the muddy country road. She half walked, half ran along the wagon ruts until she came to the barbed-wire fence. She climbed through it and in a moment she was ankle deep in the lush, black earth and glowing autumn leaves.

She stopped and leaned against the trunk of a tree to get her breath.

What was it that had happened to her? She had slipped; two strong hands had held her firmly, then set her on her feet. For an instant she had looked into two strange eyes, had felt a warm breath on her cheek, and a singing had begun in her blood which had mounted and mounted until she could hear it in her ears. She had been stupid and mute and had clutched onto the knob because of the queer giddiness that had swept over her.

She pushed the hair back out of her eyes, put her hands deep in the pockets of her coat, and trudged on toward Finnegan's.

She sat down on a great gray boulder just outside the cave and looked over the valley and the purple mountains beyond. Her eyes caught the glint of the afternoon sun on the faraway rails which wound through the hills, and the wind threw back to her the hollow sound of a train whistle in the distance.

All at once, the face of the young man rose up before her. She remembered chiseled features in a thin white face, the long green eyes with their straight lashes, and a knife blade of a smile, which was there and was gone, but not before she had noticed the suggestion of a dimple that lurked under the left corner of his mouth and gave his smile a rare sweetness.

A flock of wild mallards whirred over her head. The lilac tint of the autumn twilight began to settle down over the woods.

She sprang to her feet. She'd just have time to run over to Philip's— for a little talk, if he were in the mood for it. She was in the mood, although she wasn't sure what she wanted to talk about. All she knew was that for some reason she was wondrously, awesomely happy.

Pax jerked at the latch of Amy's front door with her elbow, pushed the door open with her knee, and ran through the hall and up the stairs.

"Philip!" she called. "Hi, Philip! You in? Open the door, will you?"

The door swung open. Philip stood there in his stockinged feet as Pax shoved past him into the room and deposited a large package on the table.

"Hey! What've you got there?"

"It's a ham. Martha baked it yesterday. We've only taken a few slices off it."

"A whole ham? What in the name of all that's holy do you expect me to do with it?"

"Eat it! You can nibble on it whenever you feel hungry. It'll last a long time if you keep it in Mrs. Sanders' icebox." She buttoned up her coat. "I thought you'd like it," she said reproachfully, and started for the door.

"Like it? Of course I like it. But you don't have to keep me, you know."

As soon as he'd said it, he'd have given anything to take it back. His mind flashed back to the conversation they had had the first night of the semester, the night he'd been promoted to a professorship of psychology and sociology—the night he had suddenly realized that his kid had grown into a woman, and not a bad-looking one, either.

"Tell me about your summer," she had said. "What did you do?"

"I worked."

Pax had looked startled. "Worked! But it was summer vacation."

"I always work in summer vacations."

"You never told me!"

"You never asked me."

"What did you do?"

"Drove a truck."

Pax's lip had quivered. "Oh, Phil."

"Nothing the matter with driving a truck. Good healthy air, see the country. Hours a little cockeyed, that's all."

Pax had thrown herself out of the chair onto the floor at his feet. She had put her arms across his knees as she used to do when she was a small girl.

"Oh, Philip, that's why you're so thin! Mrs. Sanders told me you were thin. Phil, do you have to?"

"Yeah, I have to, so what?"

"Tell me."

"What?"

"All about you. I don't know, you see."

Philip had taken her hand and laid it in the palm of his. "What do you want to know?"

"Why do you have to work in the summer? I've got some money, you know, Phil. My mother left it to me—"

"You nice kid! I don't need any money. I just need to make a living for me and my mother."

"Aren't you lucky?" she had said. "I never had one, you know."

46

Now he looked at her with something more than affection. That was why, during the last few weeks, she had made excuses to bring him a batch of cookies or a jar of soup or a whole ham. He smiled wryly to himself. How dangerously romantic she still was.

"Take off your coat while I have a smoke. Sanders won't let me have a pipe downstairs."

He noticed that she was walking nervously about the room, stopping at the window a moment, then peering restlessly at the books in his bookcase.

"Stop prowling, kid. Sit down and let me look at that black head of yours and the silly face underneath it. It rests me."

She grinned and lay down on the couch.

"What's the matter?" she said. "Tired?"

"Kind of."

"Being an honest-to-God professor too much for you?"

"Could be," he replied. "You know, it's kind of tough getting you young people to think."

"Young!" said Pax derisively.

"That's what I said. And I'll thank you to pay my twenty-eight years some respect."

"What do you teach them, Phil?"

"Lots of things. Oh, they can read books. It's their damned hearts that are tough to reach. Why, kid"—he was sitting up straight now—"I told 'em today about those trust mongers who've been entertaining newspaper readers for the last few years by jumping out of windows. I told 'em they should have been forced to live out their span of life, and those fellers just looked at me as if I'd lost my mind. Damn it, Pax! I can't make 'em see that God made an awful mistake somewhere, because the wrong guys have been selling apples. Do you understand at all what I'm talking about?"

"Nope," said Pax cheerfully.

Philip laughed. "Say, look at your shoes. They're as muddy as mine. Bet they're wet, too. Where you been?"

He went over to her, knelt down, and took off her shoes. She wiggled her toes contentedly.

"I took a long walk in the woods. Oh, Phil, wasn't it a beautiful day?"

Philip put another log on the fire and pushed her wet shoes close to the blaze. "I didn't notice it much. Looked kind of windy to me. Where did you go?"

Pax hesitated for just a second. "Oh—just in the woods. The wind didn't seem to get in the woods. It just blew over the top of them. And, oh, Phil, you should have seen the colors! It was all gold and red and brown. The leaves were all crushed into the ground and the earth smelled black and wet—it was just beautiful!"

Philip watched her as she began to prowl again. She picked up a book and began to thumb through it. Suddenly she looked up at him.

"Say, Phil, do you know a guy named Jake Felder?"

It had been a strange and unexpected day from the beginning, when she saw the letter lying beside her breakfast plate. She opened it with great excitement—she never received letters—and read in small hand-printing: "Mr. Philip Winslow cordially invites Miss Pax Gifford to tea in his rooms on Friday, the nineteenth, from four-thirty to six." Why had her serious, solitary Philip chosen to give a tea party?

Out of sheer curiosity Pax arrived at Philip's well ahead of time, to find the room painfully tidy, with a crackling fire in the grate and a table covered with Amy's best tea cloth in the corner. On the table was a bowl of autumn flowers, Amy's silver tea service, plates of little sandwiches, and a large layer cake.

Dorcas Pembroke, one of Phil's rare dates, was already there, sitting comfortably in front of the fire, talking easily to Philip. Pax couldn't very well ask him now what it was all about. She didn't think she liked Dorcas very much.

About half past four, other guests began to arrive: Priscilla Pembroke, Tiny Jarvis, Butch Masters, Emily Bascomb and Bill, and then Bob Lyttleton, that drawly-voiced Southerner who lived across the hall from Philip.

She tried to make conversation with them all, but she wasn't used to talking with anyone except the few people who were close to her. Finally she took her cup of tea, retired to the window seat, and sat there, munching a piece of cake.

Then he came in. She noticed with what grace he moved as he went from one to the other, greeting those he knew and acknowledging introductions to the others.

When he got around to her, she fumbled with her cup, which he promptly took from her with one hand while he held out the other. He flashed that blade of a smile at her, apparently not noticing her embarrassment as she clumsily transferred the bit of cake to her left hand, wiped her right one surreptitiously on the cushion of the window seat, and shyly laid it in his.

She moved over and made a place beside her on the window seat and he sat with her there most of the afternoon.

The late autumn day was palely fading when Bill Bascomb drew up a chair in front of them.

"Mind if I join you?" he said.

She minded terribly. She had never really liked Bill and this afternoon she disliked him more than ever, for he interrupted her contentment.

The conversation straggled into the news and gossip of the college. Then Bill centered his attention on the young man who sat beside her.

"And what is your particular purpose in life, my fine fellow, after you leave this holy academy?"

"Me?" He smiled lazily at Bill. "I hope to be a journalist of sorts and do a little writing on the side."

"Yeah? I imagine that would be the most comfortable profession for you to follow."

"What do you mean, comfortable?"

"I mean, you'd be your own boss, in a way. Wouldn't have to depend on other people's indulgence, would you?"

There was a lull in the general conversation. Emily, who had been concentrating on the Lyttleton boy from across the hall, stopped flirting and smiled across at her brother, whom she admired extravagantly. Philip came over and sat on the desk next to Jake Felder's chair.

"Well, I'll tell you, Bascomb," the young man said, "I hope I'll always be lucky enough to win other people's indulgence."

Philip tried to turn the conversation to Amherst, from which Bill had been graduated the previous June, but Bill stuck to his original interest as a dog does to a bone.

"What nationality are you, Felder?"

Jake Felder smiled that charming smile. "I'm an American, Bascomb. Or isn't that what you mean?"

Bob Lyttleton stepped forward and Bill rose swiftly and swung his chair behind him.

Bob said, "Why, you son of a bitch—"

"It's all right, Bertie," interrupted Jake. "The feller has an inquisitive mind, that's all. We should encourage it."

He still smiled.

The party broke up quickly after that, and Jake asked if he might walk with her across the Green. She assented eagerly and then a little frown of disappointment flitted across her face as Lyttleton, without waiting for an invitation, swung along beside them.

The first stars were spinning in the pale sky, and in the cold dusk the lamplight indolently flicked on behind the windows of the houses. The frosty air stung her face and her eyes were moist with the cold. The wind whipped their voices behind them and they found themselves shouting in order to be heard.

Pax longed to tell Jake—although she didn't understand why—that Bill's questions and his voice had disturbed her, frightened her really, but she didn't dare. She felt, somehow, that she would be intruding. Besides, that Southerner was there.

When they reached the gate, she held out her hand to Jake, smiled at him shyly, and with a casual nod to Lyttleton she ran up the stairs and into the house.

Felder looked after her for a moment, then turned up the collar of his tweed jacket, buttoned it tightly over his turtle-neck sweater, and started back in the direction of the town. Lyttleton caught him by the arm, but Jake pulled away from him.

"I've got to go home," he said.

"Come on, stop in at the Bascombs' with me. I told Em I would. She'll be tickled to death to see you too."

"Can't do it, Bertie," said Jake.

"Why not? And I wish you'd stop calling me Bertie."

"What's the matter with Bertie? It's a nice, dainty name."

"Son of a bitch!" said Bob, and laughed.

The strange friendship between these two had been going on for three years. No two men could be more unlike or have less in common and yet they were inseparable.

Jacob Felder was self-confident and proud, with an unusual reserve for so young a man. He was an avid student, a great reader, and hated anything whatever to do with sports.

Robert Lyttleton was a good-looking giant of about twenty-two, a complete extrovert. He had a bright, shallow mind and was unsubtle, obstinate, and merry. He excelled in all sports and preferred to loaf comfortably through his four years of college. He had no shyness about his lack of enthusiasm for study and was perfectly content to fumble through with a great football record and the reputation of being popular. Although slightly arrogant, he was a good-natured young tough with a certain childlike quality, and he went out of his way to be liked.

"Come in just for five minutes," coaxed Bob.

"I can't do it."

"Why?"

"In the first place, you know I'm antisocial—with some people." Jake smiled sarcastically. "And besides, I've got a hell of a translation to do."

"Oh, come on, be a sport. Say, what do you see in that stuff, anyway? Does Virgil write anything illuminating about love?"

Jake glanced at him quickly and the corner of his eyes wrinkled in a

50

sardonic little grin. He had detected the change in Bob's voice and he saw that his friend was staring eagerly at a young woman who was languidly swinging her shapely buttocks along the other side of the street.

"She the latest?" said Jake. "Better switch to Euclid, Bertie. What you need is mathematics."

"I'll walk down with you as far as your street," Bob said.

"Thought you had a date with the Bascomb girl."

"To hell with her," said Bob good-naturedly. He kept his eyes glued to the girl, who continued along a few yards ahead of them, occasionally throwing them a lazy glance over her shoulder.

Jake put his hands in his pockets and strolled on, whistling a somber lament in a minor key.

"For God's sake, Jakie, lay off that mournful tune, will you? Can't you think of anything more cheerful?"

"Got no sense of music at all, you bastard," Jake said disdainfully, and went on whistling.

Jake lived in a bare, carpetless room in the French-Canadian quarter of town, on a street that ran at right angles to the main street; at his corner was Papa Leclerc's drugstore, the most popular meeting place in the town.

Papa had crossed the border from Quebec at the turn of the century and opened a small chemist's shop. He fared badly for many years because of the obstinacy of the Mapletonians, who continued to drive twenty-five miles to Burlington to buy their drugs.

One day a traveling salesman passed through the town with samples of soda-fountain equipment. Papa took a gamble. He invested what he had left, relegated the chemist's shop to one small counter at the back of the store, and his financial troubles were over.

The placards plastered on the mirror had become fly-specked, the names of his queer concoctions had changed from time to time, and the fountain now was clumsy and outdated, but it was the favorite haunt of the students.

It had gained in popularity during the last few weeks because of a sloe-eyed nymph named Jeannine, who had come to work there.

Jeannine Leclerc was the only daughter of Papa's brother in Quebec, whom Papa had not seen for years. The girl had been educated to become a nun, but she had run away from the convent only a few months before she was to take her final vows. After the parental rage had subsided, she had induced her father to let her come to the States and take a job with her uncle.

She satisfied Papa's French thrift by being willing to work for comparatively nothing. She was a shrewd young woman, with a slow, warm, rather decadent charm, and she decided that a soda fountain in a college town would be the most satisfactory market for exhibiting her wares to young men.

Now, from behind the half-open door of the Leclerc living quarters which were at the back of the store, she watched one of these young men, Bob Lyttleton, as he lolled against the wall at the corner of the soda fountain, his hot blue eyes focused on the door.

The girl unfastened the top button of her dress, turning down as low a "V" as she dared. She strolled toward the front of the store, tying her apron.

Jeannine was a furtive-faced beauty of about nineteen. She had high cheekbones, deep olive skin, milk-white teeth, and rather heavy lips. Her hair was black and oily, still cut short like a boy's, the only remaining symbol of her original dedication.

"Hello, beautiful. Make us a couple of chocolate sundaes, will you? That all right by you, Jake?"

"Sure. Anything's all right by me."

The girl poured the thick syrup over the extra scoop of ice cream in one of the glasses, looking up at Bob from under her lazy, smooth lids with a warm, intimate smile.

"You know, you're a beaut, Jeannine. I bet all the fellows are just wild about you."

"Aw, quit it." She smiled.

Bob slipped one hand over hers as she put his glass down on the counter in front of him, but his eyes were on her full, pointed breasts under the knitted dress.

"Come on now, give! Who's your feller, huh?"

"I don't know what you mean by that remark," she said, lowering her eyes.

Jake pushed his half-filled glass to one side, walked over to the newsstand, picked up a magazine, and began to look through it.

Bob leaned over near enough to breathe in the musky perfume of her hair. "Got a date tonight, honey chile?"

"Mmm, not exactly."

"Meet me behind the administration building at nine, will you? I'll take you for a ride."

Bob was one of the few men at the college who had a car.

"Can't. Don't finish here until eleven."

"All right, eleven-fifteen, then. Don't make it any later, will you?"

Jeannine nodded, threw him a sultry look, took the empty glasses down to the other end of the counter, and began washing them.

"Hey, Jake! Come here a minute, will you?"

Jake lighted a cigarette, tucked the magazine under his arm, tossed a couple of coins on the cigar counter, and strolled back to Bob. A slow smile lighted his thin face.

"I know, I know. You've got a paper to write."

Bob shifted his weight from one foot to the other, then put his arm around his friend's shoulder.

"The answer is no," Jake said. "I will not write it for you."

Bob sighed; then that familiar, winning smile wrinkled the corners of his mouth.

"Tell you what I'll do, Jakie. I'll make a bargain with you." Jake watched him warily. "You do my paper or keep my date." Bob's smile widened. "We Lyttletons are generous fellows."

Jake said nothing, but his answering grin was all Bob wanted.

"Eleven-fifteen," he called out to Jeannine, and threw a dollar bill on the counter. "Keep the change, my child."

Twenty minutes later, Jake walked alone up the Gifford path. He went up the steps, stood for a moment in front of the door, then pushed the bell firmly.

He remembered how like a dryad she had looked in her warm autumn-red dress, and suddenly he knew he must see her again tonight if only for a moment.

The door was flung open, and she stood, just as he remembered her, in the same red dress, tall and slim against the hall light.

"Hello," she said.

"Hello." He held her hand for a moment, and then he said, "May I see you again? Soon?"

And she, Pax Gifford, soberly and in her right mind, without benefit of her father's permission—or even Martha's—asked a strange young man, whom she had barely met, to come to dinner.

But how nice he was! How very nice he was!

Late that night, Pax turned out her lights and started to feel her way to her bed. Out of the corner of her eye, she saw a small pointed white light in the sky, beyond her window pane. Shutting her eyes tight, she groped her way to the window, flung it open, and whirled around with her back to it. Carefully she turned her head over her left shoulder, lifted her face toward the sky, opened her eyes, and stared at the delicate crescent of a young moon gently floating there. Then she turned around, bowed calmly to it nine times, made a wish, and sighed happily.

She stood in her thin nightgown, unaware of the cold flooding in on

53

her through the open window. The stars were frosty white flames, out-dazzling the warm yellow lights in the neighboring windows.

Reluctantly she turned away. She crawled into bed, pulled the covers over her, her arms under her head, her eyes wide open, gazing into the soft blackness of the night.

As she lay there, her dark head cradled in her arms, her bemused memories could no longer follow the road of her day with any precision. Suddenly she realized that her arms were beginning to tingle from the frost-bitten air. She rubbed them briskly and pulled them under the covers. On the ceiling above her, the silhouette of the lacy winter twigs just outside her window fluttered gently. She tried to follow their pattern but her lids were becoming heavy, and as her eyes closed she seemed to see a remote lean face burning strangely from behind the shadow branches.

And so, for Pax, the following days and weeks began to merge into a consecutive and quiet radiance.

Her back was straighter, her long-legged stride more confident, and her face shone with a new loveliness.

She knew nothing of the flirtatious wiles of the average girl with her first beau. She accepted Jake's eagerness to be with her thankfully, and soon allowed the thoughts of her future and the strands of her life to weave themselves in and about him.

As for Jake, he loved her from that first day in Philip's rooms, and he loved her all the days of his life.

Jake was Pax's first love. She was his last.

That year spring came early and suddenly. In the orchards, the green buds burst quickly into a shower of pink and white blossoms, the new leaves on the maples were green-gold, and she knew she must share her secret cave with Jake.

One afternoon in late April, Pax and Jake wandered hand in hand through the young forest, up the sun-bathed hill, and she introduced him to Finnegan's. They sat outside the cave, he on a boulder, she with her body pressed into the warm earth.

Her upturned face was luminous in the afternoon light, and her eager thoughts flitted across it like rays of sunlight flickering on a pool. She told him how much Finnegan's meant to her and how she had always run there when she was a little girl, confused and lonely.

"Why do you call it Finnegan's, Pax?"

She frowned and considered a moment. It had been such a long time since she'd thought about that.

54

"Why?" She half smiled to herself. "Don't you remember, Jake, the story of Peer Gynt? There was a cave in the mountains, don't you remember? Finnegan's Cave. I guess I was awfully little when I heard it. I don't know, Jake, but it's just always been Finnegan's."

He squeezed her hand a little tighter, and decided he wouldn't tell her for a long, long time that what she was thinking of was probably Fingal's Cave, and that Fingal's Cave had nothing whatever to do with Peer Gynt, nor was it anything like her cave.

Day after day they went there together, and as the spring ripened they went back in the warm nights.

It was there he told her about his family and his ambitions for them, and how much they had sacrificed for him.

"You'll love Mama, Pax. She's cuddly and funny, and she loves anybody I love. Guess she'd try to mother the whole world if she could get a shot at it. And Miriam's a dear. She's my sister. Pretty, too, but shy as a rabbit. Of course, she's only fifteen. You'll like her, Pax. She's sweet."

"What's your father like, Jake?"

Jake's face glowed. "Papa's a fine man! He's simple and unselfish— and brave, too. He and Mama came over here from Germany when they were both young. Papa worked hard and made quite a lot of money."

His face darkened. "Then the crash came. Everything he'd saved for us went. Just like lots of other little people—big ones, too. Only Papa was different. He just went on believing in God and cheerfully started all over again."

"What's he do, Jake?"

"Well, before the crash he got to be quite a big shot. He was a wholesale grocer. Now he's got a delicatessen store in Worcester. Likes it, too. Says when he doesn't have to feed so many people he can feed 'em better."

"What a shame, Jake!"

"Papa doesn't think so. The only thing I worry about, Pax, is my going on here at college. I wanted to skip it and go to work, but Papa said I'd be an ungrateful son if I spoiled his dream. So here I am." He smiled. "I guess he was right, too, because I found you. I'll make it up to him, though, when I finish here."

"What are you going to do, Jake?"

"I'm going to be the best damn newspaperman in the country. And then I'm going to write books—books that'll make people think, if I can, and at the same time make a lot of money for my pa and ma."

Pax pressed her cheek against his hand, and as she smiled up at him her yellow eyes were full of admiration. She wondered vaguely if all

55

young men felt so deeply about their families. Funny to have a whole family to care about.

Once, toward the end of May, they sat there close together in the dark of the spring night. She was curled up at his feet, her black head against his knee. The hillside and the valley below them were bathed in soft moonlight that almost drowned out the stars. The black earth was dotted with wet blossoms, heavy with the dew which had fallen early. They could hear the lapping of the brook at the bottom of the hill and almost smell the mint and the crisp cress which grew along its banks. Around them was a symphony of rustling night sounds.

Jake was silent and a little remote.

"Jake," she said softly. "Jake, what is it?"

He slipped down beside her and looked deeply into her face.

"Pax, there is something about me that you may or may not know. If you don't, I think you must."

"Yes, Jake?"

"I am a Jew."

"Are you, Jake?"

She smiled serenely at him.

"Does it make any difference, Pax?"

"Why should it?" she said calmly, and put his hand against her cheek. "Is there a difference?"

"A hell of a lot of people think so, girl," he said. "If we are married you will be hurt. I don't want you to be hurt, Pax."

"I love you, Jake."

It seemed to her that there was nothing beyond this.

He took her tightly in his arms.

"I've got to make you understand, Pax, because our lives together will depend on it. Remember back, girl," he said, "remember back to that day at Professor Winslow's. You were uneasy, but you didn't know why."

"I remember," she said quietly.

"You know, Pax, men strike at men with whatever weapon they can find. The privilege of the most powerful, Pax—that's the slogan of the world!" He tried to speak calmly, but bitterness was beginning to creep into his voice. "We're a minority, and so we're unsafe. Two thousand years ago, darling, Jews were driven out from a bright land. They've had no security since. Look at me, Pax!"

He was kneeling in front of her.

"Look into my eyes, look at my face, feel my hands! Am I so different from you?"

"Yes, Jake, you are different. You're alive. And I haven't been until now. I love you, Jake."

56

"Listen, girl. You'll be hurt. You'll be hurt a dozen times a day. You'll be hurt for me, and the more you love me, the more you'll be hurt."

"I won't care, Jake," she said, and she pressed his throat with one hand and stroked his face with the other.

"Darling Pax—you with the peaceful name," he said, a little mockingly. "You don't know what in hell you're talking about. And I don't know whether I can make you know."

But he relaxed, slipped down beside her with his head on her shoulder, and lighted a cigarette. Then he went on talking, almost as if to himself.

"You see, the damnable thing is that I'm beginning to think that to try to reach men's hearts is a lost cause. I've seen a man cry over a little hurt cat that's been run over; I've seen him spend time and money to save that animal, to give it a little longer time on earth. And I've seen that same guy meet a thinking human being in his own community, and with malice and antagonism in his heart strike at him. Strike at his pride and his family and his religion, and send him forth a little more desperate and frightened than he was before."

Jake ran his hands nervously through his dark straight hair.

"They tell us we accept this," he continued. "They say we are obsequious and mute in the face of attack. But damn it, Pax, we are a handful against the world, and it's a world which hasn't suffered enough. It hasn't learned remorse. And it isn't going to get better, it's going to get worse! I can see the handwriting on the wall—"

In the flickering light of his cigarette, Pax saw that his green eyes had again taken on the darkness of the night and of his brooding thoughts. She listened but she didn't hear. She sympathized but she didn't feel. She couldn't understand this suffering of his because she had never suffered.

All she could do was to take him in her arms, press his head against her breast, and gently rock back and forth with him.

Jake could feel the quickening of her heart under her cardigan and the feathery touch of her dark hair on his forehead as she bent her head over him, and when the words came they were a child's words.

"Jake, don't be hurt! Somebody's hurt you and it's cowardly and horrid. People aren't like that. Honestly they're not! You'll see. Why, we haven't got any religion, Daddy and I. People don't pay any attention."

She pressed her lips on his eyelids. "Darling, you mustn't let people like that awful Bill Bascomb upset you. They're not worth it, Jake, really! You'll see! We just won't speak to people like that."

Jake buried his head in her breast because it comforted him, but also

57

because he didn't want her to see him smile. This girl of his was so ignorant of ugly things.

"I love you, Jake. Isn't that enough?"

"It's enough for now, my darling. I'm sorry."

"What are you sorry for?" she asked. She hesitated a moment; then she said shyly, "Jake, we can be married soon, can't we?"

He took her face between his hands. "Pax, listen to me. You know I want to marry you more than I have ever wanted anything in this world, but I'm poor, Pax, you know that."

"What's poor?" she said. "We're not poor."

"Listen, you lovely thing. I love you. You must always know that. But, hang it all, I've got to get a job first. As a matter of fact, I've got a job of sorts after I graduate. Bob Lyttleton got it for me. It's on Jim Nelson's paper in Burlington. Nelson's a friend of Bob's father. But you know, Pax, I can't support anything as lovely as you on peanuts. And then there's my family—"

"I've got a little money, Jake," she said eagerly.

"Pax, you dear fool—"

"It isn't much." She began to laugh. "It's funny, but I always seem to be trying to get somebody to take my little bit of money. I offered it to Philip once, but he wouldn't take it either. What's the matter with it?" she demanded.

"You baby," said Jake. "Life's tough and you're sweet. Just wait until I get a job and love me forever, will you?"

They clung together in the dark, but suddenly Pax was no longer unafraid. Through her confused thoughts and her love for him came a desire to dedicate herself to him for always. The houses in the valley slept in darkness. The moon was sinking over the curve of the hill; the sky over them was like the vault of a great cathedral. There was silence on the earth and the earth was theirs.

Pax sat on the steps, her head against the railing, the flowers and shears thrown carelessly on the path in front of her. She was reading over and over her first love letter, which wasn't a letter at all. Her life took on a new importance. She belonged to someone and someone belonged to her.

Her gaze traveled far into the deep blue of the mountain ridges— above and beyond them—but she didn't see them or the smoky thunder cloud which was gathering there.

Again she took out the single sheet of paper in the handwriting which she had never seen before. There were just eight lines:

58

My lonely embers of yesteryear
Are mournful ashes in the gale,
Now, in my heart, a nightingale
Sings low to her so I may hear.

Gone is my soul's black hopelessness,
Its hearth is swept, its windows wide,
The pain is done. She steps inside.
She is a haven in my wilderness.

Jake

She smoothed the paper, folded it carefully, and tucked it inside her gingham dress where it lay against her heart.

She was so engrossed in her daydreams that she didn't notice a girl on a bicycle who slowed down as she passed the house. The girl reached her own gate, jumped off the bicycle, and strolled over to the tall privet hedge which separated the Gifford and Bascomb places.

"Hi!" she called. "Mind if I come over?"

Pax shook her head, but she didn't look too pleased. Emily Bascomb wiggled through the hedge, swung her sturdy little body across to where Pax sat, and threw herself down on her stomach.

"Gee, it's hot, isn't it?"

Pax didn't answer.

"Don't you think it's awfully hot for May?"

"I guess so," replied Pax.

"You'd have thought so if you'd had to push that bicycle up the hill. I had to go get some butter for lunch. We were all out."

Em pulled on a blade of grass with her sharp little teeth, as small and pointed as a cat's. Her face was impertinent and boyishly ugly. She had gray-green eyes, hair the color of sovereigns—a little on the red side; her nose was practically nil and so snubbed that it seemed as though you could look up through the wide nostrils to the canny mind which dwelt behind her knowing eyes.

Em gave Pax a searching look, then lowered her eyes and went on pulling aimlessly at the grass.

"You look sleepy," she said flatly.

"Well, I'm not."

"You ought to be. You got in awfully late last night."

Pax frowned. "How do you know?"

"Saw you come home," said Em, and then she laughed lightly. "I was up late, too. Bob Lyttleton and I were sitting in the porch swing having a little smoke before he went home."

59

Pax said nothing.

"I think Bob's swell, don't you?" Em went on. "I guess everybody likes Bob. They say he's the most popular man in college. I guess he's the greatest quarterback we ever had. I think he's awfully good-looking, don't you?"

"I don't know him," said Pax shortly.

"Oh, you do, too. He was at Philip's that day, don't you remember?"

Pax winced. It seemed such a short time ago that she'd been reminded of that day.

"Bob's taking me to the prom!" Em's face sparkled with excitement. "You going?"

"I don't know. Hadn't thought about it much," said Pax.

"Hasn't anybody asked you yet?" Em asked.

Emily was fond of Pax, but she was jealous of Pax's physical loveliness. Even though she knew that she, herself, was more popular with the boys, when the two girls were together Em never ceased being conscious of her own plain freckled face and her short, stocky body.

Today, Pax's face seemed even more radiant than usual, and envy made Em want to strike at her.

"Of course, I don't suppose it matters to you. You're the President's daughter. You can always go and take anybody you like. Why don't you take Bill?"

"Because I don't want to."

Em's mouth tightened ominously. " 'Course it's nothing to me who you take. I only—"

"Oh, for heaven's sake, shut up!" said Pax.

She got up abruptly, picked up her shears, and began to clip the flowers. Em turned over on her side and watched her.

"Bob Lyttleton's family are coming all the way up from Savannah, though I can't see why. He's not graduating for another year. They say his people are frightfully important in the South. Wonder if they've got any money."

Pax paid no attention. She went on cutting. The clip-clip of the shears punctuated Em's next words.

"Can't figure out what Bob sees in that feller he's always running around with, can you? What's his name—you know, Felder."

The snap of the shears stopped suddenly.

"What's the matter with him?" demanded Pax. "I like him." Her heart pounded until it hurt.

"Oh, I guess he's nice enough, really. Of course, he's a Jew."

Pax whirled on her. "Shut up! Don't ever say that word!"

There was a distant rumbling of thunder and a few large drops began to fall.

"You'd better go on home and take in your butter. There's going to be a storm. I'm going in."

Without another look at Em, Pax ran up the steps into the house and angrily slammed the door.

Martha answered the bell.

"Evenin'," she said shortly.

She wondered what this strange, foreign-looking young man was doing hanging around the house all the time. Up to no good, she'd be bound. She knew his kind! Hangers-on, that's what they were. Pax, poor child, couldn't be expected to know anything about them. It was Mr. Edmund's place to—well, it wasn't any of her business—

"Where is she, Martha?"

Humph. "Martha," indeed!

"If you mean Miss Gifford, she's upstairs in the sitting room. I guess you can go up," she said ungraciously, and swept through the door into the kitchen.

Jake smiled a little bitterly, ran upstairs, and stopped at the door. Would she be sorry now that the night melted into today? Would she belong to him now, really, or had he lost her forever?

He watched her standing there in the lamplight wrapped in all the loveliness in the world. She wore a frock of periwinkle blue which fell to the ground. Her small head was held high on the child's throat; wound in her hair was a spray of bouvardia, and two or three sprigs were pinned to her shoulder. She held out both hands to him and he went forward slowly and took her in his arms.

They sat on the couch, side by side, their hands clasped tightly. The future spread out before them like a calm sea of enchantment.

"Thank you for my poem, Jake. It's beautiful."

"You're beautiful. The lamplight is shining on your hair."

Martha appeared at the door, looking at them disapprovingly. "Your father's waiting for you, Pax." And with a sniff she turned away.

"Martha doesn't like me," said Jake.

"Oh, she does too. She just hates me to grow up, that's all. Come on, let's go tell Father."

She sprang up from the couch and pulled him with her.

"Tell him what?" said Jake anxiously.

"Tell him that I've got a young man." She smiled. "Tell him I'm in love—so terribly in love, Jake."

They ran downstairs into Edmund's library.

"Father," Pax said, "Jake and I are engaged."

Edmund looked up. "Are you indeed?"

"Of course," she said calmly, "he hasn't really asked me yet."

"I see," said Edmund. "What's it going to be? A shotgun wedding?"

"What's that?" she asked blankly, and then she rushed on: "It doesn't matter. What I mean to say is, Jake can't marry me yet. He hasn't got any money. But he's got a job—after he graduates, I mean. We love each other. Is it all right?"

"Well, that depends," Edmund said. "First I'd like to know if Jake loves you."

"Oh, sir—" He gave a helpless little shrug of his shoulders. "Of course I love her! But I've told her it may be a long time yet—I mean, I don't want her to—" He paused, not quite knowing how to go on.

"I understand how it is, Jake, and if it means anything to you, you have my heartiest approval."

"Thank you, Father," said Pax simply. "I'm glad you approve, but it really wouldn't have mattered if you hadn't."

Pax didn't mean to be impertinent. It was a mere statement of fact.

"You see, I belong to Jake."

One warm night in June, Pax and Jake sat quietly swinging in the porch hammock, which Pax had moved to the side of the garden away from the Bascomb house.

Hardly a breath of air stirred. Occasionally the sleepy call of a night bird could be heard above the tree toads and the katydids. The odor of honeysuckle hung heavily in the still air, and a busy moth flashed back and forth through the darkness.

Graduation was only ten days off and Pax was as excited as a child. It was not only because of the pride in Jake which she would have on that important day, but it meant a man's job for him afterward, and her dream of a life with him would begin to take shape.

Plans had been made for dinner at the Tavern for the momentous meeting with his family. She had described in detail the new white gown she was going to wear at the prom, and she had promised him every dance except one or two which she must save for Philip.

"And now," said Jake, "back to the salt mines."

"Darling, not yet! It's only ten!" she pleaded.

"Your wiles are no good, girl! I've made up my mind I'm going to be kingpin—for you, Pax—come a week from Wednesday. I've got to go, and right now."

Pax sighed. "All right, if you've got to. Come on, I'll walk across the Green with you."

Arm in arm, they strolled through the garden, out of the gate, and along the Green to its farthest side where the road fell away from it down the hill to the town.

For five minutes they stood in the shadow of a great oak, their hands and their eyes straining to each other their long good nights. Neither of them noticed a tall figure leaning up against a fence about a hundred yards away, watching them.

Pax followed Jake with her eyes until he disappeared below the brow of the hill; then she turned and walked slowly in the direction of her house. All at once she was aware of footsteps behind her and she heard a sharp whistle. A man ran easily toward her.

"Who's that?" she called.

"Hiya, Pax!"

"Don't you whistle at me, Bill Bascomb," she said irritably. "What do you want?"

"Nothing, Pax. I just saw you were alone and I thought you'd let me walk home with you."

She said nothing. She started walking on.

"Little girls shouldn't be out all alone in the dark," he continued clumsily. "So your old Bill thought he'd kinda like to protect you."

"I don't need any protection."

"Don't be so nasty to me, Pax. What have I ever done to you?"

He hadn't done anything to her really. He'd been beastly to Jake that time at Phil's, but then he hadn't known what Jake would mean to her. She relaxed somewhat and her manner became less curt.

"Sorry, Bill. I guess I'm just tired, that's all," she said. "It's late."

They reached her gate and she held out her hand to him.

"Good night, Bill, and thank you for walking home with me."

"Listen, Pax," he pleaded, "let me come in and have one cigarette with you, will you? Please? I haven't seen you in months."

Pax frowned and walked slowly to the front steps.

"Where's the swing gone?" Bill looked around the garden dimly lighted by the lamp which hung from the porch ceiling.

"It's in the back."

She didn't tell him she'd had it moved so that she wouldn't be conscious of curious eyes from the house next door.

"Let's go round there. It's much more comfortable than these hard steps."

"No," she said curtly, and sat down on the steps.

Bill sighed and sat beside her, his knee pressing against hers. She edged away.

The porch lamp picked out his thick features, the snubbed nose, and

63

the wide, heavy mouth with its large, strong teeth. His neck was powerful and pink-white, his hair coppery like his sister's, and he had the same freckles under his eyes and across the bridge of his nose. His eyes were very blue, but the short, white lashes gave him a furtive look.

He was always self-conscious with Pax, although he showed an almost insolent self-confidence with most of the Mapletonians. Bill's father, Judge Bertram Bascomb, was one of the wealthiest men in town, and young Bill never failed to let people know it. The Judge practiced law in Burlington, Mapleton being still too small to support its own law court. Bill was his only son, and, after he had graduated from Amherst, had been installed as a junior partner.

"What do you think, Pax?" said Bill. "Dad gave me an office of my own yesterday. Got my name on the door and everything." He laughed. "I'll begin to think I'm getting to be somebody around here."

"That's just fine, Bill," said Pax indifferently. "Congratulations."

"There's one drawback, though. I have to be in Burlington every morning at nine o'clock or Dad gives me hell. Tough, isn't it? Seems to me I'm always tired—in the morning."

"Why don't you go home and go to bed, then, and get some sleep?"

"It's too early. I couldn't sleep, anyway."

He lighted a cigarette from the butt he'd just finished; then he suddenly moved closer to her and reached for her hand. She jerked it away.

"What's the matter?" he said. "Give a feller a chance, will you?" He roughly took her hand again and held it tightly in his.

His face had changed. In the dim moonlight, she could see the sudden sweat gleaming on his forehead, the dilating nostrils, and the sensual, loose mouth. His glistening eyes terrified her. He pressed closer.

"I like you, Pax. I like you a lot."

His breath came quicker and he lunged for her breast with his thick hand. She hit him across the mouth.

The surprise of the blow made him loosen his hold on her, and in that second she slipped away from him and began running toward the back of the house. She heard his muffled steps in the grass following her, and she quickly stepped behind a tall syringa bush.

Bill peered around the garden, and then in the faint light he caught a glimmer of the corner of her pale skirt. He came up to her, reached around the bush, his face twisted with anger, took her roughly in his arms, and began to press his wet mouth all over her face and throat.

She tried to fight him off. She knew she should scream—her father or Martha would be sure to hear—but she was too ashamed. Frantically, she whipped her head from side to side and then she began to cry.

Suddenly he let her go and stood there looking at her stupidly. He shook his head like a prizefighter, as if he would shake the passion out of it, straightened his clothes, and buttoned his double-breasted coat. He looked clumsy and a little pathetic and his eyes darted from side to side in foolish indecision.

Pax leaned back into the syringa bush and covered her face with her hands.

"How could you, Bill! How could you! You're horrible!"

Bewildered thoughts flew through her brain like lightning. Why, she'd known Bill all her life! Of course, he had tried to steal a kiss from her from time to time, but it had been a boy's kiss. This was ugly.

"You're horrible!" she repeated.

"Horrible, am I?" He laughed defiantly. "Well, you're not such an angel yourself. Who do you think you are, pulling this 'horrible' stuff on me?"

Bill rushed on furiously, but he lowered his metallic voice as if to point the insult straight at her. It was as though he didn't want anyone else to hear, for fear that would blunt its drive and lessen its pain.

"What's the matter with you? Do you think we're all blind around here? Do you think people haven't seen you sneaking around in the dark, kissing that Jew lover of yours?"

There was a moment's taut silence, heavy with hate. Then the words came—meaningless, incoherent words, spilled from her in a torrent of loathing.

"I hate you! Oh, God! God! I hate you! You're rotten! You're rotten all through, do you hear? I wish I could kill you! I wish I could kill you!"

She was crying uncontrollably now.

"I love him! Do you hear? I love him! And you make my flesh crawl!" Her throat was dry and scratchy, and she seemed, as if from far off, to hear words pouring from her mouth. "You low, contemptible beast! You don't hate me! You don't even hate him! It's Jews you hate! And you don't care if they die while you hate 'em!"

She couldn't stop. She stood there like a Fury, lashing at him with words. Bill began to be frightened. He'd never seen anyone like this.

"Be quiet, you little fool! Somebody'll hear—"

"I don't care!" she raged. "I want 'em to! I want the whole world to know what a vile, filthy beast you are!"

"Pax, don't! I didn't mean—Jesus—I'm sorry, Pax—"

"Go away! Don't you come near me! You leave him alone! And you leave J-J-Jews alone!"

"Pax, for God's sake! I didn't mean anything. I was angry. Everyone says 'Jew' like that if they get angry."

65

"You shut up! Don't you dare—don't you dare say that word again!"

Like the fool he was, Bill persisted. "I'm sorry, Pax, really I am. Won't you forgive me?"

Pax shook her head and blew her nose violently.

"I can't say anything more than I'm sorry. Damn it, I— Won't you please forgive me?"

"No!"

He looked at her unhappily for a moment. She had slipped down on the damp grass and crouched there, exhausted.

Bill shrugged his shoulders helplessly, crossed the garden behind the house, leaped the fence, and disappeared.

Pax didn't move. She'd had a glimpse of a world she had never seen before and it was ugly. Hate had entered her heart for the first time and it appalled her.

She knew now what Jake had meant. And with an unfamiliar bitterness, she also knew that when her rage was exhausted she would forgive Bill. She would forgive him because she had to forget.

Like someone plunging through the crest of a wave, her hands pressed together and her arms stretched to their full length, Pax found her way through the filmy clouds of white chiffon which Martha was carefully lowering over her head. When the soft puffed sleeves were drawn up to her shoulders, she rushed across the room to the little jewel box which had belonged to her mother. Martha followed her, scolding and protesting, trying to fasten her dress.

"Oh, shut up, Martha. Don't be so cranky," cried Pax. "I want to see what'll go best with this beautiful, scrumptious dress—Martha, did you ever see such a dress? How do I look? What about these pearls?" She held up a string of small imitation pearls. "Or would the cross look better? What about this locket of my mother's?"

"Well, if you listen to me, but of course you won't," said Martha tartly, "I wouldn't wear any. Not if you're going to cover yourself with all them flowers in the icebox. But you'll do just as you please—you always do." Martha finished fastening the dress. "Want me to get the flowers?"

"Oh, yes! What kind are they, Martha?"

"I'm sure I don't know. I didn't open them. They're not my flowers."

Martha started for the door. With her hand on the knob, she turned and looked her child over from head to foot.

"Well, you don't look bad," she said, "but if I were you, I'd give those ears another going over. The left one looks a little grimy."

"Oh, Martha, stop treating me as if I were ten!"

66

"Ain't got any more sense than ten."

Pax ran a comb through her hair, powdered her shoulders, then turned and twisted in front of the mirror. Her cheeks were unusually flushed, the deep rose starting from underneath the rather prominent jawbone, working its way unevenly up to the amber eyes.

She turned swiftly as Martha came in, took the two boxes from her, and tore off the wrappings.

"Oh, look, a wreath! A real wreath!"

She placed it carefully in her dark hair, where it formed a powdery white halo around the small excited face. From the other box she took a corsage of falling sprays of the same bouvardia and held it in both her hands.

"Martha, look! Don't I look exactly like a bride? All I need is the veil."

Jake was waiting for her in the hall below, a little uncomfortable in his rented dinner jacket. She smiled down at him; then with a bored, slow, almost show-girl walk, she began to descend the stairs, one step at a time, humming in her high, clear voice the first bars of the *Lohengrin* wedding march.

"Rum tumpty-tum. Rum tumpty-tum."

Halfway down, she stopped and said solemnly, "Do you, Jacob, take this woman to be your lawful wedded wife—et cetera, et cetera, et cetera?"

"I do," said Jake, in a deep phony voice.

"Do you, Pax, take this man—et cetera, et cetera, et cetera—I *do*." Pax leaned over the railing, scowled, peered around the hall, then drew herself up to her full height. "If there is anyone present who knows any reason why this man and this woman should not be joined in holy wedlock—"

She ran down to him, held up her face, and said, "Then you kiss me, Jake."

He kissed her gently, then held her off from him and looked at her. "You look like an angel."

"Do I? Do I honestly, Jake? Well, it's all for you." She touched the corsage lightly. "The flowers are lovely. Thank you, Jake. Oh, Jake, I'm so excited. I think this is the most important day of my life. You know, the prom, meeting your family—do you think they'll like me, Jake?"

Jake smiled.

"Then tomorrow," she rushed on, "you in your cap and gown. I'll be so proud! And then after that we can begin to plan. Isn't life wonderful, Jake? Do you love me?"

67

She didn't wait for him to tell her. She took his hand and began to pull him toward the library. "Come on, let's go show Father."

Ten minutes later they left the house. As they reached the Bascomb gate, a car drew up and Bill Bascomb jumped out. Pax hesitated a minute and then walked on. Bill saw her, and his face became nearly the color of his hair.

"Good evening," he said as they passed.

"Good evening," replied Pax, but she didn't look at him.

"Hello, Bascomb," said Jake, "going to the dance?"

Bill didn't answer. He ran up the stairs and into the house.

Pax and Jake walked on in silence. Jake turned his head and looked at her searchingly. Her shoulders were a little more erect and there was a frown between her brows.

"Pax, don't let that fellow bother us. You said yourself that we wouldn't pay any attention to that kind of people. Anyway, it was such a long time ago."

Ten days isn't so long, she thought, but then, Jake didn't know anything about that. She smiled and squeezed his arm.

When they got as far as Amy's, Pax broke away from Jake, ran across Amy's lawn until she was underneath Philip's window, and whistled. "Ph-i-ll! Hey, Phil!"

Philip came to the window and leaned out. "Hi, you beautiful thing, where you goin'? Off to meet the family?"

"Yes. Are you coming to the dance tonight?"

"No, I don't think so, kid. I've got some last-minute jobs to do tomorrow, and I'm kind of tired."

"Oh, Phil, please! I've saved dozens of dances for you. Jake doesn't mind, do you, Jake?"

"Fat chance I'd have of minding, Professor," Jake said, and grinned.

"Phil, will you, please? *Please!*"

"I may stroll over later on. You kids have a good time. And, Pax, you behave yourself. Don't flirt with anybody except me." He waved his pipe in Jake's direction. "That's telling her, Jake."

On the main street, surrounded by shops and one or two tumble-down houses, was the only hotel in the town. It was old and dilapidated and, except for an occasional traveling salesman, it boasted of very few guests. Two or three feet below the level of the street was the Tavern, a kind of rathskeller which had been installed mostly for the benefit of the students, who patronized it at all hours until the closing midnight order of "All glasses off the tables, please."

On this particular night each year, it overflowed with them, their

68

families, and their girls, who came from all over for the important event.

Jake and Pax pushed their way among the laughing, shouting young men who shoved each other and called out to the head waitress, offering her bribes and kisses, giving her an occasional pinch if they could get near enough.

"Hello, Jake!"

"Hiya, boy!"

"Miss Gifford."

"How are you, Butch?"

"Make way for Prexy's daughter!"

"Got a table, Jake?"

They finally made it, Jake holding his arms around her like a fence. The head waitress led them to a table almost in the center of the room.

"Do you mind staying here alone for a few minutes, Pax? I'll go up and get the family. That all right with you?"

"Of course, darling."

"Bob's over there with his mother and father. Would you like him to sit with you until we come back?"

"Oh, no, Jake. I'll be all right, really. Only hurry, will you? I'm getting scareder and scareder every second."

"I'll leave your coat upstairs, darling," said Jake, and he made his way through the crowd and disappeared.

Pax settled herself in her chair, leaned on her elbows, and looked around the room. She smiled and waved to several people she knew, then turned her head and looked over at the Lyttleton table.

Bob looked very handsome in his well-cut dinner jacket. With him was a tall, distinguished-looking man and one of the loveliest women Pax had ever seen. She was wearing a simple black dinner gown with a single strand of pearls around her throat. Her hair was short and smartly cut and the color of silver fox. Pax couldn't see what color her eyes were, but her skin was a smooth, deep cream, her features small and regular, and her smile was brightly warm. As Pax watched, Bob got up and left the table.

The minutes seemed like hours. Why didn't Jake come? She pulled the menu toward her and began to read it, but that was dull. She'd seen it dozens of times. It never changed.

The hum of the voices subsided rather suddenly and there was a moment's silence in the room. Heads turned curiously toward the door and the hum began—a little louder this time.

Two very small people stood in the doorway for an instant, then slowly came toward the center of the room.

The woman was stout and middle-aged, and not much over five feet tall. She was round and fat and she seemed to balance her weight by walking flatly back on her heels. Her thin black hair was streaked with gray and drawn tightly back in a small knot halfway up the back of her head. She wore an old, rusty black silk dress with a jet ornament at her throat, and long jet earrings hung from the heavy lobes of her ears.

The man was very little taller than she. He was thin, rather stooped; he had a long fierce nose with pointed nostrils, and a straggly black-and-gray beard. His black eyes were set deeply in their sockets, and tiny bushes of hair sprang out above ears which stuck out an inch and a half from his bony skull. His suit was dark and worn and hung slackly on his lean body, and his collar was low with a loosely knitted black tie around his stringy throat.

They both looked a little frightened, and as they stepped forward, he reached for one of her hands and held it tightly in his.

Pax felt her face beginning to burn. She looked away from them to a slight girl with a fragile, dark face, walking with Jake. He held his arms out protectingly behind them, gently pushing them in the direction of her table.

From the tables around her, she could hear whispers and a few snickers, and every face she could see out of the corner of her eye seemed to be staring in her direction.

Then the little group was standing beside her. She tried to rise, but her legs felt like lead.

Jake touched her on the shoulder. He had one arm around his mother and his eyes were full of pride and affection.

"Here they are, Pax. Darling, this is my mother. Ma, this is Pax."

Mrs. Felder held out her little fat hand and smiled warmly. The nearsighted eyes were a faded, watery blue and blinked. Her thick, steel-rimmed spectacles protruded from her bag; she had undoubtedly taken them off for the party.

"I'm pleased to meet you. Meet Jake's father—my Isaac," she said proudly, and sat down by Pax.

"Papa, you sit on the other side of Pax, will you?" said Jake, and pulled out the chair for the old man. "This is Miriam, Pax. Over here, chick. I'll sit here where I can look at all of you." Jake smiled happily on his little brood.

Pax murmured her greetings, and picked up the menu and handed it to Mrs. Felder, who fumbled with it awkwardly.

"Put your glasses on, Ma. You've made your entrance," said Jake affectionately. She flashed a smile at her son and reached into her black bag.

Pax could still feel the eyes looking mockingly in their direction, but

70

the most frightening of all of them were the ones she hadn't seen, which seemed to burn through the back of her neck.

As Jake ordered dinner, the noise of several pieces of silverware dropping on the floor startled Pax. She raised her eyes and saw the thin, tormented face of Jake's sister, which was turning a dull red. In her shyness she had fumbled with her knife and spoon and they had slipped off the table. Her large black eyes were swimming in tears, and she looked appealingly at her brother. He patted her arm and whispered comfortingly to her.

"Miriam, my own," said Mrs. Felder, "tell the young lady how you have been looking forward to the party tonight. Come, Miriam, talk now a little."

"Yes, miss," the girl murmured.

"Miss, already! You should be ashamed, Miriam!" Jake's mother chuckled delightedly. "This is our Jakie's girl. 'Miss' ain't friendly, is it, young lady?"

Pax stiffened. Miriam blushed again.

"Her name is Pax, baby," said Jake gently.

"That's a funny name," Mrs. Felder exclaimed. "Pretty, though."

"You're pretty, too," said Miriam softly.

"I should live to see the day when my Jakie married an ugly girl. Jakie don't like ugly people, inside or out, do you, son?"

Mr. Felder spoke very little. Occasionally he threw Pax an enigmatic glance and he seemed to be the only one who sensed her confusion. He watched his son proudly, every now and then nodding and winking at him when he caught his eye.

"A big day tomorrow, Jake!" For a moment he directed his attention to the uncomfortable girl at his side. "Ve haf vaited a long time for dis day, miss. Jakie, Mama und me vant you should come home for a liddle rest before you take de job in Burlington. Vat do you say, hein?"

What kind of an accent was that? Pax listened with a repugnance which she could scarcely hide. What kind of people were they? Why did they have to talk so loud? What was she doing here? In some strange way she felt betrayed.

"Pax, darling"—that was Jake's voice—"you're not eating. Don't you like it? Can I get you something else?"

"No, thank you, Jake. I'm just not awfully hungry."

She tried to smile at him, but her lips seemed frozen. Did she detect a slight, mocking gleam in his eyes?

Suddenly she felt something touch her left hand, which was drawing indeterminate lines on the tablecloth with a knife. Mr. Felder had gently covered her hand with his rough, gnarled one. It startled her.

Instinctively she snatched her hand away from his and put it in her lap under the table. Then she swiftly glanced up at Jake.

I'm lost, she thought. I'll never find my way again. Oh, wait! Help me to go back! Jake, I didn't mean it! I just don't understand! Something's happened—

Out of the corner of her eye, she saw Emily Bascomb come in with Bob Lyttleton. Em was wearing a pale green dress and had a spray of small yellow orchids pinned to her shoulder. Pax's eyes followed her red head as she and Bob made their way to Mr. and Mrs. Lyttleton's table. If she could only exchange places with Em, just until she could get hold of herself!

"Well, if it ain't Bobbie! Bobbie!" Mrs. Felder called across the room.

Bob looked over his shoulder and his face lighted. He said something to his mother, then hurried over to the table. He called gaily to Miriam as he came toward them, but he walked straight to Mrs. Felder. He gave a quick glance around the room; then with one swoop he deliberately gathered the little woman in his arms.

"Mama! *Mamele!* Well, we've got you here at last. How's my best girl?"

Mrs. Felder was beaming. Bob held her off from him a moment, then he bent over and kissed her heartily on the mouth.

"Howya, Pop?" He reached around Pax's chair and clasped the old man's hand. "Miriam, honey, you're prettier than ever, isn't she, Mama?"

He turned to a table next to them, and, with a "May I?," pulled up an empty chair. He was obviously glad to see the little family, but an unsympathetic onlooker might have wondered if he were not playing a scene and enjoying it. At any rate, his charm was putting them all at their ease—except Pax, who felt more than ever alien and alone.

"Well, you got 'em here, Jake. *Mamele,* I'm putting in for the first dance."

"Nonsense, Bobbie! An old woman like me! Such things he says!" But the little woman chuckled.

"Jake, keep her in order! *Mamele,* are you my best girl or aren't you?"

Mrs. Felder leaned toward Pax. "He likes to make jokes, but he's a good boy."

But Pax wasn't listening. A new terror had found its way into her consciousness to torment her. They were all going to the prom! Why, oh, why was it the tradition of this particular college to invite the boys' parents to the prom!

"Hello, Miss Gifford." That was Bob Lyttleton speaking to her and he seemed to be seeing her for the first time.

"Good evening," she said shortly.

Why was this young man so at home with these strange people? Where had he known them?

Mrs. Felder and Bob kept up a running conversation, with an occasional soft word thrown in by Miriam. Jake sat very still. He didn't seem to be listening and there was a brooding vacancy in his eyes.

"Papa, you-all are goin' to be right proud of that young man of yours tomorrow. Rumor hath it that the dirty dog will run off with most of the honors of his class."

"He iss a fine clever boy, my Jacob."

"But damn it, Papa, it's the beginning of my downfall," Bob complained. "Who's goin' to get me through next year, I ask you!"

"Never mind, Bobbie," said Mrs. Felder. "I want you should come home holidays like always. Mama, she bake you *cholah* and *latkes* like always, just the same—"

Bob's eyes danced. "And herring and noodle pudding and matzo balls."

So that's why he knew them. Jake hadn't told her. Had she ever really known Jake?

"Good evening. Am I intruding?"

The low, cultured Southern voice was directly beside her. Pax looked up. Mrs. Lyttleton, completely self-possessed, with a warm smile on her lovely face, stood there waiting. Bob pushed back his chair quickly and rose to his feet.

"Why, Mum! I didn't—"

Mrs. Lyttleton interrupted him. "May I have the pleasure of meeting Jake's mother and father, Robert?"

"Why, of course, Mum. This is Mrs. Felder—my mother. This is Jake's father, Mr. Felder. And Miriam. You know old Jake, of course. Oh—I don't think you've met Miss Gifford, the daughter of our Prexy."

Mrs. Lyttleton greeted them all graciously, reserving her friendliest smile for Jake's mother. Then she slipped into Bob's chair.

"I don't know how to thank you, Mrs. Felder, for taking such good care of my son the times he hasn't been able to get home. His father and I are beginning to think we have very serious rivals in Worcester. But Jake has promised to come South to us sometime, haven't you, Jake?"

"Papa and I like children, Mrs. Lyttleton. We feel that Bobbie belongs to us already," said Jake's mother, and she reached up and touched Bob's sleeve affectionately.

"And now, Robert, I think we should let these good people finish their dinner in peace. Miss Gifford, we hope to have the pleasure of seeing your father this evening." Mrs. Lyttleton stood up, her hand resting lightly on Miriam's shoulder. "We'll see you all later. Perhaps you'll let us sit with you at the dance. We're strangers here, you know. We really have no reason to be here, but we were motoring through—"

Words, words, words! They swam through her ears and through her brain like fish in a pool, with no direction, no meaning. And she couldn't find any words! And if she were able to find them, how could she use them? They would only be a flimsy evasion of the thoughts which were making little explosions in her brain as they crashed together, trying to find a way out.

Above them all, one of them rose clearly and degradingly. She was ashamed of his family. She had failed Jake.

Somehow the dinner was over. Somehow she had managed to walk out of the room with her head high. Somehow she had found herself sitting on the bed in the dingy room upstairs, waiting for a family which would someday be hers.

Mrs. Felder had made little clucking noises over her, trying to put her at her ease, her embarrassment being only too apparent. Miriam, away at last from the prying eyes of strangers, talked eagerly with Jake, who leaned against the wall smiling at his sister.

But he didn't look at Pax, and his eyes were not smiling.

Then they were out on the street, plodding up the same hill that she had tripped down so gaily only two hours earlier.

Jake was walking ahead of her with his mother on one side and Miriam on the other. She couldn't see his face, but there was a tautness in his slight body, and although he was still carrying her coat, it seemed, in an odd way, to hang detached and lifeless from his indifferent arm.

Pax walked behind with Mr. Felder, weakly pointing out the few landmarks of the town, trying to make conversation. As they reached the top of the hill, she saw that there was still a light in Philip's room. Oh, Philip! If only he'd come!

There were no stars in the sky and the air seemed still and heavy with foreboding. The lights were all on in the college gymnasium, and as they came nearer she could hear the strain of a Strauss waltz faintly wafted across the Green.

Jake found them seats at the end of the large room which had been turned for the night into a ballroom. He still carried Pax's coat over his arm; then he gave it to his mother to hold.

74

They watched the dancers for a few minutes; then the music stopped. The dancers chattered and applauded and the orchestra played again.

Jake stood before her. "May I have this dance, Pax?"

She rose and walked slowly into his arms. He put one arm around her waist, took her hand firmly in his, and guided her gracefully and surely through the maze of young dancers. Neither of them spoke. They circled the room twice in silence. The lump in her throat was becoming unbearable. She knew she must speak or die. She looked wistfully into his face. He looked back at her and smiled faintly.

"Your mother is sweet, Jake."

"I'm glad you think so," he said. "My mother is a wonderful woman."

"Oh, I'm sure she is, Jake. I'm sure she is." Her voice was tremulous and eager.

Jake didn't answer. They finished the dance in silence and he took her back to her chair. Mrs. Felder was sitting there, flushed and chuckling, fanning herself with her handkerchief. Bob Lyttleton stood in front of her grinning. He had evidently held her to her word and had danced the first dance with her.

When the music began again, Jake danced off with his sister and Lyttleton turned to her.

"Will you dance this one with me?" he said.

Gratefully she accepted, and in a moment he was whirling her around the room in a fast waltz. Pax was a beautiful dancer and her body melted into the curve of his arm. The fragrance of her floated up into his nostrils and he looked down with surprise into the weary white face and wondered why he had never realized before how attractive his best friend's girl was.

Suddenly she stopped. "Would you mind terribly taking me outside for a moment?" she asked. "It's awfully warm in here, don't you think?"

He took her arm and they made their way through the dancers until they reached the tall windows which opened out onto the campus.

"I think you'd better have your wrap," Bob said. "Stay right here until I get it for you. Don't move now," he added. "I don't want to lose you."

She leaned against the edge of the door, her eyes straining despairingly to catch a glimpse of Jake among the hundred couples on the floor. Once she caught his eye. He looked at her gravely; then he swung Miriam away from her and was lost among the dancers.

Lyttleton rejoined her, threw her coat around her shoulders, and they went out together into the blackness. They found two chairs on the grass. She turned hers around so it would face the room they'd just left.

Two or three dances went by. Lyttleton talked at random, but he was obviously admiring. She replied with polite murmurs and didn't hear a word he said.

From time to time, couples passed around and in front of her, the girls' light frocks making them look like wraiths in the darkness. From the ballroom, laughter drifted to her in waves like the echo of her lost hope, that hope which had welled up in her heart this very afternoon, spilling over in its joyousness.

How very long ago it seemed.

"Well, I like that, I must say!" It was Emily's husky voice behind her. "Bob Lyttleton, aren't you ashamed? I'm supposed to be your date for tonight and you haven't asked me to dance once."

"Hello, Em," said Pax, "it's my fault really. I wasn't feeling very well." Her voice faded away. She didn't honestly care what Em thought. "Go along with Em, Mr. Lyttleton. I don't mind being left alone. I'd like it, really."

"Won't you let me take you back to your party?"

"If you don't mind, I'd rather stay here. Anyway, I want to find my father."

She watched them go off to the ballroom, Em hanging on his arm, laughing up into his face. Suddenly she let herself go and the tears poured down her cheeks. She tried to muffle the sobs with her handkerchief. It would be too shame-making if anybody heard her.

Wasn't Jake ever going to come and find her? Had she lost him forever?

She finally cried herself out. She put the wet ball of a handkerchief into the pocket of her coat and walked stealthily over to the other side of the building. She stood on tiptoe and peered through the window into the lighted room.

The musicians had left their instruments on their chairs and had gone out for a little air or refreshments. The room was practically empty. At the far end she could see the Felders. Mr. and Mrs. Lyttleton had joined them. Jake was sitting on the arm of his mother's chair.

She gulped down a lump in her throat. He wasn't going to look for her. He didn't even seem to be bothering to wonder where she was.

She turned away from the window and wandered away. Where was Philip? Where was her father? Where was somebody who cared what became of her? She couldn't go back in. What could she say?

She stuck her hands in her pockets and walked out toward the street. She looked across to Amy's. The light was out in Philip's room.

She continued on up the street until she came to her own gate. She opened it, went slowly up the steps, and into the dark hall. There was a light on the landing and a thread of light under the door of the library. She didn't stop. She climbed the stairs wearily, went into her own room, and closed the door. She didn't bother to turn on the light.

She took off her coat, kicked off her grass-stained slippers, left her lovely white gown in a sad little heap on the floor, and climbed into bed.

BOOK TWO

5

PAX MOVED HER HEAD uneasily from side to side with the motion of the train. Her limbs felt stiff and the back of her neck ached. She looked at her watch. The pastel twilight was falling softly over the rolling hills. It wouldn't be long now; they'd be there in ten or fifteen minutes.

She smiled at the boy who sat stiffly in the seat opposite her. What an extraordinary difference a few hours and some new clothes had made in him. His gray flannel suit was well cut, his feet looked small in the shoes which were still too new, and the collar of the white shirt—a little grimy now—fitted snugly around his small throat.

His face was streaked with the engine soot which blew in from the half-open window across the aisle. She took out her compact and looked at her own face; it was even dirtier than his.

She rose, took him by the hand, and pulled him toward the washroom at the other end of the coach. It was occupied, so she steered him out onto the platform where they waited, swaying back and forth with the movement of the train.

Eventually a fat woman came out of the washroom, and Pax took the boy in and shut the door. It was an evil-smelling, filthy little hole, with soiled towels flung all over the sloppy wet floor, and she began to feel a little sick.

She pointed to the toilet, then turned her back to wash her hands and face. The slab of soap was dirty and the water was cold, but she managed to remove some of the grime. She scrubbed Jan as best she could and combed his thick hair with her pocket comb.

She looked out of the window, recognized the familiar outskirts of the town, and hurried him back to their seat. She put him into his new topcoat, stuck his cap on the back of his head, and heaped as many packages in his arms as he could manage. She picked up her suitcase and the bright new one she had bought for him, and hurried up the aisle.

81

The conductor threw open the door, calling out, "Mapleton!" and the train bumped to a stop with a bang and a screeching of brakes.

Pax jumped down quickly and looked around for Philip. The only person she could see was Lucien, the old station master, who stood watching the train, an unlighted lantern in his hand.

"Lucien!" she called. "Would you mind helping this little boy down the steps? I'm afraid he can't manage it with all the boxes he's carrying. Have you seen Professor Winslow anywhere about?"

"Saw him just a minute ago, Miss Pax, down the platform a spell," said the old man.

He reached up and lifted Jan and all his packages down from the platform of the coach.

"There comes the Professor now," he said, nodding his head in the direction of the little wooden station. "Ups-a-daisy!" he sang out as he set Jan on the ground. "Well, young feller, you're by way of bein' a stranger round these parts, bein't yuh? What's your name, eh? Here, Miss Pax, let me take those bags for you. Here's Phil now." He turned again to Jan. "Now, young feller, you just gimme some o' those bundles. That's the boy. Say, what's your name?" he repeated. Jan walked along beside him; he said nothing. "What's the matter? Cat got your tongue?"

Meantime, Pax and Phil exchanged hurried greetings, and Philip nodded in the direction of the boy trudging on ahead with the old station master.

"So that's the boy. Nice-looking chap, isn't he?"

"Oh, Lord, Phil, what an idiot I am! I forgot—Jan!" she called. The boy looked back and waited. "Jan, this is Mr. Winslow."

"Hello, Jan," Phil said casually. Then he lowered his voice. "Better for me not to pay too much attention to him, I think. It's all so new to him—so many people—"

"Oh, Phil! You don't have to whisper. He can't talk!" she wailed.

"What?" he said sharply.

"I mean he can't speak anything! I can't talk to him! I can't tell you how awful that part of it's been. I've been like a deaf-mute for twenty-four hours."

They reached the edge of the platform and got into one of the town's two taxis. The car started off along the winding road, through the French-Canadian quarter, and up the hill to the Green. Pax kept leaning out of the taxi window.

"Phil, it seems months since I left. How could so much happen in two days? How's Tubby? How's Pansy? Has Tubby been good? Has he behaved himself? Pansy have any trouble with him?"

82

"Good Lord, kid. How on earth should I know? Calm down, you dope. Relax."

The ivy-covered Colonial buildings of the college loomed out of the darkness, which was now falling swiftly, and soon Pax could see the outline of her own ugly Victorian house, warmly window-lighted, solidly sitting there in the gloom.

A warmth began to flood through her whole being. She was home. Philip was with her. She was safe.

When the taxi stopped in front of the house, Pax jumped out and ran up the path. Pansy opened the door and hurried to take her packages.

"God bless my soul, Miss Pax, you're back safe and sound. Heah, lemme take those things for you. Where's your bag?"

Then she saw Jan.

"Heah, boy! Bring them bundles heah," she called.

The child stood there looking from one to the other.

Pax ran to him, took the packages from him, put one arm around his shoulder, and guided him toward the house.

"Pansy, this is Jan. He's come to stay with us. You must take good care of him, but you're not to spoil him."

" 'Pon my soul, Miss Pax, now ain't that jes' fine. Wheah you find him?"

The young colored woman flashed a dazzling smile at the child and gave him a little pat on the shoulder. Jan looked up at her; an expression of complete bewilderment came over his face and he shrank away from her toward Pax.

They dumped all their belongings in the hall and went into the library. Pax flung off her jacket and hat and flopped into a big comfortable chair. Philip went to the side table where Pax still kept two decanters, as her father had done for so many years.

"I'm going to pour you a good stiff swig. By God, you need it."

"By God, I do!" replied Pax grimly.

She looked back over her shoulder. Jan had sat down on a straight chair just inside the door, with his coat and cap still on. With a little murmur of remorse, she jumped up and led the child toward the fireplace and took off his coat.

"Coat off, Jan."

He looked at her steadily. She held up the coat and smiled.

"*Was ist das*, Jan?"

"Co-o-at," he said soberly.

Pax laughed delightedly and pushed him into a low chair beside hers.

"Pansy," she said, "will you bring Jan a glass of milk?" Suddenly she remembered the disaster of the night before. "Oh, and Pansy, you'd better take the chill off. His tummy may be a bit nervous after the journey."

"Yes'm, I'll do that."

She smiled that wide smile again at Jan as she started for the door. "Where's Tub?"

"I don' know, Miss Pax. He went next door 'bout an hour ago to play with the twins."

"Well, call him, will you? Tell him we're home."

"Yes'm. And I'll bring the milk straight away."

Pax settled herself comfortably in her chair and sipped her drink. She smiled at Jan, who sat there as motionless as a little statue, looking at her, once in a while casting a furtive glance in Philip's direction.

"I'll just let Jan drink his milk quietly and then I'll take him up to his room." She sighed. "Oh, Lord, Phil, I'm tired."

"I know you are, kid. Now just drink up and try to relax. How did you find New York? It's been over a year—"

Philip didn't get any further.

Through the door, like a small whirlwind, came Robert Lyttleton the third, more familiarly known to his intimates as Tubby. He threw himself on Pax and wound his arms around her neck. "Hi, Mom! You're back! Gee! We missed you! Did you bring me—"

Suddenly he caught sight of Jan. He stopped abruptly and stared at him. "Hello," he said.

Jan stared back.

"Hey, Mom, who's that?"

" 'That'—as you call him—is what I went to New York for. He's a surprise. Well," she finished lamely, "aren't you glad?"

"Sure," he said. Then, with his father's charming smile, he got up and put out his hand. "Hello! What's your name?"

Jan looked at Tubby's hand, then timidly stretched out his own.

"His name's Jan."

"Mine's Tubby," he said. "How long are you going to stay?"

Jan looked from the child to Pax.

"What's the matter with him, Mom? Can't he talk?"

"Well, not very well yet, Tubby. You see, he's come from a long way off. All the way from Europe. He doesn't know how to speak English yet. You'll have to teach him."

"That's tough, isn't it?" He tipped his fair head to one side and considered for a moment. "How long is he going to stay, Mom?"

"As long as he wants to, Tubs."

"Gee!" Tubby stood there with his hands in his pockets, looking at Jan curiously.

84

"He'll stay as long as he's happy here, Tubby. And that's up to us— you and me—to see that he *is* happy, see? I'm going to try very hard. What about you?"

"Aw, sure, Mom. He'll be all right." All at once his eyes sparkled and he ran to the door. "I'll go get him my Dick Tracy book. He'll like that! He won't have to read it, see? It's got pictures! Be right back."

He raced out of the room and up the stairs with the noise and speed of a colt.

"Jan!" Pax pointed in the direction of the door from which Tubby had just left. *"Er ist dein kleines neues Bruder, nicht wahr?"* she said haltingly. Then she threw up her hands and smiled wryly at Philip. "Heaven help me with my stinking pidgin German!"

Jan looked at her with a perplexed frown, shrugged his shoulders, and shook his head.

"Oh, Lord, Phil," Pax said despairingly, "does he mean that he hasn't got a brother or that he doesn't *want* a brother?"

Philip said, "The trouble with you, Pax, is that you're dead tired and your nerves are shot to hell. You've had two days of it alone, you poor kid. You know, Pax, we've both been utter damn fools. Neither of us had the sense to realize that the boy wouldn't speak English. But it doesn't take kids long, believe me. Everything's going to be O.K."

Pansy came in with a tall glass of milk on a tray and put it on the table beside Jan. "Theah y'are, son. You drink it up now." She leaned over him. "You like milk, don' yuh? It's good for boys—makes 'em grow up into great big strong men."

She put her dark hand on his shoulder, and he jerked away from her with a little cry, knocking over the milk and breaking the glass.

"Oh, God! Oh, God!" whispered Pax to herself. Aloud she said, "What's the matter, Jan?"

The boy pressed against her knees and pointed to Pansy.

"Tch, tch, tch," clucked Pansy, and she knelt down and picked up the bits of glass which were all over the floor. "My, my, what's de matter with the boy? You ain't feared o' Pansy, are you, son? Pansy won't hurt you." She picked herself up, holding the bits of glass in her apron. "I'll just go put some more milk on the stove and get me a cloth to wipe this up."

Jan went back and sat in his chair. Pax looked at Philip; then she put her hand over her eyes.

"Oh, Phil!" she said, and her voice quavered.

"Get hold of yourself, kid. Little accident, that's all. Happens to all of us."

85

His sympathetic tone was too much for her. With a little gasp, she got up quickly, ran out of the room, and slammed the door.

Jan's eyes followed her nervously, and then he stared at Philip as though he were seeing him for the first time. He saw an unusually tall man with steady, deep-set gray eyes under heavy level eyebrows. Philip had a strong, short nose with sensitive nostrils, and deep lines on either side of his firm, serious mouth curled upward as they came to an end and gave it a certain whimsical sweetness. His jaw was clearly defined, his chin determined and a little too square.

Philip didn't speak. He lounged on the couch, with his pipe between his teeth, trying not to look at the child.

Jan was very tense. He clasped one thin hand with the other so tightly that the knuckles became blue-white, and his eyes kept darting from Philip to the door and back again, his small face getting steadily paler.

Philip got up, strolled casually over to the window, then turned and walked toward Jan. The child leaped up quickly and backed against the mantelpiece.

Philip stopped immediately and began to speak quietly to him in fluent German. Then he moved forward again and put out his hand. When the boy heard the steady outpouring of the hated language, the frightened look on his face changed to one of horror and he began to run. He dodged around the furniture until he found a clear path to the door; then he threw himself against it, frantically trying to find a way out. Not a sound escaped his lips and he groped wildly for the knob like a terrified little animal which had been trapped.

Philip quietly opened the door and stepped aside. "There you are, feller," he said in English.

The child stumbled out of the room into the hall and began turning round and round, searching for some means of escape.

The door at the back which led into the kitchen opened, and Tubby came in. He had a book in his hand which he held out to Jan. "You can have it," he said, with his charming smile. "It's Dick Tracy. He's a dick! Nobody ever gets away—"

Philip went back into the library and quietly closed the door.

86

6

PAX RAN UP THE STAIRS into her room and flung herself on the bed. Her temples pounded. Wearily she stretched out her arm and pulled on the light beside her bed. Was it only forty-eight hours since she had lain almost peacefully in this very bed?

She got up, went over to the dressing table, and peered at herself in the mirror. The face that stared back at her was drawn and there were dark circles under her eyes.

She went into the bathroom, washed her face, and bathed her eyes with cold water. She powdered her face, put on fresh lipstick, ran a comb through her hair, and tied it back with a red ribbon.

She looked wistfully at the chaise longue with its comfortable cushions. Then she listened at the door. Everything seemed quiet downstairs. Jan would be all right with Philip. Everyone was always all right with Philip. She would take just five minutes. She settled herself comfortably among the pillows and closed her eyes.

Suddenly she found herself alone, standing on the crest of a hill. Around her stretched endless plains, treeless and burnt. There was rubble and ruin everywhere, and she could hear the howling of hungry dogs beating in on her ears.

There was no sunlight and no darkness and the sky closed down to the horizon like a great empty gray bowl. She could see a column of smoke in the distance; it changed into a huge serpent, twisting and gliding slowly across the desolate steppes.

As it came nearer, she saw that it was a procession of living men and women—thousands and thousands of weary exiles, who trudged along in silence, glancing at her incuriously with dull eyes as they passed around the hill on which she stood, coming from nowhere, going into nothing.

Then a childish voice began tapping like a small hammer on her brain.

She awoke with a start, her heart thudding in her breast. She

87

listened. Everything was quiet except for that voice, subdued and monotonous, that continued almost without pause.

She leaped to her feet, straightened her untidy hair, and again glanced in the mirror. She could almost see that dream vision, the long slimy serpent of despairing, patient people, writhing its way unnoticed through the subconscious mind of the world.

She went out into the hall and leaned over the banister.

The two boys sat three or four steps up from the lower floor, where the light which hung in the well of the stairway shone directly on them. Jan was sitting with one shoulder against the newel post, and Tubby pressed his strong little body close to him, so that one knee of each boy could support the book which was open on their laps. The towhead was no more than six inches away from the brown one, and her son's childish treble floated up to the landing above.

" 'So you won't talk,' says Moonhead—Moonhead is the feller Tracy's out to catch. 'Well, we got ways to make guys like you talk, ain't we, Hatchet?' Here's Hatchet here, see? He's Moonhead's lookout man and he's awful mean—"

Pax walked down the steps past the boys and went into the library. Philip was sitting in her father's chair, reading. He raised his head when she came in and through the open door he saw the tableau on the stairs.

Pax smiled at him. "It's going to be all right, Phil," she said. "It's going to be all right."

They got through dinner easily and quickly. Jan began by drinking out of his soup plate and eating with his fingers, just as he had done the night before in New York, but he never took his eyes off the other child, and later, during the meal, Pax saw him wipe his fingers on his napkin and clumsily try to use his fork. She smiled and nudged Philip.

After dinner, they went into the library for coffee. Pansy put two cups of cambric tea on the tray for the children. Philip offered Pax a cigarette and lighted it for her. Immediately, Jan put down his cup, went over to Pax, and put out his hand.

"*Bitte?*" he said shyly.

"*Bitte* is 'please,' Jan," she said, and gave him a cigarette.

"What are you doing?" asked Philip sharply.

"Sh-sh," she whispered, "he's quite used to it. I'll tell you about it later. We'll just have to teach him gradually."

"Hey, Mom! I want one!" demanded Tubby.

"No, Tubs, you're too little."

"He's littler'n me!"

88

"But Jan's three years older, Tubby," she said lamely.

Tubby scowled and stuck his lower lip out. "Well, if he can have one, I don't see why I can't!"

"He's got something there," Philip said quietly.

"Have you ever smoked a cigarette, Tubby?" asked Pax.

"No, but I want one," he said.

"Very well, Tubby, you may try one, but I don't think you'll like it," Pax said. "Your daddy's never smoked, you know. That's why he's such a big, strong man." She leaned toward him. "That's what I thought you wanted to be, Tubs. Cigarettes stunt you, you see. You'll probably grow up to be a little runt of a man—no football, naturally. How are you going to like that?"

Tubby held the cigarette in his little fat hand and stared at it. "Well, he smokes!"

"That's why Jan is so much smaller than you are."

She knew she'd have to pay for that someday, but she went right on: "But here, Tubby, you try it. Let me light it for you."

The child stuck it in his mouth and Pax held the match to it. He puffed out his cheeks and blew the wrong way.

"Draw your breath *in*, old man," said Philip.

Jan sat there, calmly smoking and watching Tubby. Tubby pulled hard at the cigarette, choked, and began to cough violently. The smoke went up his nose, into his eyes, and tears streamed down his cheeks. No one said anything.

Tubby looked at the cigarette, wiped his eyes and his nose on the back of his hand, marched over to Jan, and said, "Here, you can have the old thing. It stinks!"

Tubby thrust his hands in his pockets and leaned against the mantelpiece, his cheeks flaming, a sullen scowl wrinkling his forehead.

"I was afraid you wouldn't like it, Tubs," said Pax. "But you were a good sport to try."

Tubby kicked the fender, looked at Jan, and an abashed grin wrinkled the corners of his mouth.

Pax decided to put the children to bed earlier than usual. She knew Jan was tired and she wanted to talk with Philip alone. Tubby protested wildly, but she was very firm.

"How would you like to sleep in Jan's other bed tonight, Tubs?" she asked, after she'd given them their baths and was about to tuck them in for the night.

For a moment she felt a little stab of self-reproach. She knew that she should be the one to be near the boy, but she mentally shrugged it aside. She was dead tired, too, and she'd had no respite from the strain of the last thirty hours.

"After all," she said, "it's Jan's first night in a new house, and if he wakes up and is frightened, you'll be there to take care of him."

"Gee, Mom! That'll be fun! Come on, Jan!"

"Jan," she said, *"gehst du mit Tubby, ja? Verstehst du?"*

She looked at him anxiously. He nodded.

Tubby suddenly snapped his fingers and a wide grin spread over his face. "Jeepers!" he yelled. "Luke! I didn't show him Luke!"

He started pell-mell for the stairs.

Philip, who was leaning against the door frame of the guest room, let out a long, low whistle. "Uh-uh!" he said warningly, and shook his head.

"What?" demanded Pax. "What's the matter, Phil?"

"I wouldn't. Honestly I wouldn't," he said gravely.

Pax ran to the head of the stairs. "Tubby! Come back here!" she called, and went back to Philip with a bewildered expression on her face. "Why?" she asked.

"Do you know whether he's even seen a dog? Since—I mean—"

She stared at him.

"You know what they used 'em for over there, don't you?"

"No."

"Guess," he said tersely, and strolled across to the sitting room.

Tubby ran puffing up the stairs. "What's the matter, Mom?" he demanded. "I'm just going to get Luke. He won't jump on anything. Jan hasn't seen him—"

"No, darling—"

"But, Mom, he'll just love—"

"Not tonight, Tubs. You save Luke for tomorrow. Jan's had quite enough excitement for one night," she said, and gave him a hug. "Now, pop into bed, both of you."

"Well, I can tell him about Luke, can't I?"

"Sure you can"—she smiled obliquely—"but I'm afraid he's not going to understand."

Two hours later, Philip and Pax were still talking.

Pax was half lying on the couch, the pillows propped behind her head. She had kicked off her shoes and was feeling thoroughly relaxed.

The window was open. A gentle breeze rippled through the leaves of the great oak outside and billowed the curtains inward. Now and then they could hear the call of some night bird and occasionally a chipmunk scampered across the roof.

Gone was the dull, sullen roar of the city, the staccato shrillness of the taxi horns. The remembrance of the cold, brilliant lights of New York was blacked out by the protective country darkness, and she was at peace.

Pax related in detail everything that had happened to her since the train had pulled out in the cool dawn of the day before—her unpredictable panics, her postponement of the dire moment. She told him about meeting the child in the surgery and of her consternation when she found he could speak no English. Philip smiled at her tale of the first dinner and her rage when Jan threw up all over her.

"That was about the worst," she said, "that is—until this morning. You know, Phil, I've never had very much of a sense of humor, and when I get scared or embarrassed, what vestige I have disappears into thin air. Well, I decided I'd shop for him at Gimbel's. I thought it was big enough so nobody'd notice how strange he looked, and then"—she hesitated—"Gimbel's seemed a Hebraic name . . ."

She flashed a look at Phil from under her dark lashes.

"Don't look at me like that, Phil. I know I should have been braver, but I just wasn't. Well, anyway," she continued, "they were trying some clothes on him, and I guess he got frightened, because all at once I saw a trickle of water seeping through the brand-new trousers which I hadn't even bought yet—running down his skinny legs into a little pool at his feet!"

Philip threw back his head and roared.

"It's all very well for you to laugh," she said in disgust. "I didn't—then. First, I wanted to kill him, and then I wished that Gimbel's floor would open and I could sink right down into the earth and never see the poor little brat again."

"Never mind, kid. The worst's over—"

"You hope!" she said.

"And you're home," continued Philip, and suddenly his face became serious. "And what's more important, so is he—at last."

"Listen!" she said.

She had left Jan's door ajar, and through and over their conversation they had been conscious of the steady drone of Tubby's voice and an occasional grunt from Jan.

Now, all was still.

Pax beckoned to Philip and they tiptoed across the hall. She pushed the door open a little wider. The light from the hall shone obliquely across the two beds. They moved quietly into the room and stood looking down at the brown head on one pillow, the honey-colored one on the other.

"What does it remind you of?" she whispered.

"I don't know. What?"

She pushed him out gently and closed the door. "It's funny," she said, "but in some queer way I seemed to be looking at Robert—and Jake."

"Yeah, I know. And now, Bob hasn't got Jake any more."

"No," she said, "and I lost him a long time ago."

Philip looked at her steadily. "Do you want to talk about it, Pax?"

"No." She hesitated a moment. "But thanks, Phil." She stopped at the head of the stairs. "How about some hot milk? Not that I think I'll need it to make me sleep—"

"Fine idea," said Philip. He took her arm and they went down into the kitchen. Pax perched on the table while Philip heated the milk.

"Phil, is it really true about dogs in"—she hesitated—"in concentration camps?"

"True? Christ!" Philip ran both his hands through his hair violently. "It was part of the regulations of those hellholes!"

"Sh-sh! Keep your voice down."

"Thank God, you don't really know everything," he said. "Neither do I. Neither does anyone yet. We've discovered the dead, but we haven't probed the living. The physical tortures we know about, but what has happened to the minds and souls of those who are left seems to be completely ignored by this pitiless world we live in."

He stopped pacing and smiled at Pax bitterly. "Sorry, kid—this isn't the time to bring up that subject. What a bloody fool I am! You've had enough!"

"No, Phil, no. That's why we've got Jan," said Pax softly. "That, and Robert, and— You know, Phil, you've told me all this before—all except the dogs, I guess—otherwise I don't suppose I'd have had the guts—"

"While we're on the subject, Pax, I'd like to say something about what you've done. It may not make any more impression in this stinking sea of mucous than the sound of a pin falling. It may even bring you a little private hell of your own. But, by God, Pax, if it were multiplied a million times, the roar would deafen the world!—Damn it! The milk's boiled over!"

"And now," said Pax, "we've got to begin all over again."

Fifteen minutes later, a pitcher of warm milk in her hand, Pax stood at the door with Philip.

" 'Thank you' seem such weak words, Phil," she said, "but with all my heart, thank you for being my friend. Always and always when I needed you, since I was a miserable kid—remember when I couldn't

92

understand my father? Remember that first and only tea party you gave me? Remember—" She stopped and blinked her eyes. "Remember that rainy day when you started out into the world for me, like my knight in shining armor?"

"Let's remember tomorrow, kid. Go to sleep now. Pleasant dreams."

Pax watched him swing down the garden path, as she'd watched him so many times, in her heart the same serenity and childlike faith that always Phil would somehow make things right for her.

Interval

THE NIGHT of the prom, she lay there in the dark until the rose-colored June dawn had seeped through the window blinds. After that, she dozed intermittently until it was time to get up.

She waited all morning for some word from Jake, her heart stopping each time somebody came to the door, then pounding painfully at each disappointment. She didn't go down for lunch.

She spent that time trying to make herself as attractive as possible. She chose a simple pale blue linen frock with short sleeves—Jake liked her in blue—and a large leghorn hat with a blue ribbon around the crown. She rubbed her pale cheeks with a rough towel, trying to get some color into them, and gazed critically at herself in the mirror. She decided that she looked quite well for someone who hadn't slept at all. She clasped a single strand of pearls around her throat, hunted for a pair of white gloves, and was off—to Amy's.

"Mrs. Sanders, may I sit with you at the exercises?" she asked anxiously. "And please, may we sit in the back?"

"Don't you always sit down front with the families of the faculty?"

"Well, yes, but today, for a change, I thought I'd like . . ." She couldn't think of any excuse. "It's a lovely day for it, isn't it?" she finished lamely.

Amy gave her a searching look. What was the matter with the girl? There was a hurt look on her young face, an aura of secretive sadness about her.

The faculty in their caps and gowns were on the dais, her father sitting in the center. There was a large man in a business suit beside him. That must be the Senator from Vermont who was to receive an honorary degree. The assembly room was crowded with students and their families.

The low buzz of conversation, punctuated with an occasional spurt of nervous laughter, stopped suddenly. Two by two, the graduates, in their gowns and mortarboards, entered at the back of the hall and walked solemnly down the center aisle.

Pax turned her head eagerly.

94

There he was! His eyes were grave, his lips firm, and he looked straight ahead of him.

She hardly heard the conferring of the degree on the Senator or his acceptance speech. But when that was over, she listened impatiently as each man's name was called in alphabetical order, and she leaned well forward in her seat when she heard her father's voice say, "Jacob Felder."

Her face beamed with pride as she listened to the reading off of his honors. More than any man in his class, she thought smugly.

She heard very little of the rest of the ceremony, but it seemed endless. At long last, the young men walked back up the aisle, clutching their diplomas.

Pax was sitting in the last row on the end. As Jake reached her, she held out her hand timidly. He broke line for a moment and that warm familiar smile spread over his face. He reached out and clasped her hand tightly. She looked up at him imploringly. He held her hand a moment longer and was gone.

A flood of happiness surged over her. It was all right. He understood. He knew she wouldn't hurt him for anything in the world. She sighed thankfully, and last night's nightmare drifted out into the limbo where it belonged.

She decided that she didn't want to see him this first time before other people. She'd slip back to the house and wait for him there; he'd come to her as soon as he could break away. She said a hasty good-by to Amy, ran lightly down the steps of the college, across the campus, and home. She dashed upstairs, humming happily, flung her hat on the chair, and went over to the dressing table.

The glowing face that smiled back at her from the mirror was very different from the wistful one of two hours ago. She brushed her hair, put some perfume on her handkerchief and a spot of it behind her ears —and waited.

She looked at the clock on the mantel for the twentieth time. Had she been home only twenty minutes? I won't look at it any more, she thought. She sat down in a chair and folded her hands in her lap.

It would take him at least fifteen or twenty minutes to receive his congratulations; then he'd have to say good-by to the different members of the faculty, get rid of his cap and gown— Oh, yes, it would be at least a half to three-quarters of an hour before he could possibly get here.

What would she do with herself in the meantime? Of course, she was hungry. She hadn't really eaten anything since last night at dinner.

As a matter of fact she hadn't eaten anything then—but she wouldn't think about that.

She ran downstairs to the kitchen.

"Martha, can I have a sandwich and a glass of milk? I'm hungry."

"I should think you would be," said Martha. "You didn't touch your breakfast and you didn't even come down for lunch. What's the matter? Too much party last night?"

"No," she said, "I just wasn't hungry, that's all. I'll get the milk."

Pax sat at the kitchen table, munching on her sandwich and gulping down the milk, watching the kitchen clock which ticked loudly on the shelf over the stove.

She thought she heard a footstep on the gravel path. She was out of the kitchen in a flash and pulled open the front door. It was only her father. He came slowly up the path, his mortarboard in his hand, his gown over his arm. He smiled as he saw her.

"Well, my dear, another year gone. I shall be glad of the rest. What did you think of the exercises? I always think it's a little sad to see those hopeful young men start bravely out into the world. By the way," he added, "you should be very proud of your young man, Pax. He did very well for himself."

"Yes, he did, didn't he? You didn't see him anywhere about, did you? I'm waiting for him. I mean—"

Edmund smiled. "No, I didn't," he said. "He'll be along soon, I expect."

He patted her cheek and went upstairs.

An hour passed; an hour and a half; then two hours. That feeling of apprehension was stealing over her again. Surely that warm, strong handclasp had meant that he'd forgiven her, that everything would be the way it was before. If she could only remember whether he'd said that his family were staying over or not. Everything seemed to blur when she tried to think back. The feeling of guilt that had stabbed at her so unmercifully last night had given way to one of sudden inexplicable fear. Somehow—some way she *had* to know.

She'd seen her father go upstairs, and she could hear Martha moving about in the kitchen. She went into the library and took the receiver quietly off the hook.

"Three-seven-nine," she said softly to the operator.

"Hello." It was a woman's voice.

"May I speak with Mr. Felder, please?"

"Just a minute."

Of course, he was probably changing into his ordinary clothes. She listened to what she thought was Mrs. Dupont's voice, speaking to someone in the room:

"What time did he leave?" A low murmur. "Did he say if he was coming back?" Another murmur.

"Hello, miss. Mr. Felder left the house about noon."

"Did he leave any message?"

"No, miss, but I didn't see him myself. Shall I give him any message if he comes back?"

"No, thank you."

Slowly she hung up the receiver. Perhaps he was at the hotel with his mother and father. What was the number of the hotel? Why didn't she know it? Frantically she began to look through the thin little telephone directory.

"Operator!" Nervously she wiggled the arm that held the receiver up and down. "Operator—please! Hello, operator? Two-two-o—and hurry, please!"

She took up the pencil that was hanging by a string from the telephone and began to draw little crosses on the telephone book.

"Hello—I'd like to speak to Mrs. Felder, please. Pardon me, what did you say?" she asked.

What was the name she'd heard Mrs. Felder call her husband?

"Er—Isaac, I think. Yes, that's it, Mrs. Isaac Felder. Yes, I'll hold on."

More crosses. In a moment she heard the same voice saying: "I'm sorry, but Mr. and Mrs. Felder checked out. What? Oh, I should think about an hour ago."

For several minutes she sat there, motionless, huddled on the chair beside the telephone, her head buried in her arms on the table in front of her. Then with a sudden movement she jerked her head up and stared straight ahead.

What was she thinking about? Why, it was all so simple! He had gone to the station to see them off. What time did that last train leave? Of course, that was it. He'd wanted to finish up all the things he had to do first, so that when he finally came to her, they could really be alone and have all the time they wanted to find their way back. Why did she always have to be so scared? Nothing had changed—how could it when she loved him so much? She'd just be patient. What was it her father had said? "He'll be along soon, I expect."

She leaned her aching head back against the wall. She wished her heart would stop thumping—she could see it thump, right through her dress. Why were her hands so cold? It was really very warm for June—

She waited.

Seven o'clock.

She wouldn't wait any longer. What did he take her for, anyway? Didn't he think she had any feelings? She guessed she'd go for a little walk. It was really very stuffy indoors; the air would do her good.

She closed the front door softly and crept down the steps. She walked on the grass at the edge of the gravel path. If no one heard her, she wouldn't have to stop and talk to anybody. Across the Green, past Philip's, to the top of the hill. She hesitated there for a moment; then, slowly, her feet automatically began to pull her down the hill.

Past the grocer and the butcher shop; Benson Road, that was the first street— "Good evening." There was the livery stable—wonder what they keep in it; not many horses in Mapleton— "Just fine, thanks, how are you?" Now the garage and the filling station— "Yes, just lovely, didn't you?"

Why did people have to keep on speaking to her?

Papa Leclerc's—her steps began to quicken. Faster and faster! Another hundred feet and she was at the corner of his street. She broke into a run. There was the house; how drab and dingy it was! She stumbled up the steps and pushed the bell. She could hear it ringing through the house. Why didn't somebody answer?

After a minute or two the door was pulled open about a foot by a small boy of eight. He had untidy, nondescript-colored hair, two teeth were missing in the front of his mouth, and his hands and nails were filthy. He was wearing a torn undershirt and a pair of faded blue jeans. He stared at her.

"I'd like to see Mr. Felder. Is he in?"

"I dunno."

"Well, is there anybody home that does know?" she asked impatiently.

"I dunno. My mama's in the kitchen. Want me t'ask her?"

A sudden thought struck her.

"No, don't bother. I think I'll go right up to his room. Could you show me where it is?"

"Sure." He opened the door a little wider and pointed up the stairs. "When yuh get to the top, go straight back, an' it's the door that way." He waved his hand to the right. "Want me t' show yuh?"

"No, thank you, I can find it all right."

She passed him and ran up the rickety stairs. She followed the little boy's directions and went to the door he'd described, knocked gently, and waited. Then she knocked again. There was no answer. She turned the knob and slowly pushed the door open.

The walls were a mustard brown, streaked and dirty. Square and oblong spots on the wallpaper stared cleanly at her. There must have been pictures hanging there before for some time. The bed was brass, with a faded, uncovered mattress on it. The closet door was open, and she could see a dozen or so twisted iron hangers hooked on a rod. In one corner of the room was a cheap oak bureau from which yawned two empty open draws, and thrown carelessly in the middle of the floor there was a pile of old newspapers and magazines.

She stood there with stricken eyes, gazing at the awful emptiness. Then she closed the door and went slowly down the stairs. The little boy was swinging on the newel post at the bottom.

"Mama says he ain't there," offered the child cheerfully. "Mama says he ain't comin' back."

"I know," said Pax dully, and walked past him and out of the house.

The plain, bespectacled young woman gave her an indifferent glance when she asked to see Mr. Nelson.

"You'll have to wait. He's busy at the moment."

And she returned to her staccato hammering.

Pax sat there, erect in an uncomfortable straight chair, her eyes fastened on the opaque glass panel of the only other door in the room. Painted on the door in black letters was the name "James Nelson," and in smaller ones under it: "Editor."

She began to regret the long journey in the bus. Her reason had told her that Jake wouldn't take up his job on the paper the very next day after graduation. Hadn't she heard his father ask him to spend a week with them before he started to work? But at the same time she couldn't believe that he'd go so silently and leave her, brooding and miserable, for a whole week. Jake was so gentle. It had all been a hideous misunderstanding. If she could only see him, just once—

The door opened and a man came out. He paused at the door for a moment talking with somebody inside; then he put his hat on the back of his head, stuck a half-smoked cigar in his mouth, and closed the door noisily behind him.

The secretary got up lazily, opened the door, and called, "A young lady to see you. What's your name?" she threw back over her shoulder to Pax.

"Miss Gifford—from Mapleton. I won't take up much of Mr. Nelson's time."

The girl repeated the name through the door. Apparently she received an affirmative answer, for she opened the door a little wider and, on the way back to her infernal machine, said laconically, "You can go in."

A nice-looking, middle-aged man rose from behind his desk and held out his hand to her. "Hello, Miss Gifford. Sit down, won't you?" He

99

offered her a chair and smiled pleasantly at her. "My secretary said that you're from Mapleton. Are you by any chance related to Professor Gifford, the President of the College?"

"He's my father."

"Well, well! I'm doubly delighted to see you. Your father and I were classmates at Harvard. I haven't seen him for two or three years. Don't get over in those parts much. How is the old boy?"

"He's very well, thank you."

"Let's see now, the last time I saw old Edmund was when I took the son of an old friend of mine, Bob Lyttleton—do you know him?"

"I've met him," she said, hoping she wasn't showing her impatience.

"Fine boy. Yes, sir, guess that was the last time. Took the boy over to meet your father—thought it might make things a little easier for him. How's he getting on, by the way?"

"I don't know, Mr. Nelson. I don't know him very well."

"Is that so? Too bad. Well, we'll have to do something about that. Bob's father and I've been pals for years—not one of my alumni, you understand. If I remember correctly, he went to the University of Virginia." He threw his head back and laughed loudly. "Damn highfalutin' Southerners—I beg your pardon, my dear young lady. Do you mind if I smoke?"

"No, of course not. Mr. Nelson—" she began determinedly.

"Well, it's a real pleasure to meet Edmund's daughter. I knew your mother, you know, beautiful girl she was. You're very much like her, my dear."

"Really? I—"

"We always used to say that the only thing your father ever got out of his Rhodes scholarship was a lot of stuffy old stones and a lovely wife."

"Yes—"

"He never married again, did he? Well, with a charming young woman like you to look after him, I can't say I exactly blame him."

Why didn't he stop? How long did she have to go on listening to this drivel? Silly old man! Shut up, shut up, shut up!

Aloud she said, "Please, Mr. Nelson, if you'll only—"

"Forgive me, my dear young lady, there was something you wanted to see me about, wasn't there? Now, what can I do for you, hmm? Thinking about a career as a newspaper woman? Well, no reason why not. Your father's daughter should have all the requisites for a good writer—"

Pax rose quickly from her chair and walked over to the desk.

"No! No! No! Please, Mr. Nelson! I don't want to be a writer. I don't want a job. All I want is to ask you something about"—she hesitated a brief second—"a friend of mine, Jacob Felder—"

"Oh, yes, Felder—"

"I know he's got a job with you. What I want to know is, has he started yet?"

"Started—"

She rushed on. "I mean, I know he was thinking of taking a little vacation first—just for about a week, you know, but I thought maybe he'd changed his mind and—"

Nelson opened a drawer in his desk and searched through some papers. "Ah, yes, here it is. Have a look at that." He handed her an open telegram. "Maybe you can make something out of it—"

Pax read it over twice. She tried to read it for the third time, but she couldn't see the words. She looked mutely at Nelson and handed the telegram back to him.

"Night letter," he said. "Got it this morning. You say he's a friend of yours?"

She nodded.

"Well, you tell him for me he's a very foolish young man. Tell him he won't find it as easy as he thinks. You see, Miss Gifford, it's this way—"

She couldn't hear any more. He continued talking genially to her as he escorted her to the door and shook hands with her cordially. She got out somehow. The last thing she heard as she felt her way down the steep stairs and out onto the strange, unfriendly Burlington street was that venomous rat-tat-tat, rat-tat-tat of the typewriter. She stumbled along to the bus terminal.

She knew now. It was all over.

I'm too tired. I'm too tired to care. When people get tired they don't care—

He wasn't coming back—ever.

She might as well make up her mind to it. Now that she knew she was never going to see him again, she could rest. Nothing any worse could happen to her as long as she lived. There was nothing left to hope for, and she couldn't be hurt any more. That was something to be thankful for.

She was so desperately tired! No good thinking any more about it. Just go to bed and sleep. It would be so wonderful to relax and drift off into oblivion—

The chimes in the church tower struck twelve. The sheets were hot and heavy and the pillow hurt her head. She turned it, plumped it up, and finally threw it on the floor. Where was that beautiful sleep she was going to have at last? Where was forgetfulness?

She suddenly leaped out of bed, pulled on some clothes, and in two or three minutes was running swiftly across the Green.

Amy's house was dark. She stood under Philip's window and whistled softly. There was no response. She waited a moment and then whistled again.

Then a frightening thought struck her. Maybe he'd gone too! He usually stayed on at the close of the year for three or four days to clean up unfinished bits of business, but perhaps he had finished and gone away like everybody else. She leaned up against the side of the house, her throat aching with self-pity. Well, she had to know.

She went around to the front door; it was open, as she knew it would be—nobody locked doors in Mapleton. Inside she found herself in utter blackness. She couldn't remember where the light was. She groped her way along the lower hall until she found the newel post; then, hanging on to the rail, she crept up the stairs until she reached the last step. She felt along the wall until she found Philip's door, and pushed it open gently. She could barely distinguish shapes in the room by the dim light that seeped in from a distant street lamp. She knew that the couch he made up as a bed at night was in the far corner of the room, but it was so deep in the shadows that she could see nothing. She walked slowly across and touched it.

He was there. He could sleep like the dead while her heart was slowly breaking into little pieces. She became so angry with relief that she began to shake him furiously.

"Wake up! Wake up! Oh, Philip, how can you? Wake up!" Her voice was getting louder and louder. "Philip! Do you hear me? Wake up! You've got to! You've just got to! How can you sleep like that"—Philip sat up slowly, shaking his head—"when you know I haven't got anybody else in the world and I'm so miserable and I can't stand it any longer—I can't! I can't!"

Pax was kneeling at the side of his bed, crying hysterically.

Philip caught her by the shoulders.

"Stop it, Pax. Stop it at once," he commanded. "What's the matter with you? Stop it! Do you hear me?"

"I can't! I can't stop it!" she wailed. "I thought you'd gone!"

Philip turned on a lamp at the head of the couch and lifted her off the floor onto the bed. She buried her head on his shoulder and went on crying out loud like a child.

"Pax, listen to me, you've got to stop this crying! What is it?"

"Jake's left me!"

"What are you talking about?" said Philip sharply.

"He's left me. I'm never going to see him again!"

"Pax, get hold of yourself! Stop behaving like a child. Jake had to leave, you know that. Listen, he's finished college, you dope. He graduated—remember?"

She shook her head violently. "No! No! It's not like that! He's gone, I tell you! He didn't even say good-by! He wouldn't speak to me, Phil!"

"Doesn't sound like Jake." Philip frowned and was silent for a moment. "What did you do to him, kid?"

"I didn't do anything! I didn't! All I did—I just—well, I think he thought I didn't like his mother and father, and he wouldn't—"

There was pity in his eyes as he looked at her.

"You poor little dope!"

She twisted her hands in pain.

"Phil, he wouldn't let me explain. People were looking and snickering—I didn't know what to do—but I didn't say a thing! Honest, Phil! I tried to tell him I thought his mother was sweet. He just wouldn't let me—"

The dawn was breaking over the hills to the east. The cool morning breeze ruffled Pax's hair, and the soft gray light picked out the hollows under her eyes. After her hysteria had subsided, she had fallen, exhausted, on the floor, leaning against Philip's knee.

In the beginning she had shied like a colt as Philip probed for the truth. She twisted and wriggled, trying in her confused way to defend herself, until at last the whole dire story spilled out—from the time she caught sight of the two strange little people, standing awkwardly in the doorway of the dining room, to the catastrophic moment when Nelson handed her Jake's telegram which said he was giving up his job.

She tried to explain how she felt at the first meaningful silence, when all eyes fastened on the small group as though they were unclean and didn't belong there, then her shame and sickening embarrassment as the awful titters rippled through the room and battered at her ears.

"Jake's mother and father, Phil! And I was as bad as the rest of them because I wanted to die then, too. It was horrible!"

"You're right, kid. It *was* horrible. You had your baptism all right. It's not pretty, Pax. But that's not exactly the point we're trying to get at, is it? For instance, when you were upstairs in the hotel room with them, away from those swine in the Tavern, did you try to be nice to Mrs. Felder—show her any affection?"

"No."

"Did you try to make the old man feel at home?"

"No, Phil."

The dark head dropped lower.

"Did you talk to his sister at all?"

"No. She didn't seem to—like to talk to anybody."

Philip sighed, got up, and began to walk up and down.

"We're all animals, you know, Pax. We're a little more aware than the four-footed kind, but it will be thousands of years—if we survive that long—before we'll really deserve to be up on our hind legs. All animals know their own kind and odor, and they don't attack their own kind, unless it becomes a personal matter like stealing their food—or their mate. But God help another species if it wanders in on their preserve. You see, that's the way it is with Jews and Gentiles, Negroes and whites, Indians, Chinese—and the majorities wield the whip, believe me. I don't mean to give you a lecture at four o'clock in the morning, kid, but don't you see what happened to you that night? You met up with a new and strange odor, so you drew back. Now, I can understand that. It was a kind of reflex action. But, honest to God, what I don't understand is your making no effort to find out what kind of people they were inside, that man and woman who conceived the boy you think you love—"

"Think?" she interrupted angrily.

"That's what I said, kid."

He noticed that her eyes were becoming moist again.

"You better get along home now, Pax, and try to get some sleep."

"No!"

"Be a good girl. It's late. Your father and Martha might get worried—"

"They don't know I came out. They wouldn't care, anyway! Please, Phil, I want to talk some more. I didn't mean it, Phil. I didn't mean to hurt him. I'll do anything. Anything, Philip! I just can't stand having him hate me!"

"He doesn't hate you—"

"You've got to find him for me! You've just got to! I haven't got anybody else but you. Find him and tell him I didn't mean it! He'll listen to you—"

"Wait a minute, Pax. We can phone his home in Worcester tomorrow."

"No. He might not answer. Anyway, he's probably told his family not to tell me where he is. Don't phone. You go."

"Suppose he isn't there. What then?"

"They'll tell you where he is. They wouldn't dare not tell you!"

"Aren't you being just a bit unreasonable? Suppose I do find him and he—"

"Oh, he'll listen to you. I know he will. Tell him I love him, Phil! Tell him I'm sorry. Won't you please, Phil? *Please?* I promise I'll never ask you to do another thing for me as long as I live! Won't you, Phil, please!"

"All right," he said reluctantly, "I'll see what I can do."

The train faded away in the gray distance, growing steadily smaller and smaller until it disappeared entirely around the curve of the mountain. There was one last puff of smoke, the mournful echo of a whistle, and all was still around the small station.

Pax Gifford was a forlorn figure as she leaned against the side of the wooden building, straining with somber eyes after the train which was carrying Philip away on her mission.

She didn't see the enormous black thundercloud which had burst several miles away, nor the wide streak of lead-colored moisture stretching from it to the earth. It was traveling fast, and suddenly she felt a large drop of rain splash on her face.

She crossed the tracks and began to trudge up the road.

At home, she wandered aimlessly around the room; then she picked up a volume of her perennial favorite, Edna St. Vincent Millay, and flung herself on the chaise longue. She opened the book at random.

"Oh, you will be sorry for that little word . . ."

The soft sound of the rain on the roof was not as soft as the sound of the tears as they dropped on the open page, making small blisters as they fell.

7

PHILIP LOOKED WEARILY at his wrist watch. Six-thirty. He stretched, then lay with half-closed tired eyes, staring at the ceiling. Why had he slept so badly?

Nothing had happened the night before that should have disturbed him or kept him awake—with the possible exception of Jan's momentary panic. He'd been a damned thoughtless fool to speak German to the boy, but he was sure he had overcome that afterward. Perhaps it was a slightly ominous premonition that a new and unexplored situation—for which he knew he was mainly responsible—now existed, which might affect the whole future of Pax and her family. Anyway, he felt like hell, but he might as well get up.

As he made his coffee and showered, he went on thinking about the girl across the Green.

For sixteen years or more, she had taken up quite a lot of room in his heart. When she was a child, he had been moved by her aloneness, then, as the years passed, by her curious dependence on him.

It was strange how two lonely opposites had clung together; he, a young man, old in knowledge of the world, with a restless and inquisitive intelligence; she, naïve, ignorant, turbulently emotional.

With a glimmer of humor, he recalled how close to the surface her tears always were, and how difficult it had always been to direct her mind in any logical sequence.

And yet, how incredibly lovely she was. How pathetically lovely.

He knew that his love for her was no longer the affection of a big brother, but she had never been aware of the change, and many years ago he had resigned himself to being what she had so childishly and sentimentally termed "her knight in shining armor."

Philip strolled over to the Gifford house. Opening the front door, which was always left unlatched, he went to the foot of the stairs and listened. There wasn't a sound. He reflected grimly that nothing had kept any of them awake. Cautiously he opened the door that led from the hall into the kitchen.

"Good morning, boss. House still asleep?"

Pansy gave a startled cry, which was immediately followed by her brilliant smile. "Lawd bless my soul, Mr. Phil! You give me quite a scare. What you doin' heah so early in the mornin'?"

"Had a rotten night, boss. Woke up early, so I thought I'd come over and see if any of you needed any help around here."

"Bless you, Mr. Phil, there ain't nothin' to do. I stole upstairs and listened at Miss Pax's door. She's sleepin' like a baby. How 'bout a little breakfast, Mr. Phil?"

"No, thanks, Pansy. I've had mine." Philip straddled a chair and leaned his arms on the back. "I'll just sit here and talk to you, if you don't mind, until somebody wakes up," he said.

"I can fix yuh a little beaten biscuit and some grits. Mighty good this hour of the mornin'. The children didn't leave a lick o' theirs."

"The children! You mean they're awake?"

Pansy laughed. "Awake, had their breakfas', and gone fifteen minutes ago."

"Both of 'em?"

"Sure, both of 'em. Tubby went flyin' out o' heah, spite of anything I could say. You know, Mr. Phil, he don't mind nobody but his mama. I can't do a thing with the chile." Energetically she began to roll out the dough on her wooden board. "Seems like to me, Mr. Bobbie should be comin' back pretty soon. That chile's gettin' out o' hand."

Philip got up, walked to the back door, and opened it. "Where's Luke?" he said sharply.

"I don' know, Mr. Phil. Somewheah about, I expect."

"He didn't go along with the boys?"

"Sure 'nough didn't. That dog skitted out o' heah a half hour before the boys was up. Tubby looked for him." Pansy chuckled. "Like to split a gut when he couldn't find him."

Philip breathed a little easier and went back to his chair.

"Mr. Phil." Pansy looked at him thoughtfully. "Miss Pax ain't told me nothin'." A little frown creased her smooth brow. "Mr. Phil, who's this yeah chile?"

"Well, boss," Phil said slowly, "he's a little boy who's lost all his family."

"Uh-huh," she said. "How long he goin' to stay?"

"You'll have to ask Miss Pax that, boss. I imagine it will depend on a lot of things."

"Why can't he talk?"

"Oh, he can talk, Pansy, but he speaks another language. He'll learn."

Pansy went through the swinging door into the dining room to lay a place for Pax's breakfast. She came back, took a batch of biscuits out of the oven, and put them on the ledge above the stove.

"Wheah Miss Pax get him?"

"In New York, but he's come a long way, Pansy. He's an unhappy boy. You see, boss, all of his people were murdered in Poland."

"You mean, he's a little Jew boy?"

"We're not sure, but we think so."

Pansy gave him a long look, pushed through the door again, and was gone for about thirty seconds.

"Mis' Pax gonna keep him, ain't she?"

It was not a question, it was a statement.

Philip shrugged his shoulders and smiled. "I don't know, boss. I hope so."

Pansy went back to her stove and began to hum in a high voice. Then just as suddenly she stopped. "Mis' Lyttleton don't eat nothin' for breakfast," she said in a matter-of-fact voice. "Wish you could get her to eat a egg sometime. Don't eat enough to keep a sparrow alive." She came and stood in front of him, her arms akimbo. "Mr. Phil, Mr. Bobbie ain't goin' to like his baby brought up with a little Jew boy."

"Nonsense, Pansy! Mr. Bobbie's best friend was a Jew."

"I don't know nothin' about that—"

"Why, boss," said Phil, "you're the last person I ever thought I'd hear say a thing like that."

Pansy tossed her head. "It don't make no matter, Mr. Phil. We don't take much to Jews in the South. My folks never did like 'em."

"But your folks and Jewish people have a lot in common, Pansy."

"Whatcha mean—my folks?" said Pansy indignantly. "My folks is Christian ladies and gentlemen!"

"I beg your pardon, boss, I thought you were talking about colored people," Philip said. "These poor Jews have been treated even worse than your people have been treated by white people. They've been tortured and killed—"

"What you talkin' about, Mr. Phil? Do you think my white folks have brutalized me?" She gave a proud little laugh. "Go on with yuh, Mr. Phil, suh, beggin' your pardon, but you're crazy!"

"Did you ever go to school, Pansy?"

"No, suh, there weren't no schools for niggers near wheah we lived. But Mis' Mary, she taught me readin' and writin' the same as Mr. Bobbie learned in school."

"The same, eh?" Philip said. "Pansy, let me ask you this: As a good honest American citizen—which you are, aren't you?"

Pansy nodded her head, but there was a perplexed expression in her eyes.

108

"Well, as far as your rights as a citizen are concerned, do you think you should be any different from—well, let's say Mr. Bob, for instance?"

"But I am different, Mr. Phil. I'm black."

Philip shook his head gravely. "It's funny, boss. But, do you know, you don't look very black to me."

Pansy threw back her head and laughed that rich, infectious laugh. "The man's mad!" she chuckled.

"All right, let's talk about the boy—you're sure I'm not in your way here?"

"Blessed God, no! I'm glad of the company! Don't get much chance to talk, except to the family. Don't know many folks around here. Funny, ain't it, Mr. Phil? I been heah close on to seven years, too—ever since Mr. Bobbie went off to join the war. Folks up heah ain't as friendly as us folks from Savannah."

"Folks don't seem to be very friendly anywhere these days, boss. Now, take Jan; he hasn't got any folks, not any at all. They were burned in a big oven—"

"My, my!"

"Why, he hasn't even got folks belonging to him like you've got—I mean, like your Miss Mary and Mr. Lyttleton and Mr. Bob. That's why Miss Pax thought she'd try to give him some, see? You and me and Tubby and herself—and Mr. Bob, when he comes back from Germany. Then he might learn to forget, and have some good healthy food that would put some flesh on that skinny little body of his. Kind of tough to think the poor kid's been starved most of his life, don't you think?"

He watched her. She gave that little cluck of her tongue, and the corners of her large mouth drooped.

"He don't like me." Her lip quivered. "Can't understand it. All children like me."

"That's because you look different, boss. He's probably never seen anyone like you before. You just wait until he gets to know you and you begin to spoil him like you spoil Tubby. What do you want to bet that you'll turn out to be the most important member of his new family?"

She smiled a little and began to bustle about the kitchen.

Pax finished her breakfast and they went out onto the front porch to wait for the children. Philip looked at his watch, then sat down beside her on the top step.

"About this job you've taken on," he said. "It's going to be tough, Pax. I don't think either of us realized how tough it was going to be until we saw the kid. If you succeed—you, an inexperienced, small-town, Gentile woman—it's going to be the God-damnedest victory for decency anybody ever heard of, and what's more, I'm pretty sure you're going to."

"Thanks, Phil," she said, "but let me put one thing straight. I'm going to try—not really because of all the things you believe in. It's because ever since night before last, when I saw him lying there asleep, when I saw that thin, shrunken arm with that awful number branded on it, and that anguished little face when he was dreaming, I made up my mind then that I was going to do it just for him."

"All right, I'll shut up. I guess you don't need any more shots in the arm. You know what you're up against, but you don't mind, do you, if I point out a few things that I think we've got to be prepared for?"

"Sure. Go ahead, Phil," she said. "Only try not to scare me too much —right now at the beginning, I mean."

"There's nothing to be scared about. It's just things like the dog, for instance. By the way, I don't think he's met up with Luke yet."

"Oh, dear."

"Let's skip that for the moment. The most important thing is, he can't talk. For some time we'll have to guess what he's really like. We've got to watch him, and we've got to be careful that he doesn't know we're watching him."

Pax nodded.

"You've got to tell him—in bad anything, French or German—that I'm not a German and that I'm his friend, see?"

"Oh, Phil," she protested, "I can't tell him all that. I don't know enough."

"Sure you do. If the language department's tough for you, it'll be all the better for him. He'll trust you more. My trouble is, I speak German too damn well and it scares him. Then, you see, we can get on to teaching him English. By the way"—Philip hesitated—"I'm going to stay on here in Mapleton this summer."

"But why, Phil?"

"Well, I haven't really got any special place to go. Now that Mom's gone, Amy's is as much home to me as any other place. You and I can get a long way with the boy. If Bob should come home, you won't need me and I can go away for a little trip somewhere." He smiled at her. "That all right with you?"

She took his hand and held it in hers. "Next," she said.

Philip smiled, patted her hand, and drew his away. He looked down and studied the toe of his shoe.

"We've got to watch him with the kids," he said shortly.

"What do you mean?"

"Take it easy, now. It's just this: when he feels a little more at ease

110

with 'em he might—" He stopped, trying to find the right word. "You see, Pax, he's seen a lot of brutality over there; it's so damn tough not to be able to talk to him and find out just what he has seen. Don't look like that, kid. We've just got to watch, that's all."

They were silent for a moment.

"Where do you suppose they are, Phil?" she said anxiously.

"Cut it out," he said. "It's time you stopped being afraid of things that never happen. Wait until they do, for God's sake. You've taken on a man-size job, Pax. Gird up your loins, you little stinker, and go to work." He grinned. "It's going to turn out swell. You wait and see."

"There's one more thing," Pax said, "and I think it's important. I've been thinking about it a lot, ever since we were in that filthy hotel." She scowled. "Anti-Semitism. What are we going to do about that? I mean, people may think he's a —" She stopped abruptly.

"So what?" he said calmly. "You've dealt with that before."

"Phil, that isn't fair."

He looked down at her with a strange expression in his eyes and when he spoke his voice had a slight edge to it.

"Maybe not, but it seems kind of a funny time to begin worrying about anti-Semitism," he said laconically. "Surely you know the answer to that one."

Pax flushed, but her answer was never given.

They became conscious of a strange sound coming from the end of the street. It was the roll and rat-a-tat-tat of a toy drum, the hideous tuneless noise of a harmonica, and over it the high treble of a childish voice.

"HUT, two, three, four. HUT, two, three, four . . ."

Around the corner marched a small gang of three. Leading it was Tubby, with a stick in his hand which he was using as a baton. Behind him came Em's twins: stocky, red-headed, freckled-faced boys of seven or eight.

Pax's heart missed a beat. She clutched Philip's arm. There was no sign of Jan.

Then they both caught sight of a frail little figure rounding the corner, strolling idly along out of step, stopping from time to time to gaze, somewhat indifferently, at the neat New England houses and the white picket fences.

"Things seem to be more important to him than people," Pax said. "Why should that be, Phil?"

"You ask me the damnedest questions," he said. "I don't know. Maybe it's because immovable things haven't hurt him. Maybe it's just people he's terrified of—and don't ask me why. Take a guess!"

All at once, Tubby seemed to forget his military authority; he broke ranks and ran to the other side of the road. The postman was coming across the Green. Tubby's sense of barter was stronger than his pride of leadership. He collected the mail and made the Gifford gate about ten yards ahead of his troupe.

"It's got an A.P.O. stamp on it, Mom." He grinned at her and kept his hands behind his back. "How much is it worth?"

Pax's eyes were on the three boys who were straggling along the sidewalk.

"A nickel," she said shortly. She looked back again at Jan. "Give me two nickels, will you, Phil?"

"A nickel?" said Tubby plaintively. "Is that all? It's from Pop!"

The twins had reached the gate, arguing vociferously. They pushed by Pax and Philip, Butch taking a swipe at Bill as they staggered through the gate.

"You gimme it now! You've had it long enough!"

"I will not! It's mine! He gave it to me!"

"It is not! And he didn't give it to you, either, you took it away from him! I saw yuh. Tub saw yuh, too. You give it to me or I'll tell on yuh! I'll tell Mom—"

Jan had followed them in, leaning against the fence in complete unconcern.

Suddenly, with a yell of rage, Bill hurled the mouth organ on the ground, turned swiftly, and threw himself on his brother. For a moment, Jan's eyes blazed as they followed the harmonica, then went dead again as he leaned down, picked it up, and returned to his position against the fence.

The twins pummeled each other, kicked, scratched, and bit. Butch got a firm hold on Bill's carrot-red hair, pulling and screaming with fury. That gave Bill an opening and with a short right he doubled Butch up with a hard blow in his belly.

For a moment, Butch looked surprised; and with an unearthly screech he turned, fell forward, and landed on his face on the hard gravel path.

Pax ran and picked him up. His eyes were screwed up tight, and the big tears streamed down his face and mixed with the blood which was flowing copiously from his nose. Philip knelt down beside him and tried to stop the bleeding. Tubby bounced up and down, completely entranced with the fight.

Only Jan remained motionless and silent. Philip saw a look of cold contempt in the boy's eyes. Slowly Jan turned away from the still wailing Butch, spat scornfully into the grass, and began to blow on his mouth organ.

The shrieks eventually diminished into choking sobs, the nose stopped bleeding, and Butch eyed the world around him with suspicion, looking up and at it from the bloody rag which had once been Philip's handkerchief.

Pax left the scene of combat and went back to the top step with her letter. She tore open the envelope and read it through quickly. The handwriting was large and round—almost like a child's, she thought.

"Phil," she called, "it's from Robert. What do you think? He may be coming home soon! Listen to this."

"Pax, I'm late now for my class."

"Please! You can be five minutes late just for once." Pax's face was shining with happiness as she held the letter out to him. Again the same thought that had been there many times before went through his mind. Amazement that this woman seemed always so eager to share these letters from her husband with him—with anyone, he reflected ruefully.

"Read it out loud," she said. "I want to hear it again."

Philip skipped the "My darling little honey chile" opening.

"I just got your last letter and it sure made me miss my sweet wife and baby. These last seventeen months have seemed like seventeen years. What am I doing this for? You can go on being a hero just so long! Country, home, and duty, as the Limies say, are all to the good but enough's enough!

"I sure want my own home and my sweet Pax and my baby son! So, honey, I've put in for my discharge. I don't know how long it will take, but get out the red carpet, baby, 'cause this Southern boy is coming home!

"War is hell, honey, as somebody once said, and nobody knows it better than yours truly. You ought to get an eyeful of this country, even now! We didn't leave nothing! Of course, we officers get plenty to eat—and to drink—pardon me! But it would just break your heart to see these poor Germans!

"Some of us fellows over here in this man's Occupation Army are just beginning to realize that the poor devils we come in contact with weren't really responsible for this war. They didn't hold with Hitler. They're polite and friendly, and honest to God, honey, the poor swine don't get enough to eat—"

"Oh, Philip! Isn't he kind—and sort of sweet?" interrupted Pax. Philip gave her a quizzical look and continued:

"We do what we can for them, but what can you do for a beaten country? Enough of that.

"How's things? Do you miss me, baby? Because I miss you like hell. Well, we'll make up for it when I get home! And no more Astors or New Yorkers, either! Joke's over! I want to come home. Give Amy my love. By the way, who's got my room this year? Tell her I still laugh about how she used to give me hell when I stayed out too late. You don't have to ask her any other questions and she won't give me away, either. Tell old Winslow hello for me, and Em and the kids and everybody else who's interested. Gee, it'll be great to see them all again!

"Give my son a big hug for me and tell him his daddy's really coming home to take care of him. As for you, my darling, we don't put any such messages as I have for you on paper. Censor might stop them! Love and kisses,

Bob

"P.S. The candy was swell! I could do with some more.

X.X.X.X.

"Only four kisses?" said Phil sardonically. "Tubby could do better than that." He handed the letter back to her. "It all sounds great, kid, especially that part about his sympathy for the vanquished. Maybe the Army of Occupation has taught him something that we don't know about."

"Phil, he never mentions Jake. Do you think he knows?"

"Didn't he say anything about it on his last leave?"

She shook her head slowly. "But we didn't know anything about it then either, remember? I just hadn't had any letters for months and I was afraid to think about it, and he didn't mention it and I didn't—"

Phil shrugged.

"But now, Phil. Surely he must know now. And yet he's never said anything in his letters."

"Have you?" asked Phil.

She sighed. "No. I've been afraid to."

She lowered her head and put the letter back in its envelope. "And if he doesn't say anything, I'm not going to either. I'll wait until he comes home."

"Sounds sensible," Phil said. "Well, so long, Pax, see you later."

Tubby and the twins were squatting in a huddle on the lawn; Butch had almost forgotten the skirmish and his bloody nose. Philip called out to them as he passed, and Jan stopped playing his mouth organ and idly started to walk up the path.

As he reached Philip, he gave him a fleeting look. He didn't smile but his eyes seemed to want to say something. Philip smiled at him but kept on going. When he got outside the gate, he stopped abruptly and turned back.

"Hold it," he said quietly to Pax. "Luke's on his way home."

Quickly, Pax went to meet Jan, who was walking up the veranda steps, took his hand in hers, and pulled him down on the steps beside her.

"Take it easy," said Philip, "it's going to be all right." He casually strolled back in their direction.

Through the gate loped the dog, panting loudly, his long red tongue hanging from one side of his open jaw. Pax saw that the child's eyes were still expressionless, but his face became very white and his grip on her hand tightened.

Luke leaped on Tubby, who welcomed him with a shout, and the boy and the dog rolled over and over on the grass, Tubby pulling the dog's long ears, the dog licking the child's face. Jan was very still, but he watched the two intently. Laughing and squealing, Tubby tried several times to get up, but Luke kept knocking him down again. Finally Tubby made it. He coaxed the animal toward the house.

"Here, Luke! Come on, boy! Come on, Luke! Hey, Jan! Here he is!" he cried, snapping his fingers and pulling at the dog's collar.

Tubby started for the steps, Luke following obediently behind him. As he reached the bottom step, a little gasp escaped from Jan's lips. He sprang to his feet and, like a monkey, he scrambled up onto the railing of the veranda, and sat there clinging to the center pillar, his thin legs dangling over the flower bed below.

Tubby immediately changed his course; he veered around to the left, still dragging the dog with him, and grinned up at Jan.

"Hey, Jan! Look! This is Luke! I told you about him, remember?"

He tried to lift the dog up against the basement lattice. Pax got up hurriedly, went over to Jan, and stood beside and a little behind him.

"Up, Luke!" shouted Tubby. "Up, boy! Up! That's a good dog!"

"Tubby! Get out of that flower bed," said Pax in a determined voice, "and take Luke out of there, too!"

By this time, the big setter was standing on his hind legs, wagging his tail furiously and sniffing at one of Jan's shoes. The boy didn't make a sound. He kept drawing his foot up higher and higher, until suddenly he toppled backward off the railing.

Pax caught him in her arms, but the surprise of it and the unexpected weight of the child threw her to her knees. She knelt there with him in her arms, pretending to laugh as though it were the greatest joke in the world.

Jan lay utterly still, his face ashen, his terror-stricken eyes looking into hers.

In the meanwhile, Philip had mounted the steps and was leaning against the pillar, calmly refilling his pipe. He began to speak in German, but in a more halting manner and with a much stronger American accent than he had used the night before. He explained that Luke was a good dog—in all probability the kindest dog Jan had ever seen—that this dog was Tubby's friend, and that he wanted to be Jan's friend, too. He told the boy that he didn't have to like the dog if he didn't want to, but that he must take Philip's word for it that the dog would never hurt him, no matter what he did.

Jan listened silently, apparently getting the gist of what Philip was telling him. Slowly he got up from Pax's arms, an expression of relief on his small white face. He walked timidly over to the top step and stood with his hands clutched tensely in his pockets, soberly watching the antics of Tubby and the dog.

"It's all over, lassie," said Philip cheerfully, "and so will my job be, if I don't get the hell out of here."

8   PHILIP APOLOGIZED to his class for being late, chatted with them for a few minutes, then proceeded to settle down to work.

In spite of himself, his thoughts persisted in wandering, and subconsciously his eye was constantly drawn to a chair under the window on the campus side of the room. As from a distance, he heard himself voicing the familiar theses; he answered succinctly the questions put to him by the students, but, time after time, his eyes strayed back to that chair by the window.

He didn't see the freshman who sat in it now. He was seeing the ghost of a young Jew who had eagerly attended his class so many years ago—not the mature Jake who had later become his friend, but the sensitive, mentally acquisitive scholar who had subsequently argued so definitely and so adamantly against his own happiness.

Suddenly Philip realized why this particular memory persisted today.

116

It was Pax's young refugee who had caused it. Perhaps, in an entirely different way, this boy might give her back some of the happiness she had lost with Jake.

"This common phenomenon of the psyche usually springs from a related behaviorism . . ." His explanation to the class continued, but his mind reverted to a vision of two young men, one only a few years older than the other, sitting beside an open window in a cheap boarding-house bedroom in Boston. That had been a stiflingly hot July day twelve years ago.

They were in their shirt sleeves, each with a bottle of root beer which they sipped through a straw, and they shared a large palm-leaf fan which Philip had bought in a neighborhood store on his way to see Jake. There wasn't a breath of air and the hot sun glistened on the pavements below.

"Suffocating, isn't it?" said Jake, as he mopped his brow with a damp handkerchief.

"It's cooler in Burlington."

Jake didn't answer the challenge. He took another sip of his root beer and stared out of the window.

"I had a hell of a time finding you, Felder."

"I know. Bad luck. You must have left the house just ahead of my letter."

"Yeah," said Philip, "I went to Springfield to the address your mother gave me—and just missed you. I wasted two or three hours before I could find anyone who knew your forwarding address."

"Forwarding address?" said Jake. "I didn't leave any forwarding address."

Philip grinned. "You're telling me! The forwarding address I finally got was back at your folks' home in Worcester."

"That was tough." Jake half smiled. "What then?"

"I waited around Springfield for a couple of days—kept in touch with your mother, of course—took in the sights, went to the movies, and eventually she wrote me that I could catch up with you in Syracuse. What the hell have you been doing, a marathon?"

Jake laughed, but there was a touch of bitterness in it. "It was awfully slim pickings as far as jobs were concerned in both those places, so I figured I'd try a real metropolis."

"Seems to me you'd stand a better chance in a town the size of Brattleboro—or Burlington."

Jake held out a pack of cigarettes. "Cigarette, Professor?"

"No, thanks, I've got my pipe. And my friends call me Philip."

"Thanks," said Jake. He finished lighting his cigarette and handed

117

the box of matches to Philip. Then he looked out of the window again.

They sat there in silence for several minutes. Philip puffed on his pipe thoughtfully.

"Jake."

"Yes?"

"She's only a child."

"I know. A lovely, sensitive child."

"Can't we straighten it out somehow?"

"There isn't anything to straighten out."

Philip's heart sank. There was such a note of finality in Jake's voice.

"Jake," Philip said soberly, "God knows—and I think you know—I'm not the kind of guy that likes interfering in other people's lives. I know it's none of my God-damn business, but it's tough, Jake." He smiled wryly. "You see, I'm her emissary. Would you mind very much if we talked this thing over?"

Jake's face became a little stern, but when he spoke his voice was friendly. "Sure. Go ahead."

"She loves you."

"Yeah."

"Christ! You're making it tough, Jake."

Jake looked at him earnestly and his voice was low and steady. "I am in love with Pax. I think I loved her from the first moment I ever saw her. I shall love her as long as I live. Is that what you want to know?"

"No. I know that." Philip waited a moment, but Jake was silent. "It's that pathetic blunder she made with your family, isn't it, Jake?"

"I wonder if you'll believe me if I tell you it isn't that."

"Go on. Let's have it."

"I'm a Jew and she's a Gentile."

"What's the matter? Are you ashamed of being a Jew?"

"No, I'm not ashamed of it. I'm not proud of it either. It's just the way it is, that's all."

"But you knew all that from the beginning."

"I thought I knew it. You know about starvation, too, but the catch is—you don't, until you've been hungry."

Philip leaned forward, his elbows on his knees, and wearily supported his head between his hands. "I get you, Jake," he said, "but you disappoint me. I've always given you credit for believing what I've always believed: that there isn't any difference in people, that they're all the same, no matter what their race or their color or their religion is."

"Sure, they're the same—underneath. But people don't look underneath."

"Jake, I don't mean to patronize you, but you haven't lived too many

118

years in this weary world. You're talking like a very old and a very bitter man."

"That's where you're wrong. I'm not bitter, but of course I'm old. I'm a Jew. All Jews are old. They're born old." Jake's mouth twisted in a derisive smile. "That's why they're so God-damned young—and hopeful and trusting! And that's why they're not trusted. Jews are loving and loyal. They're loyal to their people, their families, and their loves. But nobody else wants their loyalty—or their love!"

"And you tell me you're not bitter?"

"That's not bitterness, that's the truth. They're steadfast, God help them. And I am proud of that! Because without that quality they wouldn't exist—any more than dinosaurs exist. And that's the way the rest of the 'Aryan' world thinks of them—as dinosaurs."

Jake ripped off his tie and loosened his collar.

"It's hot as hell, isn't it?" He frowned and continued. "Then, you see —that is, if you're still interested—"

"Go on."

"The funny part is, there are good Jews and bad Jews, dull Jews and amusing ones, honest ones and dishonest ones; but it doesn't matter and it never will matter. To the world, we typify the one word 'Jew,' and the world has built—I guess—an insurmountable wall between the Jews and the non-Jews. And God help the poor devil who tries to straddle it."

"You mean Pax?" said Philip quietly.

"I mean Pax." His face softened. "My lovely, fine, innocent Pax. Don't you see, I can't do that to her. God! Don't you see I can't!"

"Isn't it up to Pax to make that decision?"

"No!" Jake said violently. "It isn't! The girl doesn't know what she's up against. I do. This isn't a crusade, you know. It's us! It's our future as normal human beings who want a decent life together—and, what's more important, it's her future. Because I love her, see? The way Jews love—"

"That's hitting below the belt, isn't it, Jake?"

"Sorry, I didn't mean it that way. But, God, I'm human, too. Because I'm giving up the thing I've wanted most in this life. And I've got to, because I couldn't see her take it."

"Jake, even if it's really what you say, perhaps the kid would prefer bucking it to giving you up. Ever thought of that?"

"Yes, I've thought of it. I've thought of everything. You saw what happened when she met my people—and they're good people, believe me. Oh, I thought a lot that night. But I didn't stop loving her and I didn't blame her either, although she thought I did. Sure, she's had her baptism. She's over the first shock, but I can give you a list of the shocks to come: a Jewish background, my family's friends, whispers, snubs and veiled insults; whispers, discrimination, segregation; hotels and clubs and whole districts closed to her; maybe children, half-Jews, to carry on her torture for generations and generations. Why, I could make you a list as long as Jehovah's beard, and if you can prove I'm wrong about a single example, I'll give you a week's salary of that job I haven't got."

There was silence for a moment. Then Philip straightened up and sat back in his chair.

"I've been listening," he said, "and I've been agreeing, but I haven't heard one God-damn word about Pax. She doesn't get a choice—because she's not a Jew. Her love can't be trusted—because she's not a Jew. She isn't given time and gentleness to get used to strangers. There's no understanding for her. She gets the book thrown at her, doesn't she?"

Jake got very white. He rose, put his hands in his pockets, and again began to walk up and down the room.

"Maybe you're right; I don't know. But there's one more thing I want to say, and then let's skip it, shall we? Let me give you the selfish side. I'm not a brave enough man to watch it for the rest of my life. I couldn't take seeing her suffer under blows that she'd try to keep me from knowing about."

"Is that where you want to leave it, Jake?"

"That's where I have to leave it."

And now, Philip mused, as he suggested a few references for next week's class, she's going to go through with it anyway, and this time I think she can take it. Christ! This unholy war must have been fought for something!

Softly, Pax closed the kitchen door which led into the hall and, for a moment, stood on the other side of it, listening. All was quiet in the kitchen. Tubby and the twins had gone off to school; only Jan was inside. She heard Pansy's rich chuckle, followed by the rumble of her cheery voice.

"What you got dose stars in yo' eyes for?"

There was no reply from the child and then Pansy laughed again. "Why, Gawd bless my soul!" she exclaimed. "Dose little insides o' yours sure is as deep as a well! You mean you want more cookies?"

Pax sighed with relief. She walked through the hall, out into the garden, and threw herself full length in the couch hammock.

She could trust Jan with Pansy and pause for a little while to take stock of this new day. Pansy adored children, and that little boy needed terribly to be adored. More than food, more than being warm, more even than being safe now, Jan needed love. He needed it the way she had needed and longed for it when she was a little girl, and had never had it.

Jan needed her love, he needed Pansy's love, Tubby's, and—Robert's when he came home.

She took Robert's letter out of her pocket and read it again. How warm and lighthearted and loving it was. It wouldn't be long now! Impulsively she kissed the four childish crosses at the bottom of the letter.

Why had Philip been so sarcastic about those crosses? Funny how bad-tempered and nasty Philip always was whenever Robert's name was mentioned. She didn't understand it; she never had. From the beginning, he'd never accepted her marriage to Robert. She had always thought it was because of Jake, but she had never been quite sure. There had been something else. . . .

She stretched out with her arms under her head and stared into the strip of blue April sky which she could see just beyond the edge of the hammock awning.

Her thoughts traveled back to that evening—how many years ago was it?—when she had had her first serious quarrel with Philip.

The journey from Cape May where she had been staying with Robert's family had been hot and tiresome, but the ache in her heart for Jake, which had been such a persistent visitor, had been dulled by the joyous secret she was carrying with her. Somebody loved her! And she'd been such a fool, thinking no one would ever love her again.

There had been the fun of telling her father and Martha, but they had both accepted it in their calm, matter-of-fact way, and she had settled down to five weeks of waiting until college opened, for the return of the one person in the world who would understand and be glad for her.

The night had finally arrived, and she, flushed and eager, had run swiftly up the stairs ahead of Philip into the little sitting room and closed the door. She turned on the brightest lamp in the room and thrust her left hand under it, wriggling her outstretched fingers, waiting impatiently for his approval.

There was a moment's heavy silence. He looked for an instant into her questioning eyes, which were glistening with excitement, and then stepped away from her.

"What the hell is that?" he demanded.

"It's a ring! I'm going to be married!"

She was amazed to see the dull red creep into his face.

"Who to?"

"Why, to Robert. Robert Lyttleton."

"That's a God-damn stupid thing to do!" he shouted. "What about Jake?"

Slowly, she sank down on the couch and stared at him.

"What about Jake?" he repeated, more quietly.

All of the happiness drained from her face. She lowered her eyes and her voice was small. "Jake doesn't want me," she said. "You know that."

"What's that got to do with it?"

He tramped up and down the room, his hands tightly clenched in his pockets, once or twice kicking at a piece of furniture which got in his way.

"By God, you get me to traipse all over the country, hunting for a guy you say you can't live without." He gave a hard little laugh. "I guess you can live without him, all right! Here I make a damn fool of myself worrying about your broken heart, and you up and get yourself engaged to a half-witted Adonis—"

"Phil!"

"A football tough without a serious thought in his head, let alone his heart! A heel who goes after his best friend's girl when his back is turned."

"He didn't! He didn't!"

"Well, what else can you call it? I didn't notice him mooning around you all the time he was inching his way through college—with God's help and Jake's."

"Phil! I've never seen you like this before. Don't! Please don't!"

"Are you in love with him?"

"Yes! Oh, yes!"

She covered her left hand with the right one, as if to protect her ring and all it stood for from this strange, inexplicable rage of his.

Philip flung himself into the big chair opposite her, stretched his long legs straight out in front of him, and let his chin fall on his chest.

"I thought you loved Jake."

"I do—I mean I did! I—oh, you're getting me all mixed up! You just don't want to understand." The tears were coming now. "Jake doesn't love me. I tried. I waited a whole year, almost two years. You just can't go on loving somebody all your life who doesn't want you. I want to be loved! I never have been, you know that. I've got just as much right to have somebody love me as anybody else. And Robert does—and he loves Jake!"

"Like hell he does!"

"He does too!" She stamped her foot angrily. "Jake's his best friend; I don't care what you say! But Robert does love me and we have fun and I love him—now! I do! I want to be happy and you're spoiling everything."

Pax buried her face in her hands and sobbed.

"Why couldn't you have waited a little while?" said Philip. "When people die you give 'em more time than that!"

"Oh, Phil!"

"All right, to hell with Jake! But why Lyttleton? There are other decent men in the world if you'd give yourself a chance. I—I—" He slouched down deeper in his chair. "Oh, hell, how stupid can you get?"

Pax jumped to her feet and pointed dramatically at the door. "Go away! Go home! I don't want to see you ever again!"

"All right, if that's the way you want it."

And he strode out of the room and slammed the door.

Philip had stayed away from her a long time. They had met, of course. They had been forced to; Mapleton was a small town and her father was Philip's boss. They had never discussed Robert or her marriage again, and Philip had never really come back into her life until a long time after she had married.

Jake had come back into it first, as Robert's friend, naturally.

And now, Robert was coming home. Home to her and Tubby—and Jan. She rolled over in the hammock and yawned lazily. She would like to lie there forever beneath the cool spring sky and dream back— and dream forward. She had had so many scrambled emotions in her life and none of them had been easy for her. Now she foresaw another one, but this was of her own making and this time she was confident it would run straight.

A small boy whom nobody wanted would grow strong and secure with her love, she thought, as she idly watched a robin, scratching in the warm brown earth of the flower bed. And, in an odd way, she wanted Jan to need her. No one really ever had. Not even her own son, who casually accepted what she gave him and then stood independently on his own sturdy heels.

A new day, she reflected, a new cycle in her life and a new vigor coursing through her blood.

She pulled herself out of the hammock and started for the house. She had really better go in and see what this new child of hers was up to. She walked around to the back and opened the kitchen door.

"Oh, Jan—" She stopped abruptly.

Jan was quietly creeping up behind Pansy's chair, scrutinizing her with great interest. He stuffed the cookies he was holding into his pocket; then, with intense curiosity lighting his face, he timidly raised his hand and felt the smooth brown cheek.

9

AT THE FAR western border of Mapleton was a pond fifty or sixty feet wide. It was fed from an arm of the large brook which made its jagged way from the mountain into a river several miles away. It was seven or eight feet deep in the center and along one side, and icy cold even in the middle of summer.

It was a favorite haunt of Tubby Lyttleton's gang, and day after day they would sneak there by a devious route—carefully forgetting to tell their parents—rip off their clothes, and plunge in from the shallow side, frolicking and romping like young porpoises.

One afternoon, about six weeks after Jan's arrival, he was sitting on a large flat stone at the edge of the pond, his knees hunched up under his chin, trailing his hand in the water; now and then he pulled at a lily pad or brushed away an occasional little island of green scum that floated in on the ripples that played around the stone.

Jan tagged along with the children wherever they went, although he never showed any particular pleasure at being with them and rarely entered into any of their games. But he still seemed to have a certain distrust of adults, and he was much more at ease when he was away from them. He was picking up English very fast, but he understood much more than he spoke.

Occasionally he glanced across to the middle of the pond where the sun-browned young bodies of the gang were dog-paddling and splashing noisily about, but he seemed much more interested in the rippling reflection of his small face mirrored in the dark water. He held out his bare foot, wiggled his toes, and almost smiled at the phenomenon of the mirrored foot which changed shape as the little curving waves maneuvered it back and forth.

Butch's high piercing voice shrilled across the pond to him. "Hi, Jan, c'm'on in! It's cold but it's great when you're in."

Jan understood, although he didn't get every word. He shook his head and went on dabbling his hand in the water.

"Aw, c'm'on, Jan," yelled Tubby.

124

"Yeah! Don't be a scairdy-cat!" Bill squealed.

Butch paddled up closer and splashed some water in Jan's face. "Scairdy-cat! Scairdy-cat! Jan's a scairdy-cat!" he taunted.

Jan wiped the water off his face with his sleeve and continued to stare at them. Then he turned his head and looked back over his shoulder. His sensitive young ears had long been accustomed to hearing the slightest sound.

There was a faint rustle of leaves and branches which came steadily nearer. In a minute or so, a black-haired boy of twelve pushed through the bushes. He grinned when he saw Jan. "Hello," he said.

"Hul-law," replied Jan.

The boy sat down beside him and began to unlace his shoes.

"Hi, Johnnie! Comin' in?" Bill shouted.

"Yeah."

Jean Pierre Baptiste Leclerc stripped, hung his clothes on a low branch of a tree, and stood at the edge of the pond, rubbing his arms briskly and staring down into the dark water. He was a sturdy, finely built youngster with deep-blue eyes and an endearing smile.

Thirteen years before, Jeannine Leclerc had left Mapleton. No one heard from or of her for two or three years; then she returned as suddenly as she had left, bringing with her a dark, curly-headed little boy.

Jeannine solemnly assured her uncle and aunt that the baby had been duly baptized into the Roman Catholic church as Jean Pierre Baptiste Leclerc, and the two were received back into the bosom of the Leclerc family. No one in Mapleton ever questioned whether the child had another name.

He had been brought up strictly and religiously by Jeannine, and, when he was old enough, she sent him away in the winters to a boarding school run by the Christian Brothers.

When he was home in the summer, Johnnie, as everyone called him, had always played with the French-Canadian children who lived in his neighborhood, until two or three years before, when Robert Lyttleton had been home on one of his rare leaves. One evening, Lyttleton found his way down the hill to Papa Leclerc's drugstore. When he returned home he asked Pax to let Johnnie play with Tubby, and to use her influence with the rest of their friends to allow their children to play with him too.

That arrangement hadn't lasted very long, mainly because of Em's protest that she would not allow her sons to associate with a little French-Canadian bastard. However, the kids loved Johnnie, so they all continued to meet secretly, at out-of-the-way places. The pond was their favorite hideout.

"Move over, will you?" Johnnie said good-naturedly to Jan. "I want to dive off the stone."

Jan got up, stood a little to one side, and watched the strong body poise there for a moment, then dive gracefully into the water and disappear for several seconds. When Johnnie emerged, he came up in the middle of the squealing group of children.

They all played around for a while; then Tubby and the twins climbed out the shallow side and leisurely walked over and sat on their haunches near Jan. They whispered and giggled and made signs to each other. Then they called out to Johnnie, who was still swimming along easily by himself.

He swam over to them with long overhand strokes, and lifted himself up onto the rock. Jan looked from one to the other, trying to understand their quick whispers. Then he gave up, strolled away a couple of steps, and continued to look down into the water, which always fascinated him.

Suddenly he felt someone push him from behind; then he was going down, down into the black, cold depths. He struggled to the surface, only to go down again and again. For a brief flash he saw a dark young face beside him and as though in a dream he felt something holding him. Then everything blacked out.

When he gradually drifted back to consciousness, he felt a painful thumping in his left side and heard a buzzing in his ears. Someone was pulling his thin little arms back and forth, up and down, and he found it agonizing to breathe.

He opened his eyes and saw four anxious faces bending over him. He tried to get up, but he fell back again; it was much easier just to lie there.

"Are you all right, Jan?"

"C'm'on, we'll help you up."

"Can you walk?"

Jan made no effort to understand or answer.

Johnnie finally got him to his feet, whereupon Jan doubled up, retched, and began throwing up great amounts of water.

Half an hour later, the five children struggled through the Gifford gate, Johnnie and Butch supporting Jan, who stumbled along weakly.

"Mom! Pansy! Come quick! It's Jan."

Tubby banged the door open and ran screaming into the house. The other children got Jan as far as the front steps, but his legs wobbled

126

badly and he sat down, feebly leaning his head against the pillar. Johnnie bent over him.

"You sure you're all right, Jan?" Johnnie asked anxiously.

Pax ran out onto the veranda, followed by Pansy.

"What's the matter? What happened?"

Johnnie Leclerc gave Jan a quick pat, turned, and without a word ran swiftly through the gate, across the Green, and down the hill.

The children all chattered at once.

"Jan fell in."

"He can't swim."

"I didn't do anything."

"He was standing at the edge of the pond—"

"What pond?" interrupted Pax sharply.

"Oh, a pond. Over there." Tubby waved his hand vaguely.

"He was standing—"

"Stop it! All of you! Stop talking!" commanded Pax sternly. "Now, one at a time. What happened?"

The children stopped abruptly and looked sheepishly at each other. Tubby pushed an imaginary something with his toe. Suddenly Butch's face brightened.

"Johnnie pushed him in!" he said triumphantly.

After dinner that evening, Philip and Pax were in the library sipping their coffee. Tubby had gone out to play and Jan was sitting on the floor at Pax's feet.

Philip spoke slowly and distinctly to the boy in English, slipping in a German word every now and then when Jan found it difficult to understand.

"Johnnie pushed you in the water?" he asked.

"I not know. *Im Wasser*—er—*Gesicht*—"

"Face," prompted Philip.

"Er—ye-es. Face—Jawhnee—"

"Yes, go on."

"Jawhnee—*im Wasser*—*nahe*—"

"All right, feller."

Philip got out of his chair.

"Pax, do you mind if Jan and I take a little walk? I think Jan deserves an ice-cream soda after what he's been through today."

"You're going down to talk to Johnnie, aren't you?" said Pax. "Why, Phil? I'm afraid Johnnie isn't a very nice boy. Anyway, he's too old to play with the children."

"I don't get it, Pax. Jan says he saw Johnnie's face near him in the water."

"Why don't we just forget it, Phil? After all, nothing's happened, and I don't suppose Johnnie did it maliciously."

"Who pulled him out? Sounds screwy to me. Want to come along, kid?"

"I don't think so, Phil. Don't stay too long. Jan must get to bed."

A little later, Philip sat at the soda fountain, Jan and Johnnie on either side of him, lapping up double chocolate sundaes.

After they finished, Philip suddenly swung around on his stool, facing Johnnie.

"Johnnie, why did you push Jan into the water? Didn't you know he couldn't swim?"

A look of amazement came into the child's face. "I didn't push him in, sir!"

"You didn't?" said Philip. "Who did?"

Johnnie hung his head.

"Come on, Johnnie, tell me who pushed him."

Still no answer.

"You know it's only fair to Jan to tell him so he can defend himself. Don't you think so?"

The child raised his eyes and looked quickly at Jan, who was painfully trying to understand.

"I'll tell you what, Johnnie, we'll promise to keep it a secret just between Jan and you and me. What do you say?"

Johnnie flushed, lowered his head again, and in an almost inaudible voice he spoke one word: "Butch."

Jan dropped the spoon he'd been licking; his body stiffened as if he'd received an electric shock and his eyes blazed for a brief second. When Philip turned to look at him, his eyes had gone dead again.

"Who pulled him out, Johnnie?"

"I did. The other boys were too little."

"Look, that was swell. Thanks," Philip said. "Johnnie, how would you like to take a ride with Jan and me over to the Lake—let's say, day after tomorrow?"

"Sure. I'd like to, sir."

"We'll go to one of the public beaches, and if Jan would like it, you and I'll teach him to swim. What do you say?"

Johnnie's eyes glistened. "Gee!" he said.

Philip and Jan walked back up the hill. Philip wasn't sure how much of the conversation Jan had understood. He decided to say nothing about it to anyone except Pax, but he was determined that she, at least, wouldn't blame the poor little tyke who lived down the hill.

"Jan."

"*Ja?* Er—ye-es?"

"How do you say *schwimmen* in English?"

Jan shrugged his shoulders. "*Ich weiss nicht,*" he said.

After that the summer passed with surprisingly few incidents. Pax and Philip tried to give Jan as much freedom as they dared, but one or the other usually managed to keep a protective eye on him and was constantly on guard for the unexpected thing that might frighten him. He was an obedient child, but that was not surprising, as he had probably never known anything in all his tragic little life but stark, horrifying discipline.

They didn't know whether he was fond of any of them or not, because he remained always detached and undemonstrative. He never volunteered any information about his past and no one questioned him about it.

Philip, in particular, watched for some signs of cruelty in his nature, but the child didn't seem to show any indication of it. However, he did catch him, one day, when he thought no one was looking, throwing stones at Luke. Philip reasoned with him for an hour.

"You wouldn't like it if anyone threw stones at you, would you?"

Philip wondered if that might not bring forth some bitter expression of remembrance, but there was no response. Jan just looked at him with a peculiar expression in his eyes and looked away again.

There was one episode which disturbed Philip seriously.

The first day that he had taken Jan over to the beach at Lake Champlain had almost resulted in a tragedy.

Along the Lake there was a winding highway which, in summer, was always thick with cars. Philip and the boys arrived about midmorning. They drew up to the side of the road and parked. Philip locked the car and he and the two boys climbed out and started to cross the road.

There was a cross section just behind where they'd parked, and in the center of it stood a State policeman in khaki breeches, shirt, and high boots. He was straddling a motorcycle with his feet on the ground as he directed traffic.

Jan was unaware of the policeman until he had almost reached him. At that instant, there was the furious, ripping sound of a motorcycle swerving dizzily at full speed, and a second officer drew up alongside the first to take over.

Jan started to run like a wild thing, dodging crazily in and out of the moving cars. Philip sprang after him, trying to call to him above the noise of the horns and motors. Both officers saw the danger, and they blew their shrill piercing whistles to stop the traffic.

That apparently familiar sound frightened Jan into a whirling, mad little animal. He began to run faster. Then he stumbled and fell right in front of a moving car. There was a screeching of brakes and the car came to a stop, one of the wheels just touching the small prone body.

Philip picked him up and carried him to the side of the road. Both State policemen hurried up to them. Philip waved them away. "Do you mind, boys?" Philip said, his voice sharp. "I'll explain later."

He knelt there holding the boy, whose body was jerking spasmodically. He wasn't hurt, but his face looked pitifully wrenched and his eyes were desperate with terror. He finally gasped one word, "Gestapo," and then went limp in Philip's arms.

But on the whole, Jan's first summer of freedom passed quite uneventfully. He became less and less a figure of curiosity to the Mapletonians, and they began to regard him as a permanent fixture in the Lyttleton household.

There had been a great deal of whispering when he first arrived. Pax Lyttleton had always been regarded as an odd, uncommunicative girl, so they were not surprised that she offered no explanation. It took Emily Masters, nee Bascomb—more mature now, but just as brash—to bring it out into the open.

"Where did you get the kid?" she asked.

Pax caught her breath for an instant, and then she took the bull by the horns.

"Well, you see, Em," she began, "Robert's brother—"

"Bob hasn't got a brother," said Em flatly.

Pax laughed nervously. "Did I say brother? Of course he hasn't got a brother. He's got a sister—you know, Nancy. What I meant to say was cousin. Robert has a second cousin who married a Polish girl he met in Paris before the war. Well, she and the boy were visiting her parents in Warsaw when the war broke out—you know, in thirty-nine. Jan was practically a baby, naturally. We don't know any of the details yet, except that the girl died and it was impossible to get the child out until now."

"Why hasn't his father got him?" demanded Em.

Mentally, Pax gritted her teeth and went in deeper.

"Oh, he's still over there in Germany somewhere."

"How did the kid get here?" persisted Em.

"They sent him over—and I met him in New York. Of course, Jan doesn't say much about what happened"—Pax looked levelly at Emily —"and we think it's wiser not to ask him any questions. As a matter of fact, we don't think he remembers—"

"Oh," said Em. Pax sighed and deliberately changed the subject.

She told Philip of the conversation and advised him to stick to the same story in case anyone brought it up.

"Did Em believe it?" he asked.

"Why shouldn't she believe it?" Pax said, immediately on the defensive.

"I don't know," he replied. "Sounds kind of lame to me. Why didn't you tell her the truth? Get scared again?"

"No! I didn't get scared," she flared. "It's just that I think we've got to give the child a chance, and you know how rotten people are—"

"Is that the story you're going to tell Bob when he comes home?" Philip asked laconically.

Pax flushed, dropped her eyes, and didn't answer.

"O.K., kid. It's your headache, but I think you're storing up a lot of trouble for yourself—and maybe for the boy, too."

"I don't care! I think it's better this way," she persisted stubbornly.

For the rest of the summer Jan didn't spend so much time with Tubby and the other boys. Two or three times a week, Philip took him —and usually Johnnie Leclerc—to the Lake, getting him used to crowds of strange people and deliberately putting him into situations that he hoped would overcome some of the boy's fears.

Curiously enough, in spite of his unhappy experience, Jan didn't seem at all afraid of the water, and the swimming lessons progressed very well. He seemed eager to learn how to swim, and he was as serious about it as he was about everything else. Johnnie would splash and dive under Phil, coming up puffing and chortling, but Jan plodded steadily along with a sober face, swimming the breast stroke, counting, "*Ein, zwei . . . ein, zwei . . .*" and later, "Wan, two . . . wan, two . . ."

One hot afternoon, early in August, a small seaplane flew low over the Lake. Jan heard the roar of the motor, looked up, gulped, and immediately went down. As he came to the surface, Philip grabbed him by the waistband of his trunks and steered him into shore. They sat there at the edge of the Lake, Jan shivering—not entirely with cold—

his right hand grasping his left arm just above the wrist. Philip tried to explain to him why there was no reason for him to be afraid of planes.

"In the first place, they're not German planes. They're not even army planes—"

Jan broke in. "Hah!" he said. "German planes all r-right! Amer-rican —English planes bomb—how you say '*töten*'? Kill!"

My God, thought Philip, that's a whizzer!

Aloud he said, "But listen, feller, English and American planes only bombed Germans, you know."

The boy turned his head and looked at him, and there was hatred in his eyes. *"Ich bin nicht Deutsch!"* he said, and he spat viciously.

Philip let it go at that. He knew it was no use trying to proceed any further for the moment, but at least he'd pulled one of the child's fears out into the open and had forced him to talk about it.

And so Jan's education of life—if not of letters—progressed in easy stages. He hurled unexpected, difficult-to-answer questions at Philip and Pax, and somehow they managed to answer them.

There was the time when he suddenly left the other children, marched up to Pax, who lay in the couch hammock reading, and looked her gravely in the eyes.

"Madame Pax," he demanded, "what *ist mein* name?"

" 'Jan,' isn't it?"

"No, oder name," he insisted.

She hesitated only for a second. "Lyttleton," she said.

Jan shook his head. "No. 'Leet-el-ton' Tubby's name. What *ist mein* name?"

"Your name is Lyttleton too." She paused. "Why? Don't you want it?"

He shrugged.

"I'll tell you what, Jan. Why don't you keep it for a while until you find one you like better?"

He looked at her long and steadily. Then he shrugged his shoulders again and walked back to the children. His voice drifted back to her.

"*Mein* name *ist* Leet-el-ton," he said.

She heard Tubby's high note of laughter. "What did I tell you?" he shouted triumphantly, "Sure it's Lyttleton! He's adopted!"

Was he? she thought. Had she definitely made up her mind? Where had Tubby got hold of that? Was she sure of it yet?

The day was hot, as only a day in Indian summer can be. The heavy white clouds hung motionless in the still air. Little ripples of heat fluttered between the sun and the earth, the gnats buzzed, and the last bees of the season sped in straight lines, despoiling the bright new goldenrod.

Jan lay on the grass on his back, his arms under his head, watching with intense curiosity a single plane that winged its way high above him to some unknown destination. He was still wary of those strange monsters, but he was no longer terrified, especially if they were high enough so that he couldn't hear the noise.

Butch and Bill and Tubby were sitting on the sidewalk outside the gate playing jacks and commiserating with each other that they had only five more days before school reopened.

Jan watched the plane until it pierced the thick clouds and disappeared. He yawned and stretched, got lazily to his feet, and strolled across the lawn. He opened the gate, closed it after him, and leaned against the gate post.

"Hi, Jan," said Tubby. "Where you been?"

"I sleep dere," he replied gravely, pointing back toward the lawn.

"Want to get in the game?"

"Naw, tank you."

He watched them for several minutes; then his face suddenly became animated.

"Hey, Tobbie! Ve go *schwimmen*, no? Hot!"

Tubby caught the ball before it bounced and looked up at Jan. Then he looked at the other two boys with a rather puzzled expression in his eyes. Since that ill-fated day, Jan had never suggested joining them on their secretive excursions to the water hole.

"What d' yuh say? Want to go?" asked Tubby. "Might be fun—and it is hot."

"Na! Let's play jacks," Butch said.

"Aw, c'm'on, Butch," Bill coaxed. "Let's!"

"Yes, I *schwimmen* now. I show to you," pleaded Jan. "You come?"

Bill and Tubby finally induced Butch to join them. Tubby hid the jacks and ball under the hedge beyond the gate and they were off. Halfway across the Green, Jan turned to the right.

"I get Jawhnee," he called back. "Ve come," and he ran down the hill.

The boys whipped off their clothes and were gingerly testing the cold water with their toes when Jan and Johnnie got there. The younger boys squealed and held their breaths, wading out a few steps and jumping up and down as the icy water crept up to their middles.

The two older boys left their clothes in a heap, and Johnnie dove off the big flat stone on the deep side. Jan followed, more slowly. He stuck one foot in, then sat down on the rock, splashing the water with his feet. Tubby and the twins watched him intently from the other side. Jan braced himself on his hands for a moment; then he slid gently into the pond, disappeared for a second, then emerged, tossing his wet hair back off his face, and began swimming slowly toward them.

"Hurrah!" shouted Tubby. "Look at Jan! He can swim!"

He and the twins started their usual dog-paddling, their laughter and shrieks ringing over the water. Johnnie turned a few somersaults, then swam gracefully around the pond, while Jan kept steadily to his breast stroke, out to the center, then back to the rock again.

After ten minutes or so, Johnnie crawled out and lay on his face in the sun. Jan walked out the shallow side, came around and sat down cross-legged near Johnnie, holding his left wrist with his right hand, as he always did if his arms were uncovered.

"Gee, Jan, you're good!" shouted Tubby. "Where did you learn?"

"Oncle Pheeleep."

"Aw, c'm'on back in! Let's see yuh swim some more!"

Jan shook his head and sat there quite still, watching them.

One by one the boys got bored with it, and joined the other two on the rock.

"That where you used to go with Uncle Philip in the car?" asked Tubby.

Jan nodded.

Tubby's face fell. "He never took us."

"You *schwimmen*. I no could."

"Aw, let's go back and play jacks some more." Butch got to his feet. So did Jan. He went to the edge of the stone, and stood there, peering intently down into the black water.

"Butch," he said, without turning his head. "Look! Vat is dat?"

"Where?" Butch came over and stood beside him.

"Down—you see?" He pointed directly below him.

Butch leaned over, trying to see, when with a lightning-like movement Jan pushed him off the ledge into the water, and leaped in after him.

It all happened so suddenly that Bill and Tubby just sat there motionless with their mouths open. Johnnie didn't even look up.

Butch came to the surface. Then Jan appeared, a split second after. He grabbed the root of a bush that extended into the pond and held on with one hand. With the other he took Butch by the hair and held him under. Butch struggled and kicked, the two boys screamed, and Johnnie leaped to his feet and stood there a moment, watching silently. All at once the struggles ceased and Butch's body went limp. He seemed to be floating there, just under the surface, with Jan still holding his head under. Johnnie glanced at Jan's face. His mouth was twisted in an ironic grin, and his brown eyes were dark with rage.

"Jan, stop!" shouted Johnnie.

Jan paid no attention. His lips tightened, and he pushed the little head in still further.

It all happened in a matter of seconds, but Johnnie realized it was serious. He jumped in and tried to break Jan's hold on the child, but Jan's thin arm was like steel. Without a moment's hesitation, Johnnie gave Jan a punch on the side of the jaw, and Jan let go. Johnnie lifted Butch's head out of the water and swam swiftly to the shallow side with him. He dragged the boy out of the water, and began working over him. The child's face was as red as his hair. The other two ran to them in a panic, trying to help.

Jan pulled himself out of the water and stood, his back against a tree a few yards away, his hands clasped behind him. He made no attempt to go near the group.

After a few moments, Butch's chest expanded and he sucked in a deep breath. When he breathed out, a feeble scream came with it. He shuddered and retched.

"You'll be all right, Butch. You'll be all right," said Johnnie soothingly.

Jan gave his friend Johnnie a reproachful look, put on his clothes, and, unnoticed by any of them, wandered away.

10

THERE WAS SILENCE in the room except for the monotonous tick of the pink marble clock on the mantel above the fireplace. The last dull rays of the late afternoon sun streaked through the dim room, tipping the carrot-red hair of young Bill Masters and turning it to copper. Bill and Tubby were standing in the west window, silhouetted against the sunset.

On the opposite side of the room, Jan sat on the chaise longue, one foot tucked under him, the other swinging listlessly. He was winding and unwinding a piece of string around his finger. The sunrays spilled over his face and stabbed into his eyes. He scowled, squinted, then moved a little to the side to get out of the way of them.

Pax sat at her desk, scribbling on a pad of paper, now and then glancing from Jan to the two children at the window but trying to avoid looking at the sullen, brazen face of Jeannine Leclerc, who sat very straight in a chair by the door, one arm around the waist of her son, who stood beside her.

One, two, three, four, five, six, chimed the little clock. The deep tones of the one in the church tower rang out a moment later. Pax got up, walked over to the other window, and stared across at the Bascomb house. The doctor had been there for twenty minutes, and as yet there was no news about Butch. Pax turned away from the window and went back to her desk.

Suddenly the telephone rang. She picked up the receiver quickly. "Yes, Em?" She listened. "Thank God!" she said. "I'll come over a little later and see if there is anything I can do." She hung up the receiver. "Butch is going to be all right, boys," she said, "for which one of you should be very grateful."

The two boys at the window stiffened. Johnnie's expression didn't change; he was watching her curiously. Jan didn't even look up.

Jeannine rose. "I take it, Mrs. Lyttleton," she said, putting a slight stress on "Lyttleton," "that my son and I can go now."

"Not quite yet, Jeannine," said Pax quietly. "You see, one of the boys is lying."

"Jean Pierre does not lie," Jeannine said arrogantly. "Jean Pierre is going to be a priest. Priests don't lie!"

Pax smiled wryly. "He has a few years to go before he takes the orders, I think, and at the moment I really need your help. Won't you sit down, please, Jeannine?"

She put her elbows on the desk and leaned forward.

"I think, children, you might like to know what happened," she said. "After Butch stopped vomiting, and your mother, Bill, had put him to bed, the poor little fellow had a heart attack."

The children drew nearer, their faces tense with fright.

"His heart became strained, struggling against one of you who held him under the water," she continued. "Now, it's not going to be very pleasant for us to sit here all night, but sit here we shall until one of you tells me who nearly drowned Butch."

The two younger boys dropped their heads, but they didn't speak. Jan reached in his pocket and pulled out a cigarette.

"Put that back, Jan," Pax said sternly. "I've told you that you are to smoke only when you're alone in your own room."

136

Jan obeyed sullenly, and she noticed that his usually pale face was flushed.

"Billy," said Pax, "was it you?"

There was no reply.

"Tubby?"

Again silence.

"Johnnie?"

"He didn't do it," Jeannine spoke up angrily, "and I resent—"

"Please, Jeannine," said Pax. "This—unfortunate accident is almost an exact repetition of what happened early this summer. The boys all said that it was Johnnie who pushed Jan in that time, but Johnnie told Professor Winslow that he didn't, and I believed him. You didn't do it this time, did you, Johnnie?"

The boy held up his head proudly and stared at her. Jan threw Johnnie a swift glance; then he raised his eyes and looked steadily at Pax.

"No was Jawhnee," he said haltingly, "was me." He smiled a grim little smile and his eyes smoldered with a dull anger. "Butch—push—me. I—push—him! Try—kill."

Pax gasped.

"No one push me any more!"

A sensation of utter frustration and helplessness stole over her, and once again that appalling stillness crowded in on her. The thumping of her heart seemed to keep time to the tick-tock, tick-tock of the clock on the mantel.

Tragedy had crept into the room, and somehow she must push it out again. There had been an awful finality about Jan's last statement, and she alone understood the source from which it sprang. Her eyes were troubled as she looked at the young cynic who was quietly sitting there, clumsily trying to make his piece of string into a cat's cradle.

Jeannine's hard laugh broke the silence. "So it was the little"—her lips started to form one word, but she stopped and used another— "foreign boy all the time." She smiled maliciously. "You would have liked to blame it on my son, wouldn't you? My son who isn't good enough to play with yours!" She took a small comb out of the pocket of her gingham dress and ran it through Johnnie's curly hair and then through her own. "Now that Jean Pierre is no longer looked upon as a culprit, I suppose we may be allowed to go?" she asked insolently.

Pax felt the blood creeping up to the roots of her hair. Why was this girl so persistently antagonistic to her? They had known each other so long, but try as she would, she never seemed to be able to overcome Jeannine's apparent resentment, which had always bewildered her.

"Why, of course, Jeannine," she said, in her friendliest manner. "It was very good of you both to come. Thank you."

For a brief moment she wondered if, in her distress, she had been arrogant or demanding when she had phoned Jeannine. She watched thoughtfully as the woman turned to go without a word. Then she saw Johnnie pull his hand away from his mother's. He walked across the room and stood in front of Jan. As Jan looked up at him, Johnnie smiled. Then he ran back and joined Jeannine.

"Oh, Jeannine!" Pax stopped her as she put her hand on the door-knob. She would make one more effort to be friendly. "Won't you let Johnnie stay here and have supper? I think Tubby would like it very much, wouldn't you, Tubby?"

"Sure would," said Tubby.

"No, thanks," Jeannine said. She looked directly at Jan. "I feel my son will be safer having supper with me."

Her sarcastic little laugh floated back into the room and Pax was left alone with the boys.

"All right, boys. Off you go! Not you, Jan. I want to talk to you."

She shooed Tubby and Bill outside and shut the door.

Jan still sat on the chaise longue, playing with his cat's cradle. Pax opened a silver box on the table beside her and took out a cigarette.

"Would you like one now, Jan?" she asked. He shook his head. She lighted her cigarette, pulled a comfortable chair up to the chaise longue, and sat down facing him.

What a fool she'd been not to have realized immediately that Jan had been the one.

We'll have to watch him with the kids. Philip had said that, the morning after she had brought the child home.

Of course, he'd planned it for weeks! He must have known from the beginning that it was Butch who had pushed him in the pond and it was Butch who had lied and blamed it on Johnnie.

In all probability, that was the kind of dishonesty that this small boy had seen punished by death.

Suddenly she felt a painful smashing pulse beat in her throat. Tubby and Bill had lied, too! Were these children in danger?

He looked so frail and innocent sitting there, so still except for those slender hands which moved incessantly with the piece of string. The brown head was bowed and the slanting lids hid any stealthy thoughts which might be lurking there.

"Jan," she said gently.

The eyelids flickered. He gave her a sly, upward glance; then he looked down again.

138

"You have been very naughty."

No reply.

"You understand? *Unartig—méchant.*"

He shrugged his shoulders.

"Butch is a very little boy. He does not understand about death."

"Yes?" He looked a little surprised. "How know he I not die?"

"He didn't mean to hurt you. That was his idea of having fun."

"Die—no fun."

Pax thought despairingly, why had Philip chosen these few days to go away? His mother's house in Lynn that he was putting up for sale could have waited. This sad little waif couldn't. The moment was too crucial. It was as if he were poised, uncertainly, on the brink between an understanding of good and a cynical acceptance of evil.

"Jan," she said, "come here."

He obeyed sullenly.

She pulled him down on her knee and gently brushed back his untidy hair.

"Jan, people aren't all wicked. You must learn to love people, not hate them."

His eyes looked into hers and they were dark with anger. "I hate," he said calmly.

She held him close and pressed his head against her shoulder. "You mustn't!"

Suddenly the rigid little body relaxed and she felt something hot and wet on her throat. Jan was crying.

She sat for some time, in the twilight, holding him. Then she carried him into his own room, undressed him, and put him to bed.

"Pansy will bring you your dinner on a tray," she said. "I want you to stay here alone, and think about what you have done. It is wrong, Jan! Terribly wrong! *Unrecht*—you understand?"

He looked at her soberly but said nothing. She took his hand.

"Tomorrow we will go to see Butch and you will tell him you are sorry."

He threw her hand away violently, and sat straight in bed. "No!" he cried. "No sorry!"

She sighed, went to the door, took the key out of the lock, closed the door, and locked it on the outside. It was the first serious mistake she had made with Jan.

Several hours later, Pax sat in front of her dressing table brushing her thick black hair. She smiled wryly at her reflection in the mirror, with its white lips and large eyes underlined with dark circles, and reflected

139

that this high-powered maternal role of hers was taking its toll. She leaned closer. There were two or three new white hairs springing up from the center parting, and a new, unfamiliar tracing of lines at the corners of her eyes.

She finished brushing her hair, turned out all the lamps in the room except the one beside the bed, and wound the little pink clock. She had just thrown her dressing gown over the back of a chair and was climbing into bed when the telephone rang. It startled her, even though it was barely ten-thirty. The phone rarely rang at that hour.

Perhaps it was Philip from Lynn. She picked up the receiver eagerly. "Hello," she said softly.

A woman's voice answered. "Is that you, Mrs. Lyttleton?"

"Yes."

"This is Mrs. Leclerc speaking."

"Oh, yes, Jeannine. What can I do for you?"

The voice at the other end of the wire was acidulous. "You can't do anything for me, I assure you, but you can do something for yourself. You can come down here and fetch that new boy of yours. I can't leave the store."

Pax sat up very straight. "My dear Jeannine, don't be absurd. Jan has been in bed and asleep for two or three hours."

Jeannine chuckled dryly. "That's what you think! The kid's down here in the back yard, trying to get my son to run away with him."

"What are you talking about?"

"It's none of my business, but I think you'd better hurry. The kid may decide to beat it on his own," continued the pert voice. "You'll excuse me. I gotta get back to my work."

There was a click on the other end of the wire. Pax hung up the receiver, slipped into her robe and mules, and went quickly across the hall. She unlocked the door. The room was dark, except for a faint glow at the far end from a light in the street. She switched on the light and looked around the room in astonishment. The covers had been thrown back, and one pillow lay there starkly in its ticking cover. The slip had been removed. The closet door was open, and two empty drawers in the bureau yawned at her. She crossed to the window. It was wide open and the window screen was lying under it against the wall. She leaned out and saw that the strong ropes of ivy were sagging and pulling away from the side of the house.

Pax hurried back to her room and into her clothes. The house was silent and asleep as she ran down the dark stairs.

The lights in Papa Leclerc's were all burning brightly when she pushed open the door. Three or four young men were lolling against the soda fountain, and Jeannine was in her usual place behind the counter, her white teeth flashing, her sloe eyes inviting their admiration.

"Where is he?" Pax demanded sharply.

"In the yard," Jeannine said indifferently, "if he hasn't already gone. You can go through the back if you want to." She pointed to the door at the rear end of the chemist's.

Pax opened the door, went in, and closed it behind her. She was in a neat little parlor, lighted dimly by one bulb which hung from the center of the ceiling over a small marble-topped table. As she walked through to the door beyond, she saw that there were three or four comfortable chairs in the room, a stiff little horsehair sofa, and an upright piano, draped in a yellow fringed shawl, on which stood several family photographs in cheap frames.

She opened the far door and stepped out onto the tiny porch. On the bottom step sat Johnnie, and standing in front of him, leaning over him, speaking slowly and urgently, was Jan. He was wearing the gray flannel suit in which she'd brought him to Mapleton, and his cap was on the back of his head. Over his shoulder, like a pack, was the pillow slip, tied at the top with a shoe lace and bulging with—she presumed—as many of his belongings as he could hastily shove into it.

As she came to the top of the steps, Jan looked up at her and his chin dropped. She descended the stairs slowly, one hand on the rail.

"Jan," she said reproachfully, "you have made me very sad."

He scuffed the dirt with the toe of his shoe.

"I take it you're going away?"

He lowered the pillow slip, rested it against the stair rail, and nodded.

"I suppose you know where you're going?"

He shrugged, and turned the palms of his hands out hopelessly, in his habitual gesture.

"Johnnie's mother tells me he's decided not to go along."

"That's right," said Johnnie. "He don't know where he's going."

"Have you any money, Jan?"

He put his hand in his trouser pocket and drew out two dimes and a nickel and held it out for her to see.

"I think you'll need more than that, Jan. That won't take you very far, you know. Would you like to borrow some from me?"

Jan frowned. "Vat mean 'bor-r-row'?" and he rolled his "r"s thickly.

"That means, I give you money and you can give it back to me someday."

He shook his head vehemently, and pointed to the pillow slip. "I give—er—sell clothes. Get money."

Pax sat down on the step beside Johnnie. "Where are you going, Jan?" she asked pleasantly.

"I go—back."

141

"Don't you like us any more?"

He shook his head again, but more slowly. "No," he said.

She paused and put her hand over her eyes as if she were hurt, but she peered at the boy from between her fingers. He was looking at her anxiously. Then she sighed and got up. She patted Johnnie on the shoulder.

"Well, Jan, I think we'd better let Johnnie go to bed, as long as he doesn't want to go with you." She started for the broken-down gate in the fence. "You could wait until tomorrow, you know, but as long as you want to go tonight, I think you'd better get started. It's getting late. Say good-by to Johnnie and I'll walk to the top of the hill with you."

Jan gravely held out his hand to Johnnie, who suddenly began to cry. "Good-by, Jawhnee. I like *you*." He threw his pack over his shoulder and followed Pax.

Silently they climbed the hill. When they got to the top, she stopped and held out her hand.

"Good-by, Jan," she said. "When you get to be a big boy and learn how to write, you write me and let me know how you are."

He took her hand listlessly and turned away. She pointed down the street that lay at right angles to the hill, past Amy's house. "You go that way, Jan, and soon you'll come to the main road. That will start you on your way to New York."

"Noo Yawk?" he repeated.

"That's right. Where the boat came to, remember? I'm sorry you were not happy with us. We'll miss you."

She bent down and kissed him on the cheek, and quickly crossed the street to the Green. She glanced back over her shoulder. The boy was moving uncertainly in the direction she had given him.

When she was halfway across the Green, she heard footsteps running. She didn't alter her step nor did she look back. Panting, Jan ran up to her. Then he slackened his pace and, without a word, walked along beside her. She looked down at him.

"What's the matter, Jan? Change your mind?" she asked casually.

"No—change!" he said stubbornly. "I go to-mor-r-row."

11

THE DARK HEAD on the damp pillow moved uneasily. The hot, early morning sun diffused its vivid white rays across the heavy lids, stabbing their way down into her unconsciousness. In her sleep she had thrown off the sheet, which was now wound uncomfortably around one bare leg. In spite of herself she was floating up, up into wakefulness. She turned on her side, out of the sunlight, struggling desperately to recapture that moment when she had almost touched his hands. But it was no good. She couldn't go back. One could never go back.

She raised her arms and lifted the wet black curls which were clinging to the back of her neck. Where had it started, this confused dream which she wanted so intensely to return to?

She had been sitting on a ledge, in that white foamy dress she had worn to the prom so long ago, and a little wind stirred the spray of bouvardia pinned to her shoulder. It was chilly and she lifted the long skirt and pulled it up around her shoulders.

She leaned over the ledge and realized that it was the ledge just over Finnegan's. To her dismay, she saw that the mouth of the cave was closed by a heap of stones which reached all the way up to where she crouched. She got on her knees and began to brush away the pebbles; they rolled down the side of the mountain, making little shuddering staccato sounds as they disappeared. As she dug her way through the heap from the top, the stones became larger and larger, and more difficult to dislodge. She felt her strength going as she moved them away and moved them away until she had reached the end, only to discover with despair that the cave was tightly sealed by a huge rock. Utterly exhausted, she stretched herself out on the ledge and buried her dejected face in her arms.

Suddenly, as if from a great distance, she heard a familiar voice. "What are you doing, girl?"

She raised her head swiftly. Standing in front of her, about ten feet away, was Jake, dressed in an army uniform. She sprang to her feet and started to go to him, but he stopped her with a warning cry.

"Look out! Don't come any further!"

She looked down at her feet. The side of the mountain was sinking slowly until there was a yawning chasm between them. It seemed as though she were staring miles down to its depths, where she saw thousands of tiny figures, milling about. They were infinitesimal in size, but as clear as though she were looking through the lens of a stereopticon. There were clashing armies of men in different uniforms, large groups of weeping women, little children, aimlessly running back and forth over prone bodies of other children. A faint moaning arose from the depths.

She stretched forth her arms to Jake, who shook his head sadly. Suddenly from behind him a small shadowy figure approached. It was a child, but she couldn't see its face. Only the outline was distinct, and misty rags seemed to float from it. Gently, it moved around Jake, toward her, and as it came nearer she could see that was walking on a thin cloud that formed a bridge under its feet. When it reached her, it pushed her gently out onto the bridge. As she made her way to Jake, his arms reached out to her, but just as she was about to touch the tips of his fingers, a flash of glaring light blinded her and she woke. She heard herself almost inaudibly breathe the word "Jake." But the voice that answered her, floating away as she regained full consciousness, was a flutelike treble voice and it said, "I go tomo-r-r-row."

She threw herself out of bed and, without waiting to put on her robe or slippers, she ran across the hall to Jan's room and pushed the door open. She hadn't made the mistake of locking it the second time.

The room looked just as it had the night before, when she'd discovered the child was gone, except that it was brightly lighted by the morning sun. Again, the bedcovers were thrown back and the room was empty, but on the floor, just where he'd dropped it, was the stuffed pillow slip with the shoelace tied tightly around its neck.

She hurried out. Her bare feet made no sound as she ran lightly down the stairs. Faintly she could hear Pansy's high voice singing, "Nobody knows de trouble I see . . ." She went into the dining room and pushed the swinging door open. The voice was louder now. "Glory Hallelujah!"

Pansy was standing at her ironing board. Jan, in his gray flannel suit, was at the table. He had a napkin tied around his neck, both elbows on the table, and was eating a bowl of cereal and cream. Pansy started the spiritual again. ". . . Nobody knows but Jesus."

Jan stopped eating, his spoon in mid-air.

"Vat iss Jesus?" he asked.

Pax let the door swing to and ran back upstairs. Thank goodness she didn't have to answer that one! But as she bathed and dressed her mind began to struggle with all the implications of the question Jan had asked.

It was one of her greatest problems, and yet it was the one to which she'd given the least thought. She hadn't sent him to any Sunday school yet because there was none during the summer. She wondered if he knew anything about religion. Where could she send him for spiritual teaching? Had he received any at all in his cruel childhood? And how was she to find out, with his, as yet, limited knowledge of English?

She made up her mind to dismiss it for the time being; until he stopped being afraid of things he could see, hear, and touch, it would be stupid, she reasoned lamely, to frighten him with anything as seemingly nebulous as a religious belief.

For the moment she'd better concentrate on the fact that Jan was still wearing his gray flannel suit. Apparently her little ruse of last night hadn't worked as well as she'd hoped it would. Obviously she had failed with the child. He had no confidence in her and certainly no love for her. Was it her he distrusted, or was it all adults?

An idea began to germinate in her mind. Of course, it was foolish but it might help, just for a start. She would dress up for him—or, rather, down to him.

Ten minutes later she walked into the kitchen with a casual hello. She was wearing white tennis shorts, a white silk shirt with the sleeves rolled up carelessly, and flat leather sandals. She had put on no lip rouge or powder and her small pointed face shone like a little boy's after a good scrubbing. She had parted her hair down the middle, and two black braids, each tied at the end with a blue ribbon, hung below her shoulders.

"Gee, I'm hungry, Pansy! What are you eating, kid?" She tried to copy Philip's offhand manner of speech.

Jan's large brown eyes looked from her to Pansy; then he held out his newly filled bowl to her. "Gr-r-rits," he said.

"Looks swell," said Pax cheerfully. "The same for me, please, Pansy."

She sprawled with her elbows on the kitchen table as she bent over her grits.

Pansy said, "Our young man tells me he's goin' away from heah dis mornin'."

Pax's heart missed a beat.

"Is that so?" she said easily. "You want some more breakfast, Jan?"

He shook his head, wiped his mouth with his napkin, pulled it from around his neck, and stood up.

"Let's have a little talk before you go, Jan. Maybe I can help you. Let's go out and sit in the sun for a few minutes, shall we?"

Pax went out the back door, Jan following her, and sat down on the grass. Jan squatted beside her. The grass was thickly spotted with clover and she began to search through it.

"Ever find a four-leaf clover, Jan?"

He shook his head in a puzzled way.

"Thought we might find one for you to take on your journey. They're good luck, you know."

"Vat iss 'go-o-od luck'?"

"Good luck is when you get everything you want. You see, Jan, you want to go away and find somebody you like better than us. 'Good luck' means that you find them. It means that you won't get hungry on your journey, or, if you do, you'll find someone who'll give you something to eat. It means you won't ever have to think of us and wish you were back—"

He turned his head away.

Suddenly she caught sight of Tubby's bicycle leaning up against the wall of the garage.

"Say, Jan, did you ever ride Tubby's bicycle?" She pointed to it.

"Not know how to ride."

"You don't?" she exclaimed. "How'd you like to learn?"

He shrugged his shoulders.

"You see, I was just thinking that if you learned to ride—of course it would take you a few days—I might get Tubby to lend you the bicycle and you could ride it to New York. It's an awfully long walk, Jan."

His face lighted.

"Come on! I'll teach you! What do you say?" She sprang to her feet, ran into the garage, and wheeled out the bicycle. "Let's take it out onto the street. It's easier than the grass or the gravel path."

He followed her eagerly.

"Up you go, boy! Now, take hold of the handlebars. I'll steer it until you get the feel. Then you can try it."

The two of them went slowly up the street, Jan pedaling with all his might and Pax, looking like a tall child herself, holding on to the back of the saddle with one hand, the other gripping the left handlebar.

When they came to the dead end of the street, Pax steered to the left down an unfrequented road. There was a slight decline, and the bicycle began rolling faster and faster until she had to hold it back with sheer strength. She was concentrating so hard on the child and the bicycle that she didn't realize for a few minutes what road she was on. When

146

it had leveled off and they had regained their normal pace she suddenly became aware of where they were.

It was her road, no longer rutted and muddy as it had been in those emotional years. Now it was smoothly and neatly paved, but the woods to its right were still there, their cool, green depths still friendly and familiar.

When they reached the meadow next to the woods, she stopped.

"Let's rest, Jan, shall we?"

He jumped down quickly and stood waiting.

"You take it, Jan. Take hold of the ends of the handlebars. Now push it along—it'll go," she said, laughing. "Now, lean it up against this tree, and we'll sit down here in the shade for a bit. Aren't you hot? I am!"

She took a pack of cigarettes and a lighter from her pocket. "Have a cigarette, Jan?" He shook his head. "No? Good boy!"

It was still and peaceful. There was no sound, except for the soft twittering of birds in the branches above them and the occasional lowing of a cow from the adjoining meadow. How strange it seemed after all these years. Bitter memories of her own failure had kept her always from coming back. It was only in dreams that she came back.

She leapt to her feet. "Come on, Jan. Let's go explore!"

"Explor-r-re? Vat iss dat?"

She took his hand and they started across the meadow.

"When I was little like you, Jan, I had a small house of my own where I used to go when I thought grownup people didn't want me." She stopped, took him by the shoulders, and turned him around, facing her. "But first, this is to be our secret! No one in the world knows where it is but me . . . and now you." She almost breathed the last word. "You won't tell, will you?"

He shook his head. She held out her hand. "Shake!" she said.

They walked on silently for a few minutes. Then she felt him pull back. He was biting his lip nervously and staring straight ahead. They were approaching the old barbed-wire fence. Just as she was about to pull the wires apart to climb through, she heard a little cry.

"No! No! Don't touch! Burn! Kill!"

She knelt down on the grass. "Come here, Jan." Slowly he came to her. She took him in her arms and held one tightly clenched little fist in hers. "Darling Jan," she said, "this is America. We don't have things like that here. Look!" She took hold of the barbed wire firmly. "The only things that could possibly hurt you are those nasty little pointed things. Might tear your pants, see? Now you touch it."

Gingerly he stretched out his hand.

"Now you help me through because I'm bigger than you and they might tear my pants."

When they were on the other side, she took his hand again and they started for the woods. Jan kept looking around and behind him.

"Nothing here but cows, Jan. That's what the fence is for, you know —to keep them from running all over town."

They wound their way through the cool woods along the little path she knew so well, until they reached the clearing at the foot of the hill. She shaded her eyes with her hand and looked up. There it was, just as it always had been. No heap of stones in front of it, no open gap below it.

She ran up ahead of him and went into the cave. The outline of her ground cradle was still there, but it was covered now with loose earth. A few straggly bits of faded paper still hung from the sides of the cave, wisps of the old magazine pictures she had stuck there. She went back to the entrance. Jan was climbing the last few boulders.

"Come in, Jan," she called. "Welcome to our house."

They sat outside the cave and she told him odds and ends of small tales of her childhood and pointed out the familiar landmarks she could always see from there.

"You know, Jan, this is a much better place to run away to than New York. I know."

Jan's expression didn't change.

"Jan," she said slowly, "do you think you could tell me why you want to go away—to go back, as you say?"

The child looked off as if into a great distance. "I go find Olga."

Pax caught her breath sharply. Olga must be the woman the Distribution Center had mentioned in his papers. This was the first time he'd ever spoken her name.

Pax didn't move, but she looked at the boy and she seemed to be seeing him for the first time. Funny, she'd never noticed before how woebegone the small thin face was. Now she knew where she'd failed. It wasn't kindness he wanted, it was love, and she hadn't given it to him. But had she got it to give? Compassion, yes, but she hadn't loved him. He was a forbidding child, and now she admitted to herself that she had always been afraid of him.

If he only would or could tell her of the horror he had seen and experienced. She longed for some knowledge of him that would fan this spark of pity into a defensive blaze. Then perhaps she could love him. The two emotions were so close.

"Jan, do you love Olga?" Again the little shrug. "Will you tell me about her?"

148

"I sleep wid Olga. She iss my friend."

"We are your friends, Jan."

"No. No fr-r-riend," he said stubbornly. "My—how you say—en-e-my iss your friend."

"Why?"

"Butch try kill me. You like Butch; you hate me." He paused. "Olga say kill en-e-my."

"But, Jan dear, to kill is not good," she said helplessly.

He didn't seem to hear. "Your fr-r-riends not my fr-r-riends. I not know your fr-r-riends. Dis fr-r-riend Jesus. Who iss dis Jesus? Pansy say He iss my fr-r-riend. He not my fr-r-riend. I not know Him. Pansy say dis Jesus not like I kill en-e-my! Why He not like? He not my fr-r-riend—"

It seemed to her as though he would never stop. She hadn't heard him say as much in the four months he'd been with them.

"He is everybody's Friend, Jan."

"No!" He pounded his knee with his fist. "Pansy say He iss my Sav-i-our-r-r. No iss true. He not save me. Olga save me! Vat iss dis Jesus vat save? Soldier-r-r?"

"No, Jan, Jesus is not alive as you and I are."

"How He save me if He iss dead?"

"Listen, Jan, try to understand. Jesus is God—"

"No God! I know God. God kill His en-e-my—"

Pax began to braid and unbraid her hair nervously. How could she make this young realist understand? For the moment it was not so important for him to know the religious story. Later he would choose his own God as all men do. But this "eye for an eye" business must be done away with somehow, if he were to live in peace with the rest of the world.

"Jan," she began, "two thousand years ago, in a country where your fathers came from—"

"I not have father," he interrupted.

"Everybody had a father, Jan," she said. "You just listen. In that country there lived a brave young Jew named Jesus. He was good and wise. He loved His enemies as well as His friends. He always said if someone hits you in the face, you turn the other cheek. You see why? Look, I'll show you."

She knelt in front of him.

"Now, suppose I hit you like that." She tapped him on the cheek. "But I'd hit you hard enough to hurt. Well, you see, if you hit me back, we both get madder and one of us might kill the other. But if you turn your head to let me hit you on the other cheek, I will have time to think and be ashamed, so I don't hit you at all, and that is wise and good."

Jan looked perplexed but he nodded.

"Now, this young man died for His people. He let them kill Him because He thought it was better to be good than to kill. So, Jan, He was so good that for two thousand years He has been remembered, and we think of Him as God, and as our Friend, yours and mine, and Pansy's and Uncle Philip's—"

"And Tubby's?"

"Oh, yes! Everybody's!"

"Oh."

"So, Butch was a naughty little boy because he pushed you in the water, and you were a naughty boy because you held his head under the water, but I am no more his friend than I am your friend, and, Jan, I love you more than Butch, and I only want you to be good and take care of those little boys instead of hurting them, because you are older and wiser and you can understand what Butch can't. See?"

The words poured out in a rush, and then she stopped abruptly. She watched the child.

Jan frowned for a moment. Then, still looking straight ahead, he shyly put his hand into hers.

12

AFTER HIS STARTLING burst of indignation, Jan returned to his customary taciturnity. When they arrived back at the house he had said "tank you" for his bicycle lesson, as he had been taught to do, and ran upstairs to his room. When he came down he had changed into his play clothes. He walked deliberately down the front steps, pushed his way through the opening in the hedge, as Pax and Em had done when they were young, and disappeared.

Em told her afterward that he had marched up to the Bascomb front door, rung the bell, and demanded to see Butch. He had walked into the boys' room and had stood for a moment looking gravely at the other child who was still in bed.

"You all r-r-right?" he had asked, and, without waiting for an answer, had turned and walked out of the room, down the stairs, and out of the house.

He made no further mention of going away, and little by little his attitude toward the boys began to change. On the following Monday they had returned to school, and he spent the mornings and afternoons with Johnnie Leclerc, whose school didn't reopen for another week. But when three o'clock came, he was home, waiting for the children. He followed them everywhere and his manner to them became a little peremptory.

After Johnnie went back to school, Jan seemed lost. He didn't as yet understand enough English to be sent to school, so Philip and Pax decided to begin some kind of lessons. Every morning Pax settled down for a couple of hours with him, teaching him elementary arithmetic and how to spell simple words. The former was easy for him and he loved it.

Amy Sanders took him for an hour after lunch, as she had taken Pax in her lonely years. Amy was a poor teacher and a worse disciplinarian, and Jan soon learned to twist her around his little finger. She told him how she had started life as a violinist, and how she'd given it up when she married her New Englander and settled down in Mapleton. She dug out her old fiddle and played for him. That was the end of all other study with her.

Jan immediately discarded his mouth organ, which he told her had been given him by a sailor on the boat coming to America, and begged her to teach him to play the violin. He loved music, and day after day he would stand in her pretty drawing room, the fiddle tucked under his small chin, patiently trying to pull out of it the pure sounds he heard when she played it.

Philip gave over several hours a week teaching him English and sneaking in bits of the history of the country that he knew would eventually become Jan's own.

One morning in October, Pax and Jan were in the library, both of them on the floor, with books and papers scattered around them. The day was clear and cold for early autumn and a cheerful fire was burning in the grate. Jan was sitting cross-legged in front of the hearth, tightly clutching a pencil which he occasionally spat on, as though that would make his problems easier.

"Five times five iss twenty-five, no?"

"That's right, Jan. Now, what's five times six?"

The doorbell rang.

"Go answer it, Jan, that's a good boy," she said. "I think Pansy's upstairs, doing the rooms."

Jan came back, his hands behind his back, a faint smile on his face. "How much?" he asked, as he'd heard Tubby do so many times.

"Oh, dear!" laughed Pax. "I'll owe it to you. My purse is upstairs. Go on, Jan, give it to me."

Jan shook his head and backed off. "How much?" he repeated.

She jumped up. "Come on, you brat! You're worse than Tubs."

He followed her up to her room and stood there waiting, his hands still hidden behind his back. She searched in her coin purse and held out a nickel.

"Ten cents, pleess. Dis one iss different."

She looked in her purse and dug out another nickel. "You little devil!" She smiled. "You'll get along. Come on, hand it over."

Jan grabbed eagerly for the money with one hand, and with the other gave her a telegram. She tore it open.

As she read it, all the color drained from her face and she began to shake. Her eyes grew dark with fear, and without a glance at the child she ran out of the room and down the stairs.

Jan didn't move. He stood there with a look of bewilderment on his small face. Then he heard the front door slam.

Twenty minutes later Pax walked up and down the floor in Amy's drawing room, wringing her hands, the tears streaming down her cheeks.

After five minutes of trying to reason with her, Amy realized that there was nothing to do but wait until she was drained dry of the hysterical emotion which always mowed her down in moments of terror. Amy had done the unprecedented thing of phoning the college and sending word to Philip to leave his class and come home immediately.

"Why doesn't he come? Dear God! Why doesn't he come?" Pax moaned. She had flung herself face downward on the couch, her body shaking with sobs.

There was the sound of footsteps running up the path. The front door was thrown open and Phil dashed into the room.

"What in hell's the matter, Sanders?" he said angrily. "Do you realize you've called me away—"

Amy pointed silently to the couch.

Philip walked over to Pax and lowered his voice. "What's happened, kid?"

Pax gulped, turned over on her side, and reached into her pocket for

152

the telegram. As he unfolded it, he took in the gray, pinched face and the swollen, red-rimmed eyes.

He read it over twice:

COLONEL ROBERT LYTTLETON SERIOUSLY INJURED STOP PLANE CRASHED OUTSIDE MUNICH THIS MORNING STOP DETAILS FOLLOWING STOP WILL KEEP YOU INFORMED. SIGNED U. S. WAR DEPARTMENT.

Philip sat down beside her and put his hand on her shoulder. "Could be worse, kid."

"He's dead! He's been killed! I know he has!" she cried. "Oh, God, Phil! What am I going to do?"

Philip lifted her up until she was in a sitting position. She tried to struggle away from under his hands. He gave her a hard slap across her cheek. She gasped, held on to her face, her eyes wide, staring at him blankly.

"Now, stop it, for Christ's sake! Behave yourself! Let's talk and see what we can do about it. Amy, got any brandy?"

They spent the next three hours in Amy's hall, Philip at the phone, Pax huddled on the bottom step of the stairs, mute and helpless. It took Philip over half an hour to reach the Pentagon in Washington, only to find out he must call the special department he wanted. Then he proceeded to go through a wild-goose chase of department after department, each time being greeted by the courteous indifference of the employees of the People, each of whom seemed to be firmly convinced that he *was* the Government.

By four o'clock, he had found out exactly what the telegram had told him.

Then he sent a cable directly to Germany, requesting detailed information. By that time, Pax was fully determined to leave for Germany at once. There were more long-distance calls. The War Department apologized profusely, but they really couldn't send a civilian across in an army plane. The Overseas Air Lines regretted that they had no space for weeks, unless there should be a cancellation. The only hope was a cabin shared with three people, on an English boat leaving in two weeks.

"He can be dead by then!" wailed Pax.

"He can be dead by now," said Philip calmly. He knew how to handle his Pax.

The fourteen-year-old who had delivered the telegram managed during those hours to act as Town Crier, his story changing with each telling, so that all of Mapleton now knew the town hero was done for.

When Philip took Pax home, the few people they met on the street eyed her sorrowfully but didn't speak. As she passed Em's house, Butch and Bill were swinging on the gate.

"Where's Tubby?" Philip demanded.

"I dunno," said Bill. "They told him about his father and he wouldn't play any more."

"Go find him, kid," said Philip as they went into the house. "Make him know that Bob's going to be all right. It's up to you now."

Pax ran upstairs and Philip went through to the kitchen. He knew he was in for another scene with Pansy. He was right. She sniffled and moaned, and Philip stamped up and down the kitchen cursing and comforting her. He finally convinced her that Bob wasn't dead yet, sent her up to her room to lie down, and offered to wash the luncheon dishes which were still in the sink.

He carried the garbage pail outside and as he returned to the house he noticed an almost imperceptible movement behind the bushes in the flower bed beside the kitchen door. He walked over and peered behind them. Jan was sitting with his knees under his chin, his back against the wall of the house, whittling a branch of a rose bush which he had broken off.

"What the devil are you doing there?"

Jan put his finger to his lips. "Sh-sh!" he said. He pointed above him to an open window. "Tubby up dere. Hiss vater killed!"

"He was not," Phil said. "Come on in the kitchen. I want to talk to you."

Jan shook his head stubbornly. "I stay here."

"What the hell do you think you're going to do there?"

"Tubby cry. He iss sad. He run away, maybe, like me." There was a little smile and then it was gone. "I watch."

Philip smiled. "Good boy! But you don't have to. Your mother's up there with him."

Jan's eyes widened. "My mudder?"

"Yes. Pax. Come on in and help me. I have something to tell you."

Jan crawled through the bushes and followed Philip. In the kitchen, Philip found another apron, tied it around Jan's neck, and gave him a dish towel.

"Help me dry these, and for God's sake don't drop 'em or Pax'll murder us!"

The dish Jan was drying immediately slipped, but he managed to catch it in time and hold on to it.

"That's just a figure of speech, son. Of course, nobody'd murder us. I mean, she'd give us hell."

"Vat iss fig-fig—"

154

"Figure of speech? Well, it's a way we Americans have of using big words when we don't mean 'em. Get me?"

Jan shook his head and reached for the next dish.

"Well, skip it! God damn!" Philip jumped back and waved his hand violently. "Sorry, Jan, but that water's hot! Now, listen. You and I are the men of the house, see? We've got to keep our heads. The Colonel isn't dead. He's been badly hurt in an airplane. But everybody's scared —me, too—but only for her sake and Tubby's—"

"Tubby's vater not dead?" Jan said, with a puzzled look. "Only hur-rt? Why ever-rybody cry?" There was a sneer on his face. "Dey not see pipple hur-rt?" He shrugged his shoulders. "Hur-rt iss notting."

The following twenty-four hours were fraught with nerves and fore-boding. Philip and Amy carried on with a false cheerfulness. Pansy sniveled as she went about her work. Jan was indifferent, Tubby sub-dued; and Pax, pale and tight-lipped, busied herself with packing to keep her nerves under control.

The next afternoon, a cable arrived from Germany, signed by some officer in Bob's outfit:

RIGHT LEG RIGHT ARM COMPOUND FRACTURES SLIGHT CONCUSSION INTERNAL INJURIES UNDETERMINED NO IMMEDIATE DANGER WILL KEEP YOU INFORMED. RODNEY NORTON—MAJOR.

13

THE SMOOTH narrow crossroads wound their way in and out, through the lush Vermont hills. Pax's 1940 Buick rolled along, hour after hour, at not too fast a pace; the interminable curves slowed her up every few hundred yards. Pax and Jan had been traveling since early morning.

The brilliant autumn colors glowed in the deep forests which stretched out on either side of the road. The early dead leaves swirled in spirals as the wind tore them from the trees, and they brushed the sides of the car from time to time and settled between the hood and the fenders.

Jan sat beside her quietly in his gray suit and top coat, his feet on his suitcase. His small trunk was wedged in the luggage compartment at the back. Occasionally he turned his head and looked out of the side window, especially when a wide panorama of the open country spread itself before them.

She tried not to think of how forlorn he seemed, being moved again with all his worldly possessions, which she had given him, into strange and unknown hands. Her throat ached a little.

When she'd finally made up her mind to leave for Germany, Philip had said to her, "What are you going to do with Jan? Pansy can't be responsible for him." It had been a shock. She hadn't thought of that. "Better start thinking," he'd said. "It's a tough one."

They had talked far into the night and had finally decided on a prep school near Manchester, in the southeastern part of New Hampshire, headed by a former graduate of Mapleton who had been a classmate of Bob's. She had phoned him long distance, giving him the rough details of her need to place the child there for a couple of months. Then had come the painful task of telling Jan that he was to be sent away from them for a time, and explaining the reasons to him.

He had accepted it as he accepted everything else. His small face closed in more than ever, and his brown eyes were inscrutable. He made no comment.

By midafternoon the round low hills began to change. The valleys were wider, the vegetation more sparse, and the New Hampshire mountains stretched their tall rugged crags skyward. It was about an hour before sundown when Pax stopped the car in front of high iron gates. She got out, opened them, then drove the car through. Again she descended and closed them after her. A straight graveled road bordered with elms led to a large country house. She pulled up on the driveway and helped Jan out of the car. He stood beside her, his suitcase in his hand, waiting for the bell to be answered.

They were shown into a small reception room to the right of the hallway by a servant, who then went to tell the headmaster that they had arrived.

"Take off your cap, Jan," said Pax. "Gentlemen don't keep their hats on in the house."

Jan sat in a stiff straight chair, his feet not quite touching the floor. He shoved his cap into the pocket of his coat, then lapsed back into immobility.

Fifteen minutes later, Pax was ensconced in a big comfortable chair in the private office of the headmaster. Jan had been taken to his room

156

to leave his coat and valise and was now waiting in the outer office while Pax and the headmaster had their conference.

"I'm very grateful to you, Dr. Miller, for letting me leave Jan with you. I know how difficult it's going to be for you. What little English he knows we have taught him, and he has had absolutely no formal schooling of any kind." She smiled. "I'm afraid you haven't a class low enough to start him in."

"Don't you worry about that, Mrs. Lyttleton. That will be our problem. You say his mother was Polish?"

Pax nodded.

"What's his name?"

"Jan"—she paused for just a beat—"Lyttleton. His father was Robert's cousin, you know." She felt her cheeks get hot and wondered if he noticed it. After all, why should they get hot? The lie couldn't hurt anybody. "He's an obedient child. Do you mind if I say he needs affection? And he's really awfully quick."

"Don't you worry about him for a minute. We've got a lot of nice youngsters here at Stratford and we'll go slowly on the discipline and the lessons at first."

"Oh! There's one other thing." She hesitated. "We don't know exactly what he's been through. He says very little and we haven't asked him. There's no doubt that at one time his family must have been captured by the Germans. You see, he has a—mark on his arm. The other boys may—"

Dr. Miller interrupted her. "Children have their own way of working things out, Mrs. Lyttleton. I wouldn't worry about that if I were you."

"Then you wouldn't mind terribly not questioning him about those years, would you? I think it's better that way. I'd like him to forget it."

"Of course, of course," he answered cheerfully. "We won't ask him anything. Now let's bring him in, shall we?"

"I'll get him," she said. She opened the door. "Come in, Jan."

The child walked slowly into the room and stood inside, gazing steadily at the headmaster.

"Come over here, young feller. Let's get acquainted. Pull up a chair."

Jan climbed into the chair and sat there, his hands lying inertly in his lap.

"Your—er—mother tells me you're going to make us a visit."

Jan flashed a quick glance in Pax's direction. It was the second time he'd heard that word used in connection with her. She wasn't his mother. His mother was dead.

"I think you're going to like it here, feller. If you don't, if anything worries you, you just come and tell me and we'll straighten it out, see?"

"Yes."

"Yes, 'sir,' Jan," Pax said.

"Yes, sir-r-r," he repeated.

"I'll tell you what we'll do. When it's time for your mother to go, you ride down to the gate with her and you can walk back. You won't get lost; it's a perfectly straight road. Then you and I'll have supper together, and tomorrow I'll introduce you to some fine fellows. We'll take a few days' vacation before we start work. How's that?"

Jan looked at Pax.

"Say 'thank you,' Jan."

"Tank you—sir-r-r."

Pax breathed a sigh of relief. This man was all right. She wasn't afraid to leave the boy with him.

"I don't want to seem inhospitable, Mrs. Lyttleton, but if you really want to get back home before dawn, you ought to be starting pretty soon."

"Yes, I guess I'd better. It's a long drive."

"Sure you won't change your mind? We can put you up for the night in the hotel in Manchester."

"Thanks, but I've really got to get back. I still have a lot to do. I sail Saturday, you know."

He walked with them to the door, his arm thrown carelessly around Jan's shoulders. "Give my best to Bob. I'm sorry he came such a cropper. He'll be all right, though. You can't kill that one, he's too tough."

"I hope you're right, Doctor. We had better news in the cable that came yesterday. He hasn't any internal injuries, thank God." She held out her hand. "Good-by, Dr. Miller, thank you for everything. Take good care of my—son. If you want to get in touch with us about anything, you'd better call Philip. He's still living at Mrs. Sanders', you know."

"Is he really?" he said. "Say hello to him for me. Great guy, Philip! Good-by, Mrs. Lyttleton, bon voyage, and don't worry about Jan. We're going to get along fine. Jan, after your mother goes, come on back here. I'll be waiting for you, but don't hurry. Good-by."

Pax got in the car and Jan climbed in beside her. She started the motor and the car rolled down the road. Again they came to the gate. The sun was setting in the west, and the soft gray twilight was gradually darkening. Pax left the motor running and jumped out of the car.

"Out you pop, Jan," she said cheerfully.

He got out and stood there looking at her. He said nothing. She knelt down beside him and put her arms around him.

"I'm depending on you, Jan, to be a good wise boy, for that will make my journey much easier. My journey is sad, Jan, and I'm only leaving you and Tubs because my husband is very ill. I know you will help me, Jan, won't you?"

He smiled a sad little smile. "I help," he said. "Who watch Tubby?"

"What do you mean, Jan?"

"I watch Tubby ven he comes home fr-r-rom school. Who watch him now?"

She hugged him hard. "Don't you worry, Jan. Uncle Philip will watch him until you come home again. We won't say good-by, will we? It's for such a little while."

She held his face between her hands and looked deeply into his brown eyes. Then she kissed him on the lips, hurriedly got up off her knees, and opened the gate. She drove the car through, then jumped out and closed it. Jan was standing on the inside, both hands clasping the iron bars of the gate.

She went up to him, put her face through the bars, and kissed him again.

"Good boy!" she whispered.

She got back in the car and drove slowly along the iron fence for twenty or thirty yards. Then she stopped and put on the brake. She turned in her seat and looked back through the rear window of the car.

The lonely little figure, his head bowed, his hands in his pockets, was trudging at a snail's pace in the direction of the school. The memory of that small, sober face looking through the bars struck at her heart. Was this to be always his fate? He'd come such a long way and he was still behind bars, even though they were friendly bars.

She put her head on the wheel and wept.

The car plowed steadily on through the night, the strong headlights picking out the curves of the lonely circuitous mountain roads. As it dropped into the valleys, the late October mists blanketed it and made the going slower and more dangerous. From time to time, Pax switched on the light in the car and looked at her wrist watch. The hands crept so slowly around the little dial.

The stretches through the mountains were interminable and she rarely passed a car. She almost wished now that she had taken Dr. Miller's advice and stayed the night in Manchester, but it would have meant a whole day lost, and she had so little time. She was sailing in a

159

week. There were still odds and ends to be attended to. Her last important chore had been to deposit Jan. Now that was done, and she wouldn't have to think about it any more.

She wished Philip hadn't been so peculiar about her going. She had faced him with it several nights ago, but she still didn't understand.

"You don't think I ought to go, do you?" she had said.

"To tell you the God's truth, kid, I don't know. I guess you've just got to decide that for yourself."

"I've got to go, Phil! I've just got to go!"

"Uh-huh," he had said. Then: "Are you still determined to go through with the surprise angle?"

"Why, yes. Don't you think I should?"

"Nope."

She had explained that she didn't want to frighten Bob with advance news of her coming, perhaps make him think he was more seriously hurt than he was.

"I'll tell you what," he had said. "Compromise, will you? Cable him a week from now that you're coming. By that time you'll know how badly off he is and so will he. Will you do it?"

She remembered putting her finger through a smoke ring she'd made. "That's for good luck. Why, yes, Phil, I'll cable him then, if you think I should."

"I think you should."

She looked at her gas gauge. She had filled the gas tank in Manchester, after a hurried bite of dinner at the hotel, and had been on her way by seven-thirty. She had stopped twice at lunch wagons for some black coffee to keep her awake, but for the last two hours she had seen nothing except an occasional darkened farmhouse and one or two filling stations which were closed for the night.

And now that awful feeling of sleepiness was stealing over her again. She mustn't fall asleep at the wheel. The mountain passes were precarious enough when she was wide awake. Perhaps she'd better draw up to the side of the road and take a little nap. But then she mightn't wake up for hours, and maybe it really wasn't safe in these silent mountains, even if she locked herself inside the car.

She lighted a cigarette and rolled down the window to let the cold wind blow in on her. The sparks from the cigarette blew all around her, and she was afraid of one getting in her eye and blinding her for a moment. She crushed out the cigarette in the ash receiver.

She'd sing—aloud. That would do it. What was that Brahms thing she'd always loved? She used to sing it to Tubby when he was little. How did it go? She began:

"Guten Abend, gut' Nacht,
Mit Rosen bedacht—"

No, that was no good. It made her think of Jan, and she didn't want to think of Jan—not now, she didn't. He was all right. Probably sound asleep in his lonely new bed— Stop it, you fool!

"I can't give you anything but love, baby—"

Robert used to sing that in his high tenor voice; it always amused her, coming out of his great, powerful frame.

"That's the only thing I'm thinking of, baby—"

Wonder how he'll look? Two years is a long time. How much had she really missed him? Oh, so much, so much! It wasn't so bad in 1940 and '41 when he was training in Canada, because he could get a week-end off every two or three weeks and come over the border to her. When he'd been transferred to the United States Air Force, he'd had leave after his first twenty-five missions and his second twenty-five. Then she had gradually grown used to the long separations.

She had been a little puzzled when he put in for Occupation duty in Germany after the war was over, but then Robert was always hot-headed and he liked living dangerously—but it wasn't dangerous after the war, was it? It was certainly taking him a long time to get his discharge papers, but of course, as he wrote in his letters, the bloody Army was full of red tape.

She had been so happy with that letter saying he wanted to come home. When was that? It must have been in April—and this was October! Was it really that long ago? Then in the next letter he'd said that the Army had politely asked for one hundred and eight days, but that it was really an order; then it would take a month or so to clear up things for the officer who would take his place. Then the crash.

Dear God! She just had to see him! It wasn't that she was sorry for herself, but, after all, how long was she supposed to go on living this unnatural life? She was still a young woman. No reason for her cheeks to burn. She was alone in a car on a deserted country road in the middle of the night. And even if she weren't, nobody could see inside her brain. Nobody, that is, except Philip.

Why did Phil have to come into her mind when she was thinking of Robert? What if it had been Phil who had crashed instead of— She was getting sleepy! Better get out of the car and walk for a few minutes.

She lighted another cigarette, turned down her headlights, and climbed out of the car. She walked up and down briskly for two or three minutes, then stood still and listened. There wasn't a sound except the rustling of the wind through the trees and the occasional hoot of an owl. She was on the rise of a hill. She walked over to the edge and looked down. The moon had gone down, but there was still a soft gray light washing the crests of the mountains, which were majestic and remote in their somber purple silence. There were a few stars flickering lazily in the pale sky; below her, an irregular sea of mist waved and pulsated over the flat lands.

She must be still a good sixty-five miles from home. She sighed, crushed her cigarette out under her foot, and got back in the car. The motor started and picked up speed.

Let's see—had she forgotten anything? Her trunk had been packed for four days; she'd already put in the bottom of her open suitcase the things she'd use on the boat; her passport was waiting for her at the White Star Line office in New York. Amy would sleep in the house as an extra safeguard for Tubby. She hoped she'd have no trouble with trains when she got off the boat; there would be no Robert to meet her, of course. The poor darling would be in some hospital bed in Munich.

No use longing to be in his arms. She'd just better stop thinking about that. One arm would probably be in a cast, and his poor leg in that what-you-may-call-it contraption hanging from the ceiling. She wondered if his good-looking face was scarred.

Ghosts of Robert began to parade through her brain. Robert in his football clothes; Robert in his dinner coat the night that Jake—no, not that! She'd rather not think of that picture. There was the night Robert had taken her for her first drive and had tried to kiss her. She hadn't liked him so much then; it was too soon after . . .

She remembered his long powerful body swimming easily through the ocean swells off Cape May, that first summer she'd stayed a month with his family in the house they'd rented for the season; and the night sitting on the deck of the small rented yacht when he had proposed. She could still see the moonlight on his fair hair, turning it to silver, and his deep-blue eyes, hot with emotion— She had married the campus hero! How proud she'd been of his strength and good looks that high noon, standing beside him at the altar. The tiny buttonhole of lilies of the valley that matched her bouquet trembled like little bells as he said "I do" in his high, almost young boy's voice—

The gray, murky dawn lay quietly over the town and the first glow in the east heralded the sunrise as Pax wearily turned her car into the garage drive.

Suddenly she put on the brakes. She took off her beret and pressed her tired temples with the palms of both hands. There was one more thing she had to do before she could crawl into bed and sleep for hours and hours. Well, she'd better go and do it, otherwise she'd lose a whole day and Philip would think she was trying to get out of keeping her promise. She knew she'd never wake up all this day. It had been nearly twenty-four hours since she'd slept.

She backed the car out of the drive as quietly as she could and drove on down the hill. She pulled up at the little hotel, climbed out of the car, and, nearly staggering with fatigue, dragged herself up the steps.

The small lobby was empty except for a bellboy, his coat and collar unbuttoned, sprawling in a big chair beside the desk, and snoring. She waked him and asked for a telegraph blank. Then she leaned on the desk, and in pencil she wrote:

Darling am coming to take care of you sailing Saturday love
Pax

14 PAX HUMMED happily to herself as she dressed. She rouged her lips with the shade of scarlet that matched her dinner dress, clasped an old-fashioned necklace of garnets around her throat, fastened the matching loops in her small ears, and then stood in front of the mirror to take in the whole effect.

The heart-shaped face with its willful pointed chin was as smooth and serene as a child's, and she wondered if Robert remembered how pretty she was when she was happy.

For the first time in nearly a year, life seemed to have ironed itself out for her.

Peace had begun slipping away from her the autumn before, when she hovered between decision and indecision about the adoption of a little refugee. Philip had lashed at her indifference to the tragedy stalking the world and had urged her on, but when she had finally taken the step, fear had entered her heart to stay.

Then she had gone through months of anxiety after she had made her application, when she was torn between hope and fear that the answer would be a favorable one, and finally Jan had entered into her life.

163

During these last six months, he had been a constant source of strain to her. It had been difficult, trying to give affection to a child who needed it so desperately and who seemed unable to accept it or return it.

Then had come the shock and terror of Robert's crash and the anxious, constant waiting for news.

But now all this was over—even the doubt and wonder as to when, if ever, she would see him again. She would have no worry over leaving Tubby—Tubby with his gay and lovable disposition—no fear for his safety, now that Jan had been taken away from him.

She told herself that Jan was all right, more all right than he had been in all his short life.

Everything was exciting that lay ahead of her. Philip was flying to New York Friday afternoon after classes and the two of them—to quote Phil—were "going on the town!" Dinner at Twenty-One, a theater, the Stork; then the next day he would put her on the boat. Europe for the first time—and Robert.

Life was good.

She took her beaver coat from the closet, snatched up her bag, and ran downstairs. Philip would be calling for her in about ten minutes. She went into the kitchen to say good night to her son.

"Tubs darling, if you want to, you can go over and play with the twins for an hour after you finish your supper, but, Pansy, see that he's in bed by eight-thirty, will you?"

"Yes'm."

"What's the matter with you, boss? What are you looking so glum about?"

Pansy didn't answer, but Tubby said suddenly, "Why do you have to go?"

"Because it's a dinner party, sweetie. Mr. and Mrs. Bascomb are giving me a farewell party so I can take lots of messages to your daddy."

"Seems kind of a strange thing to me, people celebratin' because a poor man's been all broken up in little pieces," muttered Pansy.

"Why, Pansy, we're not celebrating," said Pax with a frown. "Mr. Robert's going to be all right. You know that."

"I didn't mean go to dinner," interrupted Tubby. "I mean go to Germany."

"Darling," she said patiently, "I'm going because your daddy's been badly hurt—"

"If Daddy's been hurt, then why are you going to a party?"

"How do you know if the poor boy is goin' to ever walk again?" Pansy said.

"I wouldn't give a party 'cause somebody's been hurt," said Tubby disdainfully, with his eyes on his plate.

"Seems to me that people's mighty happy round heah when somebody's nearly got killed."

"Oh, shut up!" said Pax. "You two make me sick." And she flung herself out of the kitchen to wait for Philip in the hall.

Philip drove her car smoothly along the highway to Bill and Bea Bascomb's, who lived halfway between Burlington and Mapleton. Pax sat quietly in the corner of the seat, with very little to say. Philip made all the conversation, Pax occasionally replying in monosyllables.

"What's the matter with you, Pax? Why so quiet?"

"Nothing. Just thinking. Phil—do you think Robert's really all right? I mean, do you suppose maybe he mightn't be able ever to walk again?"

"Oh, God! Are we going to go through all that all over again? How on earth should I know? Sure, I suppose he will. Anyway, you can't possibly find out until you get there, so stop worrying about it."

"I know. But, Phil, maybe I shouldn't be having such a good time when he's—I mean, maybe I shouldn't be going to parties and looking forward to New York and—I mean—Oh, Phil! You know what I mean."

"Sure. I know just what you mean. You mean God forgot to give you any sense of values. You silly little fool! What do you want to do? Have a wake for the guy?"

An offended and dignified Pax got out of the car when they reached the house. She swept through the door ahead of Philip, gave her coat to the trim, uniformed maid, and made her way to the game room.

In a glance, she saw that Robert's gang was all there. Bill Bascomb was standing behind the bar shaking up a conglomeration of gin and orange juice, with two or three liqueurs to give it an extra kick. His wife, Bea, swathed in a black dinner dress with a strand of real pearls around her neck, jumped off of a bar stool and came to meet Pax.

Em, dumpy and matronly, her red hair still cut in a boyish bob, her cheeks flushed from several cocktails, was flirting outrageously with Tiny Jarvis, the giant who had married Em's best friend, Priscilla Pembroke. Butch Master, Senior, looked on indulgently.

Priscilla, mother of four, tiny, with her fair long bob, looking like a child in her pink taffeta *robe-de-style*, was playing Oklahoma with Joe Anders, another classmate of Robert's. His wife, Kay, sat on the arm of Priscilla's chair, kibitzing.

There were two or three other couples whom Pax didn't know so well, but they were all friends of Robert's. They all greeted Pax and all talked at once, questions about Robert flying about the room. Pax drank the cocktail that Bill gave her and he promptly filled her glass again.

"Well, Mrs. L., so you're really off," said Tiny. "What boat are you taking?"

"The *Queen Mary*," she replied a little proudly.

"I wonder if Paris has changed much," sighed Bea—she was the only one of them who had ever been abroad. "Wonder if the Eiffel Tower and the Opera and Notre Dame look just the same," she continued in a bored, slightly superior voice.

"I won't know," said Pax curtly. "I'm going to Germany."

"Well, I'm glad the big bum got out of it as lightly as he did," Butch said. "Got off with a couple of broken legs, didn't he, Pax? Always was a lucky stiff."

"I won't know until I see him," said Pax, and she carefully kept her eyes away from Philip. "They cable that they're sure he's going to be all right."

"What's the old bastard been doing over there all this time?" asked Bill. "Don't he know the war's been over for two years?"

"Yeah," chuckled Tiny. "What's he got over there? A flaxen-haired *Mädchen*?"

"Betcha he has," roared Bill. "He's certainly taking his own sweet time about coming back." And he began to sing, keeping time with a bar spoon: "Dum-dum—de-dem-dumpty—*bedeuten—dass ich so traurig bin*—"

Joe looked up from his game. "Didn't take us guys that long to get out of the lousy Army, did it?" he said.

Pax stalked over to the bar. "That's not funny. Give me another cocktail, Bill."

"We were only kidding, Pax. Where's your sense of humor?" he said, filling her glass.

Pax downed it in one gulp and held out her glass for another. Above the slightly drunken laughter, she heard Phil's voice. "Careful, kid."

"Well, here's to the blighter," cried Butch, and held up his glass for a toast.

"To his safe recovery!"

"Here's to his coming home!"

"To Pax!"

"Sure, here's to you, gal!"

"God bless Bob," said Priscilla sentimentally, and she daintily brushed Pax's glass with her own.

"Kiss the big bum for me," said Em, and she leaned over and gave Pax a ginny smack on the mouth.

Pax swung around on the bar stool. Philip was sitting quietly in a big leather chair, twirling his glass in his hand. He raised his eyes and smiled at her. "Here's to you, kid, and may good news await you at the landing."

No one seemed hungry. They reminisced about Bob, about his football days, his enlistment before America went into the war. They boasted of his bravery and his decorations and they went on drinking cocktails.

Suddenly Em cast a sly glance at Pax. "Wonder if he's seen anything of those awful concentration camps over there," she said. "Bill, Pax is empty. Give her another drink."

Pax tried weakly to refuse it. She was beginning to feel a little dizzy and miserably unhappy. She was becoming frightened, too, at the turn the conversation was taking.

"Come on! Be a sport!" Bill filled her glass and then refilled his own. "Here's to the party we'll give the mug when she brings him home."

The maid stood in the doorway. "Dinner," she announced.

Philip drove home very slowly. Pax was asleep in the corner of the car and he tried not to jolt her too much. The clock on the dashboard said eleven twenty-five, but it was at least a half hour slow.

The party had become gayer and noisier as dinner progressed. Em had insisted upon continuing the conversation about concentration camps, in which most of the others had joined, making idle and callous remarks about them and their inmates. Then, it seemed to Pax that Em had deliberately twisted the conversation around to Jan, and with her perpetual curiosity had tried to pry into the child's history. Pax, obviously ill at ease, had handled it badly, and then had become steadily more belligerent during the evening. By the time Philip had dragged her away, she had become stubbornly silent.

About ten minutes before they reached Mapleton, Philip slowed up at a crossroad. He heard a little sob.

"So you're not asleep."

Another sniffle.

"What are you crying about?"

Pax sat up straight and fumbled in her coat pocket for a handkerchief. "I don't know."

"That's silly."

"I know it," she replied. "Phil?"

"What?"

"Am I crying because I'm sleepy or because I'm drunk?"

"Little bit of both, I guess. And then, too, because you're a congenital ass."

"Yes, I am, aren't I?" she said. "Why do you put up with me?"

"God knows!"

They drove on for two or three minutes. Then:

"Phil, what did I go out there for?"

"Same reason."

"I wanted to go, Phil. I thought it would be fun. Then just before I went, somebody—said something, and I began to feel guilty that maybe I was celebrating Robert's accident instead of— Give me a cigarette, will you?"

Philip pulled a pack out of his pocket and handed it to her; then he leaned over and pushed the lighter home in its socket until it caught.

"Thanks. And then I got out there, and they all began to insinuate nasty things and Em began to poke around in"—she swallowed and went on—"concentration camps, and—Phil, do you think she suspects?"

"Suspects what?"

"Suspects that— Do you think she thinks Jan's a Jew?"

"And what difference does it make if she does?"

"Well, it doesn't but— Anyway, now I don't care if I am a selfish beast! I don't care if everybody thinks I'm taking advantage of Robert's suffering to have fun. I'm *glad* I'm going! I'm glad I'm going to get out of this rotten, stinking town with its rotten, stinking people! Damn it! I'm *glad*!"

"Uh-huh," said Philip.

"And I'm glad I'm drunk! I hate 'em! I hate everybody except Robert and you and Tubs and Amy and Pansy—"

"And Jan?"

She paused for a split second. Then she said in a low voice, "Yes, I guess so."

Philip closed the doors of the garage and walked around to the front of the house with her.

"Good night, Phil, and thanks for taking me to the rotten party. I feel awful!"

"Get some sleep, kid. You'll feel all right in the morning. Good night." He got as far as the gate. "Hey, kid," he called, "a can of cold stewed tomatoes is swell for a hangover."

She giggled, shut the door, and stood for a moment in the hall. Pansy had left one dim light on, and from the open library door Pax saw that there were still smoldering embers and a small flickering flame in the fireplace.

She felt her way into the library, stood looking down for a few seconds into the glowing coals, and with a sigh stretched herself on the rug in front of the hearth. She slipped out of her beaver coat and pulled it over her. Then everything blacked out.

From an infinite distance she heard the faint ping of a bell. Then another, a little louder and longer this time. She turned restlessly. The bed was hard. And she ached all over. Where was that bell coming from? It got louder and louder, and nearer and nearer, until it seemed to roar in her ears.

She sat up with a start and looked about her. There were ashes in the fireplace, and the hearth beside her was dusty with them, where the wind making its way down the chimney had scattered them. The windows had been closed all night and the room was stuffy. She had thrown off her coat in her sleep, and her red frock was a mass of wrinkles. She shivered.

An October storm raged outside, her head was splitting, and the world looked dismal and dreary.

Where the devil was that ringing coming from? She shook her head desperately, trying to clear it. It must be either the telephone or the front doorbell. Why didn't somebody answer it? What time was it?

She pulled herself to her feet and groaned. She was so stiff she could hardly walk.

Another long, steady ring.

"Oh, stop it!"

She stumbled out into the hall. The one light was still on. She heard padding, shuffling footsteps coming down the back stairs. Around the corner came Pansy, her hair done up in tight little braids. She wore men's carpet slippers and a plaid flannel wrapper.

"It's all right," said Pax, yawning and stretching. "It's the doorbell. I'll answer it."

The bell had stopped ringing.

"What time is it?" Pax asked as she went to the door.

"It's nearly six o'clock," replied Pansy. "What you doin' comin' home at this time o' the mornin'?"

Pax opened the door. An envelope that had been stuck in the door fell to the floor.

"I'm not coming home," she said crossly. "I'm just getting up. I slept in there."

She picked up the envelope and pointed with it in the direction of the library. She walked slowly back inside, tearing open the envelope as she went.

"It's wet," she said irrelevantly, as she crumpled the envelope and

169

tossed it in the fireplace. She went over to the window, followed by Pansy.

"What was you up to las' night that you couldn't sleep in yo' own bed? Jes' look at you!"

"There was a little fire—it seemed a good idea—oh, I don't remember. I do wish you'd shut up!"

She unfolded the telegram and began to read it. "It's a cable," she said. Then her gloomy face lighted up like a small torch. "Pansy! He's going to telephone me this afternoon! What time is it now?"

"I tol' you, it's six o'clock. Don' get so excited."

"But he's going to telephone me from Germany! At four o'clock! Look! Read it!"

15

THE STORM had continued unabated all day. The rain was coming down in glimmering sheets and the water ran swiftly in the gutters.

Philip turned his coat collar up and fought his way against the wind across the soggy Green. Little rivulets were running down his neck from his wet hair and in the short time it took him to walk home from the college the lower part of his trousers was soaked through.

He ran upstairs without stopping for his usual greeting to Amy. His room was dark and it smelled damp and musty. He lighted the lamp and put a match to the fire, took off his wet clothes and shoes, got into his dressing gown, and put some water on the electric plate to boil.

He had a couple of hours before he was due at Pax's. A hot drink and a little rest would make him feel much better. He drank two cups of tea, then lay down on the couch and began to read. After several minutes, he realized that his mind was wandering far from Thomas Mann.

It was that girl again. It would be lonely as all hell without her. What was there about her that had tied his life so completely to hers? She was bright but not overintelligent, unpredictable, lovely, emotional, and deeply in love with another man.

Of course, it was her dependence on him—that, and a certain heart-breaking quality about her, frightened as she always was by reality, but facing it like a soldier when the time came that she was forced to touch it.

Perhaps it had been a mistake for him to stay in Mapleton this past summer, where he had seen practically no one except her. He began to wonder if he were really in love with the girl. One thing he knew: he'd never been in love with anyone else.

When his mother was alive, he'd spent the summers with her, and during the months when he was away from college, he'd lived like a normal young bachelor, but no other woman had ever really had any part of his heart or his interest. In Mapleton, he practically lived the life of a celibate.

He'd been a fool to spend virtually an unbroken year with her. He was a normal man and she was a normal woman. It was perfectly natural that he should resent her going to Lyttleton. There was no use fooling himself that it would be better for her if she didn't go; he didn't want her to go!

He tried to drag his mind back to the time when she was a gangly, long-legged youngster. He remembered how she'd cried in his arms over another man. And yet he'd admitted to that other man that he loved her. He had then. And now?

To hell with it! He'd meet her Friday afternoon in New York as they'd arranged, put her on the boat, and send her off to that son of a bitch. Then he'd forget it. There were lots of pretty women in New York. There was nothing to stop his spending his weekends there.

He turned over and tried to sleep. It wasn't any good. He'd wander over to the house and see how the kid was doing after her night of debauchery. He grinned to himself. What a stupid little mutt she was!

He pushed open the front door and found the hall in utter blackness. He shook the raindrops off his hat, threw his coat on the hall chair, and pulled off his overshoes. He went over to the foot of the stairs and looked up. There was no light on the second floor.

"Hey, Pax," he called.

There was no answer.

He opened the door to the kitchen. There was a light on there, and a pot simmering on the stove, but the kitchen was empty. He went back into the hall. He could hear no sound except the ticking of the grandfather's clock which stood under the stairs. The door to the library was closed. He opened it.

The room was dark except for a flickering light from a dying fire.

The fitful glow revealed a still figure sitting in the wing chair beside the fireplace.

"Hi," said Philip.

Pax raised her head a little, but she didn't answer.

"What are you sitting in the dark for?"

There was a low murmur from the chair.

Philip crossed in front of her and knelt down on the hearth. He reached into the wood basket and threw a couple of logs on the fire, prodding them with the poker until they caught and blazed. As he got to his feet he glanced at her casually and moved over toward the standing lamp opposite her chair.

"What's the matter, kid? Hung over?" He put his hand up under the lampshade. "Do you mind a little light?"

As he pulled the lamp chain, he looked back at her. She was wearily shaking her head, but not looking at him. Her thick black hair hung loosely about her shoulders, and one untidy lock fell over her brow and nearly hid one eye. On the table beside her were two small combs, a few hairpins, and an empty highball glass. Her face was drawn and gray, what lipstick there was left was smeared, and there were two or three damp spots on the front of her sweater.

"Hey, kid, are you still drunk?"

"Not still, Phil." She giggled unhappily, "That rhymes, doesn't it? 'Not still, Phil.' Hah! That's not bad. 'Not still, Phil.'"

"Stop that," he said sharply.

"What's the matter? I'm just making rhymes. I think that's very good. 'Not still, Phil!' I'm sorry. But I'm not still, Phil, I'm again! See what I mean? I'm drunk again."

He stared at her a moment; then he got up. "Mind if I join you?" he asked.

She leaned her head on her hand and closed her eyes. "Do you mind if I don't have any more?" she said plaintively. "My head hurts."

Philip poured himself a whiskey and soda, then came back and sat down. "You've certainly tied one on," he said quietly.

"What do you mean?" she replied with dignity. "I've only had five in the last hour. A soupçon, my dear man, a mere soupçon." He waited. "Five is an uneven number," she said. "I think I'll have six."

She half rose from her chair, then fell limply back into it. Her lower lip quivered and two tears rolled down her cheeks.

"I'm not going," she half whispered.

Philip's hand tightened around his glass.

"He doesn't want me."

172

She bent over until her head nearly touched her knees and her hair fell like a black mane over her face.

Philip leaned forward and put his hand on her head. "Steady. What's the story?"

She slipped out of the chair onto the hearth rug, in her old familiar position, and threw both arms across his knees.

"I talked to him—no, I didn't! He talked to me. What's the difference? I can't go." She began to giggle hysterically. "Isn't it silly? And I'm all ready and everything."

Philip held one of her hands tightly in his. "Pax, do you know what you're saying?"

"No, I don't think so! I just know he doesn't want me to come." She looked up at him with mournful eyes; her face was screwed up like a child's, and her mouth twisted in a crooked smile. "So ridiculous, don't you think? When you've made all your plans and burned all your bridges— Please, can I have another drink?"

"Sure, but I think at this moment it'll make you sick."

"All over you?" She chuckled. "Like Jan, huh?" She tried to hold on to that for a moment. "What was the use of sending Jan away?"

"Here, take a sip of mine."

She took one gulp, then pushed the glass away. "He just absolutely put his foot down—but he couldn't, could he? His foot's up. Up in that whatcha-ma-call-it."

"Pax, listen to me." He shook her gently by the shoulder, then lifted her chin up with his hand. "Pax, Bob's going to be all right, isn't he? He didn't break anything but one leg and one arm, did he?"

"All of 'em!" she said grandly, waving her arm in no particular direction. "No place for a woman to live, nothing to eat. He wrote me a letter—"

"Well, kid, maybe he's right. We don't really know about conditions over there."

"He wrote me a letter with his feet," she continued. "His arm's broken, you see," she added confidentially. "Isn't it embarrassing?"

She put her head down on his knees and began to sob as if her heart would break.

Philip picked her up and put her on the couch. His mind went back to that summer night in his room twelve years ago when he'd lifted her up onto his bed, just as he was doing now, and she was crying her heart out just like this. He smiled ruefully. That time it had been for Jake.

He went into the kitchen. Pansy was standing in front of the stove, holding a lid in one hand and stirring some steaming concoction with the other.

"'Evening, boss," he said, and went over and stood beside her, peering into the pot. "Smells good. What is it?"

"She ain't goin'."

"So I gather."

"Mr. Bobbie telephoned her from Germany. It's too bad, ain't it?"

"What did he say to her?"

"I don' know. But when she hung up de phone, she was cryin' kind o' pitiful. Poor chile!"

"So you've been feeding her liquor?"

"I only gave her one little drink, so help me Gawd! She asked fo' it, with her po' little face all puckered up—"

"Only one, eh? You wicked woman!"

"So help me— What's de matter with her?"

"She's come over unexpectedly drunk, that's all. Give me a bowl of that soup, will you?"

Philip and Tubby had dinner together.

Instead of being delighted that his mother wasn't going, with the usual contrariness of children, he was sulking with disappointment. "She was going to bring me a Luger pistol. Now I won't get any!"

"Where was she going to get a Luger, Tubs?"

"Oh, from some German prisoner. They've got lots of them over there."

"Prisoners don't carry revolvers," said Philip, "and I don't suppose there are many German prisoners in Germany."

"Aw, she'd a found two or three. And I wanted some bones, too, for a souvenir."

"Bones?" said Philip. "What kind of bones?"

"Oh, they got a lotta old bones left over from people who were burned up in stoves," replied Tubby cheerfully. "I could give a show and make a lot of money."

"Who told you about that? Jan?"

"Naw. He's not German. He comes from Europe."

Philip suddenly felt sick. "Tubby, I'm ashamed of you," he said sternly. "How would you like to be killed and burned in an oven? Or maybe burned alive? Do you think you'd like that?"

"Aw, I'm not a Jew, Uncle Philip." His round innocent face looked puzzled.

"Ever know any Jews, feller?"

"No. They killed 'em all."

"Who told you about these—bones, Tub?"

"Oh, all the kids know it," he said, and went back to his custard.

174

Philip thought for a moment, then reached in his pocket and pulled out a box of matches. "Ever burn yourself, Tubs?"

"Yeah, sure. On the stove."

"How brave a feller are you?" asked Philip. "If I light a match and put my finger in the flame, will you do it?"

Tubby hesitated. His eyes looked frightened, but he braced himself and nodded slowly. Philip's mouth tightened and his face was grim. He struck the match, held his finger over it a moment, then held it out to the child. Tubby timidly stuck his chubby finger in the flame. He let out a piercing scream and snatched his hand away.

"Hurts, doesn't it?" said Philip. "Jews are no different than you are, Tubs. It hurts them, too. Now, whenever you hear about Jews dying— or anyone else, for that matter—you remember that match, will you?" He walked over and ruffled up the child's hair. "Now go and tell Pansy to put some butter on it. I'm going in and see how your mother is. By the way, old man, I don't think I'd say anything about bones to her."

Scowling, Tubby slipped down from his chair, and, still sucking his finger, he pushed open the swinging door into the kitchen and ran through to Pansy.

Philip stood beside the couch and looked down at Pax. She was lying just as he'd left her when he went in to dinner, on her back, with her head turned a little to one side. In the dim light of the one lamp he'd left on, he could see the tired blue veins in her white lids; her smudged lips were slightly parted and she breathed heavily.

Philip had managed to get a bowl of hot soup down her throat, in spite of her protestations that she was never going to eat again because there wasn't any food in Germany. He'd thrown a coat over her feet, and she had immediately fallen into a deep sleep.

The rain was still beating at the windows and the wind was high. Philip decided against going home for a while, even though he guessed that Pax might sleep soundly right through the night. The fire was still burning steadily, and he could read for a couple of hours and be here in case she did wake and want something.

He put another log on the fire, poured himself a small brandy, selected one of Edmund's books, and settled himself in the big wing chair. He filled his pipe and lighted it, sipped his brandy, and lazily turned the pages of the book. But his mind kept returning again and again to his conversation with Tubby.

Tubby: a normal, healthy, well-brought-up American boy, the son of a courageous man and the gentlest of women, had spoken with almost morbid relish of a human agony, the remembrance of which should be seared for all time on the conscience of the world.

It had been a great shock to Philip to hear those callous words fall casually and easily from the boy's lips. As far as Philip could remember, he'd never noticed any signs of cruelty in him. He tried to recall his own processes of thinking when he was Tubby's age. He didn't find it too easy to compare the minds of the children of his generation with those of the children of today. He had been young in a comparatively simple era. The favorite games of kids then had been cowboys and Indians. William S. Hart and the heroes of James Fenimore Cooper had inspired the small boys of his time, and their villains were Billy the Kid and the other fabulous characters of the Wild West. Their young minds were awed by the horror of Indian scalpings. Not even the age of gangsterdom had arrived.

There had been no thought, then, that a day would dawn when a homicidal maniac would stalk Europe, torturing and massacring en masse, building a gigantic funeral pyre out of which would rise the agonizing death rattle and stench of six million innocent people.

It was tragic enough to have to face the fact that this crime had been tacitly and shamefully accepted by adults, but that little boys would exploit the horror in their childish games was not to be endured.

Tubby had wanted some bones, bones of dead martyrs to exhibit. Who could have put this monstrous thought into the mind of a child? Not Jan, a lonely young survivor of the slaughter. Tubby had said no. Would Jan be safe if Tubby found out that Jan had been nearer to those stoves than he had ever dreamed? Nothing can be crueler than a child's taunts if he is curious or amused. Well, Tubby was not his problem, thank God. But, in a way, Jan was.

It was time that Bob came home.

Philip admitted to himself that he had never particularly liked Bob Lyttleton. They had nothing in common—that is, nothing but their love for that lovely drunken idiot who was asleep over there. He smiled a little ironically as he looked across the room at her. But even if he didn't like him, he knew that Bob was a kindly man. It would be up to him to steer his son's mind in the way it should go and to protect this new son who was waiting for him.

The church clock was striking. He counted the strokes. Ten o'clock. No use trying to read. He couldn't keep his mind on it. He went to the window and looked out. The rain was falling more gently and the wind had died down.

Pax was stirring. Her head moved on the pillow. Then she opened

176

her eyes and stared at the ceiling. She yawned, stretched, and suddenly sat up. "I've been asleep," she said.

"You're telling me."

"I've got to go upstairs. I'll be right back."

She stood up and weaved a little, brushed her hair out of her eyes, and started unevenly for the door. She opened it, braced herself for a moment, and disappeared into the hall.

Philip leaned down, knocked the ashes out of his pipe onto the hearth, and went into the kitchen. Pansy had evidently gone upstairs, and he imagined Tubby was in bed. He heated some milk and carried it into the library.

When Pax returned, he saw that she'd washed her face, combed her hair, and put on lipstick. She slumped down in the big chair and took the glass of hot milk he handed her.

"Drink that," he ordered. "It'll make you feel better."

"I'm cold," she said, shivering.

Philip bundled his coat around her shoulders, and put another couple of logs on the fire.

"Does your head ache?"

She shook her head. "Not much; it feels fuzzy. What time is it?"

"About half past ten."

"Everybody gone to bed?"

"Yes."

She finished the milk, put the glass on the table beside her, and stared into the fire.

"I'm glad I woke up. I'd hate to have spent two nights in this damned room."

"What did you try to do, drink up the cellar?"

"I only had—" She hesitated and looked a little shamefaced. "I don't remember how many I had."

He lighted a cigarette and handed it to her.

" 'Mapleton housewife takes to drink. Lodged in corner room in city jail.' "

" 'The woman's husband returned from the wars—and she murdered him!' " she flung back at him.

"What happened, kid?"

"Isn't it silly, I don't exactly remember all that, either," she said, and a little frown wrinkled her forehead. "Let me think for a minute."

Philip waited.

"I wasn't drunk then. I was just excited and—happy. I guess it was a shock; I didn't expect it. Well, he said I wasn't to come—something about no place for me to stay; army red tape; it would embarrass him.

Oh, I don't know. I talked with some doctor. He said it would make Robert nervous and would perhaps delay his getting well. Robert's writing—I mean, somebody's writing for him. Oh, yes, he still loves me," she added, with a derisive curl of her lip.

"I don't want to say I told you so," Philip said, "but I thought something like that might happen. We don't know what conditions are like over there for anything as sudden as a new girl's arrival in a military setup. Wait till you get his letter. It'll explain everything."

"So now I'm not going anywhere and I feel such a fool!"

"Nothing to stop us going to New York and having one hell of a good time, is there?"

"I'd still have to come back. Can you imagine what they'll all say at the next party I'm not invited to? And I wouldn't go to their stinking party if I was," she added viciously. " 'What did I tell you about the bum having a girl over there?' " she mimicked. " 'He don't wanna come home—looks like he don't want her either.' Can't you just hear them, Phil? You heard them last night." Her underlip quivered. "Why did he have to go and do this to me, Phil?"

"Cut it out, kid. Give the guy a chance, can't you? Wait until you get his letter."

They sat in silence for a few minutes.

"Well," said Philip, "there's one little guy who's going to be awfully glad you're going to change your plans."

Pax looked up at him nervously. "Who?" she asked.

"Jan, of course."

"Oh."

"What's the matter?"

"Does he have to know?" she asked timidly.

"What do you mean?"

"Well, you see, I'm so tired and everything's so awful. I thought I might leave him in the school for a while. It'll be good for him—you know, his education—and, after all, he doesn't have to know I didn't go."

Philip looked at her grimly and when he spoke his voice was harsh. "No, you don't, Pax! If you want to keep on shying at reality, go ahead. If you want to go on making up pretty fairy stories for these God-damn fools around here, go as far as you like. But, believe me, if you want to keep that kid's respect, don't lie to him. He's seen people lied right into a gas oven."

She didn't say anything for several minutes. When she did speak, her voice was sad and small. "Phil, you're angry with me."

178

"No. You go on upstairs and go to bed. You've had quite a day. We'll talk tomorrow."

"But, Phil—"

"Shut up. Anyway, you and I have a date in New York. Go on, get the hell upstairs. I'll put out the lights. Good night, kid."

Pax folded the letter carefully and put it back in its envelope. She stood at her window, tapping nervously on the sill with the letter, looking out over the Green where the white morning sun made dancing shadows of the already bare branches on the dead grass. But she didn't see them. Her mind was far away and full of confusion.

She had been waiting for that letter for over a week, trying to keep her troubled mind open to reason and closed to resentment.

And now it had arrived and she didn't feel anything. She took it out of its envelope and read it again.

Sweetheart:

Your cable came yesterday. You can imagine my happiness at the thought of seeing you again after so long. Then I realized it was just impossible. It would just gum things up beautifully. There isn't any place for you to stay. These poor people haven't any money or material to build up things and it's still largely a pile of rubble here.

What there is in the way of living quarters is occupied by the married army personnel and you couldn't live in my place because I live in a bachelor's barracks. Army wouldn't like!

Of course, if I were up and about, it would be quite different. I might dig up a room for you, but I'm one big solid plaster cast.

And the food stinks! All right for us and gobs of it, but not for a spoiled gal.

Don't worry about me, baby. Can't kill me. It was a close call. Engine conked out nearing a field, and I missed it. Tried to make the field, but hit a pile of stones and ground looped right into it. Result: Right leg fractured in three places, right arm and collarbone busted, concussion, out three days. Cuts and sprains and dislocations and God knows what. But I'll be all right.

Be a good girl and don't come. I'll come home soon as I can. Rod Norton's writing this for me. He's a good guy. You be good now and I'll be seeing you.

Love and kisses,
Bob

P.S. Have just talked to you. Understand now, baby? The Doc told you. So you stay home and wait for me, see? Love.

It was no more than he'd said over the phone, and it sounded so cold and strange. But of course it would have to. It wasn't his writing. After all, a letter to your wife wasn't supposed to be public property. Then she remembered a little sheepishly that she always showed his letters to Phil and Amy and—oh, lots of people.

Nevertheless, it troubled her. She went to her desk to put it in the drawer where she always kept his letters. She put her hand in the middle of the stack and drew out another one at random.

> *England*
> *October 12, 1941*

Darling Pax:

Well, here I am at an aerodrome not far from London [line censored]. No action yet, just practice flights. I'm glad to be here and in it, but it was awful tough leaving you, darling. Unless we get going, I don't know how I'm going to bear being separated from you.

I don't think I realized how lucky we were to be able to be together for so many weekends for nearly a year. I can't help wondering how long it will be before I see you and our baby son again.

The fellows in my outfit are swell and do everything in their power to make things easy. I don't do anything in the way of instruction here. Just getting ready for the big scrap, which I pray to God will be soon. God help those bleeding krauts (that's English, sweet) when your husband and the RCAF start after them!

I was surprised to hear that old Jake had enlisted. War doesn't seem to be his particular cup of tea (English!) but I'm damn proud of him! But you'll miss him, honey, and I won't feel quite so secure, knowing he isn't there to look after you for me. But then your Winslow fellow will never let you down. Where is Jake stationed for his basic? But then he'll write me of course and let me know.

Kiss my son for me. Keep taking photos of him so I can see him grow. As for you, my sweet, you are photographed on my heart. I love you.

> *Your loving husband,*
> *Bob*

She put the two letters side by side on the desk and looked at them. Naturally they were different. It wasn't the same writing . . .

180

She reached for another a little nearer the top. As she pulled it out of its envelope, another sheet of paper fell out.

England
Jan. 19, '43

Pax, love:
This God-damned Blitz is hell! Been up for three nights straight. Lucky to get four hours out of twenty-four. Those [censored] [censored] are [censored] but they're dynamite. Hey, pun!
Am enclosing a short letter from Jake. There goes an alert. Up and after 'em!
I love you both. Kiss him for me. (The baby, I mean—not Jake).

Bob

She unfolded the other sheet of paper.

Somewhere in Texas
Xmas, 1942

Dear Bertie:
Here I am in Texas. Hating every minute of it. My feet hurt and I'm a bum shot. I don't know where they'll ship me but wherever it is I know I'll be scared as hell.
God knows I'm a poor excuse as a soldier, but I just can't sit down and let great guys like you fight for my people, so I'm throwing my five cents' worth into the kitty.
Pax and the kid were fine when I left. She's promised to write.
Hear great things of you, you son of a bitch! But then you always liked a scrap, especially if it was for someone else.
Take care, feller, and give 'em hell!

Jake

Dear Jake, she thought, as she put the letters back and closed the drawer. Funny how Robert gradually stopped writing about him after D-Day. Maybe he'd heard and just couldn't bear it. So unlike, they were, and yet so close. Oh, well . . .

She'd better make her bed and tidy up. Pansy had enough to do. She hesitated. She went to her dressing table and felt about in the back of the top drawer. She pulled out a key chain with a dozen keys hanging on it, and went back to her desk. She unlocked a small drawer and took out another stack of letters, tied loosely together with a ribbon. Haphazardly she pulled one out.

My dear Pax:

I'm on a vast and angry sea, on my way from one place to another. The Personnel of this Army certainly changes with ungentlemanly speed. We lost too many great fellows mopping up the last atoll, but we'll pick up another lot of cannon fodder as we start all over again on the next.

It's ironical, Pax, that I'm in the Pacific. All I wanted to do was to get a chance at those butchers on the other side of the world, and all I'm doing is to dodge the bullets of those delicate little yellow men. But I suppose there's a pattern.

Today's my birthday. I only mention it because nobody seems to have birthdays over here—or maybe it's just that they have too many.

I look forward to your letters, girl. They bring normalcy right into this holocaust. Memories I have that not even the horrors we have to look at can blot out. Those weekends from the paper in Boston, with you and old Bertie; you carrying his child blissfully, like a self-satisfied Madonna; the first time my young godson gripped my finger with his little fist; Bertie's heroic enlistment in the RCAF—he's been transferred to the U.S. Air Forces now, he tells me. His last letter was just like him—enthusiastic and optimistic.

Give my best to Philip and Mrs. Sanders. I'll write as long as I have a pencil and a hand to write with.

Yours,
Jake

Those years between her young tragedy and Jake's tacit offer of steady friendship returned to strike at her with full force; not with unhappiness or regret, but with a strange wonder and a little sense of guilt that her heart hadn't broken, after all. She *had* been happy with Robert. He had given her passion, sweetness, and care, and those first three years had always been touched with excitement, owing, mainly, to the pace at which the world was moving. She recalled Robert's first love letter. It was always at the bottom of the stack.

Friday night, Sept. 16, '37

My darling, darling, darling, darling!

I am the happiest man in the world! I humbly thank God for this great blessing. The most beautiful girl is going to be my wife. My WIFE!

182

I'm sure I shan't be able to sleep, but if I do, it will only be because I shall think of the day that you will sleep in my arms.

I love you! I love you! Do you love me?

Until tomorrow. It will be a year till then!

Bob

There was another in the small drawer, on the other side. She didn't really have to look at it. It was blazoned on her memory. It wasn't very much of a letter. There were just eight lines:

> *My lonely embers of yesteryear*
> *Are mournful ashes in the gale,*
> *Now, in my heart, a nightingale*
> *Sings low to her so I may hear.*
>
> *Gone is my soul's black hopelessness,*
> *Its hearth is swept, its windows wide,*
> *The pain is done. She steps inside.*
> *She is a haven in my wilderness.*

Such a young poem. The minor strings of a Jewish harp. Not a Jew's harp! She didn't mean that. . . . Jan's harmonica! Now, what made her think of that? She must write him. She had promised Philip.

Slowly she placed Robert's last letter, in the unfamiliar handwriting, on top of his other letters. She could still see the last phrase of today's letter, before the short P.S. "You be good now and I'll be seeing you."

But she wouldn't be seeing Jake—not ever again.

Her eyes fell slowly to the envelope that lay on top in Jake's very small drawer. She took it out and walked over to the window with it. That envelope had unfamiliar writing on it, too. And it had a black border. And the postmark was Worcester, Massachusetts.

She remembered so clearly the day it had arrived, nearly two years ago. She took out the smaller envelope. She had known that writing. It just said "Pax."

Somewhere in eternity

My dear love:

If your eyes ever read these lines, it will be because I will not be coming back.

It is quiet here in my father's house, and my soul is calm and content.

I have loved you without pause. My love had to be speechless because only in that way could it serve you.

183

I have always been impatient with the lot of martyrs. Their dedication is their reward and their life. And so, I command you, girl, never be sad for me.

Deep is my longing for the peace of my people and for a dwelling place for them, but that place is not for you, my darling. Do you understand now why I could only give you my friendship, which is as great as my love?

I shall carry a photograph into battle with me. It is you in your bridal veil that you wore for my best friend. And that is good, too, for I know you will be safe with him.

Perhaps it is that love does not know its own depth until the hour of separation. But perhaps there will be no separation, and I shall burn this on my return.

If we meet again, we will meet as friends. If it should only be in the twilight of memory, we can always speak together. If our hands should meet in another dream—on another plane—we may build together in a more compassionate world.

It is dawn. And this letter is without end, my beloved.

Jake

There were no tears this time. She was growing up. Her eyes were dry but her heart was warm. The poet in a good man had spoken to her as he left.

And now she must really write to Jan.

16

THE FLICKERING LIGHT of the two candles illuminated the young faces at cne end of the smaller boys' dormitory. Each candle was stuck on a saucer and they had been put on the floor in a safe place, closely watched over by the Light Officer of the week. Another guard watched the door, which was open a crack, to give the warning in case of any suspicious signs of spies in the corridor.

Three beds had been pushed together, and ten or twelve boys were sitting on them, cross-legged, in a circle. The heat was always turned off at nine o'clock in the dormitories, and two of the open windows let in the frosty November night air. Some of the boys had their coats on over their pajamas and bathrobes; others were tucked up in blankets which they had pulled off their beds.

It was the fortnightly meeting of the Supper Club. In front of each boy was a box, in which there were sandwiches, cakes, fruit, and candy, all either sent by families or bought out of allowances.

There was one slight figure sitting there with them in his red robe, soberly watching the proceedings, but he had no box of any kind in front of him.

Jan had been at the school just a little over two weeks. The boys had paid very little attention to him during the first few days—they were somewhat awed by his strange accent and his aloofness—but they gradually had become used to him, and the small boys' hazing had begun.

Spitballs, sniped at him from unexpected places in the schoolroom, left him quite unmoved. They hid his clothes and knotted his shoelaces; his schoolbooks disappeared and the boys apple-pied his bed, until his indifference—and what they took for good nature—made them lose interest.

That afternoon before the meeting they had gathered in a huddle in the playground and decided that the foreigner was a good guy, even if he did talk like a wop or something, and invited him to join the club.

Jan's years of acceptance had made him a passive little creature so he agreed at once, although he had no idea what it was all about. No one had sent him any food from home nor had he been given any allowance. In the excitement of Robert's crash and her hurried plans to go abroad, Pax had overlooked many important things.

So there he sat, listening to the giggling and whispering, wistfully watching the exchange of food.

"Aren't you cold, Lyt?" asked one of them curiously. "I'll lend you half my blanket."

Cold? With that beautiful warm red flannel robe! For a moment he wondered if any of these boys knew what it was like to be really cold.

He shook his head and wished the boy would lend him half of the sandwich he was stuffing into his mouth. His sober brown eyes traveled around the circle, watching each morsel of food as it passed from the small hands into the eager young mouths, and his own mouth watered uncomfortably.

Directly across from him was the boy who sat next to him in class. Peter Lawson was about a year younger than Jan. He didn't look unlike

185

Tubby, not quite so husky, and his nose was shorter and snubbier and finely dusted with freckles. His hair was straight and yellow, and he wore a band on his little crooked teeth.

Peter was chewing thoughtfully and watching Jan. He was speculating as to whether he had the courage to break the rule of the club and share his supper with Jan. He had a consuming curiosity about the little foreign boy and that, combined with his natural generosity, finally got the better of his discretion. He held out a thick chicken sandwich with one hand and a piece of jelly roll with the other.

"Here," he said, "you can have some of mine."

Jan reached for them eagerly.

"Hey! Cut that out!" shouted a skinny thirteen-year-old. "He's got to bring his own grub."

"Yeah! Only keep your voice down, Mike," whispered another. "If there's any extra loot, we can do with it."

"Yeah, let him bring his own," muttered a tall boy called Dickie Jones. "You tell him, Mike!"

"Any more breakin' the rules, Lawson," said Mike angrily, "and we'll kick you out." Mike was obviously the ringleader; the others all treated him with respect.

Jan continued to eat peacefully.

"He doesn't know about the rules yet. This is his first night," protested Peter. "Next time he'll bring enough for two times, won't you, Jan?"

Jan gave his customary shrug and stuffed the last bit of cake in his mouth. He didn't care what they thought. He was eating the same as the others were, and it was good!

"Jan," said a dark boy whom they called Skinny. "That's a funny name. What kind of a name is that?"

"Polish, I tink," said Jan indifferently.

"Say, are you Polish?" asked Mike.

"I don't know. I tink so. My"—he hesitated—"mudder say so."

"Hah! That's a good one!" Stinky laughed. "His mother says so! Don't you *know*?"

Jan stood up. "I go to bett now," he said, and calmly walked away. When he reached his own bed, he took off his robe and hung it on the bed post. Then he looked back at his new friend. "Tank you, Peter."

He climbed into bed, pulled the covers over him, and turned his back on the Supper Club.

The bell had just rung for recreation hour. The boys streamed in from the classrooms, noisily shoving and pushing to get to a desk in

186

the recreation room, over which hung a small partitioned cabinet, alphabetically marked, which housed the mail. One of the older boys stood by the desk, sorting the letters, putting them in their compartments or giving them to boys who were clamoring for them.

It was the Monday after Jan had been initiated into his first midnight feast. He had just left the mathematics class, which he thoroughly enjoyed. For a boy his age, he had a remarkably logical mind and seemed to have a real aptitude for mathematics.

Most of the boys were huddled around the desk, laughing and reaching for letters from home, but Jan walked quietly across the hall and stood looking out of the window.

"Hey, Jan!"

Jan turned and looked back. Peter Lawson was waving an envelope. "It's for you. You're the same letter as me."

Slowly Jan walked over to the group and took the letter from Peter. He perched on the arm of a chair and held it in his hand for a moment. From under his lashes he threw a sly glance around the room to see what the other boys were doing with theirs.

They eagerly tore open the envelopes. He did the same. They took out the sheets of paper, most of them smiling happily, and read first one side, then the other. So did he.

The only difference was, he couldn't understand the strange handwriting, and in his bewilderment could only make out a word here and there. Nonchalantly he put the letter into his pocket and strolled quietly out of the hall and up to his dormitory. He pulled a scarlet turtle-neck sweater over his brown head, got a cap from his locker, and ran down the stairs, out of the side door into the autumn-bare grounds.

Back of the house, he found a garden seat which was hidden from the school by a large lilac bush. There he took out his letter and ploddingly tried to concentrate on each word.

"Dear" he understood, and "Jan"—that was one of the first words he had learned to spell. "T-h-i-n-g-s"—yes—"h-a-v-e," then six or seven words that he couldn't make out. He went over and over it, but it wasn't any use. He put it in his pocket and started back for the house. Suddenly, in the distance, he recognized a familiar figure going from one school building to another. He began to run. "Please! Please!" he called.

Dr. Miller turned and waited for him. "Hello, young feller." He smiled. "Where's your overcoat? Aren't you cold?"

"Not cold," Jan replied. Then he held up the envelope. "You read dis, please?" he asked eagerly.

"Of course." Miller opened it and read it through. He looked down into the small excited face. "It's from your mother," he said.

"So?"

Dear Jan. [he read]: *Things have changed, and I am not going away. Tubby's father is better, and will come home soon. If you are not unhappy in your school, it would please me very much if you would stay on for a while, as I think you will learn a great deal, and more quickly. After all, you will be coming home in six or seven weeks for the Christmas holidays, and if you don't want to return to school then, you don't have to.*

Tubby is well and sends his love; so do Uncle Philip, Aunt Amy, and Pansy. Be a good boy and study hard.

Much love,
P. L.

P.S. Uncle Philip is watching Tubby until you come home.

Jan took it from the headmaster and looked at it for a long moment. "She vant me to stay her-re?" he questioned.

"That's right, Jan. Don't you want to?"

"I stay," he said flatly. Then he frowned. "What is dis P.S.?"

"That means she thought of something else after she had finished the letter. You see, 'P' stands for 'post'—that means after—and 'S' is for 'script'—that's writing. Understand?"

Jan nodded, but he still studied the paper. "What is dis 'P.L.'?"

Dr. Miller hesitated a minute. "Those must be your mother's initials," he said guardedly. " 'P' is for Pax, and 'L' is for Lyttleton—*your* name." And he patted the boy on the shoulder. "Would you like me to write her for you, Jan?"

"No—tank you. I write."

He turned away.

"Better run get your coat. The sun's going down. See you later, old man."

"Tank you—sir-r-r."

That evening, after supper, Jan sat cross-legged on his bed with a pad in front of him and a pencil clutched in his hand. Laboriously he tried to form the letters. Suddenly he called down the dormitory to young Lawson, who was putting a toy airplane together.

"Peter, you come a minute?"

Peter put down his plane and went to him.

"How you spell 'sandwich'?" Jan asked.

188

Three or four days later, Pax opened a letter addressed to her in large, sprawling printing.

Dear P. L.

I stay. I like. I can say nine times nine is eighty-one. I have friend. His name Peter. He like me. Much love.

J. L.

P.S. Send me sandwich, candy. Other boys have. I no have money. Good night.

Pax read it twice, and a smile began to play around her lips. She couldn't wait to show it to Philip. Her mind went to those two desk drawers that contained so much of the past.

So here was another "first letter." But not by the wildest stretch of the imagination could it be called a love letter. One might rather call it a curt business note.

Pax grinned.

About a mile from Jan's school was a small Presbyterian church with the simplest of services. All of the Protestant boys walked there and back every week to Sunday morning service. The Roman Catholics were driven into Manchester for Mass.

Dr. Miller was a little puzzled as to where to send Jan, but Pax had said nothing about the boy's faith. He was sure that if he had been a Roman Catholic, she would have said so and made some provision for his attending Mass, so he sent Jan along with the Protestant boys.

Jan had become so used to new studies and new customs that he accepted them without question, and the first two Sundays passed by practically unnoticed by him.

The pictures in the stained-glass windows fascinated him. He thought the colors and the light through them were lovely, but he couldn't imagine what the men in the pictures were standing on. And some of them had great wings like birds. Most of all he liked a small white animal that looked up into the face of one of them.

He listened to the music of the little organ, and even the shrill voices of the boys pleased him. When the boys knelt down, putting their foreheads on the top of the pews in front of them, he knelt too, but he didn't bow his head. He was too busy watching the tops of their heads and wondering what on earth they were doing.

A man went up some stairs, stood behind a funny little curved fence, and read from a big book. Then he talked in a hollow singsong voice. Jan didn't listen.

By the third or fourth Sunday, he had explored to its fullest all the wonders of this weekly hour and he was becoming a little bored with everything except the music. In spite of himself, he found himself listening and trying to understand some of those big words.

There it was again! The Name of that Man she had told him about. "Our Lord Jesus"—and then a word he couldn't make out. "The Son of God." No, that wasn't the One she had told him about. She said Jesus was God. She hadn't said anything about a Son.

When the boys filed out, two by two, and walked the mile home along the country road, Jan walked steadily on, silent—even for him—and a little frown puckered his brow. The boys broke ranks when they entered the big iron gates of the school, and Jan led Peter Lawson back of the house to the long seat behind the leafless lilac bush.

"Peter," he said, "know you a man named Jesus?"

The other child looked at him with open mouth. "A *man*!" he exclaimed. "You mean, our Lord Jesus Christ?"

"What is dis wor-r-rd, Chr—?" He couldn't quite pronounce it.

"Christ." Peter's young voice was a little awed.

"Dat is dis Jesus udder name?"

"His last name? Yes, I guess so," said Peter, but he didn't seem sure.

"How you spell dis?"

"C-h-r-i-s-t."

Jan reached into his trouser pocket and pulled out Pax's letter, which he always carried with him. He opened it and studied it until he found the word he was looking for. "Look, Peter. Dis Christ-mas. Dis mean Jesus?"

"No. That's when He was born, Jan. That's why we go home. It's a holiday. Don't you know that?"

Jan looked puzzled. "Dis man, He have a son?"

"Naw! He *is* a son. The Son of God."

"No." Jan shook his head stubbornly. "My—mudder say He *is* God."

"Well, He is! He's both."

Jan persisted. "How can He be God and God's Son, too? Dis is ver-ry strange!"

Peter was becoming bored with all these questions. "Oh, why don't you go and ask Dr. Miller?"

"Dis Jesus is dead, no? He die like udder pipple?"

"Yeah. On a cross."

"Ah!" said Jan, and he nodded his head and frowned. "He is God after He is dead, no?"

"Sure. He's been dead two thousand years!"

"Look you, Peter," said Jan earnestly. "You have seen dead pipples."

"No!" replied Peter, his eyes wide. "Have you?"

Jan leaned down, and from the ground he picked up a small, twisted, dried-up bough that had fallen from the tree above them.

"Dead pipple all finished. No good. Like dis." He broke the bough over his knee and threw it away. "How you tink a dead man is God—after-r He is dead, huh?"

"I'm going in," said Peter, jumping down from the seat. "You don't know what you're talking about."

"It is funny," Jan said, as he followed his friend.

17

THE FIRST ten days of the Christmas holidays had slipped away with ridiculous speed.

It had been a white Christmas. The first great storm of the year had broken the week before and then there had been a soft fall of snow every two or three days. Mapleton nestled peacefully in a blanket of white among the snow-covered hills. From early morning until sundown, and again in the ghostly blue moonlight, the young people of the town tobogganed and skied down their steep sides.

Jan arrived from school three days before Christmas. He had stepped down onto the platform, in his new beaver-collared coat and beaver cap, the ear muffs tied under his chin, clutching in his mittened hand a piece of paper with the word "Burlington" written on it. Dr. Miller had put him in the care of an older boy who was going as far as Rutland, and Pax, Tubby, and Johnnie Leclerc met him at the station.

Pax noticed immediately the unmistakable change which had taken place in the boy in the seven or eight weeks he had been away. The guarded rigidity of movement had almost completely disappeared. His shoulders were not so hunched, and he turned his head easily when he was spoken to, instead of looking straight ahead. Only occasionally did that secretive, shut-in expression appear, and his brown eyes were no longer perpetually hidden by the slanting lids.

As long as she lived Pax knew she would never forget the look on his face when he had his first glimpse of the Christmas tree which had miraculously sprung up during the night before Christmas. He gasped, his eyes widened, and he held his head with both hands. He could hardly take his eyes away from it long enough to look at his gifts, which were stacked on one side under the tree.

There was a bob sled from Tubby, skis from Amy. Pax gave him an inexpensive little fiddle, and Philip, a small silver wrist watch with his name engraved on the back. A bicycle of his very own leaned against the wall with a card reading: "From Tubby's father with love and a Merry Christmas," and Johnnie Leclerc gave him a St. Christopher's medal.

He didn't understand any of it, but it was all magical to a small boy of eleven who had never seen anything like it in all of his short life. When he was in the house, he wrapped and unwrapped his presents and would steal up to the tree and timidly touch the gay, paper-light ornaments that hung from the boughs.

He climbed and reclimbed the slippery, snow-covered hills with Johnnie and the other children, dragging his sled after him, and came in at sundown like any other child, his stockings and trousers wet above his galoshes, his eyes bright, and his usually pale cheeks scarlet with the cold.

He overstuffed himself with turkey and repeated the performance of his first night in New York, this time all over the stairs, and again the next day when two dozen red-and-white peppermint sticks disappeared from the tree.

The second time, much to Pax's annoyance, she had to sit up with him most of the night while he held tightly on to his distended little belly, stoically trying not to show the agony he was going through with gas pains. But on the whole, he had given her much less anxiety than she had expected.

It was two days before the end of the holidays. Jan and Tubby were on their way upstairs to bed when Pax called to Jan from the foot of the stairs.

"Tubby, you run along and get undressed, darling. I want to talk to Jan for a few minutes."

Tubby went, under protest, and Jan followed her into the library and sat in one of the big chairs by the fire. He waited for Pax to speak, his eyes constantly wandering over to the corner of the room where the tree still stood. He had never liked anything quite so much in his life as that tree!

Pax studied the small face—not quite so small as it had once been—and knew she must ask the question she dreaded. She was ashamed of herself for dreading it, because the boy had been no trouble during the two weeks he'd been home, to her or to anyone else. But indeterminate worries were always with her when he was, and she knew there was nothing she could do about it.

"Well, Jan, did you have a happy Christmas?" she asked.

"Yes."

"Yes, what?" she said, with a gentle tone of reproof.

"Yes, P.L.—tank you."

"What did you call me, Jan?"

"P.L.," he replied. "Dat is what you wr-rote in de letter-r. It is not r-right, no?"

Pax lowered her eyes and felt a tell-tale flush steal up from her throat. "That's just for letters, Jan." She didn't quite know how to go on. "Tubby calls me 'Mom.' Wouldn't you like to?" she asked timidly.

There was that shut-in expression again.

"Tank you," he said. He jumped down from his chair and went over and touched his bicycle, which was still leaning against the wall. "Tubby said it is polite to wr-r-rite his fader and tank him for de bicycle."

Pax looked startled. "Yes—yes! By all means. I'll send it for you," she added hurriedly.

"Why he is in Ger-r-rmany so long time? He is in"—he hesitated, then proceeded very slowly—"con-cen-tr-r-ra-shun camp, no?"

Her heart missed a beat. It was the first time he had ever used that word. She wondered where he'd heard it in English.

"No, Jan dear. There are no more concentration camps." She knew she was lying, but she also knew she must do everything in her power to keep from disturbing him. "He is with the American Army. He'll be coming home very soon now."

She waited, wondering if he were at last going to tell her some of the horror that she was sure was always at the back of his mind, but he didn't. His eyes just drifted back to the Christmas tree.

She sighed and reached for a cigarette. She held the box out to him. "Will you have one, Jan?"

He shook his head. "No, tank you. I do not smoke."

She remembered now, she hadn't seen him smoke once since he had come from school.

"Why, that's perfectly wonderful, Jan dear."

"Mr. Adam—he is man who teach me mat-a-matic—he tell me I be gr-r-reat scientist someday. He say smoke bad for br-rain."

She didn't tell him it was not so bad for scientists as it was for athletes. She was too grateful to this man Adams—whoever he was— who had been able to do what she'd failed utterly in doing.

"Udder boys smoke behind tr-rees way down by fence. I do not smoke," he said proudly. "I will be scientist."

Now she knew why his marks for two months had been so good, especially in conduct and mathematics.

"Jan, have you decided whether you want to go back to school or stay here with us?"

She waited anxiously for his reply. She didn't have to wait long. His eyes lighted and his voice was eager.

"I go back to school, please. Mr. Adams say I be scientist."

Two days later, Pax and Jan stood on the icy platform at Burlington, waiting for the train. The white clouds rode high in the sky and the early morning sun glistened on the snow.

"Jan, dear, don't forget to watch at Rutland for your friend. Listen carefully—keep looking at your new watch. The train should arrive there about ten-thirty. You'll hear the conductor call it out when the train pulls into the station. Say 'Rutland.'"

"R-rut-land," he repeated.

"That's right."

They heard the sound of the whistle way up the tracks, and the train puffed into view.

The conductor picked up Jan's sled and put it on the platform. Jan slung his skis over his shoulder, and, followed by Pax with his valise, climbed up the steps and found an empty seat in the coach. Pax put his skis and his valise on the rack above him, kissed him hurriedly, and made her way back to the platform.

As the train pulled out, she saw his nose pressed against the window, and he was smiling.

She waved until she was sure she was out of sight. Then she breathed a sigh of relief, climbed into the car, backed it out onto the slippery road, and made for home.

18

I saw God. Do you doubt it?
  Do you dare to doubt it?
I saw the Almighty Man. His hand
  Was resting on a mountain, and
He looked upon the World and all about it:
I saw Him plainer than you see me now,
  You mustn't doubt it.

He lifted up His hand—
  I say He heaved a dreadful hand
Over the spinning Earth. . . .

Pax stopped reading. She put the open book face downward on her lap, clasped her hands behind her head, snuggled down into the cushions, and stared at the ceiling. It was the same old ceiling at which she'd stared for so many years, except that the water stain was a darker brown and it had spread a little wider.

She liked James Stephens. He was a crony of leprechauns. But sometimes, even in his Irish simplicity, he was disturbing.

"His hand was resting on a mountain. . . ."

Perhaps that was what was the matter with her. God's hand was resting just a little too heavily on her and it made her uneasy. She had taken on a responsibility and she was evading it.

From the time she had deposited Jan in school she knew that, more than anything in the world, she wanted him to stay there—or somewhere away from her. Somewhere where his presence wouldn't continually batter at her fear and sense of responsibility.

What was it she was afraid of? Anti-Semitism? In the people around her—or in herself? It was out now, and she'd better take a look at it. Jan was a Jew. She was sure of it. But hadn't she always been sure of it? For what other reason had she sought him? And yet she had constantly hedged about it, pretending, perhaps even hoping a little—

Why shy away from it? Why not accept it? Jan was a Jew—like Jake. And she'd failed Jake. Was she doing it again?

She had been so relieved when he had chosen to go back to school of his own free will. She was so sure then that she would be at peace, and the future could look after itself.

But it hadn't worked out that way. As the weeks went by, she found that the boy was continually invading her thoughts. She had taken him for better or for worse—sounded like the marriage service, didn't it? But then she hadn't really! She had another year to make up her mind.

But could you let somebody go who had no one in all the world and no place to go to?

Take your hand away, God! She wouldn't fail him!

She wondered if Robert would take the strange child to his heart as she had planned? A small Jake! Something to take the place of his best friend whom he had lost. She remembered the first time she had voiced that thought to Philip.

Fool! Why did she have to think of Philip? Far less disturbing at the moment to stick to thoughts of Jan. But she might just as well face it. She missed Philip. And she was hurt and bewildered and lonely—and she knew she was being perfectly asinine.

She hadn't actually missed him during the first two or three days after Jan went back to school. He'd gone to New York in the middle of the holidays without telling her why, but she knew he wasn't in Mapleton and she hadn't expected to see him. It was after he came back, and she knew he was just across the Green—

He only came to see her now once or twice a week, and she wasn't used to it! Perhaps he was interested in some woman; she was shocked by the little stab of jealousy which took her unawares. Well, why shouldn't he be? Why should she expect to be the pivotal point in his life? After all, Robert was the pivotal point in hers. But she *was* lonely.

She mustn't forget that the reason she'd seen him every day during the last year was because of Jan. Well, she'd sent Jan away. She hadn't any reason now to demand every minute of his attention. When was she ever going to grow up?

She smiled to herself a little wistfully when she thought of how possessive she'd always been about him. How many years was it? Must be sixteen or seventeen. What a pleasant wailing wall he'd always been for her—

What made her think of that expression?

"Mis' Pax, what you layin' heah without any light for?"

She opened her eyes. The room was quite dark. The twilight must have fallen quickly.

196

"You ain't been tryin' to read in that light, have you?"

"Oh, stop fretting, Pansy. How could I? I'm not an owl."

"Ain't no need to bite my head off. Dinner'll be ready in fifteen minutes. I'll turn on the lights."

So dinner was nearly ready. Dinner by herself. She wondered what Philip was doing for dinner. She stretched and sat up. The trouble was, she was beginning to act so like a fool when she did see him. She must stop being so dignified and self-conscious when she was with him, just because her pride was hurt. She couldn't make him want to see her if he didn't want to.

She got up, felt her way across the room, and turned on the dressing-table lights. She picked up her powder puff and squinted at herself in the mirror. She really wasn't bad-looking for an old girl of twenty-nine —well, let's face it, she was practically thirty. Her skin was good and her eyes. She wet the tips of her fingers with her tongue and wiped the powder off her long black lashes.

When on earth was Robert coming home? It was nearly four months now since he crashed. What was all that stuff about eight or ten weeks? Oh, well.

She'd just have time to telephone Philip and ask him if he wouldn't take her down the hill tonight to the movies. She'd better call up first and find out the name of the picture so she'd have the excuse of wanting specially to see it.

Nonsense! What was the matter with her, anyway? Why shouldn't she just tell him that she wanted to go somewhere and do something— tell him she was lonely. She could tell Philip anything.

How long had it been since she'd seen him? Four days?

She wondered if there *was* somebody in New York.

As Pax and Philip reached the brow of the hill, the clock in the church tower struck eleven. It was a beautiful night, still and cold. There was not the slightest whispering of a wind. The moon was full and white and it spilled its diffused light until the earth was ice blue in color, and the feathery branches of the trees covered in glistening ice seemed etched on the bright sky.

When they came to her gate, Pax went ahead and ran lightly up the steps.

"Hey! Don't go so fast! What's the hurry?"

"I'm just going to run in and get some ice, so we can have a nightcap."

"On top of hot chocolate?"

"Why not? That was fifteen minutes ago. Anyway, I want to talk to you about Jan."

Philip followed her in, and Pax's last words were said over her shoulder as she disappeared into the kitchen.

When she got back with the ice, Philip had taken off his coat and put a match to the fire. Pax breathed a sigh of relief. She did hate to come home at night to an empty house.

She put the ice bucket down on the table where the decanters and glasses stood. "How do you want yours, Philip? Long or short?"

"Long on soda, short on whiskey. I'm not at all sure whether whiskey has even a bowing acquaintance with hot chocolate. . . . Hey! Easy does it!" he said, as she tipped the decanter over his glass.

"What's the matter?" she retorted gaily. "Has New York made a sissy out of you?" She poured her own, and came over and sat down. "Em's got a new Cadillac."

"That so?" said Philip noncommittally.

"Mmm. She always hated being held up when her own car had to take the twins back and forth from school. She said she wanted a second-hand Ford, but she finally compromised on a Cadillac."

"Settled by arbitration, no doubt," observed Philip.

"Oh, Em can charm the pants off Buck." Pax knew she was making conversation, but she couldn't stop. "And it's the damnedest color! Almost the color of her hair!"

"What's with Jan?"

"What?"

"You said you wanted to talk to me about Jan."

"You needn't worry about it. I mean, it's nothing to make you think you'll have to take over again," she said with dignity.

Philip looked swiftly at her, but he said nothing.

"It's just something he said in a letter I got day before yesterday. It wasn't anything much. It was just that—" She jumped up and started for the door. "Wait a minute. I'll get it."

Philip wondered what was the matter with the girl. She seemed a bit moody lately, but then she was always an erratic bundle of emotion. Perhaps she missed Jan and wouldn't admit it. Or maybe it was just Bob she missed. The bastard was certainly taking his time about coming home.

He heard her running down the stairs.

She pulled a single sheet of lined paper out of the small envelope, and held it up for him to see. Jan had written some of the words uncertainly and printed the rest.

"Isn't it terrible?" She laughed. "He may be in the sixth grade in mathematics and get a hundred in languages, but did you ever see such writing?"

"He's in the sixth grade—Jan?"

"Yes. Don't you think that's remarkable?"

"I always thought he was a smart kid," Philip said flatly.

"After all, he's never even known how to study, no foundation, a new language. I know there are lots of American boys who graduate from grammar school at twelve—but Jan!"

"Twelve, did you say? You told me the kid was eleven."

"Well, he was, but don't you think he must be— That's what I want to read you. Listen:

"Dear P.L.— [She frowned slightly.] I am well. I hope you are well. I am in physics class. I like it. I do problem on blackboard. I like it. I begin be great scientist. Teddy had birthday Wednesday. He get big cake. 11 candle. I have a piece. I like it. He get skates. Watch. Not so good like my watch. We see movie each Sat. I like Judy Garland. She sing nice. Much love.

J.L."

Philip smiled. "Not the same kid who was afraid of Luke, is it?" he said.

"Wait a minute, there's more: P.S.—"

"He's hell on those P.S.'s, isn't he?" Philip interrupted.

"P.S. [she repeated]. Stinky Powell say I must have hair cut. Look like girl. I do not want look like girl.

P.S. Hair very short now. Stinky cut it. I like it.

P.S. When is my birthday? Good-by."

Pax folded the letter and put it back in its envelope. Then she looked inquiringly at Philip.

"When *is* his birthday, Pax?"

She shrugged. "I don't know."

"Didn't it say in his papers? No, of course it didn't. How could it?"

Philip got up from his chair, stuck his hands in his pockets, and began to pace up and down.

"Couldn't we give him one, Phil?" she said.

He stopped pacing abruptly and sat down again. He ran his fingers through his light brown hair and smiled at her. "Well, what one will we give him?"

She thought for a moment. "Too bad we didn't think of it when he was home. We could have made it Christmas, couldn't we? I mean, it would be so easy to remember—" She didn't finish her sentence and a little pink crept into her cheeks. "Oh! I forgot for a minute. We couldn't give him that day, could we? He's a —"

"That's not the point!" he cut in. "The point is that it's a lousy birthday for kids. They only get one batch of presents. No fair. Think of another."

"Well . . ." She cupped her chin in her hand and pondered for a moment. "Do they have birthdays of saints—I mean, prophets or anything—in the Jewish religion?"

"I don't know," he said shortly. "Let's stay away from holidays and give him a holiday of his own. Poor little bastard!"

"Oh, damn," she said. "It's kind of frightening to have to give somebody a birthday. It's like playing at being God, don't you think? It scares me."

"Go on, lady. Take a number from one to ten." He pulled up one cuff and then the other. "You see, I have nothing up my sleeve—"

"Shut up, Phil. I've got to pick a date that I'll remember. That's why I thought about holidays, don't you see? I have an awful time remembering all the ones I have to remember. When's your birthday, Phil?"

"I forget. Besides, that ain't no holiday," he said. "What's Bob's?"

She deliberated a moment. "Why, it's the—it's the—er—twenty-eighth or twenty-ninth—" She paused. "It's the twenty-eighth of July."

"Well, how's about that one? Bob's getting too old for birthdays."

"No," she said positively, "that wouldn't be a good one. Why, Jan doesn't even know Robert yet. Want another drink?"

She reached for his glass.

"Yeah, I think I will. You took me at my word when I said make it weak." His eyes followed her slow, graceful walk across the room. "What's Jake's?"

She wheeled around quickly and faced him, and her eyes were warm and bright. "May seventh," she said without a moment's hesitation.

A muscle in his cheek rippled and he looked at her steadily. "Well?" he said.

"I'll write Jan tomorrow. He'll like that date."

He took the glass she was offering him. "Thanks, kid," he said.

19

At the beginning of lunch hour, Henry Adams walked hurriedly from his classroom and turned into the corridor that led to Dr. Miller's study. He stopped abruptly as he saw the door open and the headmaster come out, closing it behind him.

"Hello, Adams," Miller said amiably, "were you coming along to see me?"

"Well, yes, I was. Could you give me a few moments, Dr. Miller?"

"Is it important?" asked Miller.

"Well, yes, it is, rather."

"Hmm. Thursday's my early morning class, you know, and I don't mind admitting that the inner man's feeling a bit neglected. You sure it can't wait until this afternoon?"

"I suppose it could, sir," replied Adams, "but I'd appreciate it if you could give me five minutes now."

Miller sighed, opened the door again, and let the young man pass in ahead of him. "As I passed the kitchen a half hour ago, I thought I smelled a good Irish stew. Sit down, Adams. Cigarette?"

"Thank you."

Adams took one, lighted it, and put it in a long black cigarette holder which he always carried in his waistcoat pocket.

"Well, old man, what's worrying you?"

"It's about Lyttleton, Doctor."

"Oh. What's the young feller done now?"

"Oh, he hasn't done anything, sir. He's a fine lad. It's just that—er—well, er—I'd like to try him in algebra, sir."

His face flushed a little, and his long slim fingers drummed nervously on the arm of his chair.

"You can't be serious, my dear fellow. The boy's only been here four months. He can't even speak English correctly. Next thing we know, you'll be suggesting trigonometry and calculus."

"I realize, Doctor, that it would seem utterly ridiculous to push the average boy ahead so quickly, but young Lyttleton isn't an average boy." Adams' smile was sweet and a little condescending.

Henry Adams was a Harvard graduate, a scholarship man. Miller knew very little about him except that he seemed a bit of a snob and didn't mix too well with the other teachers in the school. He did his job well, and was a great favorite with the younger boys, but somehow Miller always felt a little uneasy when he was with him.

He watched him now, with a rather calculating eye, as the young man sat there, smoking serenely, and he wondered if Jan were really as clever as his instructor believed, or if the boy were just the latest one he'd chosen to bestow his favor upon.

"Of course, my dear fellow, he's your responsibility and you must do as you think best with him, but I wouldn't push him too fast if I were you."

Adams gracefully tossed back a lock of his fair hair which was always falling over his forehead, and his voice became animated and confidential. "I may be wrong, Doctor, but I really believe the boy's a genius," he said. "At least, he is in my subject. Even when he doesn't quite understand my explanations, the moment he sees figures on paper, he seems to have an extraordinary acquaintance with them. His mind works logically and swiftly. Did you tell me he is the grandson of the late President Gifford of Mapleton?" he added.

"Hardly, my dear fellow. Lyttleton is the married name of Gifford's daughter. I presume you haven't overlooked the boy's accent?" Miller added a little sarcastically. "His mother was a Pole."

"Ah!" said Adams, "I thought for a moment he might have inherited the intellect of his grandfather."

"You believe in heredity?" asked the headmaster.

"Naturally. Don't you?"

"I can't say that I do, entirely. If genius springs from heredity, I find it very difficult to account for the Lincolns and the Einsteins and the English butcher boys who sing with the voices of angels and the majesty of God."

"But then you see, sir—if I may say so—you're a mystic; I'm a logician."

Henry Adams rose, delicately extricated the butt of his cigarette from the holder, and crushed it out in the ashtray. "Then I may enter him in my alegbra class?" he said, as he turned at the door.

"By all means," said Miller, with a suspicion of a twinkle in his eye, "but I wouldn't bother too much about Lyttleton's heredity if I were you, Adams. I'm quite sure you'll find that he isn't in any way related to the Curies."

He followed Adams out of the door, closed it, and stood there a moment, watching the slight figure move languidly along the corridor. He determinedly put out of his mind a troublesome thought that had slipped into it. Of one thing he was convinced, the fellow's conduct and manners had always been exemplary. After all, he'd be pleased and excited himself if the grubby little caterpillar came out of his chrysalis a brilliant butterfly.

He sniffed avidly, and let his nostrils lead him in the direction of the dining room.

There was no sound in the classroom except for that of the chalk moving swiftly back and forth across the blackboard. Jan stood with his back to the room, his feet planted firmly on the floor, his back straight and his head high, concentrating with all his might on the problem he was solving for the rest of the class, all of whom were two or three years older than he.

Henry Adams watched him with a faint smile on his face, as Jan, taking the shortest way, went directly and surely to the solution.

Jan had changed, even in the three months following the Christmas holidays. He'd grown a good inch, his chest had filled out, and his face was noticeably rounder. The hair, of course, or the lack of it, made a great difference. Apparently Stinky Powell had done a complete job on his head. He'd shaved it closely, and at the moment it seemed to be sprouting little brown bristles.

Jan finished his problem, put the chalk in the groove at the bottom of the board, and turned around and faced the class.

"Good work, Lyttleton," said Adams. "Now do you think you can explain to the class just how you arrived at that solution?"

A puzzled expression appeared on Jan's face, and Adams had to repeat his question. Jan wasn't used to concentrating on more than one thing at a time and at the moment he was steadily watching a large gawky boy of sixteen, who was obviously trying to signal something to him.

Reluctantly, he turned to the blackboard and haltingly explained how he arrived at his final figure, and then, with his instructor's permission, started for his desk.

As he passed the tall boy with whom he had only a "hello" acquaintance, a crumpled-up piece of paper was slipped into his hand. He sat down, and with one eye on Adams he smoothed it out under the desk and read: "Meet me after class down by the main gate. Say nothing to anyone. Come alone. P. Lawson."

Jan crumpled it up again as noiselessly as he could and slipped it into his pocket. He thought for a moment of chewing it up and swallowing it, as he had seen it done many times in his earlier years, but decided against it. He'd be sure to be right in the middle of it and Mr. Adams would ask him a question; besides, it was a pretty big piece of paper and it was thick.

The three-o'clock gong rang through the building, and the boys began to gather up their books and papers.

"Just a minute, fellows." Adams had risen and was standing behind his desk. "I think you'll all like to know that your young classmate, Jan Lyttleton, will start a course in algebra on Monday."

Adams smiled with satisfaction. There were a few feeble hand claps and one or two "Yeah?"s and the boys scrambled out of the classroom, mumbling their "Good afternoon, sir"s.

Jan seemed not to have heard Adams. He was moving faster toward the door than any of them. The disappointment on the thin boyish face of the teacher was very apparent. Knowing the boy's ambition in mathematics, he had thought his announcement would have been responded to with great excitement, but he saw that Jan was obviously preoccupied. As Jan passed him, he caught him by the arm. "Well, boy?"

"Sir-r-r?"

"I've promoted you again. What have you got to say to that?" he asked eagerly.

"Tank you, sir-r-r."

He threw Adams a hurried good-by and ran out of the room and up to his dormitory.

Ten minutes later, Jan, in his heavy coat, tasseled woolen cap, scarf, and mittens, strolled carelessly across the snow-covered lawn in front of the school. He lifted his feet high, as with each step he cracked through the dry, crisp layer of snow and went in up to his ankles. From time to time, he threw a sly glance over his shoulder to see if anyone was watching him.

When he reached the big iron gates, there was no one to be seen. He turned around slowly, in a complete circle, peering in every direction, but all he could see was an unbroken expanse of white and the bare leafless tree branches, silhouetted against the dove-gray sky.

Then, to the right of the gates and close to the fence, he noticed some freshly made tracks in the snow, making a faint path toward the gymnasium. Suddenly, in the stillness, he heard a hissing sound, and then a long, low whistle. He looked in the direction from which he thought it came.

Twenty or thirty yards along the erratic path made by the tracks in the snow, he saw a large bush, and peering from behind it the round,

204

ruddy face of Peter Lawson. Peter waved, then beckoned, and Jan plunged ahead toward him, trying to make his feet fit in the footprints made previously by Peter.

When Jan reached him, Peter put his mittened finger to his lips, his wide blue eyes peering stealthily in every direction.

"What iss dis? Something has happened, no?" whispered Jan.

"Sh-sh!" Peter whispered back, and, motioning Jan to follow, he led him along another path in the direction of a tool shed. Jan looked bewildered, but followed.

When they got there, Peter pushed open the door slowly. The rusty hinges squeaked ominously, and they stood still, like two small graven images, listening. When Peter was satisfied that they were still undetected, he pushed Jan in and shut the door.

Peter slipped the latch home, took off his cap and scarf, and put his mittens in his coat pocket. Jan did the same; then both boys climbed up on an old carpenter's horse and straddled it, facing each other.

"You tell me, Peter," said Jan coaxingly. "You have done someting? You have killed someone, maybe?"

"What's the matter with you, Jan? You crazy?" Peter said in a withering tone. "It's just that I've got something awful important to tell you, and I'm not supposed to."

"You tell me, Peter," demanded Jan eagerly.

Here was something he could understand. For him, to slip into the realms of concealment and under-cover plotting was like putting on an old shoe.

Peter lowered his voice and he leaned toward Jan with an air of great mystery. "Did you ever hear of the Skull and Dagger?"

Jan shook his head in bewilderment.

"Well," said Peter solemnly, "it's a secret society!"

"Secret society? What iss dis?"

"It's a club. You know what a club is."

"Sur-r-e," replied Jan, "it iss a bat."

Peter looked disgusted. "Aw! Not that kind of a club, dope!" he said. "You see, a secret society is like—is like—well, it's like when fellers get together—fellers like Jonathan and me and Stinky and Dickie Jones and—oh, lots of fellers! And it's secret, see? And—and we do all kinds of things—of course, I can't tell you what yet—and nobody knows but us!"

He turned his head and listened; then he put his finger to his lips again, jumped down, and peeked out of the one small-paned window. "Did you hear a noise?" he said suspiciously.

"No."

He crawled back on the horse and wriggled a little closer to Jan. "Here's what I want to tell you," he whispered mysteriously. "Cross your heart and hope to die you won't tell?"

Jan looked perplexed. "I do not hope to die," he said, and then he added proudly, "but I do not tell."

"Well, I've proposed you to be a member of the Skull and Dagger, see? The next meeting is Saturday night when everybody else is in bed. They'll put it to a vote, whether you'll be let in. Maybe you will and maybe you won't."

"Let in?" asked Jan with a little scowl. "Dat iss easy, no? But will I be let out?"

"Let out of where?" demanded Peter.

"I don't know," replied Jan.

"Oh, never mind," said Peter impatiently. "You remember, tomorrow night is Supper Club night, don't you? That's why I had to talk to you today. How much money have you got?"

"I don't know. You want money?"

"No, I don't want it. Listen, Jan. You got to get all the money you can together, and you got to bring the biggest box of candy you can buy, see?"

"Where I buy it?"

"Ask old Adams to buy it for you when he goes into the village tomorrow. He'll do it for you. He likes you best."

"Why I bring dis candy?"

" 'Cause then they'll think you're a great guy, see? And they'll let you in easier, see?"

Jan was pulling at a bent nail that was embedded in the horse. He reached over and picked up a hammer that was lying on a shelf within arm's reach and began to hammer at the nail.

"Sh-sh!" warned Peter. "Don't make so much noise! Somebody'll hear!"

"Nobody to hear," said Jan disdainfully.

"Well, will you do it?"

Jan shrugged. "Maybe," he said.

Peter suddenly got an idea. He yanked Jan off the horse and over to the window. He pulled up his sleeve and pushed back the wrist watch he was wearing.

"Look!" he said, and he pointed to something that was drawn with an indelible pencil and which previously had been hidden by his watch. "If the fellers let you belong," he said triumphantly, "you can wear one like this. See? That's a skull, and that line over it's a dagger."

Jan peered at it, hesitated a moment, then whipped off his coat and

206

the jacket under it. He rolled up his shirt sleeve and pointed to a spot just above his wrist—the spot he always kept covered with his right hand when his arms were bare.

"I got one, too," he said.

Peter examined it intently and his blue eyes widened. "Gee!" he exclaimed.

Jan reached for Peter's wrist and inspected his mark thoughtfully. "Dey hur-rt you when dey make dis—what you call—skull?" he asked.

"Naw," said Peter, "I did it myself with an indelible pencil."

"Dis one hur-rt," said Jan simply, pointing to the tattooed brand on his own arm.

"Mine's not supposed to come off, but it does. Then I draw another."

"Mine not come off," boasted Jan. "Look! You spit on it. It stay, see?"

Peter wet his finger, touched the mark with it, then rubbed it hard with the elbow of his coat. The branded flesh was as livid as before.

"Gee!" he said again. "Who drew it?"

"Bad men," said Jan quietly.

"Gee whiz! Did you ever see so many numbers!" Peter exclaimed. "What's the 'O' for?"

"Oświęciem."

"What's that?"

"Dat iss where I live," Jan replied calmly.

"Is that a city?" inquired Peter. "Where is it?"

"I don't know," Jan replied with his usual shrug. "Not a city. It iss jail—what you call—camp. Tousands of pipple!"

"A concentration camp?" breathed Peter, his eyes dark with awe.

"Sur-re." Jan put on his jacket and his overcoat. "Come, Peter," he said, "we go now. I try to get candy."

"Wait a minute, Jan," pleaded the other boy. "What was it like—the concentration camp, I mean? Come on, tell me, will yuh?"

Jan frowned, and started for the door.

"Aw, come on! Will yuh?"

He pulled Jan down on the floor beside him, and they sat under the window, their backs against the wall. Peter drew his knees up and clasped his arms around them.

"Was it bad, Jan?" he asked breathlessly.

"Bad?" said Jan, "Oh, yes, ver-ry bad. Kill—kill— Always kill pipple. Cannot get away. Fences made of wire. You touch—you are dead!"

"Where was your mother and father? Why did they let you go to a place like that?"

"My mudder was dere wit me. We *live* dere," Jan said. "Not remem-

207

ber my fadder. Remember my mudder. She always hide me, under-r her skirt, under-r bed, under-r—how you say, bar-rrel. All de same, I see ever-ryting, and I am always scar-red. One day, my mudder, she get big belly—she get another baby, I tink. Dey take her away wit udder pipple, in a big van. She iss bur-rned in oven."

Peter's small face was aghast with horror. "Did you *see* them burn her?"

"How do I see her? I am not in oven! I hide! But I know. De days dey bur-rn pipple, it smell nasty." And he made a grimace.

Then, it seemed, Jan couldn't stop.

It was as if a dam had burst inside him, and the description of the incredible, monstrous horrors he had seen poured from him. All the things Pax dreaded but wanted to hear, so she could pity him and love him, Jan told to his new friend. Beatings; his terror of vicious dogs; hangings; the griping agony of hunger and his constantly distended little belly—on and on and on.

The pale rays of the setting winter sun straggled through the window of the shed, and still he talked.

"One day, dey put many *Jude* in little wooden house and den dey burn house. Dese pipple scream and scream and scream! Dey got big horns in camp and sometime dey play music loud so you not hear screams, but I hear. One day I look tr-rough fence—I do not touch—I see many pipple dig in de ground. Dey dig and dig and dig. I hear bang! bang! You know, all dese pipple fall in hole? Den, dese bad men dig—same place—and put dir-rt on. Dese bad men are Ger-rmans, see? Everybody die, except you hide—like me. You get spots; dey kill. You go crazy; dey kill. I know! I hear Olga talk."

"Who is Olga?"

"She iss my friend. She is *blocova* in camp."

"What's that?"

"Well, it iss like dis. Here iss one Ger-rman man. He like Olga ver-ry much. She iss big and pr-retty and nice. Dey don't kill Olga! Not much!" he said proudly. "She get mor-re food dan de udders. She give me her food." He laughed grimly. "When dese bad men come, she hide me in hole she make in ground and put big piece of wood on top. Dey not find me ever-r! Den, one day, dere iss bangbangbang! outside de camp. All Ger-rmans run away. We run, too, Olga and me. Den we go to lots of camps—oh, for long time. Good camps. Nobody kill nobody. We eat more. Dat iss better, no?"

Peter began to sniffle. "Oh, Jan!" he whimpered.

"Why you cry? I do not cry."

208

"Where is Olga now?"

"I do not know," Jan replied sadly. "She go away. Home—not de camp!" he added hastily.

Jan got to his feet, stretched his arms way above his head, and yawned as if he were just waking up from a long sleep.

"We go back now. I am hungry. Come on." He wound his scarf around his throat, put on his cap and mittens, and buttoned up his coat. "You come on, Peter. It will get dar-rk soon."

Peter stood up and stared at Jan.

"You want to walk back to de house alone?" asked Jan.

"What?"

"You are afr-raid dese skulls see you wit me?"

"Naw!" said Peter proudly.

They closed the door behind them. Peter led the way, pushing under a clump of bushes that grew in front of the tool shed. "We can cut across here. It's shorter."

"No," replied Jan, "we go over to de road. Not so much snow, and hard. Den I race you."

"All right."

They crawled back through the bushes and along the little path they had made a couple of hours before. When they got to the road Jan looked at his friend and smiled.

"R-ready! Get set!" cried Jan. "One! Two! Tr-ree! Go!" And he was off like a flash, easily outdistancing the other boy.

Gasping for breath, Jan waited for Peter on the front steps. As Peter approached a few seconds later, Jan jumped up and down with excitement. "I beat you! I beat you!" he crowed.

Peter climbed the steps slowly. When he got to the top, he looked at Jan and put out his hand like a man. Jan took it, but he was puzzled by the expression on the other youngster's face. He leaned toward him and whispered, "Someday, Peter, you will go wit me while I find Olga, no?"

Peter nodded.

"Now I go get my money and I ask Mr. Adam get me dis candy, so I can be a skull like you."

"I got some money left over from my allowance, Jan. You can have it. Then you can buy the biggest box they have."

Peter Lawson stared with admiration at his best friend. He was more than his best friend now. He was a hero.

BOOK THREE

20

A FLUTTER of suppressed excitement spread through the little town of Mapleton.

Within an hour or two after Lucien, the old station master, had received the message which had been tapped out to him in his telegraph office, the news had traveled like wildfire through the community. Tim Clancy had bounced in and out of shops and houses with his news, and the small town reminisced on street corners and beside their hearths as though Lyttleton were a native son.

Through the war, they had heard of each act of heroism, each decoration and promotion in rank, until this man, who had spent most of his adult life in Mapleton, this campus hero, had become their war hero.

And so, two years and seven months after the world laid down its arms—temporarily—a postwar scene was being re-enacted as if it were being viewed through the wrong end of a telescope.

Even Amy recalled the days when Bob Lyttleton occupied her two best rooms; Em became coyly sentimental over the first time he had asked her to a prom; Philip wondered cynically why the hero had chosen a series of connecting trains that would bring him in at Mapleton instead of a direct train to Burlington, then cursed himself for the unfriendly question.

Pax shook with excitement; Pansy sniveled blissfully; Tubby, of course, was imbued with the general infection but wondered why he couldn't remember exactly what his father looked like.

And Jan Lyttleton—nee ben Rozov—in Manchester, remained comfortably unaware of the great event.

At ten minutes to five on the afternoon following the arrival of the telegram, cars were drawn up at the station side by side like sardines, and many of Lyttleton's acquaintances and most of his friends were on the platform, waiting for the afternoon train. The Bascomb crowd were in a huddle, passing back and forth between them a quart-sized flask of Bill's.

213

Pax, Tubby, Amy, and Philip were together, Pax keeping an anxious eye on her son, who, she was afraid, might fall onto the tracks in his excitement. Only Pansy was missing. She was preparing for a cocktail party at the house—Pax had hurriedly planned it; besides, as she told Pax, she preferred to greet her returning family privately.

Leaning against the west corner of the little wooden building was a woman quite remote from the others. Jeannine Leclerc, carrying a small bunch of red roses and a package which looked suspiciously like a bottle, stood alone, looking in the direction from which the train would come.

From a distance, the faint sound of a train whistle was heard. For a moment there was an expectant silence and then the noise began again. From the station door came old Lucien, his inevitable, unlighted lantern in his hand, and waved the people back from the edge of the platform.

Pax tighted her hold on Tubby's hand, Philip took a firm grip on Luke's collar, and Jeannine straightened up and shaded her eyes with her hand.

The train chugged up to the station and stopped with a jerk. The door of the third coach opened and a conductor, with a valise in one hand and an army coat over his arm, got down from the coach; then he turned and helped a tall man in uniform who descended slowly with the aid of a crutch, hopping down, step by step, on one foot.

On his shoulder he wore the single star of a brigadier general, and his broad chest was covered with War Theater ribbons and decorations. He settled his crutch comfortably under his right arm, took off his overseas cap, and the late afternoon sun glinted on his fair hair.

There was a general rush in his direction, but his blue eyes searched the length and breadth of the platform looking eagerly for Pax, who was pushing her way through the crowd with Tubby clutching her hand.

He heard her voice above the noisy greetings, and then she was in his arms. He held her close for a long moment, then he handed her his crutch, leaned down, and picked his son up in his arms. He gave him a great hug, whispered something in his ear, then put him down. Tubby pressed himself close to his father's side and proudly watched the others welcome the returning soldier.

Finally the crowd began to thin out, and Bob made his way limping to the car. Philip helped him into the front seat and lifted Tubby in beside him; he and Amy got in the back with Luke.

As Pax climbed into the driver's seat and put her foot on the self-starter, Jeannine Leclerc suddenly appeared and came smilingly up to Bob's side of the car. Pax, who did not remember ever having actually

214

seen Jeannine smile broadly before, was a little surprised to realize how lovely the woman was.

Bob quickly rolled down the window, and leaned out and kissed her. "God bless my soul! Jeannine! How are you? Still a beaut, aren't you?" He grinned. "For me?" he asked, as she thrust the package and the roses into his hand.

"Red roses for remembrance," she said gaily, "and have a drink on me."

He thanked her and she turned to go, but Pax called her back.

"We're having a little cocktail party at the house, Jeannine. The rest of the cars are going to follow us. Won't you come along with us and have a drink with Col—" She stopped short, as Bob pointed to the star on his tunic and grinned like a kid. "Oh, my goodness!" Pax laughed, her eyes widening with excitement. "With *General* Lyttleton, upon my word."

"Thank you," replied Jeannine. Her head was high and her tone was not friendly. "I can't leave the store so long."

"Oh, come along, Jeannine. Help us give him a real bang-up welcome."

Jeannine again flashed her smile at Bob. "So long, Bob, I'll be seeing you."

"Oh, Jeannine," he called. "How's Johnnie?"

"He's fine," she said laconically, and was gone.

Bob pulled his son close to him and smiled at Pax. "Home, James!"

She smiled back at him, threw the car into gear, and they were off, the other cars following in a long procession.

The car rolled around the circle in back of the station, out onto the road, and across the tracks. For a few minutes that silence which usually follows a sudden cessation of excitement descended on them and no one spoke. It was broken by Tubby, who began fingering the decorations on his father's tunic.

"What's this for, Pop?" he asked, pulling at a small bronze star which was attached to a ribbon.

"I was a good boy and came home safely as I was told," replied Bob carelessly. "Hey, will you look at old Clancey's filling station? What did the old mick do? Buy the whole block?"

"Gee, Pop! This blue one's pretty. What did you get that for?"

"Shootin' a cow off an aerodrome."

"Aw, Pop!"

Bob rumpled the boy's hair and then looked eagerly out of the window. "Papa Leclerc's! Looks just the same, doesn't it? Is that old feller still alive?"

"Sure he's alive," said Pax, "but he doesn't spend as much time in the store as he used to. Jeannine and her bar seem to have pretty much taken over in the last couple of years."

"How was the flight?" asked Philip. "I take it you did fly?"

"Yeah. Sat down at Gander. It was all right for army transportation. Not much room to park a bum leg, though. I was sure glad when I hit that Ritz bed last night in Boston. I didn't have to be rocked to sleep, I can tell you."

"Oh, darling, what a thoughtless pig I am!" said Pax remorsefully. "I never asked you about your leg. Or your arm, either. Was it awful? Does it still hurt much?"

Bob stretched his leg out straight until it touched the partition in front of him. "Take a look!" he said proudly.

Pax took her eyes away from the road for a moment and gave him a quick smile. "You look whole to me."

Philip laughed. "Yeah, she's pretty cocky about it now. You should have seen her, Lyttleton, when the telegram arrived from the War Department. You'd have been ashamed of her. She didn't act much like a soldier's wife, did she, Sanders?"

"Shut up, Phil," said Pax.

"She certainly didn't," said Amy. "We had quite a time with her for about twenty-four hours. It was like trying to quiet a calliope at full steam."

"Just love, darling. Pay no attention."

Bob put his hand on her knee and pressed it.

They reached the top of the hill and swung around the Green.

"There she is, God bless her!" said Bob sentimentally, and he rolled the window down again, leaned out, and saluted. "Good old Alma Mater!"

"Should auld acquaintance be forgot—" sang Philip softly.

Pax threw him a reproachful look over her shoulder.

"We're home, Pop! We're home!" shouted Tubby, and he wiggled around in the seat until he was on his knees. "Gee! Look at all the cars!"

They helped Bob out and gave him his crutch. One by one, the cars behind them stopped, pulling up in front and behind the Lyttleton car. Tubby opened the gate and waved them in. Bob led the way, leaning on Pax's shoulder, and the gay procession made its way up the graveled walk and into the house.

The hero had come home.

The old house which had drowsed away so many years awoke with a start as its square Victorian rooms filled with people. Fires crackled in the library, the dining room, and the staid, uncomfortable parlor; there were flowers everywhere—flowers from the Burlington florist—a buffet supper in the dining room, and an improvised bar in the library.

The men made straight for the bar, some of the women dashed upstairs to powder their noses, and Pax went into the large hall closet to hang up her coat. The closet was dimly lighted by a small window high up in the outside wall, and the daylight was fading quickly. As Pax felt her way toward a hook, she heard the door close softly and the sound of something scraping against the wall. She couldn't see anything but she felt two strong arms around her and Robert's voice whispered, "Hello!"

"Hello, my darling," she answered.

He kissed her eyelids, her throat, and her wide, warm mouth. She wound her arms around his neck and her slim body relaxed against his like a tired child.

"You're home! I've got you back! It's been a long nightmare without you, darling," she said, her mouth against his ear. "It's such fun waking up!"

"Do they have to stay long?" he said.

"Who's they?"

"Those dear friends of ours—damn 'em!"

Pax laughed contentedly. "Don't you want to be social, sweet?" she asked, pressing closer to him. "War's over! And we've got a whole lifetime to be together."

"We've got eight years to catch up with!" He found her mouth again.

"And if we don't get out of here, we won't have eight years," she said, struggling out of his arms. "We'll be smothered! Let me out of here, or I'll scream for help!"

Bob laughed, loosened his hold on her, and felt for his crutch. "All right, out and at 'em!" he said, opening the door and starting to limp toward the library.

"Hey!" she called. "Haven't you forgotten something?"

"What?"

"There's another member of your family who's been waiting many years for this moment!"

His brows pulled together and he looked at her inquiringly. Pax tipped her head in the direction of the kitchen. "Had you forgotten Pansy?" she said reproachfully.

"Oh, damn!"

He limped toward the kitchen and opened the door softly. Pax followed and pressed herself against the wall where she could hear the welcome and not be seen.

Pansy had her back to him, stirring something on the stove.

"Atten*shun*! 'Bout face!" he shouted in his most military tone.

Pansy wheeled around and looked at him. A wide smile spread over her face and she wiped her hands on her apron.

"Mr. Bobbie! Mr. Bobbie!"

Her voice broke and she dabbed her eyes with the corner of her apron as she came toward him.

"How are you, Pansy?"

"God be praised!" exclaimed Pansy. "He's brought our boy back! Began to think I'd never live to see this day! Look at yuh! All smashed up and everything! Never could take care o' yourself!"

She stretched out both hands to him, but he held on to his crutch with his right hand and extended his left.

"It's good to see you, Pansy, good to see you," he said. "What's the matter with you? Are you crying, you silly nigger?"

The colored woman's smile slowly faded; she frowned, and a puzzled expression crept into her black eyes.

Outside in the hall, Pax was a little puzzled, too. Surely she'd never heard Robert use the word "nigger" before! Funny—

"No, Mr. Bobbie, I ain't cryin'. Is you all right, Mr. Bobbie?"

"Sure I'm all right," he said cheerfully, "and I'll have you know, woman, that I'm no 'Mister'! Look at that star! I'm a general. What do you think of that?"

"My! My! Ain't we gettin' up in the world?"

"Have you behaved yourself since I've been away?"

Pansy stared at him for a long moment. "Glad to see you back, Mr. General—sir." And she quietly turned her back on her boy and went back to the stove.

Pax stood in the open doorway with Bob's overseas coat around her shoulders, waving off the last guest. It wasn't very late. She had heard the church clock strike eleven several minutes before, but it seemed to her as if the party had been going on for days.

It had been a gay one, stretching into supper and bridge and gin rummy—and a great deal of liquor.

About ten o'clock, due to the high tension of excitement, Bob had suddenly become exhausted. Pax had pleaded with him to go to bed, but he had refused stubbornly. She finally induced him to lie down on the couch, so that he could at least relax; she loosened his collar and tie, and eventually he fell off to sleep. He didn't even hear his guests leave.

Pax switched off the porch light and went into the parlor. Wearily, she took one look at the messy card tables, the empty glasses, and the

218

ashtrays filled with dead cigarette butts, and with a sense of guilt decided to leave them for the morning.

She turned off the light, went into the library, and stood beside the couch, looking down at Bob. His face was flushed, his lids fluttered now and then as though he were dreaming, and the waves in his fair hair swept back from his forehead, which was wet with perspiration.

Pax dropped on her knees beside the couch. Perhaps she should put another cover on him, open the windows, and leave him there for the night, for he was sleeping as peacefully as a child. But she hadn't really seen him yet; it was his first night home. She'd wait a little longer.

Suddenly he stirred and opened his eyes. He yawned, stretched, and reached for her hand. "It was so still, it woke me," he said lazily. "Beautiful sleep, baby!"

"I'm glad, darling."

"Everybody gone?"

"Yes."

"Thank God!"

He pressed her hand over his lips. "I'd forgotten how beautiful you are!"

"Sweet!"

"I love you, darling! It's been complete hell without you."

"Me, too!"

He pulled her face down to him and kissed her long on the mouth. Then he chuckled softly.

"What's the matter?"

"Why can't a feller think of beautiful things to say to his girl?"

She smoothed his damp hair and looked deep into his eyes. "Because 'love' is the tops, darling. It isn't words I've been homesick for!"

"Do you love me as much as before?"

"Before what?" She smiled.

"Before I stayed away so long?"

"I think so."

"No other guy?"

"What do you think?"

"Do you know, I'd forgotten how beautiful you are?"

"You said that before."

"I know. But I just want to say it over and over."

"O-o-oh! That Southern charm! What about you?"

He stretched and put his good arm under his head. "What about me what?"

"I bet you just devastated those starved *Fräuleins* over there!"

219

"That'll be the day," he said easily. "You know, baby, I keep thinking about that first glimpse of our town."

"*Our* town?" She laughed.

"My town, now. Forever and a day."

"I'm glad, darling."

"You know, it was a shock," he continued.

"Mapleton? Why? It hasn't changed."

"That's why it was a shock. You know, honey, you get so used to seeing places all smashed up. I've been flying over rubble and desolation all through Europe. Then I get off the train, and there she be! This smug little New England town, lolling on the side of a hill—same shops, same houses. The same faces—not much older than when I left, perhaps a little better fed."

"You're just used to seeing thin ones," said Pax.

"That's what I mean. I bet they don't even remember there's been a war!"

Pax suddenly bristled. "Does it occur to you—General, sir—that our guys here came home from the war over two years ago?"

"Don't get mad, baby. That's not what I mean—"

"I'm not mad! They remember all right! Maybe their memories aren't as vivid as yours, but they remember what they fought for, all right!"

Robert pulled himself up on one elbow. "They remember, but they don't *know*. I talked to a lot of them tonight."

"I don't understand you, Robert. What don't they know?"

"They haven't waked up to the fact yet that we fought the wrong guys!"

Pax looked puzzled. "What are you talking about, darling?"

"We know it over there. The British know it, too."

"Know what, Robert?"

"Those God-damned Bolshies! God damn 'em! The only people who are wise enough to know who our real enemy is are the Germans! They fought 'em! They're still fighting 'em and sooner or later we've got to help 'em finish 'em up!"

"Robert, don't get so excited, dear. The war's over, remember?"

"Over, is it? What do you people living in this whistle stop know about it? I've been living with 'em—"

"Stop it, darling. You've come home to forget all that."

"Sorry, baby. I guess I'm just tired."

"Of course you are. Let's you and me have one little drink together, now that the crowd's all gone. It'll relax you."

She crossed over to the untidy bar.

"And then bed?" he asked.

She smiled at him tenderly. "And then bed. And no more politics or you'll get yourself all excited and you won't sleep."

"Who wants to sleep?" He grinned.

She sat down on the couch beside him and tucked one hand under his arm. "What do you think of your son?"

Bob smiled proudly. "Some kid, huh?"

"He's exactly like you, the little stinker!"

"Thanks most awfully," he said with a fake English accent.

Pax laughed and kissed him.

"He looks wonderful, baby, but you know that was another shock. He's the first kid I've seen who looks fat and husky."

"I know, darling."

"Don't get me wrong, Pax. I'm delighted. But I've been so used to those poor skinny little bastards. You ought to see 'em, baby. They pick over our garbage pails in back of the Post!"

"I know, darling," she said. "It's awful! But don't let's think any more about it tonight. Let's think about you and me. It's been so long, my darling."

She bent over and nuzzled her head in his chest. He raised her chin and looked at her.

"Look at me, baby! Look at me with those beautiful yellow cat's eyes of yours, and tell me if you've wanted me as much as I've wanted you."

The amber eyes filled with those ever-ready tears, and she nodded her head vigorously. He held her close and his mouth groped for hers. "Then what are we waiting for?" he whispered. "Come on, darling, let's go upstairs."

Ding—dong—ding—dong. Dong—ding—ding—dong. Ding—ding—ding—dong. Dong—dong—ding—dong.

One.

Two.

Three.

And Pax hadn't closed her eyes.

She had changed to the side of the bed that she wasn't used to, so that Robert could have his bad leg on the outside. But that wasn't the reason she couldn't sleep. It was because her brain was on a merry-go-round.

Robert slept on her breast like a baby, his right arm thrown over her. She was getting numb, but she was afraid she'd disturb him if she moved. She turned her head uneasily on the pillow.

She was almost perfectly happy. Lord, that was rotten grammar.

Robert was home; he was safe; and she wouldn't have to be lonely any more. Why that "almost"?

Something wasn't quite the way she had hoped it would be.

It wasn't that sudden outburst of Robert's that it had been wrong to fight the Germans. It was understandable that he should have absorbed that idea living a quiet, administrative life in an occupied country governed by its conquerors. It was easy to imagine how the Germans had tried to ingratiate themselves with their captors. A remote view would probably change all that. And she had been touched by his concern for the starved kids in Europe. She could understand that. She had a refugee of her own—

That was it! That was the moment she should have told Robert about Jan. But she hadn't. She'd missed the boat. Why hadn't she? Was she afraid to? Afraid when she'd seen Robert worrying over the fate of those youngsters over there? Nonsense!

It was something else. He hadn't mentioned Jake.

Well, she hadn't either. Why hadn't she? Had she forgotten him, too? Of course she hadn't! It was just that tonight belonged to her and Robert. No room tonight for anyone else in the world.

There was always tomorrow. Tomorrow and tomorrow and tomorrow! Who had said that? Her father, of course—and someone else. Was it Shakespeare?

Ding—dong—ding—dong—

Gently she pulled her arm out from under Robert's head. He didn't wake. She edged further over onto her side of the bed and tucked the small pillow under her ear.

Robert was home!

She sighed.

21

"Peter!"

"What?"

"I will speak wit you."

Peter wandered over to Jan, who was leaning against the playground wall, scowling, his hands in his pockets, watching the other boys as they used up some of their pent-up energy during the recreation hour.

"Peter," said Jan, "you explain someting to me, no? Look, Peter, I have gave de candy, like you say, and I am not a Skull! Why is dis?"

Peter's round face began to redden, and he scuffled the dirt with his toe. "You got to wait, Jan. You got to wait for the vote, see? It'll be all right. You'll get in! I'm trying to fix it."

"So?" said Jan thoughtfully.

Peter changed the subject abruptly. "Jan, what do people do when they get shot?"

Jan frowned impatiently. "Dey fall down. How you fix it, Peter?"

"Gee!" exclaimed Peter. "Is there much blood?"

Jan stamped his foot. "Why you keep asking dese tings? I will not speak of dis! I will be a Skull or I want back my candy!"

"Don't be mad at me, Jan. I only asked because—"

Peter stopped suddenly and blinked his eyes hard. Then he turned on his heel and walked away. "Hey, Tony," he called to the boy who was waiting out in the center of the playground. "Catch!" Peter hurled the ball and ran well away from his friend as it was tossed back to him.

Jan's eyes followed him in great bewilderment; then he slowly walked back of the house toward the orchard.

All was not well in Jan's young life and he was beginning to brood. This little stoic, who had never reacted to anything beyond physical danger or his new material pleasures, was beginning to learn other values. He couldn't have explained it, but his naturally alert mind was slowly becoming aware of something called human behavior and the concessions of civilization, and he was confused.

The Supper Club had met, as planned, the night after his spontaneous burst of confidence in the tool shed. Jan put his five-pound box of chocolates in the middle of the circle and waited confidently. The assault on the box began, and Jan managed to get only two fat pieces, wrapped in their tiny brown ruffles, for himself. He rolled them around on his tongue, tasting their delicious sweetness as long as he could, wistfully eying the foragers as they grabbed the rest for themselves.

So far, everything had gone according to plan—the plan shrewdly laid out by Peter. Then everything slowed down. Jan and Peter, absurdly confident, waited for the vote that should make the former a member of the Skull and Dagger.

But nothing happened.

As yet, the disappointment of not having become a member of the secret society didn't worry him too much. It was the box of candy that rankled. He had given something for nothing and that he considered unjust.

223

Up until a year ago, he had serenely recognized and accepted perfidy. He had had to. He'd been all too familiar with the infamy of the German guards who ferreted out the weakness of internees to turn it against them and torture them for it; and he was aware of the treachery of some of the inmates who informed against their companions, in order to hold on desperately to a few weeks more of their pitiful lives.

But this was different. He had spent all the money he had left from his allowance and had borrowed the rest from Henry Adams to make a fair trade, and it hadn't been a fair trade.

Even in the concentration camps he had known, a sour crust of sodden black bread, snatched from some pile of refuse, had been exchanged for an extra bowl of watery rank soup.

Peter had planned it; Jan had followed it through, but somehow he felt he had been betrayed. It utterly confounded him.

Jan, clad in his pajamas and bathrobe, stood in the doorway and looked down the row of small white beds which ran the length of the dormitory. All of the boys in his section were in bed, some of them snoring softly. For a moment he stood on tiptoe, craning his neck to look at one particular bed. Peter was sound asleep, too, the covers tucked halfway over his head.

It seemed to Jan that the boys had all gone to sleep pretty quickly; he couldn't have been in the bathroom more than ten minutes.

He took off his robe and started to climb into bed, when he saw that there was a folded sheet of paper pinned to his pillow. He took out the pin, and in his bare feet he pattered along to the dim light at the other end of the dormitory and held the paper up. It was printed in large clumsy block letters and was unsigned.

SHOOT A JEW AND DROWN A NIGGER
POINT THE GUN AND PULL THE TRIGGER

What did that mean?

He glanced along the row of beds. Everything was unnaturally still. Thoughtfully he walked back to his bed, folded the paper, tucked it under his pillow, and got into bed. It didn't take him very long to go to sleep. He was healthily tired, and the rather hard school cot was still a luxury to him.

As for the childish, venomous verse, he didn't give it a second thought. In the first place, he didn't understand it. He just thought it was silly.

224

But there was one last thought which flashed through his head and with it came a dull sense of rage. That candy!

Then the heavy lids closed, the thin angry face relaxed, and he fell into a dreamless sleep. His young soul was at peace.

By the next day, Jan had almost forgotten it, but there was an uneasiness spreading through the junior section of the school. After school hours, the boys gathered in groups, and when Jan passed any of them, the whispering would cease suddenly, and heads abruptly turned away.

One morning, while he was dressing, he stuck his foot into his shoe and then quickly drew it out as something crackled under his toes. He smoothed it out on his knee. It was the same kind of paper as the one he had found on his pillow and it was the same awkward printing.

GROW HIS BEARD, THEN BURN THE JEW! AIN'T YOU GLAD IT ISN'T YOU?

There was a suppressed giggle from a few of the boys. Then they ran out, throwing Jan sly glances as they passed him. As the last one reached the door, Jan called to him. The boy hesitated, then slowly came back.

"What d'ya want?" he asked sullenly.

Jan folded the paper and spat on it. "Stinky," he said calmly, "you will tr-ow dis in de toilet, no? It is no good."

Then he went back to fastening his shoes.

After that, the verses made their appearance oftener and in the most unexpected places. He found them pinned inside his cap, under his plate at meal times, and, in the classroom, stuck in his schoolbooks between the pages of the day's lessons.

Jan made no comment, but he was beginning to get angry.

The next meeting of the Supper Club was canceled. But that night, when he went to bed, reposing right in the middle of it was his candy box, its red satin bow gleaming in the light of the one dim electric bulb.

For a moment he held his breath; then his small face beamed and he clutched the box to his breast and hugged it. He crawled up onto the bed and opened it.

One by one, he unwrapped layers of tissue paper until he came to the last. Slowly he lifted out of the box a little rag doll, made of a black sock stuffed with cotton wool. The doll's head was made of putty and crudely colored with crayons. It had a long hooked nose and a thick, outthrust underlip. It was bald except for a small skullcap, and two tufts of black wool were glued to each side of its head, with a long one on its chin. Tied to one of its wrists were three gilt beads, strung together to make a triangle, and pinned to its chest was another piece of the familiar paper.

Jan turned it round and round in his hand and then he read the paper. It wasn't a verse this time.

JUST TO KEEP YOU COMPANY BECAUSE YOU ARE GOING TO BE LONESOME.

There wasn't a sound in the dormitory.

Jan looked around with dull eyes. Then suddenly he ran out into the middle of the room, the doll clutched in one hand, the paper in the other.

"Wake up! Wake up! Pigs! Dogs! Get up!"

His voice was shrill and piercing and it quivered with rage.

There was an uneasy stirring in some of the beds.

"Get up! Get up! Or I kill you!" he screamed.

"Sh-sh!" whispered one of the boys. "You'll have 'em all in!"

"What I care!"

One by one the boys began to sit up or prop themselves up on their elbows. Two or three of the thirteen- or fourteen-year-olds stared at him for a moment and then their faces broke into derisive grins. The younger boys looked scared, and Peter Lawson sat straight up, his face solemn and frightened.

Jan's pent-up resentment burst from him like a flood, and he felt for words he had heard and learned during the past year. "Dir-rty pigs! Tieves! What you tr-ry do to me, huh? Why you send me dese letter-rs, huh? What I do to you? You no good! What is dis Jew-nigger-r, nigger-r-Jew business? I not know dese tings! You ar-re bad!"

Suddenly he caught sight of Peter's white face. His lip curled with scorn and he bared his upper teeth. With a swift movement he hurled the doll right in Peter's face.

The tears rolled down Peter's cheeks and he looked imploringly at Jan. "I didn't do it, Jan! I didn't do it!"

"Why you give me dis ugly ting? What is dis?"

It was fourteen-year-old Mike who spoke. "Maybe somebody thought you'd like to see one of your relatives, Yid," he said laconically.

"Yid?" said Jan. "What is dat?"

"Don't, Mike! Don't!" sobbed Peter.

There was a sound of footsteps coming nearer; one of the seniors opened the door. "Here! What's all this screaming about? What's happened?"

Jan turned on him furiously. "Get out! Get out of her-re or I kill you, too!"

The older boy went out quickly, and the footsteps outside were running.

But Jan's rage had not abated. He burst into sounds they didn't know. Polish, German, Yiddish spilled from his lips. Then, just as suddenly as he had begun, he stopped.

He held on to the foot of one of the beds, shaking and gasping; then he looked up and his eyes were still hot.

"I want back my candy!" he said brokenly.

The tempest was spent.

Two or three of the boys chuckled softly, turned over, and settled down into their pillows. Peter threw back his covers, jumped out of bed, and walked over to Jan, who was staring straight ahead.

"It's because they think you're a Jew. You're not, are you, Jan?"

Jan seemed to pull himself back from a long distance. He looked at Peter in astonishment. "Jew is *Jude*, no?" he said dully. "How I am *Jude*? I am alive—"

He stopped and frowned.

"You see, fellers," said Peter eagerly, "I told you he wasn't."

"Aw, go to bed, Pete. You're crazy! You said he had the mark on his arm," said Stinky disgustedly.

"Peter, you tell dem dis?" Jan's eyes burned with hatred.

Peter's words tumbled over themselves. "Jan, I told them you were a hero! I just told 'em the Nazis couldn't kill you. You fooled 'em! I told 'em you knew more than anybody! I wanted 'em to make you a Skull!"

"You wer-re my fr-riend. You made me buy dem candy and you tell dem dis!" Jan said, his voice cold and hard.

The tears welled up again in the other child's eyes and rolled down his face. "I'm your friend, Jan! Honest!"

At that moment the door opened and Dr. Miller stood in the doorway. "What's the trouble, boys?"

No one answered. Most of the heads were half under the covers. Only the two small boys stood in the middle of the room, facing each other.

"Evans tells me there's a row going on in here. You've been making enough noise to rouse the whole school."

"Yes, sir."

"Sorry, sir."

227

"It wasn't me, sir."

They all snuggled down in their beds and pulled up the covers. Peter crept back to his bed, whimpering softly.

Jan just stood there, his head high.

"Lyttleton," said Dr. Miller, "are you sleepy?"

"No—sir-r-r."

"Put on your robe and slippers and come along to my study." He turned to go out and then stopped. "How many of you are there in this dormitory? Ah, yes, twelve. All of you report to me in my office tomorrow after class. Come along, Lyttleton."

Jan seemed lost in the great chair. He sat there in silence, with Dr. Miller's overcoat over his knees, his chin on his breast, his eyes brooding into space.

Miller was standing at a dresser in the corner of the study, stirring something in a small aluminum pot which was heating on an electric plate.

"You like plenty of sugar in yours, don't you, Jan?"

"Yes, sir-r-r."

"I often make myself a cup of chocolate before I go to bed. It's good for you. Makes you sleep."

"Yes, sir-r-r."

He poured the chocolate in a big cup and handed it to the boy.

"Think I've got a couple of cookies around here somewhere." He rummaged in a drawer, found the crackers, then poured himself a cup of chocolate and sat down near Jan. "How is it, young feller?"

"Go-o-od."

He studied the boy for a moment. "What seems to have been the trouble upstairs, Jan?"

Jan lowered his eyes and didn't answer.

"Don't you think you could tell me? I might help, you know."

"I do not tell, sir-r-r," he said proudly. "I am not—how you say— infor-rmer."

"Of course you're not, Jan. I just thought you and I could talk things over and we might straighten everything out so nobody'd get in trouble."

There was no response from Jan.

"You see, Jan, American boys are a little different sometimes from the boys you've probably known. How about another cup of chocolate?"

"Tank you, sir-r-r."

Miller poured him another cup. No matter how Jan felt, he never refused anything that pleased his palate. It was as though he were always trying to catch up with the time and food he'd lost. He drank

228

the second cup of chocolate and then put the cup down on the table beside him. Suddenly he blurted out, "I am not *Jude*—what you say—Jew, no?"

The headmaster's eyes opened a little wider. "No, I don't think so, Jan."

"No. I am not. *Jude* old pipples! Old men, have long hair on chin. All dead. Me, I am young. Have bir-rthday soon. No *Jude*."

Then he lapsed into silence again.

Miller was beginning to understand. He looked at the child curiously. It might be— He tried to picture what might have gone on upstairs, but Jan was speaking again.

"American boys not like *Jude*—Jew?"

"Lots of American boys *are* Jews, Jan."

"No, sir-r-r. Boys not Jews. Jews old men. I know."

Dr. Miller leaned over and patted him on the arm. "Did you ever know any little boys well, Jan? In Poland, I mean?"

Jan shook his head. "No, sir-r-r. No boys. I have seen boys pass in carts. No little boys where I live."

Miller decided to change the subject. The ruction upstairs might have more serious implications than he'd first thought. It warranted thinking over.

"Mr. Adams and I are very proud of your record, Jan. I think you're going to turn into a fine mathematician, my boy."

"So?" said Jan calmly. "But I tink I go home now."

"Nonsense, Jan. You're going to stay here with us and make your mother proud of you too. You wouldn't want to disappoint her, would you?"

Jan lowered his head.

"Well, it's getting late, old man. I think you'd better run along to bed now. We'll straighten things out tomorrow."

The boy slipped out of his chair and walked to the door. The headmaster opened it for him and held out his hand.

"You and I are friends, Jan. You can always come along and talk things out with me, you know."

Jan smiled a weary little smile and put his hand in Dr. Miller's. "Tank you, sir-r-r. Good night."

"Good night, old man. Pleasant dreams."

For the following week, there was an ominous stillness at the Stratford School. Only Dr. Miller and twelve boys knew what had happened that night in Dormitory Three, and the twelve were forbidden to discuss it. They had been ordered to keep within bounds; the recreation ground for one hour a day for air, the rest of the time in the library or in their sleeping quarters; an hour earlier to bed for them each night and all packages from home confiscated for the month's duration of the punishment. Jan was included in the disciplinary measure. Miller could not play favorites, but he made things as easy for the Polish boy, outside of class hours, as he could.

Naturally, none of the boys confessed what had really occurred; all they would say was that it had been a private fight. But the headmaster had drawn his own conclusions. His conversation with Jan had been illuminating, and besides, one of the chambermaids had brought to his office the next morning a foul-smelling, smoldering thing of black, burned material and half-melted putty. It had obviously been burned hurriedly and then some water had been poured over it in the wastebasket where it had been thrown. With an infinitesimal amount of imagination Miller could easily picture the original outline and meaning of the small effigy.

Jan went on as before, with two exceptions: he refused to have anything whatever to do with Peter Lawson and he suddenly seemed to lose all interest in his favorite subject.

For several weeks there had been a daily oral routine between Henry Adams and Jan, which bored the rest of the class extremely but delighted Adams. Like two boys playing at blowing soap bubbles, Adams would conjure up a problem, toss it to the boy, who would catch it as one would catch a bubble with a clay pipe, enlarge it into a perfect iridescent thing, and blow it back into the air for the rest of the class to see.

Now, it floated in the room, was given an extra impetus by the young instructor, but finally dissolved into nothing as Jan stood there, that shut-in expression on his face, and made no comment.

Jan wanted no more of school. He wanted to go away.

He didn't know what to do. He couldn't ask this person they called his mother to take him away now. She wanted him to stay. She'd been kind and gentle to him always, especially during the holidays, and she wrote him once a month, telling him how proud she was of him and sending him his two-dollar allowance.

But slowly he began to figure out that there were other ways.

For instance, schools were to learn things in. They wouldn't like it if he got bad marks in his studies. He'd be sorry to disappoint Mr. Adams, but it couldn't be helped. He didn't like it here any longer.

If his conduct was bad, they would punish him, but he could stand punishment! And if he were too bad— Funny, he'd almost forgotten

230

what a cigarette tasted like. If you smoked in bed, cigarettes burned the sheets. They could burn other boys' sheets, too!

Then those boys had a lot of things belonging to them that they liked a lot. They'd hate to lose them. He'd never get caught—unless he wanted to. He was too experienced in things like that; he'd learned in a hard school. He knew ways of torturing people, too. Of course he didn't have to go too far, but righteous punishment must be dealt out.

She wouldn't approve of it; he didn't suppose Jesus would either—but there was nothing he could do about it. If he didn't take matters into his own hands the school would soon be turned into a concentration camp! Dr. Miller wouldn't like that, and of course he couldn't know what had been going on. How could he? He hadn't informed against those pigs.

Yes. There were other ways. He could be *sent* home!

If he only had his candy to take with him! He would give it to *her*, and to Pansy and Tubby. He wouldn't want anything else in return for it, because he wouldn't be making a trade.

He owed Mr. Adams two dollars and forty-five cents. That would be easy enough to steal, and if he wanted to buy more candy, five dollars more would do it. Eight dollars would be all he'd need; perhaps not even that much, because he'd saved his box that they'd put that nasty thing in—his beautiful box with the red bow.

Of course, he wouldn't stop at eight dollars. That wouldn't be enough to punish them. And there were always lots of things you could spend money for—

Oh, yes, there were other ways!

22

"Prosit, Pax!" Bob grinned his most charming grin at her across the dinner table and drank most of his glass of wine at one gulp. "God, Lyttleton, you bum," he continued, "what alliteration! That's what comes of returning to a college town."

Pax smiled back at him. "Here's looking at you, darling. And I really mean here's looking at you. Do you still realize how many hundreds and hundreds of nights I've looked at that empty chair?"

"It's been a long time, all right."

"But you're back, and safe, thank God, in spite of a few broken legs and things."

"Yeah," he replied, slowly twirling the stem of his half-empty glass. "I guess Old Lady Luck sat on one shoulder while the gremlins were busy on the other."

"I'm the lucky one, darling. Think how many gals are going to have to face an empty chair for the rest of their lives."

Bob's face lost its smile for a moment, and he held up his glass again. "Here's to 'em, Pax—the guys who've gone up topside for keeps. Happy landings, fellers!" he said.

Embarrassing, she thought—but Bob was like that.

"And here's to the ones who didn't get to go 'up topside' as you call it, but who didn't come back, either."

Pax paused for a moment before touching her lips to the glass, wondering if he would mention Jake, but he didn't.

"Hey, let's have some more. Pansy! Put your foot on the bell, will you, sweet?"

"I can get it, darling," said Pax, rising from her chair.

"Sit down!" he thundered, but he was laughing. "What the hell have you been doing since I've been away? Spoiling that nigger wench of mine?"

Pax frowned. That was the second time he'd used that word.

"Ring it again! She's certainly taking a devil of a time to come."

Pansy stuck her head through the door. "Yes'm?"

"What's the matter with you, Pansy?" said Bob irritably. "Didn't you hear the bell?"

"Yes, sir. But I was makin' a cheese soufflé for yuh. I was afraid it would fall."

"Never mind the soufflé. If it falls, make another one. But you come when you're called!"

"Yes, sir. What you-all want?" Her lower lip trembled and she didn't look at him.

"Get another bottle of that wine out of the icebox. Bring the corkscrew in here. I'll open it."

There was a curious expression in Pax's eyes as she looked at him, but she dropped them when he smiled at her.

"What's the matter, baby?"

"Nothing. I'm not sure I can drink any more. I'm beginning to feel a bit tiddly. Why open another bottle?"

232

" 'Cause it's an anniversary. Three days, two hours, and forty minutes," he said, looking at his watch.

Pansy came back with the bottle and corkscrew.

"Honestly, darling, I'm really feeling a little tight."

"Nonsense," he answered, pulling the cork, which crumbled a little as it came out. "A gal with a level head like you? Give me your glass."

"It is good," she said.

"Liebfraumilch, 1933. Know where it came from?"

"Wouldn't be surprised if it came from Germany, if one can believe in names."

"Right out of *Herr Reichsmarschall* Goering's private stock, believe it or not," he said proudly.

"Oh," Pax said, and she put her glass down. "What did he do, leave it to you?"

Bob laughed. "No. I'm afraid it wasn't come by as honestly as all that. When our guys caught the poor devil, the G.I.'s went through his castle like a physic and helped themselves. They couldn't manage to drink it all—anyway, they preferred beer—so eventually quite a few cases found their way to the Officers' Club in Munich. Your feller sent most of his clothes by boat, and lugged a case of this golden nectar home to his woman. Hold it up to the light, honey chile. It's almost the color of your pretty cat's eyes."

At that moment, a back door slammed, and they heard a voice in the kitchen.

"That must be Tubs," Bob said. "Maybe he's tired of visiting or Em is tired of keeping him."

"I hope not," Pax said. "Really, darling, I'm not an unnatural mother, but it's been such heaven having you all to myself these few days."

There seemed to be some kind of altercation going on in the kitchen. Suddenly the door swung open and Tubby rushed through, followed by Pansy.

"Go on, now, ask yo' mama. I ain't goin' to give it to yuh 'n'ess she say so."

"Good evening, my son," said Bob in a pontifical voice.

"Hello, Pop—Mom! Pansy won't gimme the key to the garage!"

"What do you want to do, take the car out?" said Bob, giving him an affectionate slap on the bottom.

"Aw! I can't drive a car!"

"What do you want the key for?" asked Pax.

"Jan's bicycle's in there. I want to borrow it."

The name was out.

Pax felt her face getting hot, but she answered him calmly. "What's

233

the matter with your own bicycle? And what do you want it for at this time of the night?"

Bob didn't seem to be paying much attention.

"Well, Aunt Em said we could take a little ride, if we were back at nine o'clock, and Jan's bicycle's got a light. Mine hasn't. Can't I take it, Mom, just this once? I'll be careful, honest. Jan wouldn't mind."

"Let him have it, baby. Are you a good rider, son?"

"Sure I'm a good rider. I'm better'n she is," he replied, with his father's grin, tilting his head in Pax's direction.

Her mind was running around in circles. Tubby had so rarely mentioned Jan since he'd been away at school; and she'd been counting on the fact that he was staying with the Bascomb twins. She had wanted time to break the news of Jan's existence to Robert, and to break it at the right moment.

Outwardly she seemed serene and she quietly went on with the discussion. "Tubs, darling, I'm afraid of cars at night. Couldn't you wait until tomorrow, and take a nice long ride then?"

"Naw. Aunt Em's goin' to let Butch and Bill go. I don't see why I can't."

"Let him go, Pax," said Bob. "You don't want to make a fraid-cat out of him."

Pax smiled. "That'll be the day, when your son's a fraid-cat. All right, Tubs, but will you be careful of the cars?"

"Sure."

"And I'll feel better if you'll come in and say good night when you come back, before you go to Aunt Em's. Your daddy and I'll be upstairs in the sitting room."

"Thanks, Mom!" He rushed back through the swinging door. They heard an "Annnnh—yuh see?" to Pansy and they could imagine the gesture that went with it. Then the back door slammed.

"Those kids of Em's are little toughs," sighed Pax, lifting her wine glass to her lips. "I never know what he's up to when he's with them."

"Good for him, baby! I want him to be tough. It's a tough world. By the way, who's Jan? And what's his bicycle doing in our garage?"

Here it was! She was for it now.

"Oh, I haven't told you about Jan, have I? . . . I think I'll have some more of that high-toned wine of yours."

"Sure. It's damn good wine, isn't it?" He filled both their glasses. "Give, honey chile. Who's Jan?"

"Well, he's a little European boy that Philip found for me."

"What do you mean that Phil found for you? Where is he now?"

234

"He's at the Stratford School in Manchester. He's a very good child. Smart, too!"

"What in the name of God are you doing with a European child? What kind of a European child?"

Bob was still smiling, but his voice had a slight edge which frightened her a little.

"We don't know, really. We think he's from Czechoslovakia."

"You think? Don't you *know*?"

"Well, no. There isn't any record, really. You see, he came over here with a lot of little orphans, and I thought . . . Well, darling, lots of women in Vermont and New Hampshire—and I guess other places, too—have been taking all kinds of poor kids for the summer and giving them a vacation. Some of them have adopted them and, I thought, instead of taking a little American child—a little Negro child, for instance, some of the girls have been doing that, you know—or a poor slum kid, I would take the little money that my mother left me and try to do some real good with it and I thought it would be doing more good to take a little orphan who was a victim of the war and who might never have a decent chance, and send him to school with it—"

"Have you adopted the boy?"

"No! Oh, no! I just said I'd take him for two years and—"

"And then what are you going to do with him?"

"I—I—I—" Why was she stuttering? "I said we'd see, and—"

"I think you're crazy, Pax," Bob said, but his voice was good-natured. "How long have you had him and what's he like?"

"Oh, I've had him nearly a year."

"Why didn't you write me about him?"

"Well, I thought maybe you'd think I was taking on too much—but, honestly, darling, I'm not! He won't bother you and he won't cost you anything. You see, he'll really only be here in the summer and then we might even send him to a camp."

The word had slipped out, but it struck at her heart with horror. Of course she wouldn't do that—ever! But she made a mental note to telephone the school from Amy's in the morning and ask Dr. Miller to keep him there during the Easter holidays. Jan would be disappointed, but she couldn't chance him with Robert until she prepared the way for him a little.

Her thoughts stopped in their tracks. Why couldn't she chance him with Robert?

Well, she wanted to speak to the headmaster anyway, about Jan's report card that she'd received the day before. It was the first poor one.

His mathematics marks was low, which was unusual, and he'd had a D for conduct.

"And he's a very good, obedient boy and he won't be any trouble."

"What's his name?"

"Jan"—she hesitated—"Jan van Rashoff, as near as I can remember it."

He laughed. "As near as you can remember! Isn't that the name you entered him by at the school?"

She flushed and looked down at her plate. "No," she said in a low voice.

"What name did you give them?"

"Lyttleton," she murmured.

Bob looked at her closely for a moment; then he emptied his glass. "Well, I'll be damned!" he said.

Through her fitful doze, Pax seemed to hear the voices of the twins next door and her own son, as if from a great distance. The birds were chattering in the great elm outside her window. She opened her tired, heavy eyes and looked at the little pink clock. The hands pointed to seven minutes to eight. She turned her head on the pillow and gazed at Robert, who slept like a child, his relaxed body taking up most of the bed. She slipped out of bed without waking him.

What a night! Restless, sleepless, and when she did fall off into a light, uneasy doze from time to time, dreams that made no sense and frightened her, and from which she'd wake with a start, her heart pounding. Mixed-up dreams of barbed wire and Jan; and rows of dead bodies hanging by the neck; and Robert with a gun over his shoulder and a bottle of wine in one hand, walking back and forth before the gallows.

Would this never stop? When she thought of Jan, it was almost with hatred, and she was ashamed.

She ran into the bathroom and turned on the cold shower. She shivered as she stepped under it, but she forced herself to take the icy-cold needles, hoping it would clear her brain and put some energy into her weary body.

She tiptoed around the room, so that she wouldn't wake Robert, who was in the habit of sleeping late these days, got into her underclothes, a woolen pullover, and slacks, picked up a coat from the hall closet, and dashed across to Amy's.

She made connections with Dr. Miller very quickly and put the problem of Jan's Easter holiday to him. He reassured her about the boy's bad marks, telling her that he liked and understood the child and sympathized with the strangeness of his new life, and that he was positive it was just a phase that he would come through easily. He even suggested that, with her approval, he would like to take Jan to Quebec with him for the ten days at Easter.

She was so relieved that her feet almost danced their way along Amy's front hall and out of the door. She was halfway across the garden when she heard Philip's voice from the bathroom window above. She looked up, to see him in his bathrobe, his face half covered with lather.

"Hi, kid! What are you doing here so early in the morning? Haven't seen you for at least three days." His face broke into a grin. "Have you decided to come out of your hibernation for a while?"

"Hello, Phil. I had to telephone the school—"

"Here?" he asked. "What's the matter? Your phone out of order?"

She bit her underlip, stuck her hands firmly in the pockets of her coat, and looked up at him. "No. I just didn't want to wake Robert. He isn't too well yet and he needs all the sleep he can get."

"How's things over at headquarters since lo! the bridegroom cometh?"

"You know, Phil, sometimes you're as catty as a woman," she said angrily.

"Thanks, kid. What are you up to now?"

"Nothing. Why should I be up to anything?"

"You're on the defensive again. Got fifteen minutes to spare? I can be down in ten."

"Why, yes, I suppose so," she replied ungraciously. "Is Amy up?"

"Haven't heard her."

"Do you suppose she'd mind if I made myself some coffee? I'll make you some, too."

"Good. Then I won't have to bother with my own private housekeeping." And he shut the window.

Twenty minutes later, Philip and Pax sat opposite each other across Amy's kitchen table, drinking their coffee and munching some hot buttered toast that Pax had made.

"I told Robert last night about Jan," she announced casually.

"Good for you! What did he say?"

"Oh, nothing much. Want another piece of toast?"

"Thanks. Wasn't he proud of you?"

"Oh, I don't know. After all, he hasn't seen him yet."

Philip studied her closely. "What are you hedging about, kid?"

"Well, it's funny, Phil. He hasn't mentioned Jake, and I'm sort of scared to—"

"Well, for God's sake!"

"—so I didn't tell him that Jan's Jewish—yet."

There! It was out, and she felt better.

"Not that it would make any difference to Robert," she continued. "You know how he loved Jake, and Jake's mother and father, too, but I want to use it as a kind of opening, see?"

"Yes, I see," Philip said.

"I thought I'd give him a little time, Phil. Jake's death must have gone awfully deep with him, and I can't bear to hurt him. I've got to let him mention it first, don't you see?"

Philip went over to the stove and poured himself another cup of coffee. "What were you talking to the school about? Fixing up another white lie to give you that little time?"

Pax jumped up from the table and nearly knocked over her half-filled cup. "Really, Phil, I don't understand how you can be so exasperating and so cruel to me sometimes." Her eyes filled with tears. "I was just agreeing to let Jan go to Quebec with Dr. Miller for Easter. He asked him—"

"For Christ's sake, stop shying at things, Pax. Bring the boy home and give him to Bob! Bob loves kids, and he'll know better than we do the damnable injustice that's been handed out to them over there."

"But I can't, Phil—yet. Robert wants to motor South next week to see his mother and father. I'm leaving Tubs with Em. I can't saddle her with two of them. When we come back—"

"You'll find another excuse. I know you. Pax, I'm only thinking of you. Do you know what you remind me of? Atlas trying to hold up the universe, only your universe is made of mist and shadows and fears. Put it down, kid, and hold your pretty head up! You've done a damn fine thing. For God's sake, stop being ashamed of it."

"You can go to hell, Phil," she gulped. "I'm going home."

23

It was almost like going on her honeymoon. Almost. Naturally, if it had been, Robert would be driving and she would be curled up beside him. But this was good enough, after the years of waiting and aloneness.

One hundred and fifty miles behind her, she had left her son, her fearfulness about Jan, and the provoking little speculations about this newly returned prodigal who had been her husband for nearly eleven years.

They were really alone now, starting off on an adventure. An adventure which would end up with a prosaic visit with Robert's delightful family, but there would be several days in between in which they would recapture, without any outside interference, all the qualities which had originally drawn them to each other.

The last ten days had been hectic. Robert had insisted upon waiting for his overseas luggage so that all his smart uniforms could be cleaned, pressed, and packed—the better to impress them with, she had thought wryly.

She had begged Robert to look through his old civilian suits, which she had put away for him, and wear them instead of his uniforms, but he had muttered something about the remaining weeks of terminal leave, and the fact that another war was just around the corner. He had finally settled for a pair of gray flannels, three or four white silk shirts, and a sport jacket, but all the uniforms went with them.

It had amazed her how quickly he had discarded his crutch for a walking stick which was beside him in the car now, but the last minute before they left he had ordered Pansy to get the crutch for him and put it in the back seat.

Pansy had seemed almost relieved when they left. She had sent homesick messages to her mother and father, who still worked for the Lyttletons, Senior, and her love to Miss Mary, Bob's mother.

Pax had thought a great deal about Robert and Pansy since he'd returned. In the short time that Pansy was with them before he'd gone overseas, she couldn't seem to remember his being so autocratic to this girl with whom he'd practically grown up. It was curious! Yet, seven and a half years of military discipline did make a difference, she supposed.

How lovely the countryside was. A virginal greenness was appearing in the meadows, and the buds were bursting on the maple-tree branches. The sun was mellow and a cloudless sky augured a happy second honeymoon.

It took them about a week to reach Savannah. As they pushed farther South, they saw that spring had been there well before them on its way North. They left the green-brown waters of the Potomac and the cherry blossoms of Washington, and rolled through the lush green fields of Virginia, where the orchards were heavy with pink and white bloom, and when they reached Georgia, the hills were sprinkled thickly with rosy dogwood.

Bob was tender and loving and demanding. She tried to keep out of her mind any memories that did not concern themselves entirely with him, and for the moment there seemed to be no cloud in this new sky of hers, except for momentary irritations caused by his strange dictatorial manner with people who served him.

She drew him out about his experiences during the long time he'd been away from her. She was fascinated by his stories of the blitz in London; of how his heart had pounded in his throat when he flew the first raid over Ploesti.

"The African days were the queer ones, baby. Poker at night with the commanders when they ordered you to play; dog fights at dawn, high in the sky; bombing Rommel's army at any hour—there was a guy! And what a soldier! Even Monty respected him. A God-damn shame that a political mistake cost him his life."

"But, darling," she said, "you never tell me anything about these last two years after the war. What was it like in Germany? No pretty German girls to while away the hours?"

"Pretty?" he said. "German women are blond and stocky with high cheekbones and thick ankles." He hesitated for a fraction of a second. "That is, for the most part. They're not sleek and slim like you, honey chile."

On the last day of their journey, they were speeding along in the late afternoon, the new tires on the old Buick humming on the smooth, well-paved roads.

"Look, darling," she said as they passed a signpost. "Savannah, five miles."

"Pax, honey, don't go around the town, will you? When we come to the main street, turn to the right, and let's stop at the hotel and have a last drink alone together before we greet the family."

"But, Robert, it's quarter to four."

"They'll wait, baby. Do what I tell you, that's a good girl."

When they arrived at the hotel, she parked the car up ahead and ran back to the front entrance, where Bob was deep in conversation with a colored bellboy.

"You run along to the ladies' room and powder your nose, beautiful. I'll meet you in the bar in about ten minutes."

She found a little table in a corner and waited—and waited. Fifteen, twenty minutes went by. Then she saw him.

He was coming along briskly, barely leaning on his cane, wearing a fresh uniform with a smart battle jacket, a jaunty overseas cap set rakishly on his blond head. He had transferred his wings, ribbons, and all his decorations, and he grinned at her, childishly and completely pleased with himself.

"Can't let 'em down, baby," he said as he slipped into a chair beside her. "The conquering hero has to look the part."

"Thank God, darling, you'll really never grow up," she said, and patted his hand lovingly.

They had two drinks and piled into the car again.

Seven miles on the other side of the city, they came to the gates of Brideclift. Sitting on the low stone wall was a small girl, with a faded little bunch of flowers in her hand. When she saw them turn in at the gates, she tumbled off the wall, waved to them, and ran ahead of the car, across the lawn, and into the house.

"That must be Mary Lou," said Bob.

"Mary Lou who?"

"You know, Nancy's child. They must have come over from Atlanta to see us."

"Lord, Robert, is she that big?"

"The war took up a lot of years, honey."

When they pulled up in front of the stately Colonial house with the great white pillars, the front door opened and the family rushed out eagerly. Pax got out of her side of the car, and ran around to help Bob.

"Give me my crutch, baby. It's in the back seat."

For the first time, Pax was not amused at his play-acting. He hobbled up the steps and into his mother's arms. Pax stood alone on the blue gravel of the drive and looked up at them.

There was Bob's father, standing to one side waiting to greet him. He was a tall man, with Bob's blue eyes and fair hair, now mixed with gray. He wore a morning coat and absent-mindedly swung a pince-nez attached to a black ribbon. Bob's younger sister, Nancy, a nut-brown maid, leaned against her husband's shoulder; and lined up behind them was William the butler, who was Pansy's father; her mother, Susie the cook; another colored girl; and a young Negro whom Pax didn't remember having seen before. And last, but the most vociferous in her welcome, was little Mary Lou, hopping up and down the steps, waving her bouquet, and chattering madly in her excitement.

For several minutes, no one seemed to have time for Pax, but she didn't mind. She had had her moment, three weeks ago at the little station at Mapleton. They got around to her at last, and then it was nearly an hour before she and Bob were allowed to go to their room. They insisted that Bob should rest a "little minute" on the gallery at the back of the house and that they must both have a mint julep which Susie had prepared for them.

The tall frosted silver mugs, topped by crisp sprigs of mint, were passed around by William; a toast of welcome was made to the return of the wanderer by the head of the house; and Pax thought indulgently that it was just like a scene from *Gone with the Wind* pushed forward eighty-odd years.

When they finally got to Bob's old room, Pax wanted to talk, but Bob shooed her into the bathroom after choosing the frock he wanted her to wear. He stretched himself out on the bed to wait for her. He wasn't going to bother changing for dinner. His toilet had been successfully made in the men's room at the hotel.

A half hour later, Pax stood in front of him to see if he approved. She wore a lovely clinging print of pale green, patterned in sprays of white lilac. She had gathered her shining black hair up and off her ears, and let it fall in a cascade of soft curls in the back. Her dark straight brows and her vivid lipstick set off the chalk-whiteness of her skin, and her wide amber eyes glowed—like a cat's, as Bob always told her.

They descended the broad staircase slowly, Bob leaning lightly on her shoulder and using his cane in the other hand. Ruefully she realized that he had made his first appearance the way he'd wanted it, and then, with no self-consciousness whatever, had promptly discarded his crutch. The thought went through her mind that that damn crutch would probably accompany them on every important occasion for a long time— and that it was all rather embarrassing.

The conversation at dinner drifted from stories of Miss Mary's only grandson, who had been left behind, to Bob's tales of his experiences overseas as a flier.

Then it turned to politics. Dick Daingerfield, Nancy's husband, a sturdy, unimaginative Southern citizen, and Mr. Lyttleton tossed their opinions back and forth, damning the Republicans and repudiating the Democrats because of the present incumbent. The Republicans were isolationist and stingy, besides being Northerners, and the Democrats had been completely corrupted by that thin-lipped man in the White House!

The minute the general attention veered from him, Bob turned to his mother and left the two men to it, but he pricked up his ears when his father snorted with indignant rage over the Civil Rights Bill for which —to quote Lyttleton, Senior—"that dreary gentleman, if one could so loosely use that word, was responsible!"

Bob was confused and not too interested by references to the contemptible enterprises of the New Deal, but when they discussed the

242

President's plaintive reiteration of it, by the introduction of the Anti-Poll Tax and Anti-Lynching Bills, he jumped into the conversation.

"What's the matter with these damned Northerners, Dad? Must be they haven't learned yet!" His mouth twisted with contempt and his face was set. "Instead of sitting here at home safely, thinkin' up laws nobody wants, they should have been in my place over there and have been forced to deal with those God-damned buck niggers in the Army! Damn their dirty black hides! So the Yankees want to let 'em vote now, huh?"

"Robert!"

Pax looked down the table into Mary Lyttleton's sober face and saw that her blue eyes were dark with anger.

"Robert, I'm amazed and shocked. I've always tried to bring you up to know that that kind of language belongs in the stables, not in the company of ladies and gentlemen. And in the stables only when you are alone," she continued sternly.

"Sorry, Mum," he muttered.

"Don't apologize to me, Robert. It is to William that you owe an apology," she said. She turned her head in the direction of their old servant, who was standing at the sideboard with his back to the room, uncorking a bottle of Burgundy.

"Dat's all right, Miss Mary. I understand what Mr. Bob means."

"Do you? Then you're cleverer than we are, William. I hope you will forgive him."

Bob bent his head over his plate, and murmured something that Pax couldn't hear as old William filled his glass.

Her heart ached for him in this well-earned humiliation he was suffering from the hands of his mother, in the presence of his whole family and before her; but there was one thing she knew: she would love Mary Lyttleton forever.

From that moment on, the conversation was awkward and subdued.

After they finished dinner and went into the drawing room for coffee, Mary slipped her arm through Pax's and smiled at her affectionately.

"Wars are bad things, darlin', and if my son has come through this one without compassion and understandin', I shall be a very unhappy woman."

Pax gave the older woman's arm a squeeze. "I hope someday I shall have your courage."

After coffee and brandy, everyone seemed to relax. Pax settled back on the divan, peacefully happy. She looked around the beautiful old square room, at the sconces on the wall which held real candles, and the dimly lighted lamps which threw soft pools of light beneath them and dark shadows on the walls above them, and thought how restful it was.

Nancy was at the piano playing the popular tunes of the day, with Bob sitting by her, singing in his high tenor voice. Mr. Lyttleton and his son-in-law sat together, sipping their brandy slowly, and Mary put on her glasses and worked on a bedcover she was crocheting.

The heat from the fire, the heavy odor of white lilac and freesia, on top of her long seven-hour drive, made Pax feel drowsy. She fought against closing her eyes, but her lids felt heavy. Vaguely she heard the music stop, and then she must have dozed a little. Through a kind of haze she heard Mr. Lyttleton talking to Robert.

"What are you planning to do, son, when your injuries are entirely healed? What about heading South and coming in business with me?"

"I don't think so, Dad. I honestly don't want to think about work for a while. I've had enough. Think I'll just laze along and be happy for a time, and live on Grandfather's leavin's and ol' Uncle Sam. This last crackup of mine is going to cost the ol' boy quite a penny, you know."

"If I remember rightly, weren't you thinkin' at one time of goin' in the newspaper business? Didn't you say something once about buyin' a paper in some small town with that great friend o' yours—what was his name?"

Pax's tired eyes opened wide and she held her breath. She tried to read Robert's expression in the subdued lights, but she couldn't. Instinctively she began to pray. Dear God, don't let it be now! Not before other people! Don't let him be hurt here!

She heard Robert speaking and his voice was controlled and impersonal.

"You mean Felder? Jake Felder?"

"Yes, Jake. Fine boy, I always thought."

"Yes, he was all right. They're all all right, I guess, when they're young."

"Who? Who are all right when they're young?" asked his father in a perplexed voice.

"Jews."

Pax's body stiffened and she clutched the edge of the couch with both hands. She wasn't hearing what she thought she heard. She couldn't be. She must still be asleep. She must wake up! Where was his pain—the pain she'd tried to spare him? He was speaking again.

"But with what I know about 'em now, I'd just as soon cut my throat as go into business with one."

"I'm sorry you feel that way, son. You must have had an unhappy experience to talk like that."

Robert lighted a cigarette, lifted his bad leg over the other, and leaned easily back in his chair. "No, I didn't have any bad experience, Dad. I just got to know something about the bastards over there."

"Robert! Your wife and sister are in the room!"

"Sorry, girls," said Bob casually, "but when you think that if it hadn't been for the damn Jews, there wouldn't have been this bloody war, you can't blame anyone for feelin' pretty hot about 'em!"

The blood was pounding so loudly in Pax's ears that she could count each beat. Her throat ached and she tried to speak but she couldn't. Her teeth were tightly clenched and her tongue so dry it felt as though it were glued to the roof of her mouth. She looked to the side and back of her, but Mary must have left the room when she dozed off.

Then she heard a tiny voice which she almost didn't recognize as her own. "But, Robert—Jake!"

"Hello, honey chile, did you finally wake up?"

That was the old gentle Robert speaking.

"But *Jake*, Robert!"

"I remember him, Bob, that Easter he came down here with you." That was Nancy speaking. "I liked him. Whatever became of him, Bobbie?"

"He got it in the Pacific, poor devil, just before the war with the yellow-bellies ended."

"Oh, my! Isn't that a shame!"

"Never even made noncom. No ambition. Funny."

"You mean it's funny to a brigadier, don't you, Bobbie?" Was that a faintly mocking tone in Nancy's voice?

"Don't you-all misunderstand me now. I liked the guy, all right, but maybe it was the best thing that could have happened to him. Look, what was there for him in this country if he had come back? There's not going to be any place in this new world for Jews any more than there is over there where I've come from. Of course, there's Palestine, but then the British don't like 'em either."

I'm going to throw up, thought Pax, and that's going to look awfully silly. I've got to get out of here.

She rose from the couch cautiously, as though her legs were made of wood, and in that same small voice she said, "Do you mind awfully if I go to bed? I guess I'm tired."

She tried to smile at them, but the muscles in her face were stiff. "Good night, sir. Good night, Nancy, Dick. I'll see you in the morning. It's very early, Robert. Don't you bother coming up yet. I think I feel a little sick, but I guess I'm just tired. Say good night to Miss Mary for me."

The men rose from their chairs and said good night. Robert kissed her tenderly and she had great difficulty suppressing an aching shudder. Then she drifted out of the drawing room and up the wide stairs. When she reached her own room, she slipped out of her clothes quickly and into her nightgown which was laid out for her. She got into bed and put out the light beside her.

Oh, Jake! There are worse things than being slain by little men you didn't know.

An hour or so later, when Bob came upstairs, he pulled on the light and stood looking down at her. She was lying on the edge of the bed, her pale face turned to the outside, her body drawn up in a tight knot. When he spoke to her softly, she made no sign. Her black lashes cast a deep shadow on her cheeks, and her breathing was steady and regular. He turned off the light, undressed in the dark, and slipped quietly into bed beside her.

God! If she could only go to sleep!

"Where shall I go now? What shall I do?"

She heard that long wailing cry as though from far off, not realizing that it had come from her own tortured throat. She sat huddled on the bottom step of the hall staircase where she had toppled, her head against the newel post, her eyes dry and burning, her slight body convulsed with shuddering sobs.

Around her, on the steps and on the floor, torn envelopes of advertisements and household bills which she had opened first had fluttered down and lay all about her. In one hand she held a black-bordered envelope; the other clutched a single sheet with writing on both sides.

The first line of the letter was branded on her brain and she couldn't seem to think beyond it: "If your eyes ever read these lines, it will be because I am not coming back."

All day, she kept the pain locked within her heart, moving about the house like an automaton. There was no one to share it with, neither the present sorrow nor the poignant memories. Robert was overseas, her father was dead, and Martha was old and no longer with her. There was Philip, of course, but she couldn't face him with it today. She always felt that he thought she had betrayed Jake when she married his friend.

It was a dismal, autumnal day in nineteen hundred and forty-five, with a sad premonition of winter in the cold air. The sky was overcast and the wind whispered ominously.

She made her way through the woods along the path, which was almost obscured by dead leaves and twigs. The stripped branches tore at her hair as she walked numbly ahead, feeling no cold except the cold inside her.

She climbed the boulders, and sat on a rock at the mouth of the cave, gazing out over the cursed familiar landscape. There was no brown-gold, no flaming scarlet, no beauty today; it was flat and colorless and empty, as though no living thing moved there. As she looked into the vacant distance, the picture began to fade. Then in her mind's eye she saw, instead of bare maples and oaks, tall palms bending in the wind under a slate-blue sky and, in the lush green of the expanse, thousands of little white crosses.

Then, like the lens of a camera closing in, there seemed to be only one cross left, inscrutable and accusing.

In the fading light, she read his farewell letter again, and for the first time she began to understand his fierce pride and his great understanding of her. Yet he had gone, with his life and his love unfulfilled—because of her. Nothing left now of their young hunger and desire or the shining hopes of those few months they had spent together.

She had taken his decision about them with a sorrowful acceptance, but now that it was too late it seemed an intolerable agony.

If she could only stop thinking of him under that white cross. But perhaps he wasn't there. Perhaps he never reached that atoll. Had he been on a ship, lonely and intent against the rail when it went down?

She must stop thinking of him like that. She had always been afraid of death, or was it the "too-lateness" of it that terrified her?

The burial of her young love had been tragic, but this was different and a thousand times more unbearable. And yet this grief was not just because of a love which was lost. It was deeper than that.

One thing was so terribly inevitable. She would never see him again. The words he had spoken to her had vanished; the grace of him had vanished; but somehow, she knew, she must keep alive the memory of his fineness and his sacrifice. She must find a way.

She must give him something—even in death. There was nothing she could do for his father and mother. Once she had hurt them irreparably. They wouldn't want her. Nobody wanted her. . . .

Her attention was caught by one lonely leaf on a dead bough which was being tossed about by a little wind. She was the leaf and Jake was the bough, and something must live beyond the wisps of memory and the sad tenderness of inanimate things which would always remind her that they had once loved each other.

She stood up and brushed from her eyes the first tears she had shed since the arrival of the letter. She wondered if Robert knew. Well, she would face his sorrow when she met it. Her grief belonged only to her tonight.

As she climbed down from Finnegan's, she thought of the hush of time over the small wooden crosses, but she knew that Jake would be alive in her heart forever.

"Where shall I go now? What shall I do?"

That was Robert shaking her.

"Wake up, darling! You're dreaming!"

"Am I?"

"You must have been having a nightmare, baby. You cried out."

"I'm sorry. Did I disturb you?"

Robert leaned over and kissed her shoulder. "Me? Of course not, honey chile!" He turned over facing her and snuggled down under the bedcovers.

Pax lay very still until his breathing became heavier. Then she quietly got up, put on her dressing gown, and sat in a chair by the window, watching the dawn break over the magnolia tree which stood just outside their room.

24

Dr. Jim Miller paid for his gas and waited impatiently for the filling-station attendant to fill his steaming car with water. It was ten minutes to four and he had only ten more miles to go, but he found himself again speeding along at sixty. The sky was losing its limpid April blue and was turning into a colorless gray, the forerunner of another shower, but that was no reason for his haste.

As a matter of fact he had none. He was returning two days ahead of time; the school would be comparatively empty; and he had plenty of time to unpack and freshen up before dinner. Rather annoyed with himself, he slowed down to thirty-five and took the rest of the way easily.

As he pulled into the school grounds the April shower had turned into a dismal downpour. He put his car in the garage, turned up his coat collar, and with a valise in each hand he sprinted across the lawn and into the private entrance of his study.

He put a match to the fire, then unpacked, showered, and changed, and rang the bell for some tea.

"Everything all right in the school?" he inquired of the manservant, after he'd given the order.

"Yes, sir. A little quiet, sir, with most of the boys away. Four or five of them returned today. I must say, we were all glad to see them, sir."

"By the way, after you ask Katie to make me some tea, see if you can find young Lyttleton and send him in to me."

"Yes, sir."

Miller lighted a cigarette, threw himself into an easy chair, picked up a book, and waited.

In about twenty minutes, George reappeared with the tea.

"Sorry, sir, but we can't find the Lyttleton boy. We've looked everywhere, but no one seems to have seen him around today."

"That's all right, George, it's not important. I'll see him later."

After he'd had his tea, he strolled down the hall and into the library. Two or three of the older boys were there reading. They jumped to their feet to greet him.

"How have you been, boys? I hope it wasn't too dull for you, not being able to go home for the holidays."

"Oh, it was all right, sir," said one. "We didn't mind it, really, did we, fellers? The weather was swell, and we hiked about the country quite a lot."

"By the way, have you seen young Lyttleton around anywhere?"

"No, sir, can't say that I have. Either of you fellers seen him?"

"Not for the last few hours, anyway. I think I saw him at lunch."

No one seemed to remember seeing Jan during the past week, except at meals. Apparently he was always there when the dining room opened and then disappeared again. The maid who made up Dormitory Three hadn't seen him at all. The only information she could give was that there was one bed every morning that had been slept in, but she didn't know which boy it belonged to.

Dr. Miller finally gave up the search and went back to his study. At six o'clock, he returned to the school dining room. The older boys were all at one table together. Sitting alone at his own table was Jan, eating steadily.

Jim Miller pulled out a chair and sat down opposite him. "Hello, young feller."

Jan looked up, but his expression didn't change. "Hello," Jan replied, and returned to his dinner.

"How was your vacation, Jan? All right?"

"Yes."

Miller remarked the omission of the "sir," but he said nothing about it. "When you've finished, come along to my study, will you, Jan? We'll have a little talk."

The boy nodded, but he didn't look up. Dr. Miller sighed and left the table.

Fifteen minutes later there was a knock at his door. "Come in, Jan," he called.

Jan came in slowly, his eyes down, and quietly closed the door.

"Sit down, old man. How've you been?"

"All r-r-right." He stood there, looking at the floor.

"Sit down, Jan! Sit down!"

Jan went to the chair opposite the headmaster and sat there, motionless.

"I think you made a mistake, Jan, not to go to Quebec with me. I think you'd have liked it."

There was no answer.

"What have you been doing with yourself since I left?"

"Notting."

"It must have been lonely for you without any boy of your own age to play with."

"I not play wit de boys. Boys no good. Dey hate me. I hate dem."

"Jan," Miller said thoughtfully, "I'd hoped that you would have had time to think things over during these past ten days and that you would talk to me when I came back. Don't you see, I can't help you, boy, unless you tell me what's troubling you. Can't you tell me, Jan?"

Jan said nothing.

"I thought you and I were friends."

Jan shrugged.

"It makes me feel bad to have to send poor reports to your mother.'

"She is not my mudder."

"She's your mother now, Jan. I haven't talked to her, but I'm sure she will feel very sad when she learns how unhappy you are."

"Not un-happy," muttered Jan.

"You are a clever boy, Jan. Mr. Adams and I have had such great hopes for you. But you must see that it isn't much use for you to go to school if you refuse to study."

The boy's face lighted for a moment and he looked up swiftly at the headmaster, but the light vanished as quickly as it had appeared and he lapsed into the same immobility as before.

Jim Miller had always thought that he knew how to handle young boys, but this foreign child completely disconcerted him. He would have found it easy enough to cope with an open resentment or a real defiance, but Jan's passive resistance defeated him.

He watched the child closely, but he was careful to keep the same friendly smile on his face. He decided that he would try to trick the boy into some sort of admission about what was troubling him.

"Jan," he said, "I wonder if you could help me out a little. You see, being away for over a week, I really haven't had time to find out anything that's happened in the school since I left. Now, don't misunderstand me, Jan, it's not a question of 'informing,' as you once called it, because you have been practically alone here except for several of the older fellows. But I wondered if you had missed anything belonging to you since we've all been gone."

Jan looked at him inquiringly. "Missed?" he asked.

"You remember, Jan, that some of the boys complained that a few of their belongings had disappeared, and they seemed to think that someone was stealing money that they had saved from their allowances. Have *you* lost anything, Jan?"

A stealthy expression slipped into the boy's eyes. "I lose notting," he said deliberately. "Dese tings—dey have not been found?"

"Not that I know of."

"Den how you know someone steal? Maybe dey just lose dem, no?"

"We haven't any proof, Jan. But so many things have disappeared suddenly that we can't help being a little suspicious."

"Please, what means 'suspicious'?"

"That means we think there may be a thief in the school."

"Oh."

"Well, Jan, you keep your eyes open, will you? You don't think it might be one of the boys in your dormitory, do you?"

For a moment Jan's eyes glittered, and a shadow of a smile played around his lips. "Maybe." He got down from his chair. "I go now?"

Miller went to him and put his hand on his shoulder. "Of course, if you want to, Jan. But it's very early. What are you going to do with yourself all evening?"

"Notting."

And without a look back, the boy walked out of the room and closed the door.

He wandered slowly along the corridor and up the stairs to his dormitory, his back very straight and his fists clenched. It was strange, but his throat ached, there seemed to be water in his eyes, and he couldn't see very well. With his fists still tight, he rubbed his eyes angrily. He wished he could have told Dr. Miller that he had really wanted to go with him to that place with the funny name, but he couldn't. That would spoil all his plans. Someday he would tell him—

when he was grown-up, maybe—and he'd tell him that he thought he was a nice man, too. But not now—oh, no, not now!

He stopped when he reached the dormitory door and cast a stealthy glance around him and listened. Then he tiptoed down the back stairs and out into the misty twilight. The rain had stopped and a little wind had sprung up. He made his way through the orchard to the far end, until he came to his favorite tree. He shinnied up it until he reached a long sloping "V," made by the juncture of the trunk and the largest bough. There he curled himself up, one arm twisted around a smaller branch. The wet leaves moved gently in the April breeze and dripped on his brown head. He lifted his small face to the cool drops and peered through the branches, watching the huge red sun sink behind the warm horizon.

"Sit down, Adams, make yourself comfortable. Let me give you some of this brandy. It's very good—quite old. I brought it back with me from Quebec. They seem to be much better off as far as liquor is concerned than the rest of Canada."

"Thank you, Doctor."

"Have a cigar? They're Coronas."

"No, thanks. I'm afraid I'm allergic to cigars. If you don't mind, I'll smoke one of my own cigarettes."

Adams pulled out a gold cigarette case and his long black holder, settled back in his chair, and looked inquiringly at Miller.

"I'm sorry, Adams, if I've taken you away from a bridge game, but I wanted to have a little talk with you."

It was the third night after the reopening of school and Dr. Miller had asked the young mathematics instructor to give him an hour in his study after dinner.

"I'm in something of a quandary about young Lyttleton and I thought perhaps you might help me."

"Me, Doctor?"

"Yes. I think you've known the boy better than any of us, and he's always had confidence in you."

Adams smiled. "Not any more, I'm afraid. As a matter of fact, Doctor, I was going to ask you to put him in a lower class. I'm rather ashamed to admit it, but I'm afraid I let my enthusiasm run away with me. I was too ambitious for him."

"And I think you're wrong, Adams. I don't think it's a question of his brain. He's a clever boy—always has been—but something is bothering him, and I thought he might tell you what it is. You see, Adams, an odd thing occurred several weeks ago and I can't get to the bottom of it."

The headmaster related the story of the quarrel in the dormitory as far as he knew it, telling about the half-burned effigy that was found in the waste-paper basket and the wall of silence of the entire twelve which he couldn't break through.

Adams listened intently, puffing on his cigarette and blowing smoke rings, which he watched as they floated up toward the ceiling and disintegrated into a soft cloud of smoke.

"So he's a Jew, is he? It had never occurred to me."

"I don't know that he is, Adams, and I don't think it matters whether he is or not."

"But this school is supposed to be strictly for Gentiles, isn't it? At least, I was led to believe that when I accepted the post here."

"That is not the question."

"Well, it would account for the boys' dislike of him, wouldn't it?"

The young man's eyes were hard and he smiled superciliously. Miller had always suspected that the snob was rampant in Adams, but he was quite unprepared for this virulent racial prejudice.

"The fact of the matter is, Adams, the boy is the adopted son of Mrs. Robert Lyttleton, who is a daughter of a very distinguished scholar, a man whom I admired tremendously," Miller said. "Besides, I like the boy. I don't want to expel him from school, which I may be forced to do, but only because of his conduct and his refusal to conform to rules. I assure you it wouldn't be because of his being a Jew."

Adams said nothing. He simply shrugged his shoulders.

"I know the child likes you and believes in you, and I think you could talk to him. Do you want to have a go at it?"

"I can try, Doctor, but I don't think I shall meet with any glaring success. If he is, as I suspect, a—a non-Aryan, I should hardly know how to approach him. However, I can try."

Miller suddenly got to his feet. "Don't try, Adams, don't try. I don't think you are the man for the job. I'm sorry to have taken you away from your bridge."

"You misunderstand me, sir—"

"I don't think so, Adams." He went to the study door and opened it. "May I ask you not to repeat this conversation?"

"Naturally, Doctor."

"Good night, Adams."

Adams pulled his slight body out of the chair, acknowledged his dismissal with a faint smile, and left the room.

"One hundred and ninety-six, divided by seventeen and a half, multiplied by fourteen and a half is-is-er—"

Mike weaved from one foot to the other, his face screwed up with concentration.

"Come, come, my dear Michael, the answer is perfectly simple if you know your—"

"—is—is a hundred and sixty-four and a fifth."

"Dat is wrong," said Jan impulsively from his desk in the center of the classroom. "It is one hundr-red sixty-two and two-fits."

There was a moment's hush in the room, then Henry Adams turned with a sarcastic smile and looked long and fixedly at Jan. He put down the piece of chalk he was holding, brushed his long, slender hands delicately, and glanced with narrowed eyes around the classroom.

"Has our young Einstein deigned to speak to us at last?" he said. "May I humbly suggest that you wait until you are spoken to, Lyttleton? All right, Michael, that was a good try, my boy. I'll give you another."

The mathematics hour droned on to its close, Jan having again retired into his customary immobility. When the hour was over, Adams held up his hand as the boys scrambled to their feet.

"Just a minute," he commanded. "Will the young genius, who has so consistently refused to co-operate with us during the last few weeks, kindly remain behind? I mean you, Lyttleton."

As they left the room, several of the boys looked at Jan and grinned scornfully, and the whispering and snickering which began just outside wafted back to the man and the boy, until the last pupil shut the door behind him.

Adams stared at the child, who looked back at him with calm, steady eyes, but the man's mood, brought on by Miller's reprimand the night before and his own emotional disappointment and petty resentment of his favorite's abrupt change, did not alter. He refused to recognize the warmth and admiration in Jan's eyes, now that class was over and the boys had disappeared.

"Lyttleton," he said, "your manners are unspeakable! First, you obstinately persist in refusing to conform to class rules; you are disobedient, and impudent when I speak to you; and then, when it pleases you, you interrupt me and embarrass both me and your fellow-student."

Jan continued to look at him, but he didn't answer.

"What's the matter, Lyttleton, have you lost your tongue again?"

"I do not understand dose big wor-rds."

"Do you understand this?" Adams asked disagreeably. "You are a bad boy!"

"So?" said Jan.

"If you intend remaining in this school, I should prefer that you do not attend my class."

254

For the second time, the boy blinked away something hot and wet that blinded him. Slowly he walked to the door, but when his hand was on the knob, he turned and looked inquiringly at his instructor. "Mr-r-r. Adam," he said, "why you call me Einstein? Dat is not my name."

"Didn't you ever hear of Einstein?"

Jan shook his head.

"Well, Einstein is a Jewish genius such as you might turn out to be, under some other teacher, if you behave yourself."

Adams turned away from the boy and began looking through some papers on his desk.

The lonely little figure still stood there, leaning against the door. "I do not know dis wor-rd 'gen-i-us'—"

"Skip it!" said Adams impatiently.

"And why you call me 'Jew'? Ever-r-ybody call me 'Jew.' It is funny," he continued, wistfully.

"Aren't you a Jew, Lyttleton?"

"I do not know."

Adams looked up at this boy who previously had moved him so deeply and felt a little ashamed of himself. The child's sorrowful brown eyes, fixed steadily on him, confused him, and when he spoke his slightly effeminate voice had lost its rasp.

"You may go now, Jan. And as long as you are in my class, I hope you will change and try to study the way you used to."

"Tank you. I do not come again," he said in a low voice and he went out quietly and closed the door.

He stood for a moment on the other side of the door, mute and motionless. He looked up and down the empty corridor. Which way should he go now? His new world had crashed about his ears and there seemed no escape—no exit from this concerted treachery.

Somewhere in some remote channel of his small, slowly awakening brain, a new word was pounding: the word "why." It was a word he had never learned in any language. His existence had always been one of acceptance, but now, little by little, he was becoming conscious of the fact that they had given him something and then taken it away. Why?

All the "why"s began to take human form and stalk through his mind. The first "why" was the pretty, kind lady who had taken him and then sent him here away from her, where all the other "why"s—the boys in his dormitory, Peter Lawson, and now Mr. Adams—could hurt him. They had even taken Olga away from him and he couldn't find his way back to her.

Why? Oh, why?

255

He wandered down the corridor, out of the little door at the end toward his favorite hiding place in the orchard, blind with a new pain he didn't understand. He climbed up into the tree clutching his small safety branch with both hands, his little thin body shaking with dry sobs which he couldn't control. If he could only find the way, he would even go back to that camp with its beatings and torture and death, just so he could feel Olga's strong arms around him and her great, full bosom under his head.

One thing he knew: he would not stay here now! He would not wait to be sent away; he would go, quickly.

This man, who had given him food for his brain and confidence in himself, had fallen from the pedestal he'd put him on. He would not stay in the school and see him lying there, day after day.

There was no kindness here, so he would go.

He must steal again. Food, this time. He couldn't take his trunk, but his suitcase would hold all that he needed—the food, too. He had enough money.

He put his small hand deep in a hole in the trunk of the tree, which at one time must have been a haven for wild bees. Out of its blackness he drew an old soiled sock, which he stuffed in one of his pockets. He didn't have to count it. He knew the exact amount, twenty-three dollars and eighty cents.

It was a long walk into Manchester, but he was used to walking. Hadn't he walked miles and miles in Europe? Of course, Olga had always been there to carry him when his legs couldn't move any more—but he mustn't think of Olga. He must think of his plans.

All afternoon, he stole in and out of the dormitory. When no one was there, he went to his locker, and each time he slipped something into his suitcase. He hung around the back door, and when Katie left the kitchen, he would dart in and snatch any article of food he could see, then be off like an arrow to hide it under the lilac bush just beneath his window.

It was well after midnight and all the boys were sound asleep when he slipped out of bed. He put on his robe, took his shoes in one hand, his suitcase which had been under the bed in the other, and in his bare feet he stealthily tiptoed out of the dormitory, closed the door, and ran down the stairs. The house was completely silent and dark, except for a dim light in the upper hall and a lighted bracket in the lower, next to the front door.

He took off the chain, opened the door as quietly as he could, and closed it after him. Hurriedly he went around to the lilac bush, opened

256

his suitcase, and stuffed the stolen food into it. He put on his shoes, and began running swiftly on the grass along the edge of the graveled road toward the big gates.

Once outside the gates, he stripped, put on a shirt and tie, trousers, socks, jacket and overcoat, put his pajamas and robe back in the suitcase, which was now much easier to close, stuck a cap on the back of his head, and stood for a moment looking back through the gates. He was sorry he couldn't have said good-by to Dr. Miller. Deep down inside him, he felt that Dr. Miller would understand.

As he walked down the country road, he looked up into the clear April sky at the stars, which twinkled approvingly at him, and the pale full moon, which cast a friendly shadow of himself beside him to keep him company. He walked slowly along, glancing at the occasional dark houses which took no notice of him as he passed. The dirt crunched cheerily under his feet, and he whistled softly to the rhythm of the sound. He quickened his pace. He was going home.

25

THERE IS A MISTY moment between the dark shadows of sleep and the bright, hard reality of wakefulness that a troubled mind clutches desperately as a means of escape. For Pax, that moment stretched into a nebulous two weeks during her visit in Savannah. Day after day, she deliberately tired herself out; in the afternoons, golfing with borrowed clubs or riding in Mary's riding clothes; at night, dinner parties at the homes of Bob's friends or at the country club, dancing until her feet ached, drinking a little too many of those fragrant juleps, so that when the thoughts did come they were hazy and dulled.

The visit that she was never able to remember very clearly finally came to an end. She went with a sense of release and thankfulness that she was going home to familiar surroundings—and to Philip, who could always straighten things out for her.

The journey back was made swiftly with few stopovers. During the last ten miles, she kept her foot steadily on the accelerator, leaning forward on the edge of the seat, her hands tense on the wheel.

The car hummed along the last winding roads, up the hill and around the Green. There it was. The old Victorian house, friendly and ugly; her son would be inside, Philip two minutes away—and time! Time to think and to talk to Philip; to tell him that after all Robert didn't miss his friend; that there was no reason now for a small Jake; that she was desperately in need of help.

It was during dinner that night that the next blow struck. Everything had been warm and natural and gay. Even Pansy seemed glad to see them, smiling her old brilliant smile, chuckling and hovering over them just as if they had been her own children coming home. Robert was relaxed and happy, and Tubby hung around her neck, kissing her over and over again.

And then it came.

Tubby dropped his spoon in his soup plate with a loud clatter and clapped a chubby hand over his mouth, his blue eyes round with remembrance.

"Gee, Mom! I almost forgot," he squealed. "Somebody telephoned from the school at Manchester this morning at eight o'clock. There was nobody here but me and Pansy, so the man said I was to tell you to call him as soon as you came, and that you were not to worry and that they were doing everything and I forgot what else, and I told him I'd tell you and I guess you'd better call him—"

Oh, God! What now?

"Thank you, darling," said Pax, smiling easily at him. "I'll call after dinner. It can't be anything that won't wait. Robert, do you suppose we could have some of that fine Nazi wine of yours to celebrate our first night home?"

Bob raised his brows at the word "Nazi." A little frown flickered across his face and was gone.

"Sure thing, honey chile. Tubs, go see if Pansy's got a cold bottle on ice."

But she wasn't going to telephone—not tonight, anyway. She had told Tubby it could wait, and it could wait. Couldn't she have at least one night off this treadmill?

She wouldn't think. She didn't have to think; she'd trained herself in the last two weeks not to think. Another night wouldn't hurt. Robert was probably tired from the long trip and very likely would want to go to bed early, and if that wretched little boy insisted upon parading through her brain, she could wait until Robert was safely in bed, and then she could run across to Philip and telephone from there.

But Robert wasn't tired. The old clock on the Green pealed forth its ten bells and they were still playing—it seemed to her—their hundredth hand of gin, when the library door opened quietly.

Standing in the doorway, the hall light shining on his touseled brown hair, was Jan. His small face was drawn and white, and deep blue circles were under his eyes. A valise was in one hand, his cap in the other.

Pax's eyes widened, and she stared over Robert's shoulder at the still little figure at the door.

"Hello," Jan said.

Bob dropped the cards that he was holding and turned quickly in his chair. "Hello," he said, "who are you?"

Jan looked calmly from one to the other.

"Why, Jan!" Pax said. "Where did you come from?"

"From school. I have come home."

Bob got up from his chair and stood, leaning on the back of it, smiling at the child. "Well, come in, feller! Sit down. We've just come home, too."

There's no doubt about it, thought Pax, God certainly has an ironic sense of timing! What do we do now? Where's that time I was figuring on?

"How did you get here—er—Jan—is that your name?"

Jan turned his tired brown eyes to her. "I walk, den I take tr-rains, den I walk some mor-re."

Bob laughed. "The kid can certainly take care of himself, can't he, baby?" he said good-naturedly. "What did they do? Send you away?"

Jan stuck his sharp little chin forward and his eyes flashed. "Nobody send me. I come. I do not stay der-re any mor-re."

"Well, that's very interesting," said Bob. "Are you hungry? You look hungry."

"I am hungr-ry," he replied flatly.

"Oh, dear, are you?" said Pax, starting for the door. "I'll get you something to eat, Jan. You stay here with—" She stopped and laughed nervously. "I didn't introduce you two! Jan, this is Tubby's father. Now, you stay here, and I'll be right back."

Pax ran from the room, her heart pounding.

"Come over here, kid, let's have a look at you." Bob looked at the boy quizzically. "How old are you?"

"I do not know. She will tell you. I have bir-rtday soon."

"What's the matter, didn't you like it at school?"

"No."

"But Mrs. Lyttleton tells me you're so smart."

259

"I am smart. I will be scientist—but not in de school."

"Is that so?" said Bob curiously.

"School no good. Ever-rybody cr-razy. Dey call me—" He shut up suddenly, walked away from Bob, sat down in the straight-backed chair by the door, and retired into his usual silence.

"What do they call you, young feller?"

"Notting," said Jan sullenly.

Fifteen minutes later, Pax stood by the table making the last sandwich from the chicken left over from dinner. She had arranged a tray, with a large glass of milk, a peach, and a piece of chocolate layer cake, and was just getting ready to take it in to the boy when she heard Robert's footsteps hobbling along the hall.

She looked at him anxiously as he came through the door. He was smiling, but there was a strange glint in his eyes.

"It's taking you a hell of a long time, baby," he said.

Then he took her by the shoulders and turned her around to him. She could feel his fingers press into her flesh and he looked down at her and grinned oddly.

"He's a Jew, isn't he?"

The kitchen was making a fast rotary motion in front of her eyes. Her knees seemed to have no relation to her legs, and there was an odd humming in her ears. She put the sandwich on the plate and picked up the tray, the milk swaying dangerously in the glass. She heard herself saying foolishly, "Who?"

She pushed by him into the hall, clutching the tray in her hands, calling back to him as she went into the library.

"Put out the light in the kitchen, will you, darling? I won't bother cleaning up tonight."

Jan was still sitting in the chair near the door, twirling his cap between his two hands.

"Sit over here in this big chair, Jan, so I can put the tray on the table," she said cheerfully. "Think that'll be enough for you? It's pretty late, and we don't want any upset tummies during the night."

"Tank you," said Jan.

Bob followed them in, and sat down opposite the child, leaning forward, his forearms on his knees, his big hands clasped in front of him. Pax flashed a look across at him from beneath her lashes. He was gazing steadily at Jan and smiling, but the smile was fixed and without warmth.

If only Philip were there!

A sudden feeling of anger at herself assailed her. Was she going to spend the rest of her life running to Philip, making a bloody nuisance of herself, asking him to help her out of messes and then stubbornly refusing to follow his advice? It was senseless and she had to stop it! He had showed her plainly during the last few months that he was tired of it—and of her too, she guessed.

Her hand shook—damn it—as she handed the glass of milk to the boy, and then curled herself up on the floor between the two of them.

"Not so fast, Jan! You'll be sick!"

"Do you eat chicken that isn't kosher, feller?"

That was Robert's voice, soft and caressing, but there was a bright hardness in his eyes that frightened her.

Suddenly she reached into her need for Philip and felt an unfamiliar strength course through her veins. After all, this was her house; her money was taking care of this child; he was hers—for the time being, anyway—and it was up to her to protect him.

"Stop that, Robert! Stop it at once!"

Was that Pax Lyttleton, nee Gifford, the perennial coward speaking?

"What's that?" asked Bob, and she could hear the edge in his high tone.

"I said stop it! That's enough! It's more than enough, if you really want to know!" She turned to Jan. "Finish your supper, sweetie. It's time for small boys to be in bed."

"What means 'kosher'?" asked Jan, his mouth full. "I have heard dat wor-rd, I tink."

"I really don't know, Jan dear. It's probably some German word that Tubby's dad has picked up. And you and I don't like German words, do we, Jan?" she said.

"Did you run away from school, kid?" Bob said.

Jan looked at him indifferently. "I do not run. I walk."

"Jan dear," said Pax hurriedly, "I'm not going to ask you any questions tonight, except this: Did your coming home have anything to do with Dr. Miller's message this morning? I mean, does he know where you are? Because if he doesn't, I want to phone him that you're all right —that you're with us. Then we'll talk tomorrow."

Jan shrugged. "I come home. I do not say I come."

She jumped to her feet, took the napkin off his lap, and wiped his greasy little face.

"Up you go, Jan! You may take your peach with you. Start to get undressed and I'll run a warm tub for you. It'll make you sleep. Robert dear, I think, at this moment, you're rather a small, weary boy yourself, after that long trip. Why don't you go to bed? I'll put out the lights and phone Dr. Miller; then I'll tuck Jan up and be with you in half an hour."

She was pushing them both out of the room—and Robert was going! How easy it was! This new power was making her very pleased with herself, indeed. She would talk to Robert firmly before they went to sleep. There were many things she wanted to tell him, and many questions she wanted to ask him—about Jake, mainly. She would demand to know, once and for all, the reason for his disloyalty to his friend. She would have the whole thing out with him tonight!

She hummed softly to herself as she drew the water for Jan's bath, and pulled out of the bathroom chest a toweling robe to wrap him in. Then she went into his room.

His open suitcase was lying on the floor, his clothes flung untidily— half of them on the chair, half on the floor—and his robe and pajamas were over the foot of his bed.

Sprawled across the bed, sound asleep, with only his shirt on, Jan lay on his face, the half-eaten peach still clutched in his hand.

Pax stood looking down at him a moment; then she gently turned him over. His brown hair was clinging to his forehead in damp ringlets; his face and lips were dead white. She took the squashy wet peach away from him and, holding his slight body in one arm, she pulled off his shirt and managed to get him into the coat of his pajamas. She put his tired little head on the pillow and pulled the covers over him.

Impulsively she leaned over and kissed him on his dirty cheek. Jan sighed, and the eyelids lifted for a second, the brown irises floating upward sleepily in the milk-white mistiness which was his eyes. A mysterious little smile touched the corners of his mouth for an instant and was gone.

He murmured one word, "Olga," and, flinging one thin arm across the pillow, he turned away from Pax in his sleep.

Pax drew back, and a sudden pain stabbed at her heart. She felt the new-found strength ebbing away.

She turned off the light, closed the door softly, and tiptoed back into her room.

Robert was asleep too, lying nearly on her side of the bed, his arm wound around her pillow. She stopped short and a bitter smile spread across her face.

Her two protagonists had walked out on her!

She knew she should feel relieved—time had been given back to her again—but somehow she wasn't. What was she to do with her new strength now? Would it be there in the morning?

She lit a cigarette, stuck it in the corner of her mouth, and sat down in a chair to pull off her stockings. She got one off, then leaned back, and with her eyes squinting against the smoke which was curling up and around her head, she looked off through the walls of her room, through the walls of Jan's room, into the future, seeing shadowy changes faintly outlined there.

Suddenly she felt the old self-pity stealing over her. She tried to push it away but she couldn't. Here she was, in the middle of the night, all ready to go into battle, with no one to fight for—or with!

And the next day, the battleground was still receding; Jan had risen early, breakfasted with Pansy, and both he and his bicycle were missing. Bob asked casually for her "foundling" and when she told him just as casually that he was "somewhere about," he dropped the subject.

And so Jake was left, sleeping peacefully, and all the brave unsaid things of the night before remained in the limbo of another commonplace day that went straggling on.

Tubby rushed home from school that afternoon in unaccustomed haste, leaving his gang to play by themselves.

"Where's Pop?" he asked as he ran breathlessly into the kitchen, where Pax was taking time out to give Pansy messages from home.

"Upstairs in his room resting, I think," replied Pax. "Do you want something, Tubs?"

"I want Pop."

"I wouldn't disturb him if I were you, Tubby."

"I'm not goin' to disturb him, Mom. I've got a 'pointment with him."

He started out of the kitchen, Pax following him.

"I think your 'pointment can wait, Tubs. He won't run away, and he needs his rest."

Tubby's good-natured face became set and stubborn. He swung on the newel post, frowning down on her.

"That's just like a woman," he said, with the arrogant lift of his head so like his father's. "They never keep 'pointments. We men are different."

He began sneaking up the stairs, one step at a time.

"Tubby, come back here! Don't you realize that your daddy's had a very bad accident and we want to get him completely well—"

" 'Daddy'!" he said scornfully. "That's a sissy thing to call him!" He slipped up another step, then smiled that ingratiating, sweet smile she knew so well. "Anyway, Pop won't mind. He promised." He scrambled up the last few steps and she heard him running along the upper hall, heard the door of their bedroom flung open, and his high voice floating down to her.

"Hey, Pop! Wake up! You promised! You promised before you went to Granny's—" and the door slam cut off the rest.

I certainly have a way with the Lyttletons, she thought. One word from me and they do exactly as they please.

Ten or fifteen minutes later, Tubby tumbled down the stairs and into the kitchen, his round face aglow with excitement.

"See? I told you! Come on up, Mom, he's got sumpin' for you, too!" and he flew back upstairs.

Pax smiled at the two fair heads bending over Robert's foot locker. Old soiled army shirts and linen were strewn all over the floor, and a heavy German beer stein had rolled toward the door and was lying in her path.

"Hello, honey chile," said Bob, grinning at her. "We got presents. This is for you, baby." He handed her an untidily wrapped package tied with a piece of knotted string. "That's not all! I've got some perfume for you somewhere, if I can find it. It's black market, but you don't mind that, do you, darlin'?"

Pax unwrapped her package and held up two prewar nightgowns, made of shiny bright pink satin and coarse lace.

"They're lovely, darling. Thank you, Robert."

She went on admiring them extravagantly, but she smiled to herself and wondered what in the world she was ever going to do with them.

"I know they're not as pretty as French ones, baby, but then, you know, we weren't occupying France."

"Mom, look! Medals!" Tubby held out a handful of metal disks and ribbons for her to see. "German ones! Pop says all the big German generals had 'em! And I got a trench coat! Pop had it made for me. It's just like the ones the Storm Troopers wore. Look, Mom!" He wriggled in and out of a gray coat which came down nearly to the tops of his shoes. "It's a little big for me, but I'll grow into it, I guess."

They heard the sound of footsteps coming along the hall.

"It's Jan!" yelled Tubby. "Where yuh been, huh? Come on in."

"Hello, Jan dear," said Pax. "Did you know Jan was here, Tubby? He came last night."

"Sure I knew. I saw him this morning before I went to school. Come on over here and have a look, Jan. Pop's brought the most wonderfulest things home!"

"Hello, boy. Have a good day?" said Bob.

"Tank you."

"My goodness, Jan, just look at you! Where on earth have you been?" exclaimed Pax. "Don't tell me you haven't had a bath yet!"

Jan smiled faintly and looked down at his knees. They were black

264

with dirt, his slender knuckles were grimy, and he had a dark smudge across his cheek.

"I go on de bicycle, and den I go in de woods."

"Jan dear, you haven't had any lunch."

"Oh, yes, I have lunch. Aunt Amy, Uncle Philip give me lunch."

Bob looked up sharply and frowned. "'Uncle Philip'?" he said. "You've taken on quite a family for yourself, haven't you, kid? You and I are going to have to get acquainted." Bob went back to his foot locker and began rummaging in it. "Well, we'll have to find you a present, too, won't we?"

Jan looked at him gravely. "Tank you," he said.

"What about this?" asked Bob, holding out a wrist watch. "It's an old wrist watch of mine. It isn't going now, but it's a good one and we can have it fixed. Want that?"

"I have wrist watch. Uncle Philip and she give me watch, for Chr-ristmas."

The boy rolled up the sleeve of his shirt to show it, but he rolled it up a little too high. He pulled the sleeve down quickly, but Bob's eyes had already seen the livid mark.

"What's that, kid?"

"What?"

"That mark on your arm."

"Oh, dat? Dat is wher-re I live in Eur-rope."

"Oh, let me see, Jan!" cried Tubby. "I never saw that!"

"No!" said Jan, and retreated a little way toward the door.

"You see? The mark of Judea, just as I told you, my darling," said Bob, and to Pax his voice seemed to purr with satisfaction.

"What's Judea?" asked Tubby.

"You tink I am *Jude*, no?" said Jan to Bob, and then he looked wistfully at Pax, who stood there as if she were made of stone. "Dis man not like *Jude*?" he asked.

"Hey! What's *Jude*?" said Tubby.

"*Jude* is Jew," replied Jan. "Ever-rybody say I am Jew. It is funny. I guess I am Jew, no?"

He didn't look away from Pax and a painful, crooked little smile curled the corners of his mouth.

"That's right, kid," said Bob softly.

Pax suddenly found the will to move. She went swiftly over to the boy, knelt down, and put her arms around him.

"You are our boy, Jan," she said, smiling into his bewildered eyes, "and we love you. But at the moment you're a very dirty one! You go in and wash your face and hands, that's a good child. Then when you come back, we'll look at all the strange things that Tubby's dad—I mean Tubby's pop—has brought home to us." She kissed him lightly on the cheek and gave him a little shove. "Oh, Jan," she called as he walked slowly from the room, "I'd wash those knees too, if I were you."

She looked at Bob and her yellow eyes were dark with anger.

They sat there for a moment in silence and then Tubby's high voice broke it. "Is Jan a Jew, Mom?" he asked curiously.

"I don't know his religion, Tubby," she replied coldly. "I think he's too small to have one. When you know a little more, son, you'll learn that people's religions belong to themselves. When Jan's older, I think he'll probably tell us if he knows. But until he does, Tubby, don't let me hear you use that word again."

"So you think it's a filthy word, too, Pax." Bob had a mocking grin on his face.

Her lids fluttered nervously and then she raised her eyes and stared straight at him. "Filthy, no. Unpleasant, yes, when it's used to hurt someone. I'm afraid Tubby isn't old enough yet to know the difference. So until you do, Tubby, don't use it. Do you understand?"

"Yes, Mom," he said, but he looked at his father as he said it.

"That goes for you too, darling," she said calmly to Bob. "Would you mind giving me a cigarette?"

"Sure thing, baby," replied Bob, and he held out his cigarette case to Tubby. "Give this to your mother, son. Here, give her the lighter, too. Forgive my bad manners, darling. I'd light it for you, but my damn leg, you know—"

"That's all right, Robert, I've been lighting them for myself for a long time," she said.

"Is that so?" said Bob. "I always thought Philip had good manners. Didn't he light 'em for you?"

"Oh, yes. But then, you see, I haven't seen as much of him lately as I would have liked."

For a moment there was a strange, new antagonism between them. Then Bob turned back to his foot locker.

"Come on, son, let's see what else we can find."

Tubby sat down on the floor near his father, his knees tucked under his chin, his arms around them.

How alike they are, thought Pax, and I don't think I really know either of them.

"This is an S.S. dagger, Tubs. They always carried them in their belt. Here you are, son. It's for you."

"Gee, Pop!" breathed Tubby.

266

"Robert! You're not going to give him that, are you? He'll hurt himself!"

"Nonsense, honey. Think we can trust you not to cut yourself with it, son?"

"Aw, Pop, what do you think I am? A baby?"

Pax sighed and gave up.

Jan slipped back into the room and, for the first time that she could remember, he came of his own free will and stood close beside her, and she felt his slight body press against her shoulder.

Out of the foot locker, Bob pulled a strange-looking flying helmet and goggles. They were stained and torn, caked with something stiff and dark that made Pax instinctively shudder.

"There's a real souvenir for you, Tubs," said Bob. "I pulled it out of the wreck of a plane I shot down over England, before the row really started. It was my first plane. I was as proud as hell! The poor bastard gave me a rough ten minutes. They were great fliers, those fritzes."

"Mom! Look! Pop shot him down!" cried Tubby, holding it out to her.

"Take it away, Tubby. I'd rather not see it," she said, and she turned her head away and put one arm around Jan.

"Mom's a softie," taunted Tubby. Then he caught sight of something his father was turning over in his hand. "What's that, Pop?" He tried to snatch it, but Bob held it away from him.

"Oh, gee! It's a Luger! I've always wanted a Luger! Aw, gimme it, Pop, will yuh?"

"I'll do nothing of the kind. That, my son, is *verboten*. No firearms for boys. They're apt to go off when you're not looking, even with grownups."

"Aw, please, Pop! I'd be careful, honest! I've always wanted one! Please, *please*, Pop, won't yuh, please?"

"No, son. Definitely, no."

"Can't I hold it just a minute, Pop? Is it loaded?"

"Yes, it's loaded. But it's not going to be for long." Bob removed the cartridge clip from the gun, and put them both back in his locker.

"How did you get it, Pop? Did you capture that, too?"

Bob laughed. "No, Tubs, I didn't. I'm afraid the *Luftwaffe* used heavier guns than that. No, I traded it with a German officer for a carton of cigarettes. It was a good trade." He dug down into the locker again. "Here's something for you, son. You can have this if you want it, or you might give it to Jan. He might like it." And again that strange glitter came into his eyes.

It was a Nazi arm band with a large black swastika.

267

Pax felt a little shudder pass through the body of the child who was leaning against her; his hand gripped her shoulder and the nails pressed into her flesh. She looked up at him quickly, and the old panic which she hadn't seen for so long was in his dark eyes. She got to her feet abruptly and took his hand in hers.

"Come along, Jan, let's leave these two bloodthirsty wretches to their gory loot. You'll excuse us, boys? You see, Jan and I prefer to remember the Germans when they were people, not brutes. Come on, Jan dear, let's you and me take a walk."

For two or three days there was a feeling of quiet in the old Gifford house, but it was that breathless stillness which comes before a storm, when no leaf flutters and great dark clouds hang motionless in the sky waiting to release their force.

It was an armed truce.

Between Pax and Bob an ominous spark had been struck which she was certain would, one day, take fire again. His first suspicion of jealousy toward Philip had amazed her. She decided, cynically, that it couldn't possibly be due to any new growth of his love for her. It was probably resentment because it was Philip who had helped her bring Jan into his house.

Occasionally, Bob couldn't resist trying to win the boy to him. Bob's native desire to be liked by everyone—even by those whom he disliked —would come to the surface in spite of himself. But he soon gave it up because the child absolutely refused to be won over. He was like a young animal, instinctively sensing the smoldering hatred that was in the man.

Jan clung more and more to Pax, when he was in the house—which wasn't often—but he was still unwilling to confide in her. She tried repeatedly to find out from him why he had run away from school, but she was always met with the same stony silence.

Dr. Miller had been able to tell her very little. He told her what he thought was the reason, but he couldn't be sure.

"May I speak to you very frankly?" he had said.

"Of course."

"Is Jan a Jew?"

"I don't know for a fact, Dr. Miller," she replied, "but I think he is."

"I want to assure you, Mrs. Lyttleton, that it doesn't make the slightest difference to me whether he is or not. I hope you won't mind if I suggest—for his sake—that you be quite honest about it." He had hesitated for a moment. "I don't think, if I were you, that I would send him back this term—not for that reason, believe me, but he was unhappy

268

here. Don't worry about his studies. He's way ahead in those. If he wants to come back next semester, I shall be only too glad to have him. I believe in him and I like him. Let him make up his own mind. If I know the boy, I think he'll come. Be gentle with him, Mrs. Lyttleton. He's a sensitive child, and I think a hurt one. How's Bob? Give him my best."

And so Jan had stayed. He kept out of their way a great deal. He would go spinning away on his bicycle, a sober little fellow, very intent on his own affairs.

Jan and Tubby grew further apart. Pax wondered if she imagined it, but she was quite sure that she noticed a difference in Tubby's attitude to Jan, and in the attitude of the other boys with whom Tubby played.

There was one thing which bothered her greatly. She had told her son never to mention the word "Jew" before her again. She had made a great mistake and done a dangerous thing, and her weak explanation hadn't been good enough. Her thoughts went back to that day in the garden so long ago when she'd said the same thing to Em. She'd been so ignorant then. She was ignorant now, but one thing she'd learned; not to say the word "Jew" didn't solve anything.

Tubby had not referred to it again before her, but she wasn't sure of what he said outside. She hesitated to bring the subject up again; she was afraid of its ramifications. Better let sleeping dogs lie! It would be stupid of her at this point to unleash the malice which she knew was lurking just beneath the apparent placidity of this little family of hers.

26

THE RADIANT day dawned at last; radiant on the soft-colored horizon, but a thousand times more so in Jan's heart-tripping anticipation.

It had been difficult for him to go to sleep the night before, and when he did his short spans of sleep had been interrupted by the striking of the church clock. He lay there, counting the bells, trying to urge the night along to the wonderful day he had been waiting for so long.

It would be silly to get up and dress and wander about the still house, so he lay there as the laggard sun climbed the skies, thinking, thinking, wondering if she would remember this moment which she had given him.

Of course, it really belonged to him as other days belonged to every other human being, but he hadn't known it, or else he'd forgotten.

He thought back as far as he was able to; to the grim, grassless compound where he had spent most of his life; the barbed wire and the huts, dreary and stark in the daytime, splashed with blinding electric searchlights at night; the howling of the dogs who were less hungry than he; misery and death, hovering, hovering—each day taking their toll of the only humans he had ever known. Naturally, his mother, in the short time he had known her, hadn't had time to remember. Olga hadn't had time either—or else she had been too engrossed with the fight for her life, and his.

But it was here now! And then his young mind began to wonder cynically if *she* would forget it as it had always been forgotten before.

At seven o'clock, he couldn't bear it any longer. He got up, dressed, and quietly stole down to the kitchen, where he was sure Pansy would soon be moving about.

There she was, sitting in the open doorway, the sunlight warming her smooth brown skin. She was beating something in a large yellow bowl.

"Hello, son. Ain't you up early?" she said. "You got to wait a while for your breakfas'. I got sumpin' t' do."

"What's dat you make?"

"I'm bakin' a cake. You don' like cake, do you?"

A slow smile broke over Jan's face. Maybe—

For the next half hour, he wandered in and out of the kitchen, eating a banana, trying to behave as if this was a perfectly normal day—and trying not to hope too much. When the cake was in the oven, Pansy offered to get him some breakfast but he refused it, saying he guessed he'd wait for the rest of the family this morning.

"Where's your bicycle? You-all goin' be late for that date you have every mo'nin', ain't yuh?"

He smiled again, then looked up quickly. Those were footsteps on the floor above! Then he heard them swiftly running downstairs.

"Jan! Jan!"

It was *her* voice. That's what he'd been waiting for. In a minute he'd know.

She pushed open the door of the kitchen with her elbow, and stood there, her face as shining and eager as his own.

"Many happy returns of the day, Jan!" she said.

270

He turned the words around slowly in his mind. Yes, that's what she meant. It was his birthday, and she had remembered. She was thrusting some packages into his arms.

"Go on, open them! They're for you!"

He sat down at the kitchen table and unwrapped them. A pair of swimming trunks from Tubby. Laboriously he read "Happy Birthday" in Tubby's childish scrawl. A gaily painted top from Pansy; a Brownie camera from Pax and two rolls of film—"Love and many happy birthdays to my Jan from P.L."—and a box containing parts of a toy airplane to be put together. "To Jan from Uncle Robert." He turned the card over slowly and read it, then he put it face down on the kitchen table. It was in *her* handwriting.

"Do you like your presents, Jan?"

How pretty he is when he smiles, she thought.

"Wait a minute, Jan! There's something else! It came in the mail yesterday. I'll get it," and she ran out of the room.

When she returned she was carrying a large round parcel, sealed with red wax, and covered with bright-colored stamps. The shape and size felt familiar. She cut the string for him and his hands shook a little as he opened it. Off came the paper. There was a red bow, in all its beauty, and when he lifted the cover, his nose breathed in the warm, musky smell of chocolates. He stood there motionless, looking at it.

"Aren't you going to read the card? Do you want me to read it for you?"

He nodded and lowered his eyes; they felt hot and sticky.

" 'Dear Jan: This is for your birthday. I had to wait and save my allowance to buy you what you wanted. I hope you like them. Very truly, your friend, Peter Lawson.' "

He didn't speak, but Pax looked at his face closely and thought to herself that it wore happiness like a benediction.

"And now one more thing, and then I must go take my bath. You are going to have a birthday party this afternoon, sweetie. It's all arranged, only you must choose your own guests."

He looked at her strangely, but said nothing.

"Come on, Jan, who do you want to come to your party?"

"You," he breathed.

"Thank you, Jan. I'd love to! Who else?"

He thought for a moment. "Pansy. Uncle Philip. Aunt Amy. Johnnie Leclerc—"

"Not Johnnie, Jan. He is still away at school."

"—Tubby." And he stopped.

"Don't you want any of the boys?"

He shook his head vigorously.

"Tubby's father?"

"No," he said calmly.

The sunlight seemed to fade out of the room and an invisible finger of danger pointed significantly at her. Her mind traveled in swift circles. Robert took his afternoon rest about three.

"All right, Jan. The party's at three-thirty in the library. Be sure you put on your best suit. Wash your hands and brush your hair. I'll invite your guests."

"I have a cake wit candles?" he asked eagerly.

"What you all think I'm doin' in the kitchen at seven o'clock, boy?" chuckled Pansy.

"Twelve candles, Jan. You're growing up!" And Pax left him sitting at the table, one hand clutching the box of candy to his breast, the other happily fingering his other presents.

For Jan, sitting in the library at the small card table, presiding over his birthday party, a pointed red paper cap cocked jauntily on his brown head, it was as if the gray pitiless world which was his prison had split open a little to let in a shining chink of heaven.

They had sung *Happy Birthday to You*, which to his unaccustomed ears seemed the most beautiful sound he had ever heard. Amy and Philip had brought him presents—some marbles from the former, from Philip a small leather wallet, with "J.L." printed in gold letters. The wallet was almost his favorite because of the initials. It meant that Uncle Philip had remembered too, and had planned ahead for his day.

There was ice cream and his own cake, covered with white icing, with his name in chocolate letters and those candles which he'd blown out all by himself.

He'd spent some time, making up his wish. As always his instinct was to wish for Olga, but today he was torn between wishing for her and wishing that Pax would really like him. He finally compromised. His wish was that his guests wouldn't eat all of his lovely candy.

He exulted in the knowledge that this was really his party. He was sure of it, because they all talked just to him, and as he looked from face to face, they were always looking at him—not at Tubby, not at her, at *him*! He didn't know that his own small face so fascinated them that they didn't want to look away, because it was the first time since they'd known him that it was alive with interest.

They had pulled the bright-colored snappers, read the fortunes out loud, and Jan had anxiously passed his box of candy around once, when they were aware of footsteps and a tapping sound approaching the closed library door.

The door opened and Bob stood there, leaning on his cane, his curly fair hair rumpled, his blue eyes swollen with sleep.

Amy and Philip greeted him in their usual friendly manner, Pansy seemed obviously nervous, Pax looked a little anxious, and Tubby welcomed him with squeals of joy.

Only Jan showed no emotion whatever. It was as though an invisible shade had been drawn down over his face, shutting out the shimmering mobility that had been there a moment before, leaving it again lifeless and remote.

"Well, well, well! What is this? A party?" said Bob with an amiable grin.

"Yeah, a birthday party, Pop."

"Whose?"

"Jan's, of course. Didn't you know?"

Bob turned deliberately and looked at Pax, and his eyes became two steel points.

"Is that so?" he said, still grinning, "May seventh, isn't it?"

"That's right, Robert," said Pax gently.

Bob gave a short, hard laugh, and sat down near Jan. "Are you sure they're not putting over something on you, kid?" he asked.

Jan didn't answer. His eyes were so lowered that his long lashes brushed his cheeks.

Again Bob looked at his wife. "Well, boy, if they're not, it sure is a coincidence! Or could it be that it's just a Jewish holiday! I wouldn't know about those things."

Tubby looked puzzled. "You gave him a present, Pop," he said.

"Did I, now?"

"Robert," said Pax, "I don't believe you've had your sleep out."

"How could I, with all this noise?" he replied, reaching for a piece of cake. "Well, I'm awake now—even if Jake isn't."

"Will you excuse me, Jan?" said Philip, patting the boy on the shoulder. "It's getting late and I've got some papers to check. It was a fine party, Jan—just about the finest party I've ever been to." He rose and started for the door. "You going my way, Amy?"

"Yes. Jan dear," Amy said, "if you'll walk over with me, I've got another little present for you. It isn't much, but I think you'll like it. Come along, dear. You can come right back."

Silently, Jan climbed down from his chair, took off his paper cap, and followed them.

"So long, Pax," Philip said. "See you later, Lyttleton." They left.

Again Bob laughed. "Guess I broke up the party, didn't I?"

"How could you, Robert? How could you! A little boy!"

"Pansy," Bob said, "you'd better get back to your kitchen. I didn't know that you made it a habit to sit down with your white folks."

"Robert, you weren't invited to this party. Pansy was. She accepted and she will stay here as long as she pleases." Pax's voice was staccato and cold. "Why don't you go away for a little while and get over your bad temper? I think you've done enough damage."

Bob's answer was to get up lazily, stretch himself out in the big chair in front of the fireplace, and light a cigarette, but his hands were trembling.

"Come on, Tubby. Come out of this room," said Pansy. She took the child by the hand and with a scornful glance at the man she had grown up with, she took Tubby out and closed the door.

There was an ominous stillness in the room. Pax picked up Jan's gifts and put them on the chair by the door, then started to clear the table.

"Well, I was right," said Bob softly. "The son of a bitch double-crossed me even after he was dead."

Pax looked up, startled, and a plate she was holding dropped from her hand and smashed on the floor.

"Robert, what are you saying?"

"I'm saying that I've had enough of the Jew department."

"Robert, don't! You're not talking about Jake! Not Jake!"

"I'm talking about all Jews! Jake, and this little kike who's taken his place with you. To hell with 'em! Slimy bastards!"

As though from far off, through his dammed-up fury, he saw the stricken expression on her face and her eyes blazing with pain and anger; and yet he couldn't stop.

"I should have known then that a Jew can't be a friend to anyone except his own kind! But I was too God-damn innocent and trusting to know it! I had to find it out for myself in a country we cheerfully licked, by God!"

"Stop it, Robert!"

"He gave me his blessing, did he, when I married you? Yes, he did! In a pig's ass! How did he get around you those two years when I was off fighting for Roosevelt's Four Freedoms—and for his Jews and his coons! Plotting and planning, clinging like glue to you, worming his way into your sympathies as they always do, making sure his stinking race would survive—at least in this house! Sure he's dead! But he made sure he'd leave you his heritage—leave it to me, too—another little kike to grow up with my son and torment my life!"

274

He stopped through sheer exhaustion. There was a deathlike silence in the room. Then he heard her voice, sorrowful but aloof.

"Jake was your friend and mine. I don't know you, Robert. Maybe I never did. You are Mary's son. You were born pure in heart. When did the corruption set in?"

"You don't know 'em, baby, as I've grown to know 'em over there. Why haven't you got the guts to admit it?"

"No, I don't know 'em. I only know human beings. That must be a world of hatred over there, Robert. I don't know that world and I don't know you."

"And you don't want to!" He limped over to her and stood towering over her, the anger which she'd never seen before still in his eyes. "You're afraid to slug it out! You run away from things!"

"I can't fight you back, Robert."

"What am I supposed to do, huh? Sit back quietly and take this little Jew into my life?"

"Robert, he's—"

"Because he is a Jew," interrupted the man, "and you can't romance Jews out of existence, you know."

"I don't want to, Robert. That's why I took Jan."

"Fine homecoming he's made for me!"

"What's happened to you, Robert? Have two years over there so distorted your mind that you've forgotten? What are these new values you've learned? I don't mean values! New shames, Robert!"

"Listen to me, Pax. Ask anyone in our Army over there. They'll tell you! They're all slackers! They're no good! They chose all the cushy jobs in the war. They hate us—"

"I don't blame them! Wouldn't you, if someone dug and prodded and tore open your heart as you've been doing to that little boy?"

"Darling, I didn't mean to." His voice was shaking. "Yes, damn it, I guess I did too. Darling, I've given you a son, a fine strong son. I can give you another if you'll take him. Pax! Send that Jew boy away—"

They both heard it at the same moment, a faint shuffling sound near the door. They turned their heads and looked.

Leaning against the jamb of the door, his hands in his pockets, his thin face expressionless, was Jan.

"Hello, Jan," she finally whispered. "Did Aunt Amy give you your present?"

Jan said nothing. He just stood there, his big brown eyes staring at her.

Had he heard? She tried her best to smile at him.

"Jan, why don't you take the rest of your cake out to Pansy and ask her to put it in the icebox for you? Then you can have it for dessert tonight."

Without a word, he marched across to the card table, took up the cake platter, and walked to the door. When he reached it, he glanced back at Bob with a look of utter hatred. Then he balanced the platter precariously in one hand and closed the door after him.

"Robert." Her voice had a command in it. "I have known one Jew well. Jake. Your friend. He was a fine man and he loved us both. You have let him down. I shall not."

He wheeled around at her.

"You may be right! Maybe he was all of that when he was young. I'll give him that! But they learn their lessons from their own pretty God-damn quickly. For God's sake, don't wish another one on me!"

She gave him a look of cold contempt and walked slowly to the door.

"For Christ's sake, Pax! Don't leave me like that!"

She swayed a little, but she didn't stop.

It was then that he exploded.

"God-damned kikes!" he screamed. "They smell! Like bedbugs they smell! Don't you see? You've got to step on them, like bugs!"

Then he burst into sobs and threw himself face-down on the couch.

She hesitated and looked at him. There was utter disbelief in her eyes. She went to him and put her hand on his head.

"Why, Robert," she said, "you're sick. I didn't know."

She sat down beside him waiting for the paroxysm to pass. She looked back along the long avenue of their past. Quite clearly she saw the stupid, good-natured, good-looking boy she'd married. She saw his easy devotion and friendship for Jake, his constant demand for affection; even with Jake's parents it had been a demand for affection, not a giving of it. Her mind traveled back to that night in the Tavern—his condescending charm, the way he made sure that no one would miss the demonstration of his friendship for them. She remembered his anxiety to get into the war. She had thought it was his hatred of injustice as well as his courage. She knew now that it was his restlessness, his love of excitement that made him such a fine soldier.

Then she came to the dark vacuum of the war years. She would never be able to pierce that wall. And now, this stranger; his ferocious, blind hatred. Was this man she was married to a psychotic? Was this vicious prejudice a result of those war and postwar years that she hadn't been a part of and didn't understand?

276

If he were mentally ill, could she bury this hurt he had just given her and help him to recover?

What was she to do now?

She didn't know. But Philip would know.

27

BUT PHILIP didn't know because she didn't tell him. She didn't run across to him that night because the conflagration was spreading.

The children had gone to bed. Bob was reading in the library. He seemed subdued and sorry, and she felt, for the time being, anyway, that his contrition was genuine.

She was in the kitchen when she became conscious of footsteps overhead that pattered back and forth hurriedly and continuously. Pansy must be up awfully late. What could she be so busy about at that hour of the night? A faint sense of foreboding struck at the pit of her stomach.

She ran quickly up the back stairs and tapped at Pansy's door. For a moment there was no answer. Then a muffled voice said, "Come in."

"Pansy! What on earth are you up to?"

The woman didn't answer. She went on folding clothes and cramming them in an old square trunk that was open in the middle of the room. She kept her face averted from Pax, trying to hide her eyes, which were red-rimmed and swimming in tears.

"Pansy! Answer me! What's the matter?"

"I'm goin' away from you-all," she said in a choked voice. "I'm goin' home!"

"Pansy! Stop being a baby! I thought you were a strong woman."

"I'm strong, all right, Miss Pax, and I'm black, but I ain't goin' t' be treated like I was dirt by my own folks! I'm goin' away!"

Pax sat down on the edge of the narrow bed, twisting her slim hands and silently praying for the right words.

"Your boy's sick, Pansy! I really believe he's sick. You and I have got to try to understand and help him to get well."

Pansy looked up at the other woman from the trunk before which she was kneeling and she curled her lip scornfully. "He ain't sick! He's just bad! I've watched him with the li'l Jew boy. He's bad!"

"Oh, no, Pansy!"

"Yes'm, he's bad! You jes' believe Pansy. He's from the South. And when you from the South and treat your black folks like he treat me, you bad! You think I ain't learned nothin' up North? Maybe it took me a long time, and maybe I jes' learned it, but this I know: White folks up North can treat the Negroes bad, but they wouldn't a known how if it wasn't for the South!"

Pax slipped down on the floor beside the colored woman.

"I think that's true, Pansy," she said sadly, "but if it is, why do you want to go back there?"

"I got my mammy and pappy down there—and Miss Mary. Miss Mary won't like Mr. Robert turnin' out bad. I ain't goin' to tell her, but I got sompin' t' tell those other Negroes down there! I'm goin' to tell 'em that it's too late for us grownups, but they gotta open those black babies' eyes, and make 'em know that white folks is bad for us, and they ain't t' believe in 'em like I done."

"Am I bad, Pansy?"

Pansy squatted back on her heels and looked at the girl shrewdly. "No, you ain't bad, but you're a fool! Mr. Bobbie's goin' t' spoil your life. You'll see." She considered a minute. "No, you ain't bad, and Miss Mary ain't bad. She's an angel. But you-all cain't do it by yo'selves."

For a few minutes neither woman spoke. Pansy continued to pack, moving back and forth from the closet to the trunk. Suddenly Pax sprang to her feet and threw her arms around Pansy.

"Pansy, don't leave me! You're the only woman friend of my own age I've got. Stay and help me!"

"Help you do what?"

"Help me with Robert! Don't you see, I've got to believe he's ill! I've got to find out for myself. If he is, he's only got his family to help him. You're his family, Pansy—and you're my friend. Please don't leave me!"

"You goin' to go on lettin' him hurt that li'l Jew boy?"

"No. I'll fix it somehow. I'll find a way—if you'll help me!"

Pax stood there with her arms around Pansy, her head on the woman's shoulder like a tired child.

Pansy hesitated a moment; then she gently stroked the girl's black hair. "I'll stay for a while. But I'm stayin' for you, Miss Pax. Mr. Bobbie ain't sick!"

Again the household returned to its previous surface placidity. Bob paid very little attention to Jan and steadily kept his eyes turned away from him when they were in the same room, but he no longer attempted to bait the child as he had constantly done before.

In spite of her talk with Pansy, and Pansy's belief that Bob's ruthlessness was innate, only coming to the surface in the years he had been away from the guiding hand of Mary Lyttleton, Pax herself was convinced that this late obsession was a result of war fatigue which had turned into a real psychosis and must be dealt with and cured.

So again Pax retired to her usual middle-of-the-road attitude, and tried to give Bob the love and care she would give a sick child.

But a curious change was taking place in her without her being aware of it. In the first place, down into a dark corner of her mind, she had thrust the knowledge that she was not in love with her husband. After the painful scene on Jan's synthetic birthday, she recognized the fact that not only was she not in love with him now, but that she never had been.

She had been miserable and lonely after the cutting short of her first young love. Bob had been Jake's friend and he had also aroused her passionate nature in its youth and unfulfillment. So she had married him. Her New England background told her it was for better or for worse, and she meant to accept it.

But now things had been brought out into the open. Ugly things, sentimental things, emotions and memories; and a pattern of truth was forming about her.

Since Bob had openly linked the small refugee with Jake, the boy was subtly changing into an avenging symbol that she was beginning to fear. Pax's reasoning mind had always been lethargic; and now these disturbing thoughts which she could not dismiss were confusing her unbearably.

She was becoming more and more uncomfortable every time Jan was in the same room with them. At first it had been merely uneasiness lest the battle between him and Bob start again. But now he was beginning to turn into a living reproach. If she was affectionate and tender to Bob, the brown eyes in his still, small face seemed to change into those long-remembered, narrow green ones that said, "Why?"

When she said good night before she closed the bedroom door upon herself and Bob, he seemed to be standing always at his own door watching; and to her troubled mind it was as if, instead of a little foreign boy of twelve, it were Jake standing there, relentlessly disapproving.

She began to wonder how much more of it she could take. She was indeed on a treadmill, two treadmills, which never stopped and which left her always in the same place. One was Bob's illness and misery; the other was the little boy's visible unhappiness.

279

What was she to do?

When he was with her, Robert's devotion and sweetness seemed to increase, but he left the house oftener and stayed away longer, and she knew it was because of the child whom she had taken into his house.

After all, she was his wife and the mother of his son; the house was his house, his home, but he found no peace there. He had been away from it—and her—for so long. He had fought so hard and served his country so well: nine of the best years of his life had been lost; he had had a bad crackup; and now that he was back from the war he had a right to be happy.

On the other hand, Jan was a pathetic little remnant of a murdered people, and he had no one in the world but her. But did he want her? Was it right for her to sacrifice her home and her family for a child who seemed to care nothing for her?

Obviously, Jan had run away from school because of the sudden blossoming of anti-Semitism there. It would only be a matter of time—especially if Robert went berserk on the subject outside the house—before it started here in Mapleton. How could she protect the boy then?

Would it be better for him if she took him back to Mrs. Harris and admitted defeat? Wouldn't he be safer and happier in some family of his own people who would understand him and whom he would perhaps love?

These constant and churning thoughts were slowly driving her crazy. And there was no one who could help her solve them. Philip had never liked Robert and he would be on the side of the boy. Amy would think as Philip did. Pansy's love for her white brother had completely turned into hate. She would have to work it out herself.

The treadmill went on.

It was a warm, late May day.

Pax stood in the middle of the lawn, her feet bare, hosing the garden. Tubby was in school, Jan had disappeared after breakfast as usual, and Bob hadn't come down yet. She automatically watched the rainbows in the arching stream of water, but her mind was, as always now, battling with her problem. She heard the screen door slam, and Bob, still in a summer army tunic, leaning on his cane, limped down the front steps and came along the path.

"Hello, darling," she said, "where are you off to?"

"No place in particular."

"Will you be home for lunch?"

Bob poked with his cane in the brown earth at the edge of the flower bed. "Will the kids be in for lunch?"

"Now, Robert, you know Tubby's in school," she said. Then she added casually, "I suppose Jan will be, though."

"Well, don't wait for me, honey chile. I may get a sandwich and a glass of beer in the village. Hey, turn that hose away! I just put on a fresh tunic."

He smiled at her, went through the gate which swung to after him, and disappeared.

Pax dropped the hose, which fell at her feet, making a dark, wet furrow in the clover-dotted grass. No place for him here!

She walked back toward the house and turned off the water. She sat on the bottom step, put on her sandals, and she, too, went through the gate.

This couldn't go on! This treadmill must stop, even if she got caught in it.

Pax made her way down the tree-bordered country street, turned left down the little hill, along the main road with the woods at her right. Strange she should think of her sanctum today. Only twice since she had shared it with Jake had she been there. So far, she had failed to find an answer to this racking problem of hers. Perhaps Finnegan's would give it to her.

She had been walking along for about five minutes when in the distance she saw a whirl of dust and the sun glistening on metal. As it came nearer, she saw that it was Jan, his bare legs working up and down energetically, his feet pushing the pedals with all his strength, as he forced the bicycle up the slightly uphill road. When he saw her, he jumped off and stood there, unsmiling, panting a little.

"Hello, sweetie, where have you been?"

"In de woods."

"Got secrets in the woods?"

He nodded, and a ghost of a smile brightened his eyes for an instant. "Wher-re you go?" he asked, but without much curiosity.

"I was thinking of going in the woods, too. I'd ask you to go along with me, but you'd go too fast for me. I haven't any bicycle."

"So?" he said, and for no reason he pressed the little bell which was attached to the handlebars, and its high tinkle echoed in the still air.

"Where are you going now, Jan?"

"Nowher-re."

"Why don't you sit down here and talk to me for a while? Here's a fine, flat rock we can sit on. It's in the shade, too."

Jan put his bicycle down on its side at the edge of the road, then came and sat beside her. They didn't speak for several minutes. She gazed upward, over the tops of the trees, while the boy veiled his brown

281

eyes, his slim fingers playing idly in the earth, pulling up little sweet blades of grass and chewing on them.

"Look, Jan," said Pax suddenly, "look at that great cloud over there. Doesn't it look like a ship? See the full-bellied sails? I wonder where she's going."

"She?" he said, and looked at Pax questioningly.

"The ship. We always call ships 'she.' I don't know why, but we do."

"It is strange," commented the boy.

"Did you ever think you'd like to get on a great ship like that and sail to the other ends of the earth?"

"Where I go?"

"I don't know. Somewhere where everything would be beautiful and happy for you."

He looked up at the cloud, then turned and gazed at her soberly. "But you think you go somewher-re and maybe you not get der-re, because de ship, she tur-rn into a camel." He smiled and pointed upward. "Look! She has got two humps now!"

"Jan," Pax said suddenly, "you are not happy with us. Could you tell me why? It makes me very sad to think you are unhappy."

He shrugged his shoulders and the veiled expression came over his face again. "I am not un-happy."

"But you always go away by yourself, Jan. You don't stay with us, and you don't play with Tubby or the boys any more. Don't you ever get lonely?"

"Tubby's fadder-r go away by himself, too."

That was one she couldn't answer—not to Jan. But she didn't have to. He was answering it for her.

"Tubby's fadder-r go away because he hate me. I go away because he hate me. It is better-r, no?"

She took the boy's chin in her hand and looked steadily into his brown eyes. "Jan, do you hate him, too?"

There was no answer. The long lashes brushed his cheek.

"Jan, tell me the truth. Do you hate Uncle Robert?"

The dark eyes flashed upward. "I hate him," he said. "He is not my Uncle Rober-rt."

Her heart gave a great thud that hurt. "Do you hate me, Jan?"

"No-o-o."

"But you don't love me, do you?"

He didn't answer. He just went on pulling at the grass.

"Jan," she asked desperately, "do you want to go away from us? I mean, would you like to go and live with somebody else that you don't hate?"

"Wher-re?" he demanded.

282

"I don't know, Jan." She paused. "I don't quite know what to do with you, sweetie! Don't you see, I can't find out what you want! You didn't like school. You ran away. Dr. Miller said he'd like you to come back next year, but I don't suppose you want to, do you?"

"I do not go back," he said flatly.

There was another silence; then Pax took her rather fierce and problematical bull by the horns.

"Jan, do you remember Mrs. Harris?"

"No. Who is Mrs. Har-ris?"

"She was the kind lady you met when you first got off the boat, remember? The one who let you come and live with me."

"So?" he said indifferently.

"Well, Jan, I've been thinking a lot about Mrs. Harris. You know, I haven't seen her for over a year, and I think somehow she'd like to see you and know how you're getting along."

The boy looked at her questioningly.

"Do you know what? I think it would be fun if you and I went away for a little trip. We can go to the circus and see all the animals and the clowns and things, and then we can—"

"Please, what is clowns?"

"They're men, Jan, just like other men, except they paint their faces with white paint and put black on their mouths and noses, and wear great big shoes and baggy pants and—"

"Why dey do dat?"

"To make us laugh. It's good to laugh."

"So?"

"You never laugh, Jan. I'd like to hear you laugh."

"And den what we do?"

"Well, then"—she hesitated—"I thought we might go to see Mrs. Harris and have a talk with her. Maybe she could—well, help us."

"You leave me der-re wid dis Mrs. Har-ris, no?"

"Oh, Jan, that isn't what I meant." She felt her throat tightening, and the palms of her hands were wet. "You see, if you hate Tubby's father so much and—"

"He hate me mor-re because I am a Jew. You tink he hate me so much dat he kill me one day?"

"Oh, Jan dear, don't say things like that! People don't kill other people unless they're very wicked."

"Maybe he kill me. I have seen people kill when dey hate."

She was becoming frightened.

"You must promise me not to think about killing, Jan. It's bad and it's silly," she said. "You know, baby, you and I both need some fun! Let's go away for a few days. We'll see the clowns, and Mrs. Harris, and we'll go find a merry-go-round—I'll bet you've never seen one of those—and then maybe when we come back you and Tubby's father won't hate each other quite so much, and we'll all be happier and—"

"You tink I come back?" he asked wistfully.

"Of course you'll come back, sweetie," she said uncertainly, "if you want to."

Abruptly, he sprang to his feet, picked up his bicycle, threw one leg across it, and looked back over his shoulder at her with an enigmatic expression in his eyes.

"You go to de woods now?" he said.

"No, Jan, I don't think I will. It's getting late. Come on, let's go get some lunch. You ride on ahead, Jan. I'll catch up with you at the house."

As he sped off, she thought she heard his voice drifting back to her, but she was sure she was mistaken in what she thought she heard.

"I do not tink I come back—ever-r."

No, she couldn't have heard that, because that wasn't what she meant —or was it?

She picked herself up off the rock, brushed off the dirt and dried bits of grass, and started back up the road.

But she didn't catch up with him at the house.

She waited and waited, and finally had lunch alone on a tray in the garden. Nor had he returned when the three of them sat down for dinner at seven. She thought she heard him come in and go upstairs, then come down, ten minutes or so later, but he didn't come into the dining room. He often stayed over with Philip and Amy, and she wouldn't have worried if it hadn't been for the memory of the expression in his eyes when he bicycled off.

After they had finished dinner, and Bob and Tubby were in the library playing a game of cards which Tubby called "fish," she went to the telephone.

"Of course, I know he's all right, but send him home early, will you, Amy? He's been out all day and I think he should get some sleep."

She didn't hear him come in, but at about nine o'clock strange sounds floated down from upstairs. Jan was playing his violin. Funny, he hadn't touched it since he'd come home from school. Bob stopped his game, listening to the mournful sounds, and then she saw him wince as the child hit one sour note after the other.

"Gee! Jan's playing! Go on, Pop, it's your turn. I took it with the ace."

Bob wriggled in his chair and kept changing position as the odd improvisation from upstairs continued. Finally, he threw down his
284

cards. "Tubs, for the love of God, go upstairs and tell that kid to either shut his door or stop that damn noise!"

Tubby slipped down from his chair and his eyes twinkled. He leaned over to his father, and Pax heard his loud whisper as he half covered his mouth with his hand and chanted: "I'll get a piece of pork and put it on a fork, and give it to the Jew boy, Jew!"

Pax jumped up from her chair, flew across the room, and gave the child a stinging slap across his face. He burst into tears.

"Aw, Mom!" he wailed.

"I told you never to let me hear that word again!"

"I was only talkin' to Pop."

"You're a bad boy, and I'm very angry with you. And if you ever say that again, I promise you, you will get much more than a slap!"

"Oh, come now, Pax," and Bob put his arm around the boy.

"You keep out of this, Robert!"

Tubby gulped and rubbed his eyes. He threw his mother a hostile glance and walked slowly to the door.

"Never mind, Tubby," she said. "I'll go up."

Wearily she climbed the stairs, tapped lightly on Jan's partly open door, and went in. Jan was standing by the open window, the violin tucked under his chin.

Pax closed the door quietly and smiled at him. "What are you playing, Jan?"

"I do not know. Sounds." He drew the bow across the strings again and smiled wryly at her. "Sometimes good sounds, sometimes bad, no?"

She sat down on the side of the bed. "You stood me up at lunch, Jan. Why did you do that?"

"Stood you up?" he asked. "Why you not sit down?"

Pax threw back her head and laughed. "Oh, Jan! It's a funny language, English, isn't it? That's slang!"

"Slang?"

"What I mean is, you didn't keep your luncheon date with me."

"Oh," he said, and played another melancholy chord.

"Let's shut the sounds out for tonight, Jan, and you come on downstairs with me, and I'll teach you a good game."

Obediently he put his fiddle and bow on the table and walked over to her. "What game?"

"It's called parchesi," she said. "You play it with dice and a big board and little colored ivory disks—"

"When we go?"

"Now, Jan. We can play for half an hour and then it will be time for you to go to bed."

285

"No. When we go away to see"—he stopped a minute—"the funny men wid de white faces?"

Her heart skipped a beat. "Do you want to go, Jan?"

He shrugged his shoulders, but he didn't answer.

"Maybe we'll go in a week or so. We'll have to see that your clothes are all clean and we've got to make plans—"

"Please, when is Johnnie come home?"

"Johnnie Leclerc?"

He nodded and looked at her anxiously.

"Let's see, he should be home in about ten days, I think. Why?"

"I would see him before-re I go away. Johnnie is my fr-riend."

"Of course, sweetie. We won't go until you want to. Let's go downstairs now, shall we?"

He followed her quietly.

When they got to the library, she found that Bob had disappeared. Tubby was sitting alone at the card table, awkwardly trying to shuffle the cards. He gave her a sulky glance as she came in.

"Where's your father?" she inquired.

"Gone upstairs."

"I'm going to teach Jan parchesi. Want to get in the game?"

"No."

He flung himself on the floor with his back against the couch, and began laying his cards out on the floor. Pax went to the desk and took out the parchesi board from one of the drawers. She had just opened it on the card table, and was sorting out the red disks for Jan, when Bob stormed into the room.

"Who the hell's been in my foot locker?" he demanded.

"What's the matter, Robert, have you lost something?"

"No, I don't think so. But that isn't the point. Somebody's been in it. It's all upset, damn it! I've kept things in that foot locker for nine bloody damn years and I know where they belong! I don't want anybody going in that foot locker!"

She laughed lightly. "Well, there's nothing in your foot locker that I want, darling. What are you looking for?"

"I wanted to get a letter that I've got to answer from"—he hesitated just a second—"from a guy in Germany. It was all mixed up. The letter wasn't in the right place, and damn it—"

"You don't want anybody going in your foot locker!" she finished mockingly. "Tubby, have you been in it?"

"No, Mom. What do I want in it?"

"Jan, you haven't, have you?"

He seemed to hold his breath for a moment; then he looked away indifferently. "What is dis foot locker?" he said.

"No culprits here. Sorry, darling."

"I'm sorry, too, honey chile. I didn't mean to blow my top," he said. He leaned over her, kissed her on the forehead, and started out of the room again.

"Oh, damn!" she suddenly exclaimed. "Where did you find it? In the closet?"

"Yeah. Up-ended, too."

"I'm the guilty one, darling. Now I remember, I found it under the bed. I don't like things under the beds. Nobody cleans properly when there are things under beds. I moved it. I won't do it again. Am I forgiven?"

Bob laughed. "I'll be back, baby, when I've written my letter."

Pax pushed the disks over to Jan's side of the board.

"Here's your shaker, sweetie. Now. You start with your men home—"

"Foot locker-r," said Jan softly. "Do not people ever-r lock foot locker-rs?"

28

Pax sat straight up in bed. What had she heard? The creaking of a floor board? The muffled thud of a closing door? She shook herself awake and listened.

Nothing.

She looked over at the marble clock. Only quarter to seven? What had waked her? Had she been dreaming? No. Something had drawn her out of a feathery cloud of complete unconsciousness.

It was too early to get up. She turned over on her side, adjusted the pillow, and tried to sleep again. But sleep slipped away, as thoughts began marshaling themselves in a disorderly array and began marching round and round her brain.

Everything was ready for them to leave tomorrow. Everything but the laundry, and that would arrive today. Jan must have plenty of clean shirts. It was starting to get hot in Mapleton. It would be worse in New York.

No one knew yet that she was going—no one, that is, except Jan. She didn't much care whether Robert knew or not. She hadn't told Tubby because he would beg to go along and she didn't want him, not this time. It was to be Jan's holiday, and perhaps a solution at the end.

She'd tell Philip today. It would be too late for him to object and talk her out of it. All her plans were made. She smiled crookedly to herself. She'd show 'em all that she could find a way out by herself and make everyone happier.

Why in hell couldn't she go back to sleep? The sun was shining in her eyes. That crack of light between the pane and the window shade was like a knife blade piercing through her lids. She got out of bed, went to the window, and tried to press the shade against the sash, but it wouldn't stay.

She looked back at Robert and decided that she really didn't want to get back in bed. She'd go in and take a shower.

She opened the bathroom door. The other door leading into the hall was ajar. That's what she had heard when she wakened so suddenly. She started over to the wash basin to brush her teeth. What was that box doing there? She lifted the cover with its dashing red bow and looked inside. It was empty.

Then she saw the note.

It was propped up against her toothbrush mug. It was addressed in printed letters to Mrs. Pax Lyttleton.

She walked over to the bathroom window and raised the shade. Then she broke the seal.

Dear P.L.

You do not want me any more. How I know Mrs. Hares she want me. I go away. Much love.

Jan

P.S. *I tell Jonnie he can have my sled and skees. Please send my watch to Peter Lawson Stratford School.*
P.S. *You can have my box. Good-by.*

She ran into his room. Everything was in order except his unmade bed. One quick glance told her that this time he had taken no clothes. The sled and skis were leaning against the big chair. On the dressing table was a small group of his possessions; his wallet, his top, his marbles, and two or three books. His violin in its case was just underneath on the floor, and on the other side of the dressing table was the wrist watch, all by itself on top of a piece of paper that read "for Peter."

She didn't waste a minute. This was serious. She had had no warning and she didn't know where to look for him. She dashed into her clothes and raced across the Green, through Amy's always unlocked door, up the stairs to Philip's room, and knocked sharply on the door. Without waiting for an answer, she flung open the door. Philip was still asleep.

"Phil! Get up! Quick! Jan's gone!"

Philip sat up and stared at her. Her face was drawn and tight and drained of all color. Her eyes were dark with fear, and her whole body was trembling.

"Where's he gone? What's the matter, kid?"

She thrust the note at him. "I don't know. Phil, I'm scared!"

He began reading it, saying absent-mindedly, "He can't have gone far." Then as he finished it, he jumped out of bed, crumpling the letter in his hand. He stood motionless in the middle of the floor for a moment, scowling, his teeth clenched. "Go get the car, kid! I'll get some clothes on and join you. Beat it, and hurry!"

Five minutes later she pulled up in front of Amy's and honked the horn. Philip ran out of the house and jumped in beside her.

"Which way, Phil?"

"God! I don't know. How long has he been gone?"

"I don't know. Not very long, I don't think. It must have been he that waked me up about twenty or thirty minutes ago. I heard something and—"

"There aren't any trains yet. Let's go down the main road for a bit."

She turned the car, put her foot on the accelerator, and they were off.

"What made him go? Anything happen?"

Philip's eyes were searching the road on both sides.

"No. Nothing happened that I know of."

"Something must have upset him. Think, kid!"

"Nothing, Phil. Honestly. Phil, he didn't take anything with him."

"He didn't? That's funny. Turn around and go back. There are no signs of him on this road."

Again she turned the car and started back.

"Where will we look now?"

There was a catch in her voice, and as Philip turned his head and looked at her, a tear rolled down her cheek.

"Stop crying! What did you do to him?" Philip's voice was harsh.

"I tell you nobody did anything. We were getting ready to go to New York tomorrow—"

"Who was getting ready to go to New York?"

"Jan and I. I was going to give him a little holiday. We were going to go to the circus—"

"You damn fool! There isn't any circus in New York. It's over."

"And then we were going to see Mrs. Harris—"

"Look out for that corner! Did he know you were going to see Mrs. Harris?"

She made the corner around the Green on two wheels and then speeded up the car.

"Why, yes, Phil. He wanted to go."

"Stop the car!"

She pulled up short and looked at him anxiously.

"He hasn't run away!"

"What do you mean, Phil?"

"Let me have another look at that letter!" He read it, then crumpled it up and stuck it in his pocket. "This is the letter of a condemned person!" He laughed harshly. "Don't you see? He made his will—poor little God-damned kid!" His voice broke. "Quick! Where would he go?"

She bit her lip, and the knuckles of her hands on the steering wheel were white. Suddenly her face showed some signs of life.

"I know where he is, Phil!"

She started the car again with such force that he was thrown back against the seat and bounced forward again. She drove past the house, turned at the corner, down the hill, and along the road at sixty until she came to the end of the woods. She stopped the car, put on the brake, and jumped out.

"Come on! Follow me."

They hurried across the meadow, climbed through the barbed-wire fence, and made for the woods. She ran stumbling along the path, stooping under some of the low-hanging branches, then going forward again, Philip right behind her. When they came to the clearing she paused long enough to point upward to the mouth of the cave.

"Wait a minute, Pax. Let me go first."

"No," she said. "It's my cave."

He pushed her aside, and climbed up ahead of her. She saw him stand motionless for a moment at the entrance, looking in and downward, and then he seemed—from her position below—to lean down and out of sight.

It seemed an eternity before she heard his gruff voice.

"Come up, kid. You'll have to help."

She took one step and her legs seemed to buckle under her. She hung onto an overhanging crag and pulled herself up. For one split second of horror, her terrified eyes took in the scene.

Philip was kneeling beside the prone body of the boy. A small stream of something thickly dark was trickling slowly from a spot at Jan's waistline on the left side. His eyes were half closed and his face was colorless. His arms were outstretched, the palms of his thin hands turned upwards. On the ground, about a foot from his right hand, was Bob's Luger.

She clapped her hand over her mouth and gagged.

"Stop that!" commanded Philip. "Get over here and hold him up. I can't get his shirt off."

"Is he—is he—"

"Not yet. Hold him steady now. Wait a minute."

Philip stood up, ripped off his own shirt, knelt down again, and began wrapping it tightly around the child's stomach.

"Sorry you have to see this, kid, but I can't do it alone."

"Oh, God! Phil! Will he—"

"Stop talking! There's no time for that!"

He pulled the shirt tight, tucking the end in at the boy's back, then began lifting him slowly into his arms.

"Gently now! All right, I've got him. Go on ahead. I'll come as fast as I can."

Pax scrambled down ahead of him. They started back through the woods, Pax holding back the branches, kicking aside what she could of the small stones that made the path rough. She put her foot on one barbed wire, holding the one over it high so he could climb through. Then, whimpering like a puppy, she raced for the car. Philip strode along more slowly, his face set and hard, carrying the limp body of the child.

Pax started the car, then jumped out to hold open the rear door. Philip settled himself in the back seat with the boy in his arms, pressing his hand as firmly as he dared over the spot where he knew the wound was.

"Burlington—the hospital! Never mind the cops! Step on it!"

Pax sat alone in the corridor in the straight-backed chair pushed up against the wall, just outside the door of the operating room.

One hour passed. Then two.

How long, oh God, how long?

Why didn't Philip come and tell her something? Was Jan going to die? Dear God! Don't let him! Don't let him die! If he did, she'd be a murderess! She was anyway. It was she who'd killed him! Not Robert, not Hitler, she thought foolishly, she! He'd known she didn't want him. Nobody wanted him.

She'd thought he was a little boy. He wasn't. He was old. Death didn't mean anything to him. He could face that. But he couldn't face loneliness and no one to care. She had shown him that a little boy could be loved, and then she'd snatched it away. She had been about to send him on his way again from nowhere to nowhere, and he was tired. . . . Where was Philip? Why didn't he come? Why didn't somebody come?

Oh, God! God! God! Let him live! He thought nobody wanted him. She wanted him now! How she wanted him!

Nurses passed back and forth along the corridor, going in and out of the swinging half-doors of the hospital rooms. Another little group huddled at the desk of the floor nurse at the other end, whispering over charts. But nobody spoke to her. The big clock on the wall said eleven-thirteen. She wanted a glass of water, but she couldn't move from there. Something might happen.

The door of the operating room opened, and two nurses, still masked, wheeled out a table, followed by the surgeon. She turned quickly and looked at the small figure covered with a white sheet, his head turned to the side, his matted hair buried in the thin pillow. He was wheeled away. Pax went back to her chair.

Ten minutes later, Philip came to her.

"He'll live, if he can take transfusions," he said. "He's lost a hell of a lot of blood."

"Phil! Let me! Let me give him my blood! Please!"

"Sure, if yours is the right type."

"It's got to be, Phil! It's got to be!" she whispered. "It'll be the same! He's mine! He belongs to me!"

Pax buried her face in her hands and her body shook with sobs.

"Cut it out, kid! That won't help. Come on, let's ask the doctor to have a look at your blood."

Fifteen minutes later, she sat in the small anteroom with Philip, waiting to know the result of her blood test. Philip begged a cigarette from a visitor who passed through the hall, stuck it in Pax's mouth, and lighted it for her.

"Do you think he's going to die, Phil?"

"It's a question of stamina, but I don't think so. He aimed for his heart, but the gun must have bucked—thank God—and the bullet didn't hit a vital spot. He knew how to load the Luger, all right, but his hand was weak." He smiled ironically. "I wouldn't wonder if he'd been shot at in his time, but I don't think he'd ever tried it himself before."

Her mouth began to quiver again, and her blue-circled eyes swam with tears. "I did it! It was my fault—"

"Stop that! Stop it at once. Suppose you did. You didn't mean to. You're a lovely fool, Pax, you always have been, but don't dwell on that. Think about what you're going to do for him if"—he stopped abruptly and changed the word—"*when* he gets well."

29

Pax's body was so numb with weariness that she was sure she would feel nothing if someone stuck pins in it.

She hadn't been to bed for three nights. Except for a couple of hours each day, when she had driven home for a bath, a change of linen, and a few moments with Bob and her son, she had stayed in that little visitors' room just opposite Jan's. Once in a while, she kicked off her shoes and lay on the wicker settee with a pillow under her head, and tried to doze. But the minute she closed her eyes, she was wider awake than ever.

Philip spent as much time with her as he could spare, but except for the strength and comfort of his presence, there was nothing either of them could do but play a waiting game.

Jan seemed to have no will to live.

From time to time, she stole into the room and watched him from behind a screen as he lay there, motionless, his eyes closed, with no flicker in the blue lids; or wide open, looking at the ceiling but seeing nothing.

Today he had taken a slight turn for the better, and Philip and her doctor insisted that she go home and get a night's sleep. She was too exhausted to argue. She dragged herself into the car and drove slowly away from the hospital.

As she turned in the direction of her house, the street light caught two figures hugging the wall. She glanced at them indifferently, and saw that they were Bob and Jeannine Leclerc. She saw Bob lean over, kiss the woman, and walk away from her.

Pax stopped the car and leaned out of the window. "Robert," she called, "want a lift?"

He limped up to the car, his face a dull red, opened the door on the far side, and climbed in.

"Hello," she said, "I was just driving home. How's everything there?"

"All right," he said. "How's the kid?"

"There's a little improvement, but he's not out of danger. Oh, Robert, what have we done to him?"

"Nothing. The kid's crazy. I tell you, they're all crazy! A normal American boy like Tubs wouldn't—"

"That's enough, Robert! I'm too tired and too sick at heart to listen to any more."

She drove the car into the garage.

"Get out, Robert. I'm going in to see Tubby, if he's still awake, and then I'm going to bed. Can you make it by yourself?"

"Sure, baby. I'm sorry. I didn't mean—"

"Stop being sorry. I'm sorry, too."

He followed her into the house and shut the kitchen door. She stopped at the door going from the kitchen into the hall and faced him.

"Will you put out the lights when you come up? And, Robert, I'm going to sleep in Jan's room tonight."

"Pax, honey! Please! I didn't mean—"

She laughed shortly. "Darling, don't be a fool. I'm just tired, that's all. I'll sleep better in a bed by myself. Good night, Robert. I may not see you in the morning. I'll be off early. Sleep well." And she disappeared around the bend in the staircase.

Jan improved a little each day for a few days, then stopped. As far as the doctors could tell, he was out of danger, but he didn't get well. His pulse and respiration were regular, but he just lay there, silent, staring into space.

Once, Pax thought she saw a flicker of recognition in his eyes, but when she spoke gently to him, he didn't answer.

"He doesn't want to live, Philip."

She shook her head mournfully. Philip had brought her home from the hospital, after a particularly discouraging day, and they were sitting on the front steps.

"I don't know what to do. I can't get through to him. Nobody can. Can't you think of something, Phil?"

"I guess he's just lost faith, Pax. Wouldn't you?"

"I can't give it to him," she said. "He doesn't want it from me."

"You're the only one who can, Pax, but I can't tell you how."

294

She was silent for several minutes. "It's got to be a major operation, I guess, Phil."

"What do you mean by that?"

"I don't know yet. All I know is, I can't go on playing both sides against the middle any longer. Right's right, and wrong's wrong, and somebody's got to get hurt."

Her eyes looked steadily into his. "I've come a hell of a long way in the last several days, but not long enough. How many years have you told me I had to grow up?" She got to her feet, leaned down, and kissed him lightly on the top of his head. "Don't be afraid for me, Phil, I'll make it. I've taken the blinders off my eyes—for the first time in my life, I guess. But it makes you feel awful kind of naked, doesn't it?"

She turned when she got to the door.

"Good night, Phil, and thanks. Don't bother to come over for me tomorrow. I'll be doing fine."

Pax shivered a little. She looked down at her forearms and saw that they were covered with thousands of tiny goose pimples. It was absurd to be cold in June. Then she remembered that it had been a quarter of an hour or so since she had heard the old clock on the Green chime eleven. She must have been lying in the tub for over an hour, and the water, which had been warm an hour ago, was nearly cold. She turned on the hot faucet and settled deeper into the tub.

Over the sound of the water flowing from the tap she heard a knock on the bathroom door.

"Yes? What is it?"

"It's me—Robert. Are you all right, baby?"

"Sure I'm all right. I'll be out in a minute."

"I brought up some whiskey and the fixin's. Will you have a drink with me?"

Pax lifted herself out of the tub and reached for a towel.

"Sure. Take it into the sitting room and pour mine for me. I'll be right there."

She came through the door out of the dark hall, like a white wraith, her nightgown showing beneath the hem of her tailored white bathrobe, her damp black hair falling loosely to her shoulders. She dropped into the chair, her arms outflung on its broad arms.

"Drink your drink, honey chile. Maybe it'll put some color in those pale cheeks."

She reached for the glass, held it up to him, and smiled wanly. "Cheers," she said.

She took one or two swallows, then put the glass down, sitting there

295

in silence, half listening to the early summer night sounds which came in through the open window. Bob's sharp eyes watched her closely.

"You're tired, aren't you?"

"Yes," she said quietly.

"The kid have a bad day?"

She looked at him steadily. "Every day's bad for him."

"Forget it, baby. Think of yourself a little."

She wanted to say, "Don't you mean, think of me?" but she didn't. Stillness enveloped the room again.

Bob got up from the couch, put two cigarettes in his mouth, lighted them, and handed her one. She shook her head. He finished his drink, poured himself another, and sat down on the couch again.

"Come on down out of the clouds and talk to me, will you, baby?"

"Yes. I've got to." She sighed, and dropped her head. Then she lifted it and looked directly at him. "Robert, I want a divorce."

The piercing trill of the tree toads grew louder. At the far end of the room a window shade banged. The tension was broken by the slow strokes of the church clock striking a monotonous twelve. Both of them vaguely counted them. Then Bob laughed.

"Who do you think you are? Cinderella in reverse?"

He reached for his glass which he had put on the floor beside him, but he knocked it over.

"Not in reverse, darling," she said, with a smile. "I've really got to go back to sackcloth and ashes—if you want to be fancy."

"What have I done now?"

"It isn't what *you've* done, it's what I've done. And the answer to that is, nothing."

"What are we playing—riddle me this or something? Talk plain, can't you?"

"I don't know. I'll try, but you know it's never been very easy for me to talk sense."

He leaned forward, his elbows on his knees, his chin cupped in his palms. "Go ahead and try. I can take it."

"You see, Robert," and she hesitated, trying to find the right words, "everything I've touched in my life—in my whole life—has always gone wrong. I guess it all comes from the fact that I'm a very stupid woman. And when things went wrong, I was afraid to look at them straight. I lied to myself, or else I straddled them—you know, compromised. Well, I can't compromise any longer, and I've got to begin with you, Robert."

"I see," he said sarcastically.

"No, you don't see, but that can't be helped."

296

"The thing is, you don't love me any longer. Is that it?"

"No, that isn't it. The thing is, I never loved you, Robert." She saw him wince, got up and sat beside him, and put her hand over his. He snatched his away.

"God damn it! I don't believe that!"

"You don't want to believe it, darling, but I think you know it's true. I think you've known all along—even before I did."

"Pax—"

"I think that's one of the reasons you were willing to leave me again after the war, and put in for an Occupation job over there, and why you stayed away more than two years. I think that was why you wouldn't let me come to you when you crashed—"

"Stop it! For God's sake! You're twisting it, damn it! What you're saying is that I haven't loved you."

"Why, yes, Robert, I'm saying that, too. You see, I'm through with lies. I've used 'em so long. They're an escape, for the moment, but, boy, how they let you down afterward."

"I don't understand any of this, Pax. You can't mean it." He looked at her searchingly for a moment. "Look here, did somebody tell you there was another woman over there?"

Her eyes widened. "Why, no, Robert. Was there?"

His face reddened a little. He got up abruptly and strode across the room. "No. Of course not. You're the only woman I've ever really loved." He sat down again and bowed his head on his clasped hands.

"Funny," said Pax slowly, "I never thought of that, but I suppose there must have been—not that it matters." Then she smiled bitterly. "If I'd thought about it much, I'd have guessed this education in bigotry must have been given you by some individual who was close to you. It's too deeply ingrained for you to have picked it up generally."

She went back and sat in the chair again, and the painful silence stole over them once more. Bob was the first to break it.

"So you never loved me and yet you married me."

"I never loved you, Robert," she replied sadly.

"It was always Jake, wasn't it? Christ-bitten fool that I was, I should have known it!"

He didn't realize it, but he was making it easier for her. When she spoke, there was a quiet strength in her voice that hadn't been there before.

"Yes, it was Jake," she said calmly. "What I mean is, it began with Jake. I was in love with him—but not enough. You see, I failed Jake with the same kind of wickedness that you've shown since you came back. He had warned me! He had said I couldn't take it and I didn't believe him. But when I came face to face with it the first time, I reacted like all fools do. I hurt him terribly. When I realized what I'd done, it was too late. Jake didn't want me."

She stopped for a moment and put her hand over her eyes.

"I should have gone after him," she continued, "but, you see, I was always afraid to face things, so I didn't. I sent Philip instead." She paused. "So I lost him. I don't think I ever got over it."

"Then you married me."

"Yes, I married you."

"Why? Glamour stuff, I suppose?" he said sarcastically.

She looked at him steadily.

"That's right. Glamour stuff, but not the way you mean. I was awfully young and lonely. You were sweet and attractive, and I thought I loved you, really I did, Robert. And the glamour stuff, as you call it, was that you were Jake's friend"—she paused—"then."

"So you've taken eleven years of my life."

"The war had eight of 'em, Robert, and I didn't know you—until now. I'm not trying to excuse myself! I did you a terrible injustice by marrying you, I'll admit that. God knows I'm sorry. But it doesn't do much good to be sorry, does it? All I can do now is to give you your freedom so you can find the kind of woman you should have married. You're still awfully young, darling."

"Thank you very much," he said. "Perhaps you will be good enough to tell me the kind of woman I should have married."

She got up wearily and moved toward the door.

"I guess it isn't any use."

"Darling, don't go! I'm sorry. Please come back and sit down again." She hesitated, with her hand on the knob. "Please! You don't mean it, baby. You don't really mean you're going to leave me."

"No, Robert." She looked at him with a shade of humor in her sad smile. "I want you to leave me."

He pulled her down on the couch beside him. "Pax, are you sure it isn't because you think there's another woman?"

"I don't know any other woman, Robert."

"But last night"—he fumbled for the words—"when you picked me up at the corner of Papa Leclerc's, you may have thought that—"

"Do you mean Jeannine?" She laughed softly. "Oh, Robert—"

"Because that was all over before I ever knew you, baby. It was all over and done with—" He stopped short, realizing from the expression on her face that he had admitted something she had never known.

"So that's why she's always hated me," she said thoughtfully. "No, darling, it's not Jeannine. As a matter of fact, I feel very grateful to

Jeannine, because, you see, the only person who has never let Jan down is her son." She looked at him suddenly, her eyes large with wonder, "And yours, Robert! Johnnie is your son, isn't he?"

Bob dropped his eyes and didn't answer.

"Funny, I should have known it. Funny, I don't care. That proves it, doesn't it, Robert? I couldn't love you or I'd care terribly. Johnnie's a fine boy, Robert. A son to be proud of." She looked at him soberly. "No, it isn't another woman. It isn't as simple as that. But I don't think I can ever make you see."

"All right," Bob said, and his face was strained and frightened. "So I'm a no-good son of a bitch, but I love you, Pax. Couldn't we try to make a go of it?"

"Robert, my dear, I know you won't believe me, but I've tried ever since you came home. Really I have! Your cruelty to Jan, and to Pansy, too, hurt like hell. But I convinced myself that you were ill. You are ill, Robert, but I think it's incurable. You've been ill always, but it wasn't apparent until now. You're like a little boy with a weak stomach who has eaten too much of something he was allergic to and hadn't known it. They fed you hate over there. You've been made to believe that black people are all black and white people are all white. You think all Jews are bad and all Germans are right. In other words, they've done a great job of turning you into a first-class Nazi."

"That's a lie."

"I tried to make myself believe that there were two sides, and I tried to see your side. But, Robert, anyone who can see two sides when it comes to a question of human decency is a coward and a fool."

Unconsciously, she was using Philip's phraseology and his ideas, but she was gaining freedom as the words poured out.

"Pax, it's not like you not to give a feller another chance."

"You won't change. It's too late for that! The bitter thing is, Robert, that you've given eight of your best years fighting for all the things you really hate now." She patted his hand and there was a certain melancholy humor in her eyes. "Somewhere, darling, you must have had an ancestor who trafficked in slaves."

He muttered something under his breath; then he made a brave attempt to smile his charming smile.

"But, baby, you don't divorce a man just because his ideas are different from yours."

"You're wrong, Robert. That's just why I've got to. I can't go on any further with you, darling. . . . Give me a cigarette now, will you?"

He put one in her mouth, lighted it, and in the flame of the match, his eyes studied every feature and expression of her tired face.

"You see," she continued, "without meaning to, I've made every person in my life miserable. You, and Jake—even Philip, because I'm a helpless fool and he's been stuck with me. Now I'm going to see that there will be at least one happy person in my world. I know it's no excuse, but in a sort of way I was a waif, too. Nobody ever wanted me when I was a child, but it's only now that I'm beginning to understand waifs. That kid's going to have a chance, if it's in my power to give it to him!"

Bob walked nervously up and down the room.

"But you don't understand Jews. He'll turn on you! They always do!"

"Robert, did you ever see a lonely little cur in the street, that nobody wanted, no home, hungry, kicked at by everyone? Sure, he'll snarl and bite. Well, there are Jews like that—non-Jews, too. Jan isn't going to be like that. He's going to have a chance to be a good Jew. I don't mean that, either; I mean a good man. He's going to have that chance if I have to sacrifice everyone around me who won't help me to give it to him!"

"So you're beginning with me."

"I'm sorrier than I can tell you, Robert, but I'm beginning with you. All my life, when things were difficult, I've looked for a way out. I hated to face reality. I've always thought in terms of Finnegan's—but you don't know about Finnegan's, do you? It's a cave where I could always go to dream. Well, I've found out that dreams are for doers, not for fools like me."

She clasped her hands together, pressing the blood out of them.

"I showed Finnegan's to Jan. I told him that it had always been my escape place. I was the one who took him there. It was there that he tried to—" She stopped and held her underlip between her strong white teeth. "He'll be coming home soon, and I've got to clean house before he gets here. That's the first step, because, you see, Robert, he doesn't want to live, and I've got to give him peace, so I can find some way to make him want to."

"Pax, don't do this to me! I love you."

"No, you don't, Robert. It isn't any use. Please go away. Go quickly! Go back to Miss Mary. Don't make it any harder for me. Let me go now, darling. It hurts—"

Then the tears came like a flood that had been undammed, and she ran down the hall into Jan's room, shut the door, and locked it.

30

PAX TRIED to read. She sat in her father's chair in the library; beside her was an ashtray filled with cigarette butts faintly tipped with lip rouge. Occasionally she would look up as an unusually loud thud came from the floor above.

Bob was packing. He had been packing for three days.

Slowly she turned page after page. Suddenly realizing that she had turned over at least four without having read a word, she flung the book down impatiently and jumped up from the chair. She felt desperately lonely. Since the painful scene with Bob, she had seen no one outside of her own household, with the exception of the still, silent little figure in the hospital bed and Philip, who stopped in for a few minutes every day to see Jan.

She looked longingly out of the window, thinking how much she'd like to go outside and cut the grass, just for something to do, but it was still raining, so that was no good. It would be an hour and a half before dinner, and she began to wonder what she'd do about that.

Bob and Tubby and she had dined together the first two nights, but there was little or no conversation except from Tubby, and the atmosphere was so taut and unhappy and confused that the night before she had made the excuse of a headache, and had her dinner served on a tray in her room.

There she had thought of her explanations to Tubby—that his father was ill, not yet recovered from the crackup in Germany, and that he was going down to stay with Granny for a little while. Lies—but Tubby was only nine. It would be best for him to learn the truth gradually. She had also told him that if he missed his father too much, he could go there too and stay with him.

Now she leaned her head against the back of the chair and closed her eyes. Thoughts of that conversation with her son, of the uncertainty of its ultimate result, of the way the boy stayed close to his father; memories of the scene with Robert and of the near-tragedy of Jan's attempted suicide, that she herself alone had been responsible for, raced through her head. She opened her eyes and sighed. Those ghosts would be haunting the house of her mind for a long time.

Suddenly the door of the library was flung open, and Tubby dashed in, his face black as a thundercloud.

"Why didn't you tell me that you and Pop weren't going to be married any more?"

"Who told you that, Tubby?" she asked calmly.

"Pop," he answered, and his lip quivered.

"I see," she said. "What else did he tell you?"

"Pop said you didn't love him any more. He said you didn't love me any more, either. He said Jan was the only one you loved, and I'd grow up without any father and—"

The sobs were coming fast now, and the tears made a grimy path down his round cheeks.

Pax stretched out her arms to him. "Come over here, darling, and let's talk. Don't cry, baby."

Tubby stamped his foot. "Don't touch me! I hate you!" he screamed. Then he turned and ran out of the room and up the stairs.

Pax followed him. When she entered what had been their joint bedroom, Tubby was lying face down on the chaise longue, banging at it with his fist. Pansy was kneeling beside an open wardrobe trunk, hanging in it the suits that Bob handed her from the closet. As Pax closed the door, Bob dropped a coat over the top of the trunk and turned to comfort Tubby.

"Come, come, son, don't do that. Your old pop's going to see that nothing's going to happen to you."

"Pansy, would you mind going downstairs for a little while?" Pax said.

Her face was pale and her chin was raised angrily. Pansy said nothing. She got up off her knees, looked at Bob with an expression of active dislike, and left.

"Sit down, Robert. I want to talk to you," Pax commanded. "I think you're hitting below the belt, don't you?"

"What do you mean by that?" he demanded curtly.

"Do you have to hurt everybody about you—even your own son?"

"When it comes to that, you've been doing a little hurting around here yourself, haven't you?"

She began twisting her handkerchief, trying to control her anger.

"Why couldn't you have gone quietly, Robert, and left some friendship between us? Don't you think there's been enough hatred around here?"

"Tubs is old enough to know," said Bob. "He's old enough not to be lied to!"

"I haven't lied to him," Pax replied quietly.

"You haven't? Did you tell him that his father has been kicked out for a little kike?"

"Robert, don't let me answer that before the child."

Bob went over and sat down on the edge of the chaise longue, with his hand on Tubby's shoulder.

"Damn it all! I don't see any reason why he shouldn't know the truth. He's my son, and you're trying to take him away from me."

"I've said nothing about taking him away from you. After all, he belongs to both of us. And we both love you, Tubby darling," she added, as the child continued to cry.

Bob gave a bitter, almost inaudible laugh. Pax ignored it.

"Tubs," she said, "why don't you go downstairs with Pansy, and leave your father and me alone for a little while?"

"No! I don't want to go away!" He sat up, rubbing his nose on his sleeve, a scowl on his small, tear-stained face. "I won't leave Pop!"

"Let him stay! Let him hear the truth! He's got a right to. It's his home you're busting up."

"Very well," she said, "if you want it that way."

"I do want it that way!"

"Tubby, I told you that your father was going down to Savannah because he is ill, and I think your granny can take better care of him at the moment than I can. That is the truth, but not all the truth."

"Now we're getting to it," Bob broke in.

"The truth is, Tubby, that we decided that we are not happy together. And when people are not happy together, it's better to go away and try to be happy someplace else. We decided—"

"You mean you decided!" said Bob harshly. "You decided that you were through—"

"Oh, Robert—"

"—and I'm supposed to walk out of here, abjectly, like a little boy who's had his bottom spanked, and leave everything, including my own son!"

"Robert, can't you spare Tubby this?"

"You decided, by God," he continued furiously, "but the final arrangements haven't been decided! I never told you I wouldn't fight for my son!"

"There's no reason to fight for anything."

"Do you think I'm going to take this lying down? Do you think I'm going to walk out of here and leave my son, when I haven't done a

God-damned thing but object to taking a strange little Jew boy into my house?"

"Please, Robert, please—"

"My son doesn't like Jews any better than I do, do you, Tubs?"

The boy's eyes never left his father. He screamed, "I hate 'em! The dirty kikes!"

Pax's face had a stricken look.

"You should be very proud of yourself, Robert," she said, "teaching ideas like that to a small boy who doesn't know what it's all about."

"Well, it's time he did know," he replied.

"This is all very horrible. I should have preferred to go into the legal matter alone with you, but if you want it this way, I suppose there's nothing I can do about it."

"Let's bring it out in the open! It's about time you thought of somebody—"

Pax interrupted him wearily. "Let's not have any more recriminations. It makes me sick to my stomach." She paused for a moment. "Robert, I think that any court, knowing the facts of our life together, I should say of your life, during the past few years—which, believe me, my dear, I'm not blaming you for—would award me the custody of my child."

"Religious up-bringing has a lot to say in the decision of a court, don't forget."

She looked wistfully at Tubby's small, enraged face, which was so like his father's.

"You mean, I'd be a Jew, Pop, like you said?"

"Did you tell him that, too?"

Bob didn't answer.

"Do you know, I'm beginning to wonder if it's worth while fighting." She smiled a twisted little smile. "He seems well on the way to becoming truly your son, doesn't he?"

Pax looked at her son reflectively. "Tubby, now that this unhappy situation has been forced on you, now that you know how things are between us, I think you are old enough to make your own choice."

She made no move toward the boy, nor attempted to touch him.

"Do you want to live with your father, Tubs, or do you want to live with me?"

She saw her husband's hand tighten over his son's, and she watched closely the child's frightened face as he looked from one to the other.

"Go ahead, Tubby. Don't be afraid of hurting us," she insisted gently. "Do you think you can decide which of us you want?"

There was a moment's tense silence; then she heard a little cry from the boy. Tubby threw himself across his father's knees and buried his face in his lap. In muffled tones he wailed, "I want to stay with Pop!"

The painful, choking sobs of the child struck at her ears with the sharp precision of a drill. Instinctively her hand went to her throat, but her eyes were hot and dry.

"Very well, Tubby," she said quietly. "Stop crying now, darling, that's a good boy. We'll fix things somehow so you'll be happy. You run along now, and wash that dirty face. Everything's going to be all right! You'll see! And, Tubs," she said softly, "grown-up people sometimes forget themselves just like little boys do. Your pop and I don't hate each other, really."

Pax went over and knelt beside her son and tried to dry his eyes with her twisted rag of a handkerchief, but he whipped out of her arms and ran out of the room.

Her eyes followed him sorrowfully. Then with a little sigh she rose and turned toward the door. Bob put his hand timidly on her arm and stopped her. All the anger had drained from his face, and he stood there, looking sheepish and hurt and ashamed.

"Pax, honey, I—I don't know what to say. I never thought—I'm sorry, baby! I'm a heel."

She turned her head and looked at him, but she seemed to be looking through him rather than at him.

"Stop being sorry! You're always being sorry and it isn't any use. You've done what you set out to do. At least, have the guts to stick to your guns!"

"But Tubby's yours, too, Pax. I don't want to—" He hesitated, and she saw the muscles in his throat ripple as he swallowed painfully. "You can have him, Pax! Whenever you want him you can have him, you know."

"But apparently he doesn't want me," she said meditatively. "Take your son, Robert." She held her head up proudly. "I'll get along. You see, I have another son, now, who . . ."

She didn't finish. She turned away from him and walked slowly out of the room. Bob heard the latch click with a terrible finality.

31

THERE WAS a faint lightening of color around the gray edges of the sky, but it was still drizzling; the grass was sodden, and the garden flowers hung heavy and bedraggled with rain. Pax had to content herself with the library, that comfortable, much lived-in room which, up to the time of her father's death, had been so free from agitation, and, since the advent of Jan, so seething with emotion.

Pax walked nervously up and down, continually looking at her wrist watch, checking it with the church clock each time it chimed, listening to the sad sounds of the house, as it prepared itself for the approaching hail and farewell.

Her own son didn't want her. But wasn't it better this way? He was more Robert's son than he was hers, Robert Lyttleton III an exact replica of Robert II, both with infinite charm and good nature—when things went as they wanted them; both friendly and craving affection, except from unfortunates whom they considered not as good as themselves.

Robert had not been anti-Semitic when she married him. He could have had no intolerance in him when he was Tubby's age. But then, he hadn't been nine years old in an anti-Semitic era! When Robert was a child, anti-Semitism had been a dormant canker. Now, it was an active cancer. With the malignant disease unabated in a self-conscious world, mightn't Tubby be just like his father—or worse—when he was grown?

She tried to swallow a very large lump in her throat when she thought of the aching loneliness she would feel without him. After all, she'd carried him beneath her heart, she'd given birth to him, she'd cared for him tenderly, and, except for a day or two, he'd never been away from her for nine years—but he didn't want her. It would be hell to go into his empty room, which had always been so untidy.

Never mind! She'd give it to Jan. He'd make it his own. A wave of shame stole over her as she thought that his room had remained the unlived-in guest room in the plain Victorian house. She hadn't even bothered to take the extra bed out of it, or to fix it up with all the intimate things which are dear to a small boy.

She listened to the rapid footsteps of her son as he ran up and down stairs, into and out of his room, where he was putting his last-minute toys into a duffel bag, which his father had bought him for the journey. She was conscious of an occasional creaking overhead, and the remote tapping of Robert's cane as he moved across the floor. Robert, her husband for eleven years.

Today would take him away from her forever. But she had no regrets. For the first time in her life, she knew she was right.

Had she ever really loved him? She didn't think she had. Had she ever loved anyone?

She had loved Jake, but only for a moment, when you figured in terms of a lifetime. What was it he had said in that last tragic letter? "Somewhere in eternity." Hers had been such a little love in such a great timelessness. Was she destined to have no love in her life at all? She was barely thirty, she was not too difficult to look at, but she guessed she was a bore. She was sure Philip thought so.

Philip. He was the one she had always needed. Sixteen years and more of her life had been lived beside him, if not with him. As she sat there in the empty room, she felt her face getting hot. Silly to blush, when there was no one there to see your innermost thoughts.

But she was blushing, just the same. What was she? A wanton? A strumpet? Thinking of another man in terms of love, with the man who was still her husband not yet gone from her house, her bedroom?

Yes, admit it! Wasn't she facing truths now?

The front doorbell rang twice, sharply. She heard Pansy answer it, and then disappear upstairs with heavier footsteps following her. The footsteps traveled up and down several times, and she presumed it was the elder Clancy, who was to drive them to Burlington, carrying down the luggage. Then there was silence. She guessed that Clancy was waiting in the car for them, and she knew that the inevitable moment was near. She was almost conscious of holding her breath.

Then the door of the library opened slowly, and Tubby stood there, cap in hand, eyes lowered, his underlip thrust forward.

"Good-by," he muttered sullenly.

His mother smiled at him lovingly. "Don't I get a good-by kiss?"

Tubby raised his eyes and stared at her for a moment; then he ran across the room and hurled himself into her arms. She felt his strong little arms tighten around her neck and he buried his face in her shoulder. She tried to loosen his hold, to pull his face around so she could look at him, but he pressed his chin in further. Then she heard a muffled murmur from behind her ear.

"Oh, Mom!"

307

Finally, she pulled him around onto her lap, where he sat very stiffly, his fat, bare legs swinging two or three inches from the floor.

"Look at me, Tubs," she said softly. "Stop it, you big baby! Aren't you ashamed of yourself? This is a holiday!"

She smoothed the fair curls off his hot forehead, and went on talking to him quietly, as if this were an everyday occurrence.

"Give my love to your granny, darling, and do everything she tells you to do. She's a very wise and lovely lady. Don't forget to write me lots of letters; I'll be looking for 'em. Now, you have a wonderful summer, Tubby, and you take great care of your pop, won't you? I'll be seeing you before school starts." She wondered what made her say that. "Off you go, now! You haven't got too much time, you know."

He clutched her desperately around the neck again and gave her a wet, teary kiss on the mouth.

"Good-by, Mom," and then in a low voice, as though it were an afterthought, he whispered, "I love you an awful lot!"

He raced out of the library and she heard the screen door bang.

She sat there a moment in silence, her elbows on her knees, her hands over her eyes. Then she listened again. That must be Robert. She heard the tap, tap, tap of his stick, as he slowly descended the stairs, but the footsteps didn't stop. They continued past the door of the library.

She ran out into the hall and stood there, clasping her hands together, watching the broad back in its army tunic, as he turned the knob of the front door.

"Robert!" she cried.

He wheeled around and looked at her for a long moment. Then he clicked his heels together and saluted her smartly. He bowed, turned on his heel again, and opened the door. Without a word or backward glance, he walked down the steps and got into the car.

She followed him out, and stood on the top step. Clancy geared the car into low and, with a loud whine, it was off. She listened to the rapid change into second, then high, and the purr of the motor as the car disappeared swiftly down the street through the trees, in the direction of the main road. Suddenly she was conscious of the damp mist of the slackening rain on her face. She went in and closed the door. As she wearily climbed the stairs to her own room, she heard the echoes of her quiet footsteps through the nearly empty house.

Pax and Philip had finished lunch. Philip was sitting in her father's chair in the library, she in her usual place on the floor, leaning against his knee.

They sat for several minutes before speaking, and Pax watched the uncertain sunlight flickering on the wet leaves outside the window.

"It's awfully still, isn't it?"

"Lonesome stillness, kid?"

She smiled at him. "A little, I guess."

She felt him instinctively draw his knee away and she looked quickly up into his face. The line of his mouth had become straight and taut.

"What happened?" he said. "Did you forget the human equation when you turned your life upside down?"

She smiled to herself as she thought, with a certain amount of pleasure, that Robert had always been Philip's Achilles' heel, and she reached for his hand and pressed it.

"It's not the way you're thinking it, darling. It's just that Tubby is my son," she said.

She turned her head and put her cheek against his knee for a moment.

"Pax. Do you mind if we talk a little about all this?"

"I'd like to," she said. "But get one thing straight, mister. I'm not unhappy. I'm just a little sober, that's all."

"I know, Pax, and I'm sorry. It's just that I don't like the guy!" he said. "I never did like him! I'm as jealous as hell and if you ever regret giving up the son of a bitch, I'll break your neck!"

Pax threw back her head and laughed delightedly. "O.K. And now what did you want to talk about, Phil?"

"Oh, yes," he said, scratching the back of his head. "It's this: You've made a tough decision. Tough and swell. So I think this is the moment to go after something that's been at the back of your mind for twelve or thirteen years. Let's dig it out and have a look at it."

"Fire ahead, Phil. I'll listen." She added wryly, "I always do."

"It's the reason for your taking Jan."

"Yes," she said, in a low voice.

"Why you nearly let him go," he continued. "Why you made the final choice between—the man you were married to and a little refugee whom nobody wanted."

"Oh, I'm trying to be moderately decent, I suppose. Is that what you're talking about?"

He took her hand and held it firmly. "I'm talking about Jake," he said quietly. "You loved Jake, didn't you?"

"Yes," she said. "Do you mind, Phil?"

His hand closed more tightly around hers. "This all has to do with Jake, hasn't it, Pax?"

"Yes."

309

"You never said anything. Neither did I. I knew you had to work it out your own way."

"I guess everybody does, Phil."

"And Jan was your answer to it," he said. "Have you known it all along?"

She shook her head. "Not all along, Phil—or if I did, I didn't admit it, even to myself."

"I know. For a long time I listened to how it was your great humanitarian urge." His eyes twinkled. "God help me, I guess I even helped put some of that into your mind."

"That must have sounded funny. Me, that never thought of anything but myself," she said grimly. "Then I found a better one. I was going to have a young Jake for Robert when he came home. Well, I found out that that was the last thing in the world he wanted. Then I was sunk."

"I know you were. And I couldn't do a damn thing to help you."

"No. I just had to face the truth: that I had to pay for what I did to Jake and I wasn't paying it. I guess you'd call it a guilt complex, wouldn't you, Phil?"

"That's it."

"And it was a guilt complex a mile and a half wide! The thing was, I knew if I gave up I'd have to live with it all the rest of my life."

Phil nodded. "Sure. It started the night you thought you let Jake down."

"Thought!" she said.

"Do you remember that I told you once, a long time ago, that what you had was a perfectly natural reaction? Well, now I want to tell you something else. Jake was my friend. I liked him as well as any man I ever knew. But, believe me, it was as much his fault that night as it was yours. More, I think—and I told him so."

"Oh, no, Phil!"

"He was wrong, kid. He had no right to spring something so utterly alien, so different from anything you had ever known—and the way he did it. In a public place! It was brutal, to you and to his family. And only his youth and the hurt inside him excused him."

"Oh, no!" she protested.

"Oh, yes! Jake knew it—after he'd grown up a bit."

"Just the same, I failed him."

"You've got to stop that now," he commanded. "You're grown-up, too."

"I failed him because I didn't love him enough. I guess, when you come right down to it, I've never loved anybody enough, Phil."

310

"What in the name of God are you talking about?"

Pax looked at him steadily. "You see, I've always wanted love so desperately that I don't think I've ever had time to give it. Even with Jan. I wanted him to love me and need me—and he didn't. Well, now I'm going to love him for his own sake, not mine, not Jake's. Maybe it's more fun to love than to be loved," she added thoughtfully.

"Well," said Philip, "you've come of age, woman."

Pax smiled. "Not quite, Phil dear. Not quite. There's something else I've got to do. It's going to be a tough one, too. But I guess nothing that's right is ever very easy," she said.

"Can you tell me, Pax?"

"I can always tell you, Phil. I've got to get my son back. You know that, don't you? And what's more, I'm going to get him back. I'm going to fight for him—in every court in the country if I have to! I'm not mixed up about this. When I kissed that stubborn little face of his I knew that I had this to do."

Philip was looking straight ahead and frowning a little. "But he chose Bob."

Again she smiled and it was a very serene smile. "Yes, I know. But, you see, it was the timing that made him do it."

"I don't get you."

"Tubby's only a little boy. If, fifteen minutes before, I'd given him two ice-cream cones, it might have been me. You see, Robert's all new and shiny to Tubs. He's a big strong male and he wears decorations and ribbons and medals! He's a little boy's dream. At the moment I'm a comfortable old shoe. Oh, I was hurt at first, but I'm not any longer. I'm going to get him back."

"I don't care what you do if it makes you happy. I don't want anything to make you miserable any more."

"Oh, I'll be miserable lots of times. I'm prepared for that. But I'm going to do my damnedest to make Tubby Lyttleton an alert citizen of the world." Then she smiled. "I'm talking like you now, aren't I? But you know what I mean, don't you? I may not find out the result for another twelve or thirteen years. Do you think I can take it, Phil?"

"I know you can take it."

"Thanks, dear."

They sat quietly for a few minutes. Then Pax sighed and pushed her hair tightly behind her ears.

"I think it's going to be hot," she commented.

"Yeah."

"Jan's room is cool, though. I guess it's the coolest room in the house." She hesitated a moment. Then she said, "I wonder if he'll speak to me."

311

"Yes, I think so."

"I think so, too. After all, Phil, the hospital was another strange new place for him, and filled with pain; and his poor little heart had been swollen with misery for so long."

She stopped for a moment, and pulled up her knees and clasped her arms around them.

Philip said suddenly, "Jake'll be pleased. Can't you just see him walking through those pretty fields of Elysium? Could be he's got that Shakespeare feller with him. Remember how Jake always wanted to be a poet?"

"He was," Pax said softly.

"And old Jake is shaking his finger in the guy's face—as if William didn't know all the answers! And Jake's saying: You see, Mr. Shakespeare? How far that little candle—and so on and so on and so on—so shines a good deed in a naughty world end of quotation period."

Pax laughed, but her eyes blurred. "Phil! You sweet fool!"

Far away the lazy sunlight, shimmering across her ground cradle at Finnegan's; far away the winding train carrying her son; far away the past; and far—oh, far away Jake! And although her soul was serene and at peace, she clung to Philip's strong and gentle hand.

Suddenly she raised her head and her hand went to her throat in that instinctive gesture of hers.

"Listen!"

It was the sound of a heavy car approaching. She heard the soft purr of the motor, and the sudden cessation of sound as it stopped at the Gifford gate.

Philip leaned over, kissed the top of her head, and went to the window. He pulled the curtain aside and looked out into the country garden, where the changing lights and shadows played on the cool, wet grass. His eyes traveled down the gravel path to the gate where the hospital car stood.

"Get up off that floor, Pax, and open the door. Your son's home."

ABOUT THE AUTHOR

Ruth Chatterton is one of the most famous actresses America has ever produced. Not so well-known is the fact that she has done directing in the theatre and has translated a number of plays from the French.

Miss Chatterton was born in New York City where she makes her permanent headquarters, although her work takes her all over this country and frequently to Europe. One of her ancestors was the poet Thomas Chatterton.

Homeward Borne *is her first novel.*